HUMAN PAGES

HUMAN PAGES

BY JOHN ELLIOTT

CHÔMU PRESS

HUMAN PAGES
JOHN ELLIOTT
PUBLISHED BY CHÔMU PRESS, MMXII

Published in October 2012 by Chômu Press.
by arrangement with the author.
All rights reserved by the author.

ISBN: 978-1-907681-18-9

First Edition

Design and layout by: Bigeyebrow and Chômu Press
Cover Illustration by: Torso Vertical

E-mail: info@chomupress.com
Internet: chomupress.com

To Jenny, Lindsey and Poppy for Maggie.

CONTENTS

ONE

Town of the Verdiales.
Who could carry you
Tight in his pocket
Like a slip of paper?
(Popular Verdiales)

Slowly, wait another moment.

Your eyes have long been accustomed to a lack of light, but given time the darkness will resolve itself into the physicality of this place. Your skin is newly refreshed by the cool, moist air that its thick walls ensure. Beneath the soles of your shoes you can feel the debris of peanut shells, cigarette butts and empty bean pods.

Listen, the voices resume.

You can see the way now. Edge along the narrow corridor taking care not to bump into the sitters on the bench by the wall. The bar counter is on your left. Its cracked white tiles support Paca's chubby arms as she hears and then forgets the everyday sounds of glass clinking against glass, descending on wood and tile, the taps of sticks, paper rustling, the splutter of matches, the faltering click of lighter tops.

Sit down. There's a place for you at the table at the back. You untie and spread out the cloth to reveal the food you've brought: a piece of bread, a sliver of dried cod, a mound of broad beans.

A nearby hand passes you a flask of red wine. Another offers a paper wrap of salt. It's as if you had never been away, as if you weren't a stranger unrecognised in time.

Vincenz and Tony Pigeon are sitting with you. My Son is standing at the bar. He looks over. It's only a matter of moments until he addresses you as 'my son' too.

'Have you eaten?'

Your throat remains dry in spite of the wine. You aren't sure, after such a long silence, after your mouth had been stuffed with stones, your lungs filled with blood, that you possess the breath and saliva necessary to utter the required reciprocal question. Each syllable seems to die on your lips before it is rescued by its halting sequel.

They smile in response and point to the rinds and crumbs in front of them. You wait for their traditional encouragement to eat. It doesn't come so you unclasp your knife anyway and pare a fibre from the cod. They nod as they watch you eat and drink. They take pleasure in your every bite, your every swallow, as if it were one of their own, for they still remember the years of hunger that you never knew.

You ease open a bean pod with your right thumbnail and extract five beans: four large, one small. You dip them in the salt and share the common thought that links broad beans, their shape and texture within the pod, to female genitalia.

'Your sister's,' says Vincenz.

Paca laughs. Tony lowers his comic book. You can see it's a favourite from the old days: *Jim, the Fastest Draw in the West*. Nothing has changed. The past loiters here. You and those around you use the same phrases, the same curses. They still include you in the daily communality of their memory.

Now Vincenz, his arm draped about your shoulder, relives in thought the day when, as boys, you, he and Tian, aware of the approaching storm, clambered panting onto the sloping shelf of a cave, high up in the hinterland above Cirit.

None of you could remain upright for long against the wrenching buffets of wind. A curtain of driving rain obliterated the whole of the sky. The three of you, one by one, were forced to crawl back into the farthest recess of the rock. There, through the gloom suddenly illuminated by forked lightning, threading its way between the mountains down to the river gorge, he caught sight of your face. Your mouth was agape. Your eyes were ecstatic. He felt his shivers of cold begin to mingle with your fidgets of exultation, and in the shared nervous excitement he was seized by a desire, a prayer, which he sensed you completely desired and prayed for too, that the storm be everlasting, the rain and lightning inextinguishable, that you, he and Tian live in and revere this moment forever.

Tony pushes Jim and the treacherous desperado aside. He lays his hand on yours and says, 'We were over at the chalets Gusaro started to build before he ran out of money. It must have been around mid-morning. We were grafting at digging up and resurfacing the south road when a man came out of one of the doorways. Somebody called out. I forget who. Anyway, I looked up and watched him as he moved off. He had a slight limp, but it was the way he held his head, the set of his shoulders, the way his hands turned outwards at the end of each stride. Christ! I said. Well, I'll shit on the host! I said. Nolo! I shouted out your name again this time louder. Manolo! That made him stop and turn. Then Orange Miguel spat and said to me, "Can't you see? Are you blind? It's Pablo from the forge at St Mateo. I recognise him. My cousin knows him well." At this, the guy came over. It turned out he had a brother working in Germany who was interested in buying some land. But I truly thought it was you, Manolo. That you had come back to us and were going to go away, for some reason of your own, without even saying hello.'

Behind the bar, Paca washes and dries glasses. My Son has gone, as, by now, have most of the others. You can rest your bones in the quiet. No need to stir. It's safe. History has evaporated. From here the silence extends into the street and from the street into each house.

It's better not to think. They carry on pretending that no choice has been made, but the names they say and those they don't, like the erstwhile name of this wine shop, which you knew and now cannot be said, betrays the reality. After all, a sobriquet which inflames hatred in some and instils comradeship in others is better dropped. The official name was hardly used anyway. Here in Llomera, as you

3

know only too well, people, places and even objects are designated by other names, little names which imply a kind of ownership, some tenderness. They vary according to who speaks. In this case, Pacetta's or The Widow's are the most common, but not alone. No doubt, My Son would say, 'My daughter's.'

Take another drink. Vincenz and Tony have returned to work. There are more chemicals in the wine than before, but don't worry. Take a long good slug. You won't have to pay. Christ knows you paid enough in the past.

You wonder what Paca's thinking as she twists and turns the cloth and stares so intently into the bottom of each glass. Well, imagine it for yourself. Maybe she sees the night you and the others left, repeating itself again and again, over and over, as she lifts one and then another up to the meagre light before, satisfied with their cleanliness, depositing them on the shelf behind her head. It was dangerous to go then and just as dangerous to stay.

'Life,' she mutters.

It's time to go. Only you, Paca and Uncle Jaume, sitting there on the bench, his head permanently bent over his stick, blind these many years and forgetful of which voice belongs to which body, are left.

'Watch out for intruders,' Paca says. 'There are strangers about nowadays.'

Say something to her. Even if it's only to say you'll return, God willing.

She chides you gently. 'You don't believe, Manolo. You used to boast about it in here.'

When you go out, Jaume imagines you were Tian Marva. 'Good riddance,' he mumbles, 'that boy was a menace. Although someone did say he'd turned out well.'

＊ ＊ ＊

A telephone rang. At first he could not locate the source. The direction of its sound suggested one of the offices to the rear of the open-plan area where, for some reason, it had not been picked up by an answering machine.

Reluctantly, he started to make his way towards it, negotiating his passage through the empty workstations, pausing at one of them to bend down and retrieve a fallen folder. My last good deed on earth, he thought, as he placed it on the desk. One less thing for the cleaners to do.

They were already in the building. He had heard them singing and vacuuming ten minutes ago on his way up. On second thoughts, he reflected, better make it my penultimate one. After all, his final good deed awaited him at home.

The possible location of the phone was now narrowed down to the two central cubicles on the right. Another persistent ring guided him into the second one.

'Harvard Smith's extension. Sonny Ayza speaking.'

A woman's voice spoke, calm and unhurried. Her inflection and the manner of her delivery gave him the impression that she was reading from a prepared text or, which seemed more unlikely, she was reciting well-memorised lines.

'This is Sonny Ayza,' he repeated. 'Harvard isn't here at the moment. He'll be back on duty at, hold on,' he paused, checking the rota details pinned to the noticeboard behind the worktop until he found the entry for Wednesday, 15. 11. 83, '8.30 a.m. tomorrow.'

Her voice continued without hesitation, ignoring his intervention. Then, after a brief silence, she said, 'In conclusion, I will recap the main points so there is no misunderstanding or ambiguity between us.

'Item one: the instruction manual for electrical installations at Gallo Mart, Depot 4, Old Station Yard, Panalquin, does not include the extension built in 1971.

'Item two: the Fitzhugh family's Alsatian was called "Rusty" not "Polka Dot".

'Item three: ex-colleagues of Fernando Cheto Simon look forward to a forthcoming reunion.

'Item four: the colour coding for Blatteriblax record labels 1953 to

1968 was as follows (a) magenta—Chicago South Side Rhythm and Blues, (b) oxblood—Texas Tenors, (c) emerald—Race Re-Issues, (d) gold—Kansas City After Hours, (e) fawn—New Thing.

'Item five: at the height of his reign of protection terror, Ute Manoko controlled 1316 pachinko parlours in Greater Osaka alone.

'Item six: Vera Sowenwell continues to think highly of her late lover, Conrad Terence, in spite of the serious allegations of his fascistic connections outlined in the 1978 biography by I A Graz.

'This is Elizabeth Kerry on behalf of the executors of Amadeo Cresci. Please confirm you have received this message.'

Sonny looked down at the jottings he had made on Harvard's scrap pad. He had topped and tailed each item with a quick thumbnail sketch: a monkey on a tree branch, a swing bridge, a car on a road between high hedges, a cheval mirror, a cut-throat razor, a leaf, a frog on a lily pad, a valve wireless.

'Let me remind you, you are calling Harvard Smith's extension, Chance Company, Greenlea Division.'

She had gone. The line went dead.

Her message contained none of the standard procedures laid down by client contracts. Obviously, she was neither a prospective buyer nor a company employee. She had made no specific reference to Harvard, yet she must have already possessed his number or else requested it from the switchboard.

He scanned the names she had mentioned. Fernando Cheto Simon—a Mirandan like himself? Possibly. Panalquin, of course, lay on the other side of the estuary, and Gallo Mart, the only other local connection he could detect, was a chain of low-grade convenience stores. The rest meant nothing except, in his time, during the interminable, neon-suffused nights in downtown Yokohama, when he had frequented several pachinko joints in the forlorn hope that he, too, might catch the adrenalin rush of their adepts and votaries. Ute Manoko. Some Yakuza or big criminal with friends in the right places? Presumably. Enough, he thought. It's not my concern. I don't have the time. If it's important she will ring again.

Adding a final outline of a large dog with a lolling tongue, he pulled the sheets of paper together, folded them neatly and then tucked them in his shirt pocket. After all, the call might well have gone unanswered. Only he and a cleaner, who by now had started work in the outer room, were present, and anyway Harvard would not see him alive again.

Outside, large snowflakes began to materialise in the black pool of the high window. These were the moments he once used to savour, the in-between times, the doldrums, when the bulk of the indoor staff had left and the few night operators had not yet arrived. He watched as the now steady flurry of flakes spiralled out of view. They struck him as somehow apposite, as though they might help to shroud his final journey and bury his tracks for once and all. Although separated from them by the glass, he felt as if they were already pressing lightly on his eyelids, moistening his eyes until his pupils were bleary and unfocused and his very existence was dissolving into nothing other than falling snow. The feeling was so real that his body gave a sudden, involuntary shiver, and in its tiny spasm he remembered, or perhaps imagined he remembered, the experience of his flesh's first encounter with the searing kiss of ice, the soft, deep embrace of snow.

As he recalled it, he had fallen over and over again in his attempt to toddle precariously, screaming all the while with delight, along the slippery newness of the transformed street. Had it been in Llomera or later in Orias? He could not say for sure. In the event, Rosario had picked him up, easily curtailing his futile struggles. Laughing, she had let his face dangle closer and closer to the wonderful white surface, which was so tantalisingly near. Then, giving in to his insistent wails, she had plopped him down so that to his heart's content he could gather and lose and gather again and lose again the precious unknown stuff. Why are there things in the world? Well, he would never know the answer now.

Outside Harvard's door, a black woman he had seen before was busy vacuuming the strip of carpet. On an impulse, he asked her name. Taken by surprise at the sound of a voice, she looked up and switched off the machine.

'Hallie. Hallie Briggs. Is something wrong, Mr Ayza?'

'No. Far from it. Should there be?'

'Well, that's alright then.' Her thumb rested on the switch, but she did not release it.

'You know who I am. I'm surprised.'

'I've seen your desk, though they don't call them that anymore, do they? I mean, I've seen you at your desk. Yours is always one of the tidiest. All of us say that. We know the desks better than we know the people.'

Sonny smiled. I've tidied it all away, he thought, but where's the difference?

He put on his jacket and took down his overcoat from the peg.

'You going now, Mr Ayza?' Hallie called out.

'Yes. I'm going.'

He walked over to the lifts and pressed the summons button. Once inside, he momentarily saw her stoop as she picked up something in her way, then the sliding door elided all her future movement.

By the time he got outside, the snowflakes were melting on the pavement. On this evening, of all evenings, he could have taken a taxi home, but instead, after a few unthinking minutes, because he had already passed their rank, he decided to stick to his customary routine. Indeed, the way was so familiar to him that he found he had crossed Prospect Street, had traversed the precinct between the Kyro Corporation building and the new Issa Tower and had climbed the four flights of shallow steps which led to Argonne Boulevard and the Inner Ring Road before he forced himself to take full account of his surroundings for one last time.

Accordingly, his cheeks dampened by the remaining recalcitrant flakes, he descended the stairwell of the subway and looked self-consciously into each preoccupied face he met in the tunnel below, listening religiously to their footsteps echo and fade as he mounted the opposite side.

On a large gable wall to his left the legend, 'WE STEPHEN KRAUS', had been, since morning, sprayed in irregular, sloping black characters. It was a further manifestation of the so-called Kraus Fraternity, who had been proclaiming their recent existence in the southern and eastern districts of the city during the preceding fortnight. Their aims, whether benign, malign, cultural or criminal, remained as yet unexplained. Some wiseacres he knew put them down as merely an old-fashioned and not very original advertising campaign, which, after the requisite period of titillation, would unveil its product.

Continuing, he skirted the right flank of the disused tobacco factory, still awaiting a new property developer after the financial collapse of the previous consortium, and cut through Vinegar Alley to Salonika Street. Twenty-five ironmongers lined its somnolent length. Each one presented an identical window display. The only outward distinguishing marks Sonny could see were the names of the owners and the years in which their businesses were founded. As he had never had the occasion to go inside any of them to make a purchase, their interiors stayed an unsolved mystery.

Beyond Salonika Street, the roads and pavements became increasingly congested with traffic and pedestrians; so much so that he was obliged, whether he liked it or not, to adopt the slow, cumbersome, shuffling gait that Greenlea's inhabitants used to minimise body checks and avoid unsettling eye contact.

Annunciation Square now lay immediately ahead. It formed a kind of antechamber; an intimation in its length and breadth of the greater open space of the Rag Market which, in its turn, funnelled and ballooned from its eastern corner. Bearing in mind his internal injunction to look and see, Sonny dutifully paused in front of the two adjacent buildings, which the civic authorities had respectively favoured with a historic plaque and an architectural interest roundel. The first adorned the rebuilt Greek Orthodox Church whose original structure had been destroyed by fire in 1876, the second the 1908 apartment house façade designed by the minor art deco architect, Alan Emscot.

The head of Walter Grebbel, the eighteenth-century mathematician, surmounted on a huge granite block, chiselled with his dates and doctorates, situated on the northern side of the square, had been, by general consensus, poorly executed and had therefore been spared official recognition.

One substantial edifice remained, namely the nondescript Agricultural Savings Bank, before he gained the Rag Market. Its sidewall was buried under an overlapping plethora of competing fly posters. As he passed, Sonny let his eyes wander over each of them, backwards and forwards, from top to bottom. One in particular stood out. Against a white background, thick red letters, printed as though they were dripping blood, shrieked, 'FREE ALBERT WENDE!' Drawing closer, small black print revealed it to be the handiwork of the 'One in a Hundred Committee'. Various scribblers had added their own names around the 'ALBERT' and the 'WENDE'. The two posters underneath unsurprisingly plugged hopeful pop singles, but the third, which he almost overlooked because of its unprepossessing layout, made him stop and stare. In two nights' time, Wilson Loumans, on his only Greenlea appearance, was going to play solo piano at the Veterinarian Hall, sponsored by the Amadeo Cresci Foundation.

He took out the pages of Elizabeth Kerry's message and studied them again once he had reached the counter of the Sunrise Tea & Coffee stall, a convenient vantage point in the Rag Market for the departure islands of tram routes 4, 9, 11 and 14, which radiated out to the northern suburbs. It was his habit to stop there most evenings, and Sylvia, on seeing him approach, had already prepared his espresso.

Under her teasing gaze, he unwrapped a lozenge of sugar and dipped its tip slowly deeper into his cup, watching it change colour until it had all disappeared. The discarded wrapper dropped on the paper in front of him obscuring the words 'on behalf of the executors'. Tonight, they were using 'Black Cat' brand. Within a cream rectangle, bordered by a green serrated line, a black cat's head faced him with its ears pricked. Thinking about Ute Manoko and the melting sugar, in his mind's eye he saw it change shape, grow a body and a tail and resolve itself into maneki neko, the Japanese warning cat, whose replicas he had often stopped to admire in Yokohama all those years ago. Its eyes became large and piercing. Its paw was raised for all eternity to warn others, not just the travelling monk, of imminent danger.

Manoko, Fitzhugh, Cheto Simon, Sowenwell, Terence, Alsatian dogs, Blatteriblax records, depots at Panalquin, Amadeo Cresci. The list was intriguing. With his pen, he drew the two versions of the cat at the foot of the page. My signature, he thought. These drawings belonged to him. They were his marks, but the meaning of the words, like the shops in Salonika Street, whose thresholds he had never crossed, whose arcane secrets he had never breached, remained out of reach, both opaque and unyielding.

'Let me see.'

He had been about to crumple the lot up and toss them in the litter bin when Sylvia spoke. He handed her the final page and then the others.

'I've never seen anything like these. I mean with this detail. You did them all?' She seemed to be only interested in the drawings, ignoring the surrounding text.

Sonny nodded. 'Since I was a boy. It's been a weakness of mine.'

'Well I think they're fine,' she said, handing them back as she moved off to serve another customer.

Sonny and Sylvia, he thought, Sylvia and Sonny. They sounded like a forgotten adagio twosome; a relic from the era of cheap dance halls, long since knocked down or converted into second-hand furniture salerooms.

He had known her name from their first encounter. Each Sunrise employee was required to wear their badge whilst on duty. Sylvia's was pinned just above her right breast. A breast he had looked at a moment too long as he imagined it unsupported and free from the encumbrance of her bra and the folds of her blue and white striped smock. She, on the other hand, had had to wait to know his until the day when, inadvertently, he had forgotten to take off his identity clearance. Leaning forward towards him, so that he had been able to smell her perfume, a kind of faint honeysuckle, and feel the softness of her breath on his face, she had deciphered and read out Roberto Ayza from under his security photo. 'You're Mirandan?' she had said, and when he nodded she had added, 'Me too.' Whereupon she had stuck out her hand and had clumsily shaken his. 'Call me Sonny,' he had said. 'Everyone does.' From then on they had never mentioned Miranda again, but had always confined their chat to life in Greenlea.

'Are you in a hurry?' Sylvia was back in front of him. She began to hum a tune he did not recognise.

'No. I'm in no hurry. There'll be other trams.'

'Okay then, let me help you pass the time. There doesn't seem to be anyone heading our way. I know, let me do something I'm good at. Let me tell you a story a customer told me yesterday. Would you mind?'

'No. I don't mind,' Sonny replied. The jar of pills and the bottle of brandy would still be there even if he was later home than he had intended.

'You might not like it. It's a woman's story.'

'Go on. Tell me what it is.'

'Very well.' Sylvia paused, drew breath, then started on her tale.

'It had been dark all day. The rain had begun in a half-hearted drizzle, but by lunchtime a gusting wind was drenching the city in unremitting squalls.

'Inside the electrical goods shop on Lower Market Street, Victor Larries, the owner, debated for several minutes whether to miss his scheduled appointment before deciding he would brave the elements and dash to the Pheasant Bar and Grill on the corner of Trevern and Williams Street. As it proved impossible to hoist an umbrella in the high wind, he was soaked through his green loden coat and brown leather shoes by the time he reached his destination.

'Monica Randell, his shop assistant, was glad to see the back of him, and, because the rainstorm deterred customers, she was soon able to slip into an uninterrupted reverie in which, buoyed up by pleasurable anticipation, she saw herself and her new-found lover, Ivo, undressing one another, garment by garment, in a room on the second floor of the Old Russia Hotel.

'In her vision, the rain was still pattering against the window when Ivo closed the curtains and joined her on the bed. The sound of voices in the corridor outside only emphasised the depth of their own tender silence, which they prolonged and nurtured, even when it was assailed by a burst of angry shouting from the adjoining room.

'Ivo raised his arm above her head. She snuggled against him, rubbing her lips along its underside. She squeezed his penis gently and lowered her head to kiss his balls. How young he was, she thought. How oblivious to the meaning of their being together. His flesh was firm beneath her fingers. The hairs at the base of his enlarged cock, which throbbed and stiffened against the encouragement of her palm, were golden. He was, as yet, untainted by the weariness of self, the erosion caused by all the nights and days, which imperceptibly made you not quite yourself, not quite someone else. "Not a word," she would say as she put her hand to his lips and then laughing softly, "not another word."

'When Victor returned at 1.30, grumbling on and on about the accursed weather and the lousy state of trade, Monica withdrew to the sanctuary of the storeroom to eat a tub of cold beans and rice. Once there, within its dingy confines, she lovingly ran back future time so that now she was on the point of coming out of the lift and catching sight of Ivo, who was already waiting expectantly for her on the fourth floor of the multi-storey car park by All Saints Station. Just as we planned, she thought. Exactly as it was meant to be.

'Once beside him in his car, as its tyres threw up water from the road and the steady to and fro of the windscreen wipers fought in vain against the deluge, she felt they were both enclosed in an aquarium of love, where their mutual desire plunged them deeper and deeper, never regretting, in the charged intimacies of their bodies, the light they had abandoned at the surface. His face was so close to hers as he switched off the ignition and turned towards her. His kiss, oh his kiss—was interrupted by Victor standing in the doorway.

'After she had answered his query and he had gone, she turned on the tap and rinsed then dried her fork. She sipped a second glass of water, secure in the knowledge that the afternoon would pass. The mundane work hours would give way to the rapture to come.

'The evening, night and early morning she had connived to spend with Ivo had only been made possible by the announcement of the proposed strike by the Ferry and Tram Workers on the following Tuesday. On hearing the announcement on television, she had not hesitated in seizing the opportunity to say to her husband, as they cleared away their evening meal, that she would spend that night in the city. She had been ready to argue with him that the alternative bus journey over the bridge and the subsequent train were too long and fatiguing, but he had merely nodded okay. "I'll stop with Elena," she had explained. "We haven't had a chance for a real get together for ages. You know how rare it is nowadays for me to go out on the town with friends."

'Whatever his thoughts might have been she never knew because at that juncture they had been interrupted by loud cries from Henry, their eight-year-old son. Rushing upstairs to his bedroom, they found him writhing on the carpet, clutching his stomach and complaining of terrible pains. After they had called the doctor and he had assured them that it was only a bout of colic, they had spent a restless night trying to get the invalid off to sleep before, in the small hours of the morning, giving way and letting him settle in the haven of their own bed. When he awoke, he seemed recovered, and, in spite of his long protestations, Monica decided to send him to school.

'Now in the shop, she began to wish the remainder of the afternoon away, but time refused to pass. She felt more and more marooned between each slow, desultory shudder of the minute hand of the large oval clock on the wall behind the microwave cookers. The few customers who did turn up were soon dealt with and gone. Victor, meanwhile, was closeted with a rep and then with the half bottle of whisky she knew he always kept in his left-hand desk drawer. The continuous rain, she sensed, was holding the hours in abeyance, pitching time a little forward, but then driving it back like a never-ending cycle on a faulty washing machine. A minute seemed to arrive then stick, devoid of progress. In this wearisome hiatus, the sustaining thought of Ivo's body, the ardour of his breath on her cheek, began to evaporate as soon as it came. She tried to resuscitate how he would look, what he would be wearing, what he would say, but instead images of Henry last night and this morning crept in to displace Ivo's touch, Ivo's smell, Ivo's face and then they, too, faded away, only to be replaced by another barren round of clock watching.

'Of course, as is the nature of the world, her deliverance came at last. Out in the street, she waited impatiently at Victor's side as he stooped to lock the door. First, he fumbled with the key, then he pushed twice against it to make certain before finally lowering and securing the metal shutter. They embraced perfunctorily. His breath smelt of booze. She watched him hurry off round the corner, noting to her surprise that the rain had stopped. By now, the strikers, she reckoned, would be at their rally at the Red Windmill on Central Avenue after their march from City Hall. With an uplifted heart, she at last set off on her unaccustomed route.

'She had only turned into Upper Market Street and walked half its length when the realisation that something was wrong seeped ominously into her happiness. A low, steady grumble of clanking and grinding was getting louder and louder. To her horror, the front of a tram came into view as it laboured and protested towards her up the steep incline. Two more had passed by the time she got to All Saints Station where headlines on news vendors' boards mockingly confirmed what she already knew: "Industrial Peace Ferry & Tram".

'She had to see Ivo desperately. She had to tell him she could not stay all night. He was not waiting for her on the fourth floor of the car park. His car was nowhere to be seen. She watched and watched the upward ramp, but the sound of ascending vehicles grew more and more infrequent. She would phone from the hotel, say that the chance to meet Elena for the evening had been too good to miss, and catch the last ferry home. A man was looking at her as he unlocked his car. He seemed on the verge of coming over and saying something. She turned away towards the lifts. This was a bad place to be alone. Moments later, she went back to the ramp. He had gone. Time began to race like the twitch of the warning pulse on the back of her hand. Nausea beckoned. Most of the parked cars had left.

'She called Ivo's flat from the station. There was no answer. She returned to the car park, but he still was not there. She phoned again. No reply. At the concierge desk at the Old Russia Hotel, no reservation in his name, her name, or any of the jokey pseudonyms they had laughed over, was held. She left the lobby; her face flushed as though the man had leaned casually over his counter and slapped her hard.

'The fo'c's'le of the eight o'clock ferry was almost deserted in marked contrast to the shoving, bustling throng of commuters and the perennial kaluki players fighting for their customary tables, which she suffered evening by evening. Through the windows, the waters of the estuary ran pitch black. Renewed rain trickled in rivulets down the glass. The harbour lights of home were more than an hour away.

'Her husband was sitting in the dark in Henry's room when she got in. He reached for her hand and put his head against her thigh. "He's had a slight temperature. Nothing to worry about. He's better now. Look," he whispered, "see for yourself. He's sleeping peacefully."

'Two months later, the three of them took a picnic in the woods below the Belvedere. They glanced up when an exuberant band of young people spilled along the path towards them. Ivo was amongst them. He had not changed. His every movement exuded vigour and beauty. The sun was glistening through the trees, and, in mid-exclamation, raising his hand to shield his eyes, he momentarily turned and caught sight of Monica. His already upraised hand sketched a kind of salutation before it dropped to his side then he was gone.

'She listened as their mingled shouts and the thump of their ghetto blaster died away. Birds called. At her feet, Henry was busily playing his new Game Boy console. Her husband, his back supported by the slender trunk of a silver birch, read his newspaper. Time progressed on an even keel, letting those alive live, aiding those who, weary of the city streets, sought an hour's respite in the woods and walkways of the Belvedere's environs.'

Sylvia had reached the end of her story, but her concluding words were half lost as she left Sonny in order to serve two impatient new customers. Laying their orders down, she smiled over at him, encouraging him to say something, to comment on what she had just related. The bell of a departing tram provided a timely footnote to her theme.

'Don't waste your youth,' Sonny managed at last.

Sylvia laughed. 'There's no point in not wasting it.'

'You can go where you want. Do what you want. It needn't be this.'

'But I like it here, Sonny. Just as well as I like it back in Miranda.'

It was his turn to smile as he watched the sugar wrapper from his second coffee revert to its original shape of a black cat's head. 'Naturally. You see Miranda full of living people. People you knew only a short time ago. I see it populated by ghosts.' He got up. 'Goodnight, Sylvia, and thanks.' He had nearly blurted out goodbye.

17

'Goodnight, Sonny. Till I see you.'

He heard her laugh ring out once more as he quickened his stride to board a number 11 tram, whose driver he had seen stowing his knapsack under the control panel.

Electricians were busy testing the display lighting when Harvard Smith pushed through the doors of the Lorelei Suite at the Berengaria Inn, home next day to an exhibition celebrating Chance Company's twenty years in business.

He had ring-fenced the funding six months ago, but was now only too aware that, in the recent climate of disappointing out-turns, he and it faced possible challenges at national level. At the best of times, overt publicity was likely to discomfort the vocal rump who preferred the clandestine route; at the worst of times, well, he would not dwell on it, he simply hoped that the generally anodyne style of presentation would deflect any overzealous scrutiny, especially now he had agreed to involve Cresci Foundation money.

A series of large mounted photographs depicting Joe May, Chance Company's founder, at various stages of his career, signposted the visitors' path through the show. The first, which had achieved cult status, was a full-length portrait from the early sixties. It showed May sheltering from a snowstorm in the entrance of a pawnshop on Columbus Circle, New York City. The clothes he wore looked as though they had been assembled from the remnants of the scummiest kind of yard sale. A neon dollar sign floated above his head. This *mise en scène* had been meticulously reconstructed by the super-realist painter and photographer, Isa Karlowski. As the accompanying rubric explained, it had been one of her *Twenty Great Ironic Pictures*.

Harvard leant forward to study some of the late-period Madcap Enterprise adverts displayed in the cabinet below Joe's feet. He had always enjoyed them.

'Tired of the Tarot?'

'Ideologically opposed to I Ching?'

'Face down your anxieties through rigged events.'

'Be imaginary histories with our connivance.'

'Get insane with Madcap!'

Carefree days, he thought, but the amiable anarchy of Madcap had seeded the birth and growth of Chance Company, and he and his future both belonged under its control.

A semi-darkened area beyond another Joe May, this time as hippie entrepreneur, enshrouded the following section. Aleatory music, triggered by the tread of feet on a thin metal strip on the floor, played in the background, dissonance seeking and finding resolution, then dissonance again. An intermittently darkened and lit screen showed the first austere declarations of Chance Company's existence: 'Don't leave it to chance. Contact the Company.' A separate monitor relayed a loop of Joe May's charismatic keynote speech, 'Uncertainty is our greatest asset', delivered on the company's second anniversary at Scranton, New Jersey, November '65.

With a barely suppressed sigh, Harvard sprawled into a convenient club chair. A feeling of incipient lassitude started to distend his limbs and loosen his focus. He shut his eyes for a moment. His task could wait. As a sop for something to do, he picked up a pair of adjacent headphones, put them on and half listened, half catnapped, as an actor, whose name he could not remember, read Item 16 from the company's *Stories We Tell Ourselves*.

'Sheer Cliff Company faced many difficulties in the wake of its founder's suicide. A hostile take-over bid from Whisper Long Corporation put its continued existence in jeopardy. Hard timber extraction, one of its key raw materials, was threatened by draconian quotas imposed by the new coalition government. Added to these, along with several other multi-national conglomerates, it had recently bled financial resources in a sequence of ill-judged arbitrage manoeuvres, while internally the task of appointing a successor to the chairmanship had sharpened the power struggle between the "New Day Hour One" faction and the previously dominant "Scatter the Stones More Widely" policy adherents.

'Conscious of these ice floes in the river, the defunct leader had wisely stipulated in his final testament that a series of colloquies must be held, representing all divergent opinions, on the future course of the organisation, and that they be transmitted live to every factory, office and workplace.

'The first meeting took place at Osaka shortly after daybreak in late autumn. Present were Yuta O, Finance Division, Taku M, Production Engineer, Moe S, Export Director, Ayno F, Pension Fund Representative, Harold L, Australian Sales.

'Taku M opened proceedings. He said, "A twenty-six stone player can meet a one stone player. Together, out of civility and love of Go, they decide to spend time at the board. Both of them are willing to learn. In the future, twenty-six will boast I had the honour to play against so and so. He showed me non-attack, non-defence. The one stone player will relax at chess."

'Ayno F chose to project a film about R Temple. It consisted of a variety of establishing, long, medium and close-ups, pans, fades, stills and crane shots. When its credits rolled, she said, "New wood, new architect, new site. Forever the same, unchanging idea temple."

'Harold L followed her. He stressed, "Stories about the loyal ronin are still popular. Tradition holds. When each factory thinks it alone knows the best way to make our products, it is time to stop making those products."

'This point of view drew an angry rebuttal from Moe S. She shouted, "No slogans! No targets! Work with workers' knowledge!"

'Throughout the proceedings, Yuta O had sat quietly, saying nothing. From time to time, he had removed the top of his felt pen and had replaced it with a faint click. Now, he laid the pen without its top on the table, got up, left the room and did not return. After a pause, Ayno F said, "He showed us in this state the pen will not write for so long."'

Harvard opened his eyes, stretched his arms and took off the headphones. He rose and ambled onwards round a tight chicane, whose walls were covered with the printed testimonies of grateful celebrity clients, to the library section. Above its entrance, a less well-known Karlowski portrait of Joe May stared down. She had taken him as he sat alone at the head of a long boardroom table. His torso was draped in a loose-fitting red and black dashiki. In front of him were arrayed a ring of keys, a bunch of yellow and white roses wrapped in cellophane and an expensive gold wristwatch. His poised right hand was frozen in the act of writing in his appointments diary. The partially formed word 'vanit' was clearly visible on the open page. The portrait's date and the fact that it was here on loan were stated below, but not that it was the property of the Amadeo Cresci Foundation.

And there is more inside, Harvard thought, appreciating the irony of the situation. After all, what better than to see Cresci heresies being legitimised amongst Chance Company folklore? He pictured his co-conspirator, Evangeline Simpson, standing beside him in obeisance before the image of her god. How triumphant she would be rootling among her donated artefacts, unearthing gleefully the video of *Chance Company: Control Through Anarchy*, a TV exposé in the Open Windows series, Bishop Albiol's Easter address condemning the dangers of addiction to fantasy lives, Oscar Tuve's apologia for the failed Cresci lawsuit conjoined with Umberto Vitale's article, 'Chance Company has been and continues to be infiltrated by The Company'. K Wiener's book, *Chance Company Does Not Exist: A Syncretic Fable*, and Abdul Abdullah's notorious pamphlet, *Master Chuck's New Toy*.

Once, he thought ruefully, she would have dropped them all readily and let him embrace her, but in those days he had not known how to give her his love, and she, in spite of welcoming his caress, his kiss, and for that matter any other's caress or kiss, only really loved and was in thrall to the man she suspected of being her father.

With the seductive image of Evangeline still in mind, his hand alighted on a copy of Alvin Medcorev's 1981 authorised *History of Chance Company* which he saw was included, at a specially reduced price, amid the items for sale spread out on a trestle table. Recognising that it would be of use in his immediate task and that it was a long time since he had last flicked through it to read about the early days of Evangeline's mother, Joe May and the rest of the crew, he picked it up and took it over to the study bench on the opposite side of the room.

He had logged on and was about to activate the file he had brought with him when his attention strayed to the map, which extended along the wall above the row of computers. It delineated throughout the world the spread and penetration of Chance Company in a range of blues: sky to midnight indigo, according to the density of operations. An infrequent scattering of white patches indicated countries and territories that still refused entry. Miranda, directly above his head, which until recently would have been white, was now a Wedgwood blue in recognition of the lifting of its long imposed embargo. Now is truly the time, Harvard reflected. We are zoning in on the synchronicity to finally track down and nail our Mirandan apostate, settle his hash for good and all, and simultaneously introduce his fellow countrymen and women to the joy of realising that life can indeed be a dream if they are willing to pay for it. Added to that, he has chosen to return here and give me the sweetest opportunity of my career. 'So, thank you, Greenlea,' he said aloud, and inwardly, and thank you Evangeline and Cresci. Together they could pull it off. He would make damn sure of that, even though their aims were radically opposed. Separate paths led to their quarry, one of which, appearing on the screen in front of him, was coming to fruition.

Client Name—Agnes Darshel

File Name—Emily Brown

Supervisor—Roberto Ayza

He entered the agreed cost-centre number. Under its cover, the Cresci Foundation would pick up five sixths of the tab. The remainder was down to the client. Hopefully, she would find her long-lost father in a matter of days, before Sonny Ayza returned to work. Another fortunate piece of synchronicity that Harvard had enjoyed when he authorised a week's leave in the perfect date slots. He began to sing as he worked. If Agnes did not trace him then one of the others would, just so long as it was not Evangeline on her own. 'Is coming to town. You'll never guess who. Lovable, huggable Emily Brown. Miss Brown to you.' She needed a guide for the labyrinth, a helpmeet, a *fidus Achates*. Following company practice, he ordered up all the EB entries from the city telephone directory and opened the copy of Medcorev at random. His finger rested on page 41.

The details began to sort themselves out. Forty-first on the list was Emmet Briggs. A match between him and the client seemed promising. He was a long-time resident of the city. He had been married for years and still lived with his wife, Hallie. The fact that they had no children and that he had no previous Company experience was not relevant. He had been out of work for the last three months, a plus as far as Harvard was concerned. Then, as the years scrolled back on the monitor, Briggs's sustained history of crime and violence, coupled with four terms of incarceration, emerged relentlessly. Harvard paused and stared at the map. Briggs still might be okay but was he controllable? He returned to the keyboard and typed in 'known associates'. The answers were more reassuring. Briggs's whole catalogue of brutality, apart from juvenile delinquency elsewhere, had taken place in the context of local organised gangsterism. He had hurt and maimed only when ordered to do so by protection racketeers or as a means of pre-empting rival antagonists. Let's go with the system, Harvard decided. Briggs's record was clear for the last five years. It was worth taking a chance. Accordingly, with his eye already scanning the text on page 41 of Medcorev's book, he keyed in 'contact' and 'offer'.

The first sentences he glanced at did not interest him, so he turned back a few pages and then back again until he came across a passage dealing with the ur-history, as Medcorev termed it, which he knew would lead him sooner or later to the appearance of Evangeline's mother.

The room was quiet. The lighting subdued. Nobody knew he was there apart from the concierge downstairs and the electricians. Home could wait. Its incumbent pain could be postponed for at least a little longer. He slipped off his watch and began to read attentively.

Chance Company started up, not surprisingly, in a tenuous and disjointed way. It had several progenitors, which flickered, sputtered and faded in the years contiguous to the emergence of Madcap Enterprise—the organisation which above all nurtured and inspired its eventual founders, Joe May and Evangeline Simpson.

Two of these progenitors merit further comment at this stage—namely the Tokyo-based home restaurant phenomenon and the European Dog Activists.

The former involved like-minded individuals who provided specialist meals at highly variable prices in their own homes. The food ranged from one ingredient themes, e.g. beef, chicken, garlic, chillies, chocolate etc. to versions of European cuisine such as English institutional, Scots high tea, Dublin pub snacks, Mediterranean fish stew, *mâchon Lyonnais, le 4 o'clock,* Austrian dumpling fest and German breads with Dutch cheeses and Mirandan hams.

Other participants relegated food to second place. They concentrated on imposing a specified ethos accompanied by its corresponding etiquette. Diners, therefore, were able to eat meals according to the customs and manners borrowed from and approximating to Louisiana plantation owners (pre-Purchase), contemporary London Pall Mall (gentlemen only), Korean and Manchurian Spring Festivals (liable to disruption by hired left-wing student brigades) et al. In one celebrated instance a vertical approach was decreed so that, as each successive course was introduced, the appropriate 'mores' regressed a century at a time.

The majority of houses, apartments and shacks used for home restaurants were presided over by single women. Colloquially, they became known as Widow So and So's—the second name denoting location and ambience. Some of these women had travelled in their lives, and they sought to recreate what they had experienced. Most, however, relied heavily on magazines, movies and television for their inspiration with the result that their 'Po Valleys', their 'Minnesotas' and their 'Lancashires' were particularly poetic.

Apart from a handful of habitués and their initiates, putative patrons and their guests found their way to these establishments with great difficulty. They were all in the suburbs, and, as they did not want to attract the attention of the fiscal authorities, they did not advertise openly. Some risked a brief display for an hour in the early evening by hanging a banner in the doorway if they were traditional or by putting plastic replicas of dishes in a window if they were modern, but this practice was unusual and probably indicated a judiciously placed protective friend. The rest were effectively underground and unknown. A situation which, especially during the infancy of the phenomenon, gave rise to many non-participating households being interrupted, chivvied and placated or otherwise by roaming groups of pleasure seekers. The most resourceful of these households responded by improvising what they understood their unforeseen visitors wanted in a symbiotic forerunner of Chance Company process.

This period of charming anarchy, however, was not conducive to effective business and was soon supplanted by an oral network of guides and helpers. In each locality, for a small sum, street sweepers, railway ticket clerks, insurance salesmen and flea market vendors could usually be relied on for accurate information. The final codification arrived with the publication of The Widow's Room by Liam Fitzhugh in Southern California.

Fitzhugh had gone to Japan ostensibly to research a monograph entitled, *Trailing Gary Snyder*. On his way back from Yoshino Mountain, he spent the night at a traditional inn. Immersing himself in the communal tub, after washing, he listened to his fellow guests discuss the merits and demerits of a succession of widows. Intrigued, he, as politely as he knew how, enquired into the provenance of their remarks. Because of his fluent command of their language, his obvious bear-like clumsiness and his praiseworthy determination to eschew all things western, they laughingly put him straight, thus planting a seed which came to fruition on his return to Tokyo when, one fateful afternoon, he quit on Gary Snyder and set off on his quest to find the widows.

During the ensuing nine months, he assiduously combed the suburbs, storing up his database and paying for his meals, travel, rent and hire of office equipment by a mixture of busking, shoe shining and teaching business American. On one of his busking forays, he was mistaken for the celebrated street musician and composer, Moondog, which gave rise to an apocryphal story of an unreleased Tokyo recording session.

The publication of *The Widow's Room*, the finished product of Fitzhugh's labours, immediately slotted into the zeitgeist of America's West Coast. Subsequent editions penetrated the remainder of the States. Owing to its success, Fitzhugh was able to recruit and maintain a corps of Japanese researchers who kept abreast of developments, ready to update each planned yearly guide.

Fitzhugh had a personal horror of value judgements, so his work stayed refreshingly free from rating systems of stars and rosettes. His guide's users, therefore, were able to discover for themselves wonderful, enriching experiences or conversely indulge in relating the number of occasions they had wasted on dire, tedious and uninspired venues. On one thing though they were unanimous: his chapter on settling the bill was indispensable. Within its bullet points, he led them through a maze of foreign customs, philosophical disjunctions and plain physical discomforts to a step by step mastery of insouciance, timing and, if need be, hard-nosed bloody-mindedness. His readers recognised that without his help they would have been completely adrift. They could never have paid up so confidently and have felt so good about it. A proprietary pat on the cover of his book struck them as a fitting tribute.

In the days of his air force tour of duty, Curtis Simpson regularly dipped into the pages of the guide. One evening, as his wife, Yvonne, was unexpectedly indisposed, he accompanied his daughter, Evangeline, to Widow Saka—Otoshi Alley—Godaigo Primitive. Evangeline, who was in her final year at Columbia, experienced a new rapprochement with her father from whom she had been alienated throughout her teenage years. She later described the journey and her emotions in some detail in an interview she gave to *Alternative Business Review*.

'The encompassing darkness in the back of the staff limousine. The smoothness of its onward glide. The subtle way my father's posture began to loosen and change. His almost boyish glance as he half turned his face close to mine. I felt as though the years were slipping away from him one by one and that he had retrieved the form and substance of the young man who must have so fascinated my mother in the days when, I guessed, their love was new. I sensed he was on the dangerous verge of mistaking me for her or, if not her, then for someone else. I almost expected him to lean across and put his hand on my knee, but, of course, he did no such thing, although the imaginary grip of his fingers on my stocking was faintly palpable. His smell was alluring and exciting. A knot twisted in my abdomen. Then he spoke, and the knot within me slowly dissipated, and we began to talk as we had never really talked before, not as father and daughter, but rather as if we had only met each other for the first time and had found, to our surprise, that we shared a love for pistachio ice cream, the Brooklyn Bridge, the New York cityscapes of Frank Stella and the bleakness of the New Jersey flatlands across the river.

'By now, our driver was completely lost. We shuttled up one dingy street after another, only to find ourselves back where we started. Seemingly interminable factory walls petered out into vacant lots which led to more factory walls. Then at last, coming towards us across uneven hillocks, squeezed between a cluster of dilapidated shacks and an elevated railway bridge, we saw two men flashing torches in our direction. They motioned us down an unsurfaced track to a raised one-storey building bordering a brickyard.

'Once inside, the widow greeted us personally. She was a short, dumpy woman somewhere in her late fifties. She wore a forties-style American frock. It had, I remember, large white gardenias on a purple background. As she took us to the mats we had reserved, she shuffled and swayed in front of us, pausing every now and then to turn and look coquettishly over her shoulder in the manner of the onnagata I had seen in the kabuki. Monotonous drumming heralded the commencement of a halting, almost static dance performed by our two former guides. Their movements and the meaning of their dance were incomprehensible, not just to me, but to the whole of the audience, which consisted of non-Japanese rubber-neckers. Father surmised that it was about a lion and a ghost. I told him that was simply his fallback position. He was as much in the dark as the rest of us. We laughed and the widow laughed too as she beat on a wooden block. Then she rose from her crouch and, with a small hammer, broke a hand mirror into two pieces. One half she discarded on the floor, holding the other aloft. Gently, with her fingers, as if she were releasing a small bird, she propelled it upwards and walked away somewhere behind the scenes. At that very moment, I realised that people are at their best, at their happiest, when they're not themselves.

'I told all of this to Joe May shortly after I'd met him. Some days later he said to me; "Come and see. I think I've found the widow's mirror." I don't remember anything else about that evening, neither the food nor the drive home.'

Harvard stopped reading and leafed towards the back of the book to find the relevant note. How typical of Evangeline's mother, he thought, to call her daughter by her own name. Two Evangelines. Two pieces of the mirror.

Medcorev's source was 'Interview with the Invisible Woman' by Hilary McPherson 1970 (*Alternative Business Review* vol. 3 issue 9). He read the following note as well.

It is worth emphasising from a wider perspective that Fitzhugh's intervention had an inevitable consequence. Patrons of the home restaurants became predominantly foreign. Commercialised standardisation replaced sporadic, haphazard amateurism. The fruit withered on the vine. Today, all that is left of the phenomenon is the ailing Ten Widows franchise, whose flagship used to be in Fukuuara Shopping Mall.

Dismayed by the turn of events, Fitzhugh abandoned the guide. He withdrew from TV chat shows and retreated to live quietly up country in Washington State. Siobhan, his youngest daughter, in time became a respected authority on Gary Snyder. She studied acting and toured the Midwest in the ill-fated production of *Kerouac, The Mother and The Priest*.

Harvard looked at his watch then returned to the main text, reading the top paragraph twice before succumbing to the flow.

The second progenitor, so-called Dog Activism, occurred from March 1951 to November 1954 at Louvain, Duisburg, Udine,

Meppel and Chateauroux. Contemporaneous accounts consisted of local and national newspaper cuttings, photographs, tape recordings, eyewitness depositions, prize-cup engravings, certificates, posters, pamphlets, memento badges and other lesser ephemera. They showed, or purported to show, that the following events had taken place.

In Louvain 18.3.51, a dog show without dogs was held at the Winter Circus. Men and women, old and young, accompanied by their handlers, were displayed, judged and awarded marks in eight dog breed categories.

In Duisburg 4 and 5.9.51, at the municipal greyhound track, an extra race was staged after the completion of the normal card. Six male adolescents paraded, entered specially constructed traps and raced on all fours. No Pari-Mutuel betting was allowed. Two months later, 1.11.51, an abbreviated performance of Schiller's *Marie Stuart* played to an audience restricted to dogs only at matinee prices.

During proceedings at the provincial court of Udine 18.1.52, Pietro Sacromonte, 59, the accused, was found guilty of imprisoning Antonia Biagi, 17, against her will, and subjecting her to unnatural acts, one of which was using her as a truffle hound. Various denunciations of similar abuse continued to trouble the authorities in subsequent years.

Throughout July 1953, public places in Meppel were bombarded with a poster and graffiti campaign urging 'Bring Back Executions For Dogs!' Crimes punishable by the death penalty were declared as follows—fouling the footpath, rubbing genitals against human legs, trailing behinds across designated non-dog areas, excessive barking, yapping and whining during dog curfew hours. The final exhortation read 'If Your Dog Resembles You, Kill It Or Kill Yourself!' Enraged dog lovers took to the streets in protest. Neighbourhood vigilantes organised night patrols in an attempt to apprehend the perpetrators. The then mayor had himself photographed self-consciously patting the head of Simba, a German shepherd, specially loaned for the occasion.

Finally, at Chateauroux 30.10.54, in the Agricultural Hall, an international dog show, inspired by Louvain, but this time judged by dogs, took place. An M. Leo Junot was barked best of show. Concurrently, one Daniel Siffra, an artist, displayed rows of tinned dog shit at the Zone Gallery.

In June 1960, Ellie Furstemburg, a Parisienne notary, stated that none of the aforementioned events had happened. Their 'news' had been invented, manipulated, inserted and documented by a group calling itself 'Dog Activism'. Members of the collective had signed a sworn affidavit in her presence. From this date, she added, 'Dog Activist memorabilia would be on sale to collectors.'

Harvard sighed and skipped pages until he came across the names he was looking for. He shifted to make himself more comfortable and resumed reading.

Selly Rycart and Joe May met regularly, night after night, in the Borough of Queens, New York City. Their conversations happened during long circular hikes, if the weather was bearable, or, if not, holed up in Selly's cold water apartment above Mantli's Deli on Sherman Street.

Rycart had recently entered partnership with Norman Cherway at Madcap Enterprises. Joe May was the poorest young American he had ever met. May slept on the streets most of the time, foraging for food day by day. Because of his insalubrious appearance, Selly initially had great difficulty in persuading Al at Mantli's to let him in. He passed Joe the necessary money to cover the tab when they had eaten, but, in the event, Joe went to the can and on his return informed everyone loudly that he had wiped his ass with it and flushed it down the john, leaving Selly to settle up and Al to beseech heaven.

Selly's unconcealed chagrin at Joe's eccentric behaviour, however, had one positive offshoot. It triggered their ongoing debate on waste as defined in open systems theory and the key role of finance in business. The theory, using biological analogies, stressed the interconnectedness of systems in transforming input into output. It stipulated that the cost of waste had to be monitored and controlled by correct identification, minimisation, efficient disposal and the exploitation, wherever possible, of by-products. As far as Joe was concerned, waste, as such, was an erroneous concept, a flaw of a too-rigid production process overview. He argued that a more fluid, sophisticated approach would not necessarily cost waste as a deficit because it did not fit a designated product but would utilise it as a potential new input ripe for transformation. He went further and pointed out that the majority of the world's population lived on waste. Recycled urine could be drunk by the person who had pissed it. The brand allure of an artist's name could transform his shit into a prized commodity. This last reference struck a chord with Selly regarding an article he had seen in *Investor Magazine* about cans of dog shit for sale and a nebulous outfit called Dog Activism. He promised to investigate and report back.

Over subsequent weeks, they both amassed as much information as they could unearth about the shadowy group. Selly concentrated on tracking the price fluctuations of the released artefacts in relation to their targeted and realised markets, while Joe set about unravelling the working methods and organisational links of the self-stated collective.

A letter they sent c/o E Furstemburg merely produced a standard reply, thanking them for their enquiry and assuring them that previously unissued goods would soon be available. No further statements were forthcoming, nor did any new items go on sale. After that, the trail went cold, and they left the field to the occasional academic commentator who was willing to pick over the bones of mass hypnosis, press gullibility, European dog cults, animal terrorists and the mulch of apocrypha and modern myth.

Joe May summed up their mutual interest, at the end of the day, by stating, 'No matter what the truth, whether the events were planned, took place or not, a named organisation gave them meaning by grouping them together, branding them and offering a commodity that potential customers could recognise. They transformed the unlikely into reality and added value.'

The following spring, a newly graduated Evangeline Simpson joined the Madcap partnership. Within a matter of weeks, Selly Rycart had become hopelessly infatuated with her. During one of their increasingly intimate *tête-à-têtes*, he told her about Joe May. She was intrigued and soon persuaded Norman Cherway, with her not inconsiderable charm, to convene an exploratory meeting. The four of them gathered for the first time at the Battery on the morning of May 11th 1963.

'And the rest is history,' Harvard muttered, as he closed the book. Time was moving on. He retrieved his wristwatch, put it on, rose and replaced Medcorev on the items for sale table. At the exit, he paused for a moment in front of the photo that culminated the exhibition. The great man lay crumpled on a day bed, a tartan shawl about his shoulders, his face bloated almost beyond recognition. Indeed, Wiener for one had typically claimed that this was not May at all but part of an agreed stunt to convince the company's shareholders, employees and clients that he was a completely spent force. Whatever the actual circumstances, however, not even Wiener had been able to dispute May's death three months later.

'She's baby to me,' Harvard sang softly, reprising the Emily Brown song. He was alone. The electricians had packed up and left. The suite was ready for tomorrow's audience. Another story from the *Stories We Tell Ourselves* came into mind. Joe May had said, 'Wherever technology takes us, there will always be people who will solely rely on real experience.' Evangeline Simpson and Selly

Rycart, who had been with him at the time, had burst out laughing. May had not joined in. Looking at his face, which had remained set and contemplative, they had concluded that no irony had been intended.

Home beckons, Harvard thought, when he took the lift down to tell the duty manager they had finished for the night. Home, as far as he was concerned, was only too real.

<hr>

'Oh! How the ghost of him clings and sings!'

'It was last autumn in Beijing.'

'You're like me. I can see you're like me. You did what I would have done.'

'Through my tears I thought I glimpsed his face and that we were both together again in our old house at Eltville.'

'Days of boredom. Running the office alone. Hardly going out at night. Staring at the compound walls.'

'He said, "Girl I don't know you. I can't understand you. You're all wrapped up."'

'Literally counting the days but resisting the temptation to cross them off the calendar. Money in the bank, of course, but a prisoner, a prisoner at heart.'

'It turned out he'd changed his name. Leila'd known. She didn't let on. Jackie told me to expect the worst.'

'Who knows? I got there and the only seats left were . . . '

Time was slowing everything around Sonny Ayza, prolonging each shake and judder, in the same way as it had cocooned the daydreams of Monica Randell, waiting behind her shop counter, in Sylvia's story. He felt as though the tram was running on two separate parallel tracks, somehow fated to pursue its twin journeys ad infinitum. On one of them, he was condemned to go on living in a present surrounded by these same passengers, repeating these same conversations, snatches of which he would hear for all eternity, whilst, in his mind, he endlessly disinterred his long dead father's bones, filling them with the possibility of life, only to have them perpetually enter and leave Paca's wine shop in Llomera: a place which Manolo had probably rarely frequented in his short existence. Whereas on the other he was carried prosaically homewards to a destination where he, himself, became a ghost without memory, oblivious to the futile resurrections of those who continued to see him in the streets and squares of Greenlea or standing opposite the lycée Jean Moulin in Lyon or shaking poker dice in a string of 'mama san' bars in Yokohama or running away in Orias or sitting on a wall dangling his legs in Llomera.

He shifted in his seat with an involuntary shiver. Something was sticking to the sole of his left shoe. Crossing his leg over his right knee, he prised off a wad of greyish beige chewing gum. He looked for something to wrap it in, but finding nothing, unlike the litter-strewn floor of Paca's, he rummaged in his pocket, detached one of the Elizabeth Kerry sheets, tore a corner off, enclosed the gum and transferred it back to his other coat pocket.

'I wouldn't go. What was the point?'

'But tonight's a different story entirely.'

A hand brushed the nape of his neck and lightly touched his shoulder as the woman behind him got up. He watched her sway down the aisle and wait at the exit doors. Two men standing beside her burst into raucous laughter. The tram stopped. They all got off, and while the tram picked up speed again he remembered the grasp of Mado's hand when she had balanced against him, lifting her leg to inspect the broken heel of her shoe.

The trivial, and till now forgotten, accident had happened in Rue Barème on their way back home from Parc de la Tête d'Or. Empty chestnut husks had lain in the *allées* where they had strolled arm in arm through the dank autumnal air, seeing the park and the suburbs of Lyon transmute into their park and their suburbs, a place where they could be with one another without thought for the future.

'*Anne, Anne fuis sur ton âne,*' she had quoted in his ear before moving off down the slope in her stocking feet. '*Ô saisons Ô chateaux,*' the words of the poem came back to him now. Truly,

'*Quel âme est sans défaut?*' Not his that was for sure.

His sister, Veri, his mother, Rosario, and now Mado, his one-time lover in the youthful days when he had quit Miranda, three women he seemed to be summoning as witnesses to his demise; one from Orias, one from the grave and one from he knew not where. His letter to Veri was at home. He had written it last night, but now the vision of her opening the envelope and holding it in her hands made him grimace and turn to the reflected smear of the street lights in the window. Better to see her as a child again and to recall childish tears, which left no lasting hurt.

They had been playing together under the table. As usual, Veri had pestered him to join her game. She had amassed a pile of pine cones by her side and he had had to say how many he wanted, while she made up the price and waited for him to hand over his imaginary money. Her sale completed, she stretched out her arms and scooped them all back in order to begin all over again, until he had seized several himself and had refused to let go. In vain, she had tried to wrest them away, her eyes dark and alive with concentrated purpose, her cheeks puffing out with her efforts, her tongue popping out of the side of her mouth with exasperation, then, realising she could not match the strength of his grip, she had subsided into mighty, wrenching sobs, punching and kicking at him as he crawled out of reach.

The roar of an accelerating motorcycle, gunning ahead of the tram, disrupted his reverie. They were approaching Lagran at last. The majority of the remaining passengers descended at the three stops that served the Sander Housing Project. He let his images of Mado and Veri go with them, then pressed the bell and left his seat. Once the tram had rounded the corner at the junction of Castle Street, he got off and watched it make its way to the terminus, the last one he would board.

A sudden, biting wind made him hunch his shoulders and increase his pace when he strode uphill alongside the perimeter of the Recassier Hospital. His eyes stung in its icy blast. Through the

36

railings, the blurred lights of the orthopaedic and geriatric pavilions were shining across the darkened lawns. The elements, at least, were providing some sensation.

A file of cars entering and leaving the Green Elf petrol station halted him momentarily before he reached Holmoak Road. He crossed it and took his usual shortcut over the waste ground behind the Lindmoor Laundry. He passed the fence of the allotments and went into the park, which lay in an extended semi-circle round the nineteenth-century buildings of Lagran Castle. Below him, the muffled rush of a stream, its waters swelled by recent rains, flowed towards the culvert at Prospect Field Business Park.

Five minutes later, when he reached the summit of the path, the city's glow, surrounding scattered pockets of darkness, filled the horizon to the south. Beyond lay the black void of the estuary and beyond that the faint glimmer of the far shore.

He had the view to himself as he went down the broad avenue lined with beeches that curved its way to the bottom gate. The clang of his footsteps echoed behind him as he crossed the iron footbridge. The grass on the other side was lumpy and partly frozen under his uneven tread. He passed the shuttered kiosk and the now derelict lavatory block. As he thrust his hands deeper into his pockets for warmth, his fingers contacted the wrapped up piece of chewing gum he had forgotten to discard when he left the tram. At this hour, no dogs bounded towards him over the open ground. No Alsatians called Rusty or Polka Dot from the cryptic message. There had been a song whose full title eluded him: Polka Dots and something. Well, whatever the something it scarcely mattered now. He reached the gate and swung it open.

The traffic lights on 14th May Drive were in his favour so he gained Cicely Way unimpeded and quickened his pace downhill. At the third turning on the right, he entered a short spur of a cul-de-sac with two small stone cottages, each with its narrow strip of garden abutting the road on one side and a row of lock-up garages on the other. The time had finally arrived. He was home.

He fumbled with his key, holding it out between his index finger and his thumb, ready to insert it in the lock. Its shape and weight seemed unfamiliar as if it were smaller, yet heavier, than before. This was it. He was at the threshold. Only two shallow steps and a doorway lay between him and his lack of future. He glanced down at the iron grid of the shoe scraper, which he practically never used, and drew one foot after the other backwards and forwards over its bars. A tiny hiccup of hysteria fluttered in his stomach. Could the household gods, if they still existed, the *lares et penates* of the Romans, guard him from his chosen course? He noticed the venetian blinds at his neighbour's windows were closed. He felt the need to urinate. Two steps to cross, a door to unlock, then a piss and the road to oblivion was easy. He mounted them in one stride, turned the key in the lock, opened the door and went inside.

The brandy bottle stood where he had left it, next to a tumbler and a full jar of aspirins on the kitchen table. He pressed down the foot lever on the rubbish bin under the sink and tossed in the remnant of gum, secure in its bit of paper, then, taking off his coat and laying it carelessly over a chair, he emptied the contents of his other pockets out beside the brandy. It was time to pee.

His flow of urine started at once. As he watched it stream away from him and hit the back of the toilet bowl, he felt an animal sense of easement, a bodily rightness. No doubt defecation would come later, but whether his brain would still register shame or relief he was not sure. He shook off the last remaining drips, did up his zip, washed his hands and returned to the kitchen.

The brandy was 104 brand, a long-standing Mirandan favourite. He picked up the bottle, broke the seal and poured it out until the glass was quarter filled. One hundred and four reasons, he thought. For what seemed like an age, he fiddled with the top of the aspirin jar, trying to get the requisite alignment and exert the right pressure to unscrew the cap. Once open, he let twenty to thirty tablets spill out. He got up again and filled a separate tumbler with water. Moonbeams. 'Polka Dots and Moonbeams', that was the title which had slipped his memory. Something about an evening encounter in a garden. He took a sip of brandy and then a larger gulp. The sensation in his mouth and throat was good. The pills lying in the palm of his hand looked so small and inconsequential. He swallowed five; one after the other and drank some of the water. He took five more. At some stage, he would go upstairs and lie down. His letter to Veri was propped on the bedside table. Everything would be tidied away.

When he raised his second tumbler of brandy to his lips, Mado's youthful form, as he remembered her, sat opposite him. She cupped her chin in her two hands and said earnestly, 'You can always ask for forgiveness.' There was no reply now, just as there had been no reply then. Hastily, he swallowed the alcohol and took another five pills. He glanced at the unimportant scraps of paper, the bits and pieces lying on the table, stuff which he had carried on his last day, stuff that would become part of the evidence, the things found at the scene when his body was finally discovered.

Everything was very quiet. There was no sound from outside. He moved his right foot about, pressing it down until he succeeded in getting a floorboard to creak. '*Pour passer le temps il faut passer le temps*.' Another of Mado's sayings. He felt the urge to eat something. There was food in the fridge, but it would be pointless. He took two more pills instead and washed them down with water. When would he begin to feel something, become drowsy or start to be overcome with what was happening to his metabolism? He couldn't say. Even in this, one had to continue. He could get a pen and a fresh sheet of paper—that would pass the time, the way he had done on so many previous occasions throughout his life. The mere act struck him as too ridiculous. More brandy was the answer. More brandy and more aspirins.

The telephone rang in the hallway. He had forgotten to disconnect it. He swallowed two more pills. By the time he had topped up his brandy glass and taken the next batch, the ringing would have stopped. 'Last autumn the ghost of him running the

39

office.' 'Hardly going out from Eltville but then I thought you were like me.' 'A prisoner all wrapped up and the only seats left.' Fuck. He was still on the number 11 tram. Its bell was ringing incessantly, but for some reason the driver refused to stop. Manolo came out of Paca's and took his hand. 'I'm going,' he said softly. 'You'll be safe, you and Veri and your mother. Tian will look after you. You'll see. Don't forget. I'll come back.'

The bell was still ringing. Was it real or something inside his head? Without thinking, he got to his feet. His legs moved okay. Like an itch, he thought, answering it is just like scratching an itch. One way or another, what could it matter? He picked up the receiver and put it to his ear.

'It's Monse.' There was the sound of piano music in the background and another voice calling.

'Monse,' he said. How calm his voice sounded. His breathing came light and regular.

'I've got something for you, something that will really interest you. Have you eaten yet?'

Laughter bubbled uncontrollably in his stomach. Like an intoxicant it glided through him, contorting his larynx and forcing his eyelids shut with hot, pricking tears. I am hysterical, he thought. This silence cannot go on. I will burst. 'No,' he managed to get out before his laughter escaped and erupted.

'You're in a merry mood. I'm glad.' She laughed to herself. 'Please come round and have some supper. We haven't seen you for ages. Albert keeps saying we must phone Sonny. It's important we expats keep in touch and, of course, when I came across this. Well, anyway, I'll tell you all about it tonight. I don't want to spoil the surprise. In about half an hour then?'

'I've,' he was about to say, 'I've got other plans,' but the truth was he realised he no longer did. This particular situation was no longer sustainable. Its moment had passed. It had been broken. He knew now he would put the pills back in their jar and screw down the lid until the next time. 'I'll be there,' he said. 'Thanks for the invitation.'

The kid had been with him again since the beginning of the evening. He had stood over in the corner by the window, protecting something in his cupped hands.

Emmet Briggs had imagined that it was trickles or beads of sweat. Later, when the kid had limped nearer the bed, first teetering perilously on his shorter leg then dragging the longer one behind, they had become a pool of water, so clear, so tempting, that he had wanted to stir and break its surface with his breath.

The sounds of the ocean accompanied the kid's halting movements. Emmet gently felt himself lost in the boom of its waves, the seductive tug and then drift of its undertow, the beguiling sigh and emphatic hiss as it captured and surrendered its farthest shore.

During these strangely euphoric interludes of submersion and flotation, Emmet sensed he knew exactly who the kid was, even though his features kept changing; now dark and flattened, now aquiline and girlish with two small, pointed breasts rising and vanishing into the smooth black contours of his chest. The kid had moved his own lips to help shape the name Emmet's lips had finally uttered. The name he could not remember. The name, by now, he was only dimly aware of trying to remember.

Throughout the time they had been together, Emmet had wrestled to stay awake, afraid that the kid would sense his need for sleep and depart. He had been glad, therefore, for the sporadic bursts of laughter coming through the partition wall, the sudden banging of adjoining doors, the sobs of drunks in the hallway, followed by the creak and stumble of uncertain footsteps on the stairs. From outside the building, he had welcomed the approaching drone of airplanes and the faint bass rumble and jolting shudder of goods trains as they clacked and rattled over the points down towards the junction. They had all aided his necessary vigil in spite of his realisation that his eyes must have closed sometimes when the kid's presence had waxed then waned.

In those moments, a foreboding of the kid's unavoidable absence began to agitate Emmet's limbs. While he attempted to beg the kid to stay, he found to his horror he had lost his power of speech. His facility to make words, at the very worst time, had deserted him. Mercifully, the kid proved to be stalwart and patience itself. His attendance persisted. His store of water, his treasure, remained uplifted in his outstretched hands.

Emmet wanted badly to show him Ogun's staff, to take him to the forge where the blacksmiths' hammers beat out and tempered the molten rods, but the kid only smiled and shook his head. With the tips of his fingers he parted the water to reveal a cluster of palm nuts. Mischievously he jumbled them up then rearranged them so that Emmet could read their meaning one by one. Kernel and shell, they spelled out—O L O K U N.

In vain Emmet tried to scoop them up, but, with his first blundering struggle, the kid finally disappeared to be replaced by a fitful dream. The sounds of the sea subsided into his own shallow breathing. Vague outlines, white and yellow lozenges of light and misplaced encounters stole over him, engulfed him and transported him to another day, another evening and another awakening.

Radio voices and the hiss and splatter of Hallie frying something encouraged him to get up and pull on a pair of slacks. She was standing at the stove in the kitchen with her back to him, wearing the red kimono he had bought all those years ago when he had gone with Jimmy Massoura to the east coast.

Business seen to, and with Jimmy safely relaxed in the company of a couple of teenage trades, he had left their hotel to track down the obligatory shit. On the way back, his attention had been caught by a black and grey kimono, visible to the rear of a Japanese five-mat living display in a store window. On an impulse, he had gone inside and asked the price. The assistant had explained that it was not a real article for sale but a specially created mock-up. She had then shown him what else she had in stock and he had picked out a red one.

Once back in Greenlea, he had driven straight over to Hallie's, the kimono resplendent in its box beside him. Twice he had honked the horn of the two-tone Oldsmobile he owned at that time, waiting for her to come down the steps.

Now, looking back, he could say, strangely and perversely, it had been one of the happiest moments in his life. Strange, because when he had climbed out of the car, she, without saying anything or even embracing him, had clambered behind the wheel then had reached over and opened the lid, only to purse her lips, shake her head and adamantly refuse to accept his gift. Perverse, because he had been obliged to take it, and himself, away. Sourly he had stored it in the back of a cupboard in his apartment where it languished on top of a suitcase, waiting, like him, for the day it could be redeemed.

One year later, when he had been released from prison and was looking after Minty Wallace's protection interests in the new West Bay tourist development, she had finally relented and had paid him a loving visit. In return, he had found the kimono and spread it out for her on the bed.

Seeing her wearing it now made him feel more than okay. True, it had seen better days. Its cuffs were worn and frayed. Time had leeched the colour's original vibrancy, but then nothing remained the same, not it, not himself, not Hallie. Trailing his fingers across the thinness of its material, he traced the outlines of her shoulder blades and lowered his forehead against her neck. Time, he thought, I'll always have time for this. He decided not to say anything about the kid. After all, what good would that do?

Hallie turned and embraced him. 'Did you get some sleep? I still don't like them, you know, these new associates of yours. I don't trust them. I never will.'

'Everything's all right. I'm more than on top of it. They just need me to be there. Use my name. Business as usual.' He pulled her close to him, soaking up the warmth of her body, waiting until the warmth of his permeated her to her very core. 'Stick to the here and now. That's what we need.'

'Take a gun with you,' she said. 'I don't want to say it, but I'd be happier if you did.'

'No. I won't need one. It won't be that kind of shenanigans. Anyway, Jacky Millom's bringing some. It's been arranged.' 'Keep on hammering,' a voice whispered in his skull. Hammering, as if he could do anything else, for Ogun was his guardian and his guide. He was Ogun's child.

'It'll be a long night. Don't forget I'm going to do another shift.'

He nodded. 'Remember, I'll see you at the restaurant tomorrow before two. Let's eat.'

Hallie dished up. They sat down together and ate. As he chewed his steak and looked into her eyes, Emmet felt the hammer momentarily loosen in his grasp, and fleetingly he saw himself standing on the bank of a flaccid, scarcely flowing river. Suddenly, he did not know what came next. He only knew that his brow was bathed in unaccustomed sweat and ahead he had work that must be done.

Three glasses, a three-quarter full bottle of Algama wine, a clear bottle with a residue of brandy in it and a broad-necked jar of raisins, macerated in grape spirit, adorned the table.

They had eaten frugally, enshrined in the joke of parsimony that Monse always liked to play on Sonny. Bread and garlic soup had been followed by a fried egg each: all of it redolent of Mirandan nights long ago, meals that they had consumed without thinking, surrounded by family, friends, fellow students, work colleagues, each one of them, then as now, adept at mopping up the runny yolks with dabs of bread.

'You're not drinking, Sonny.' Albert's hand, holding the wine bottle, hovered over his glass.

'No thanks. I don't feel like it tonight. Please don't let me stop you.'

'No chance of that.' Albert laughed and filled up Monse's glass and then his own. 'Is it too sweet? Help yourself to brandy if you prefer.'

Sonny shook his head and raised his open palm. Monse leant across and gave his arm a squeeze. 'Are you well? You look quite pale. Are you taking enough care of yourself?'

Sonny smiled. 'I'm quite well. A little touch of cold. It's nothing. I just can't seem to shake it off. I took some pills before I came out. That's the only reason.'

His answer seemed to reassure both of them, for Monse began to chat happily about the various people she and Albert had met on their recent trip back to Miranda. The strange thing was he felt so remarkably well considering the circumstances. Let this day finish, he thought, and tomorrow we'll see. Accordingly, he looked on indulgently, while their animation markedly increased as they both extolled the unsurpassed joys and many virtues of their homeland.

Albert Roig, Monserrat Selle: their names had followed one another in the ritual taking of the class register from their very first morning together at secondary school. Even now, forty years on, they still maintained and nurtured links with those who had shared their schooldays group, an exchange of holiday postcards here, a telephone call there when a grandchild was born or a death occurred.

Their flat was littered with related mementoes. Every surface sported framed photographs of individuals, families alone or united with other families, group reunions, gifts from hither and yon, souvenirs and knick-knacks, which, on the slightest touch or most cursory glance, triggered off a spate of memories of such and such, anecdotes about so and so. Desks, occasional tables, chairs, sofas and, no doubt, cupboards and drawers as well, brimmed and sighed under a shifting cargo of correspondence containing fascinating accounts of chance meetings, unforeseen confessions, complaints, desertions, illnesses, changes of address, gossip, work plans, anticipations of high days and holidays, celebrations that went wrong. Others that succeeded, vagaries of the weather, too hot, too cold, too much the same, aftermaths and consequences, reasons for silence, failure to keep in touch, depressions, grounds for jealousy, men going off the rails, estrangements, sulks, happy tidings, women's problems, scribbles and scrawls from children eager to mark the paper and bestow the xxxxs of kisses to their, until the next time, far-off auntie and uncle, Monse and Albert.

Religiously, they returned to stay with their old schoolmates at least twice a year. Monse, who taught at the Greenlea Conservatoire, enjoyed generous holidays, and Albert, who owned a small printing firm, organised things to fit in. This continuous, engrossing involvement with their place of birth and the lives of their contemporaries, into which they had poured so much energy and love, stood in stark contrast to Sonny's diffidence on all matters Mirandan: to their knowledge, he had not set foot there nigh on thirty years.

Monse had studied harmony and composition with Nicolas Ferens in Orias. During that time, she had also attended Sebastian Marva's lectures on the origins and development of Mirandan song forms. In turn, he had been guest of honour when she had participated as an oboist in the music college's performance of his suite, *Western Pilgrimages*. On that particular night, he had been accompanied by Rosario, his wife, and Sonny and Veri, his stepchildren.

Years later in Greenlea, while searching for the telephone number of the Azimuth Company, she had come across a single entry under Ayza. Vaguely recalling something about the name, and overcome with her natural curiosity about all possible things Mirandan, she had dialled several times before, in the end, Sonny answered. To her surprise, after she had talked about Orias, Ferens and Marva, he had remembered the occasion and the evening in question. She had taken a lively interest in him ever since.

'To the city of green hills!' Albert raised his wine glass in a toast. 'I should say to the two cities, Algama and Greenlea!'

'Oh green, how I love you green. Green wind. Green branches,' recited Monse.

'To the land of nothing for us,' rejoined Sonny ironically, picking up his own empty glass.

'Come to me healer and heal my griefs,' Monse crooned, looking into Sonny's eyes mockingly. She was getting slightly tipsy.

'Isn't that usually sung by a man to a woman?'

'Those griefs of yours are over,' Albert said. 'Everyone is free to return. Everyone has returned.'

Sonny did not reply. Albert coughed and poured more wine. Monse emptied some of the raisins onto a saucer. For an instant, the angel of death hovered above them and they fell silent in its presence.

'Silence, for it is night-time. Silence, the darkness,' Albert sang. He had a pleasant tenor voice and would have continued with the remaining couplets if Monse had not signalled to him to desist.

'I was thinking about my father today,' Sonny said.

'Sebastian? Tian?'

'No. Manolo Ayza, my natural father. In my thoughts, he hadn't died, or at least he had been able to leave his grave on the other side of the border and return to Miranda. I pictured him sitting in the wine shop I remembered as a kid, a few streets away from our old home in Llomera. I thought, let him rest there and drink for a moment in the company of those who still knew of his existence, where some kind of continuity had been preserved in contrast to the perpetual start from zero. Needless to say, it was only a daydream, an idle passing of a minute or two.'

'Your job weighs you down, man. It's not healthy dealing with clients who pay money to pretend they are someone else.' Albert had a hobby horse about Chance Company and he was about to ride it full tilt when Sonny interrupted him.

'Yes. Everyone can go back, but it's a question of choice. I choose not to.'

'You're still bitter about Sebastian and your mother,' Monse said.

Sonny shook his head. 'No, Monse, that feeling died a long time ago. I don't blame Rosario or Tian. They loved each other. It's my father I can't understand.'

Without a word, Monse suddenly got up, as if his words had reminded her of something, and began rummaging in a pile of envelopes and sheets of paper on the lowered shelf of the writing bureau behind the table. 'It was here an hour ago. I had it by me after I phoned you.' She raised her hands in exasperation then switched her attention to a different pile, which had started to sprout on the floor on the bureau's far side.

'Try the kitchen,' said Albert. 'You'd something in your hand when I was peeling the garlic.'

Sonny scooped up a handful of raisins from the saucer and held them in his cupped palm while he chewed them one by one. They tasted increasingly rancid. He felt a cold sweat begin to dampen his brow. A nagging pain flitted behind his retina. The aspirins were having a delayed effect. 'I must be going,' he said. 'I'm tired. You see I can't keep up with Mirandan hours. I'm used to being in bed by now.'

'Work tomorrow?' Albert drained his wine.

'No, I've got a week off. It's been owing me for some time.'

'Hah!' A triumphant cry emerged from the kitchen. Monse reappeared clutching a large manila envelope. 'Here it is. I got it yesterday from an old Orias newspaper cutting. I knew you'd be interested so I made a copy for you.' She handed it to Sonny. 'It's about someone you met. Someone I know you have always admired.'

First Elizabeth Kerry, then Sylvia, now this, Sonny thought. The steady drip of accretion of things people want to give me never stops. 'Thank you,' he said. 'I'll read it tomorrow. I'll have some time on my hands.' A car, its headlights dipped between high hedges, an open cut-throat razor against a strop, the last, inadvertent, shameful glance in the mirror in his hallway, the brandy bottle here on the table, he felt the day's memento mori were spilling from his brain for all to see. 'By the way,' his voice sounded as though it had emerged from the reanimated corpse of his father, 'have you ever heard of someone called Fernando Cheto Simon?'

Neither of them had.

<hr />

'Let me go in first,' Walter Sembele said, as he eased past Emmet Briggs and cheerfully pushed his way through the crowded hallway into the room on the right.

Following Walter's retreating back, Emmet dutifully accepted the cautious looks that came his way. They were his reputation's tribute, his ambiguous dues. The day he failed to arouse the familiar mixture of wariness, contempt and fear they displayed was, he knew, the day he would have to quit the life for good.

He glanced back over his shoulder in order to remind Antoine Viall, who should have been immediately behind him, to stick close and be clearly seen as part of their entourage. Instead, the young man had drifted away towards the doorway where he was now attempting to meet and greet new arrivals.

Shit, thought Emmet. His priority was to be by Walter's side. He did not have time to babysit anyone else. He gestured to Antoine to get a move on, but his signal was ignored. Fuck him, let him stay, Emmet decided, though the guy worried him. He had done right from the start four days ago. He just did not fit in. Now, for instance, his body posture was all wrong. His hands did not move right. There was no unrolling of the wrists, no spreading of the fingers. Instead, they jabbed and patted feebly at the sleeves and arms extended to them, plus he failed to meet and hold people's eyes long enough. Why him? Emmet wondered. From the little he had overheard, Viall was not Walter's choice. He was too young, too callow, too white, for the glad-handing, the flesh-pressing, the schmoozing with malice aforethought, the calling in of favours and staking out of markers, that Walter required. Somebody related to the money side? It was a possibility. Or simply a private matter of sex? If so, the signs were well disguised. Whatever the answer, one thing was for sure, he would not let up until he had it. Patrol the boundaries, Minty Wallace used to say, and he, over time, was an expert boundary patroller, especially when fitted up with a set of knuckledusters and a razor in his pocket.

The gathering had closed in a circle round Sembele when Emmet entered. Judiciously shifting a few intervening bodies, he elbowed his way to the front. Word quickly spread to the uninitiated about the degree of respect and the space he should be given. A thickset man beside him, whom he had not seen before, grinned and muttered, 'Hi.' Emmet cut him off with a slow, steely stare.

'Party! Party all you want and more!' Walter was building up his spiel to hit the high notes. 'There's everything you desire for right here tonight,' he yelled, positively luxuriating in their attention, 'and if you don't find it just let poppa know. Cos I gotta make it all right. I gotta see you right for the Old Man's sake. For, before I set out on this memorable journey, he said to me, "Walter, let the joy be unconfined, man! Let that blessed milk and honey flow! Tell them the news in Greenlea. Take them the glad tidings that I will repay them. Their abiding faith in me will be rewarded. Their votes cast on that forthcoming, fateful day will always be remembered. They will be duly recognised and most solemnly honoured. For they are truly our citizens and our brothers and sisters in the flesh and spirit." So you see, good people, I'm here to bring his message to you,' he sidled over to a shortish man and his taller woman companion, 'and you, my friend, and you, my sister,' then darted back to hold his audience once more. 'Eat as you want! Drink as you like! Substance your soul in the way the Good Lord intended! And, ladies, there are gentlemen here for you. And, gentlemen, look around you in the house, there's AC/DC. Good poontang,' he whispered in a nearby male ear. 'Good highflying,' in another.

Right on cue, Latin music started up. Still alternately shouting gleefully and joking confidentially, Walter shook his hips and danced and weaved amongst the growing crowd. He smiled and ducked and bobbed like a feinting lightweight, just as he had ducked and bobbed round Emmet two days ago when he had introduced himself and Antoine Viall at Panalquin racetrack.

'Know anything in this one, brother?' he had opened. 'No. Well don't worry. We may be in a foreign land, far away from the old country, separated from our beloved places, but this baby's got enough poke to go round.' He had reached out to find Emmet's arm, but a withering bull-pen glare made him think twice and drop his hand to his side. 'No offence, Mr Briggs. Let me introduce ourselves and explain. I'm Walter Sembele. This is my associate, Antoine Viall. The Old Man sends his greetings. Through me he's of a mind to bestow good fortune on our people here and, if I may say so, you in particular.'

Without answering, Emmet moved away from the two of them to the far side of the pre-parade ring, where the entrants for the last race were being led round by their lads and lasses prior to saddling up. Arkansas Highway, a grey four-year-old mare and likely favourite, jig-jogged past, unresponsive to the soothing words of her attendant. Patches of white sweat spread between her hind legs.

'Not today,' Johnny Karim said, standing guard as usual over the wheeled basket in which the truncated body of his brother, Billy, gesticulated and mouthed repeated 'fucks' at the leaden expanse of the darkening sky.

'No,' Emmet agreed. 'We've got to look elsewhere. Pinpoint's the one for me. It's his time of year, and he goes well after a break.'

Johnny laughed. 'Save your money, Emmet. His trainer isn't here. No, the whisper is My Myosotis. Billy here says it's fucking nailed on.'

Tucking a win ticket for Pinpoint into the band of his pork-pie hat, Emmet left the totalisator hall and climbed to the top of the grandstand. Sembele and Viall eyeballed him from a barrier below. Only when the last of the field had cantered down to the start did Walter nudge Antoine and get him to reluctantly switch his attention to the track.

Away from the stalls, Pinpoint was slow into his stride and soon had to be ridden by his jockey to pick up the early pace. Swinging round the final bend, he came back on the bridle but was forced wide, and after improving halfway up the straight his challenge petered out. He trailed in seventh of ten. Meanwhile, Do The Time, an unregarded outsider, got up close home to beat My Myosotis by a head.

'I don't give a fuck for politics. Your Old Man is shit to me,' Emmet said, when the pair accosted him again.

Walter smiled deprecatingly, 'You do yourself a disservice. Sure, on behalf of the Old Man, I can give you and your wife a good time, but I'm not here for that. I'm here to offer you, as a favoured son of our soil, a very rewarding position. Will you do us the courtesy of hearing us out? Let's have a drink. Now, where's the harm in that?'

They made their way together to the Cyclops Bar. At the counter, Walter cheerfully ordered three large rums. 'Ourselves,' he said, clinking his glass against Antoine's whilst Emmet's remained on the bar. 'As you know,' he continued unabashed, 'the election is nigh and the Old Man's set his heart on a final term. He's achieved so much recently, but he needs more time to bring his grand design to fruition. We're gathering in the sheaves, brother, Antoine here and me. Those already on board, of course, will stay on board, and for those who in the past were undecided, those with outside interests, those fickle multi-national corporations, well, he's got plans. He's changed, you know. You'd warm to him. Now he's got a new history and new friends. Believe me the old ways are dead, the ways you perhaps regretted. At home, he'll win for sure. There he's laying as the house, but abroad, and especially here, there's a big vote, a floating vote if our forecasts are correct, and there's a lot of dirty tricks. There's lying propaganda, which we will have to face. There's people's untutored memories that we will have to instruct. The opposition's got influence and serious funding. It's clear we must stand and fight. That's why the Old Man needs emissaries, like myself and Antoine, to go out spreading the truth, so that errors can be rectified and tragic misjudgements avoided. Frankly, he'd like it if you joined us. I'd like it. Your reputation brings us to seek your help. Now, what do you say?'

As Emmet did not immediately reply, Walter hastily bought another round of drinks. 'Why Cyclops?' he said, noticing the legend suspended above the barman's head. 'Does it honour Polyphemus, our one-time colonial captor?'

'The best seven furlong horse that ever raced here,' Emmet said. 'Before my time.'

'Listen, let's forget the crap. We know all about you. We know your wife. We know where you live and where she works,' Antoine Viall suddenly spat out, almost knocking over his glass in his newfound agitation.

Walter fluttered his hands angrily in front of the young man's flushed face. He turned apologetically to Emmet. 'You see how badly he does it. He's still a youngster. This is his first time. Don't you see the reason why I need you and your experience? Think about it. Apart from the money I'd guarantee, you could go home again, even get into the States if you wanted. Believe me, the Old Man paves the path for those who support him. All your past problems with the law could be set aside. The hour is striking for the gravy train's departure. Say the word and hop on. Give us your vote and you're welcome to enlist in our crusade.'

The following morning, Emmet met Walter alone at his newly instituted campaign headquarters, located in two dusty, high-ceilinged rooms above an ironmonger's shop at 31 Salonika Street. Once he had checked his initial retainer by riffling through the notes and scrutinising their watermarks, they got down to negotiating terms for more positive interventions. Business concluded, Walter smiled and floated a further proposal.

'That's too dangerous. Usually, I avoid killing people and I certainly won't do it for any of this political shit,' Emmet replied.

Walter extended his arms and spread open his palms. 'Like yourself, I'm a percentage player. The matter can wait.' He got up from behind his desk. 'Now let me give you a couple of lists. This first one contains the names of weaker brethren who would benefit from your guiding arm. I leave the style of conversion to you. This other one consists of malcontents and wreckers. Take the fight to their homes and hearths. Smite these philistines so they can no longer congregate and spread their lies.' He chuckled. 'You know, with this new, rosy future waiting for us round the corner, I wouldn't be surprised if, on the day, the dead men and women who voted for us in the past didn't revive to the glad sounds of trumpets and abandon their graves to record their shining votes. You'll see, we'll get along just fine.'

'And Viall?'

'Leave him to me. He's my concern. The important thing is we have an understanding.'

Now, looking about him, with the two lists in his inside pocket, and surrounded by people eager to enjoy the party, business was taking care of itself. Walter, as good as his word, had ensured they had ample rations, convivial company, a variety of drugs and a leavening of female and male prostitutes to discreetly cruise the territory. All he had to do was to keep an eye on those who got too close and wait for Jacky to bring the guns.

In the event, they arrived sooner than expected. Within an hour of the shindig properly kicking off. Jacky Millom, grasping a canvas bag tightly in front of him, poked his head round the doorway and, on spying Emmet, jostled into the packed crowd. Emmet quickly alerted Walter, and, to curious glances, the three of them pushed out to the stairs. Jacky looked as whey-faced as ever. His blue-grey pupils were dilated, and Emmet guessed that under his long black leather coat his skinny legs were trembling. The charade was Walter's idea. When Emmet had protested, he had been adamant. 'A show,' he had said. 'I need people to see we're armed and ready.'

Seeing them approach, Antoine disengaged himself from a knot of revellers, who were drinking rum out of a Green Bush bottle on the first landing, and joined their cortège. Walter opened the door of the master bedroom. 'No fuss, brother,' he said, as a man's head swivelled round from the prone, naked body of a light-skinned woman. 'We won't interrupt long. Just hold it fine and dandy and we'll be gone.'

Jacky turned appealingly to Emmet. Emmet gripped his arm. 'It's okay, Jacky.'

Almost on the verge of tears, Jacky's left knee shook violently against his bag. A posse of men and women had followed them into the room. Others gathered at the threshold.

'Dump them over there,' Emmet ordered, indicating the dressing table.

The woman on the bed raised her pear-shaped behind, allowing her sexual partner to release the coverlet and drape it over their bodies. Jacky took out four automatics one by one. He unwrapped them and laid them in a line, then he placed clips of ammunition beside them. Conversations froze as Emmet inspected each in turn. He had already made up his mind, but Walter wanted a show and now the audience was assembled. Slowly, he meticulously tested each one's weight and balance, sliding their mechanisms back and forth before assuming the firing position.

'Another?' Walter asked, when he indicated his choice.

Emmet shook his head. Walter pulled out a roll of banknotes from his trouser pocket and began to pay Jacky.

'Wait a minute. I'll take this one. It might come in useful. It reminds me of the one I used to carry in New York City.' Antoine's remarks went down well with his immediate onlookers. Two of them hugged his shoulders. A little cheer went up.

Walter shrugged, 'So be it.' He finished counting out the extra money. Jacky half managed a wan smile in return. While he wrapped up the two remaining guns and stowed them back in his bag, Antoine crooked his right index finger, aimed at the couple in the bed and slowly pulled the imaginary trigger. A burst of laughter erupted as the company trailed out.

'A word, Jacky,' Emmet said when they were outside the door. 'I'll want you to buy the gun back at a fair price. I'll let you know when. You know my word. I won't bring it if it's been used.'

'I don't know, Emmet. Don't do this.'

'I hope you're not forgetting we go back some. I came to you. I gave you the business. Now I don't want to go out of my way to find you. So tell me you'll be around when I call.'

'Please! This is crazy enough in a house full of tourists. Christ knows how many of them are police informers. Throw it away like normal. Come on, man, you didn't pay for it.'

Emmet raised him off his feet and shook him. 'I'm glad you see it my way. The piece is more valuable than I first thought, but between buddies there's always an accommodation.' He lowered Jacky's shaking frame and enveloped him in a bear hug. 'Good to see you, citizen. I'll be in touch.' His grip relaxed. Without replying, Jacky seized his chance and fled.

Downstairs, the party was cranking up a notch. A thin young woman with ash-blonde hair, scarcely filling out an electric-blue strapless dress, asked Emmet to dance. Satisfied that Walter was okay a few feet away, he held her to him and guided her through the breaks of 'La Isla Encantada', a recently revived rumba hit. He had a gun. Antoine had a gun. Walter did not. Whatever their plans were, he aimed to be at least two steps ahead. He guessed the unnamed target whom Walter had proposed, and he had rejected, was the key. The subject was bound to resurface in spite of Walter's casual acceptance of his refusal, probably as a definite order rather than a tentative request. He whispered in the young woman's ear. Following his gaze, she nodded and shimmied over to Walter, who was locked in conversation with a group of the party faithful. A courtly bow greeted her arrival, and, taking her outstretched hand, he let himself be led into the choppy rhythms of a merengue.

As Emmet had expected, Walter proved to be a lissom and subtle dancer. Each of his moves perfectly complemented and underscored his partner's now blossoming verve. For a brief moment, she began to exude a demonstrable grace, which he counterpointed in the sway and thrust of his jutting hips. Then the music changed, and, with a nonchalant wave of his hand, he moved aside to backslap another potential supporter. Her eyes still shining, she rejoined Emmet.

'Thanks,' she said. 'That was a good idea. Can I get you something? Something to drink or do something for you?'

'No. Don't worry about me. Relax. I'm hired help. I'm Emmet Briggs by the way.'

In an unguarded second, she flashed him the look then recovered her composure. 'I've heard of you. I'm Corinne. Just Corinne. That's how people know me.'

'Where you learn to dance like that?'

She laughed. 'You don't have to be black to shake it. I practised is the answer.'

Emmet nodded. 'It does make perfect.'

'Shall we sit down? I could do with a break.' She left unsaid the thought that, with him, none but the foolhardy would be likely to demand her services. 'Tell me if it's not okay.'

'It's alright, so long as I keep an eye on Papa Le Bas over there.'

'Why do you call him that? He's Walter Sembele isn't he?'

Why indeed, Emmet thought, for Walter was all too human, a trickster certainly, but in no sense, in spite of his religious jive, a divine messenger. It was the kid's doing, he realised. Somehow the memory of the kid had prompted him to use the name. Granma used to know all about it, but what it was he did not seem able to retrieve. 'Only a way of speaking,' he said. 'Let's sit here.'

The image of a smiling Antoine Viall, pulling the trigger of his newly purchased automatic, flitted into his mind. There was no sound and no visible target, just the memory of the two bodies, now fused in coitus, in the bed upstairs, then, as suddenly as it had come, it went. He felt Corinne's hand slide into his trouser pocket, and he became aware that she was starting to tell him about her childhood in Veldar, a place he had good reason to remember.

' . . . in my home town of Veldar when I was twelve. They were busy building the extension spur to the North-South motorway at the time. Gangs of construction workers were billeted in a trailer camp near the site. In the evenings and at the weekends especially, when their shifts were finished, they came into town to get drunk, get stoned and, if possible, get laid. Naturally, this often resulted in fights with our local youths who had not been hired for the job. You could say the town was equally divided between those who benefited from the extra business and those who increasingly resented the disturbance of our somewhat somnolent everyday tranquillity.

'During the preceding years, the closure of first the shoe and furniture factories, and then the tanneries and sawmills, had dramatically changed our way of life. Long gone were the days when Veldar's slopes and riverside hummed with industry, and its sons and daughters followed their fathers and mothers into the same work. As a very small kid at play in that disappeared world, I can still see my two older sisters watching over me, while I toddled freely, my hair crowned with daisy chains, amongst the lads and lasses sunning themselves on the riverbank. Then the hooters sounded, telling them that their lunch break was at an end, and they rose and left us to our skipping and chanting outside the factory gates.

'From drip to increasing flow, that comforting bustle and commerce was replaced by stagnation, followed by migration, until the time arrived when Greenlea commuters, seizing the chance of improved road communications, began to buy up rundown properties.

'They brought with them a new level of expectation and sophistication. One of the old tannery buildings on the north bank was converted into a disco-cum-nightclub called My Friend Felicia's. Normally, it operated a policy of selective membership coupled with a strictly enforced dress code. However, in their wisdom, the owners decided to cash in on the short-term construction boom, so, for the month of September, they threw it open for anyone over twenty-one. The first body was discovered there on the morning of Wednesday the fourth.

'The story went like this. Mary Langlands, a bag lady of no fixed abode, had wandered in through the open door of the service area. Whilst George Aarons, the bar manager, was angrily escorting her off the premises, she told him that she had seen a corpse in one of the rooms. Unlikely as it seemed, her information proved to be correct, for, on later inspection, there in the general manager's office, sprawled on the floor, was a cadaver.

'The deceased, whose identity was never satisfactorily established, was a Caucasian male of around twenty-five to twenty-nine years of age. The cause of death, surmised by the police doctor and then confirmed by the pathologist, was drowning in fresh water. DI Pinson of the local force led the inquiry.

'The second body was found ten days later, lying beside an earth-moving machine at the roadworks. It had been a clear, moonlit night with the onset of hoar frost already whitening the ground when Lewis Wilson, one of the security guards, made his way round along the western perimeter of the site. Scarcely needing the beam of his torch, he thought he had come across simply another drunk as he glimpsed a slumped, comatose figure on the ground. Swearing, drumming on his shoulder and poking with the toe of his boot for encouragement, he tried to lift him to his feet. The clothing he grasped was soaking wet. The drunk felt limp and lifeless. Then, according to Wilson, an extraordinary thing happened. The man groaned, escaped from his hold and staggered away round the digger, where he collapsed again.

'Of course, after the police and the doctor had examined the body, his testimony was discounted. Wilson was tested for drugs and alcohol, but the results were negative. Once more, death was by drowning. The deceased had been in fresh water for at least four days.

'This time, however, dental checks got an identification. The dead man was Ezzard Ambilene, age forty-three, a sales representative employed on commission-only by the Steady Drift Insurance Company. He left a widow, Catherine, and two children, Lois and

Maurice. For most of his life he had lived in Greenlea.

'The last known sighting of Ambilene alive was at My Friend Felicia's in the early hours of Tuesday morning, tenth September. Three people remembered him there. Vera Sowenwell, the part owner and general manager, had been cold-called by him on the previous afternoon, a fact that he mentioned when he introduced himself to her in the club later on the following night. George Aarons, under questioning, produced Ambilene's business card; he vaguely recalled chatting to him about vintage cars and life insurance some time after midnight. Finally, Liz Congreve, a local supermarket checkout woman, stated that someone resembling his description had propositioned her on the dance floor around 1.30 a.m. She had not seen him after she had refused his offer. Meanwhile, Lewis Wilson stuck vehemently to his preposterous version of events.

'The appearance of the third body raised a complete furore. Tragically, it was that of an eight-year-old child, Alice Michaels, whose parents had reported her missing a fortnight earlier. In truly heartbreaking circumstances, she was found being nuzzled by the family dog, an Airedale terrier, in the backyard of her home. Its frantic whines and yelps brought first her mother and then her father to the scene. She, like the other two, had been drowned, but on this occasion her body had only been in the water briefly. Up to an hour, it was reckoned.

'Mounting suspicion, rapidly overtaken by hate and execration, fell on the poor child's parents. Rennie Michaels was well known as a blustering bully. He had numerous convictions for aggravated and grievous bodily harm. Milena, his cohabitee, had a history of credit card theft and petty fraud, supplemented in hard times by casual prostitution.

'Accordingly, from day one, the media stoked up the fires against them, with the unsurprising result that their house was soon besieged by enraged locals bolstered by a contingent of rubber-necking ghouls. Dog and human excrement was regularly deposited through their letterbox. Fascist inscriptions bedaubed their walls, and, for their own protection, they were ferried to a safe address somewhere out of town. The national police force, much to Pinson's chagrin, now took charge of the investigation.

'Their operation was headed by Superintendent "Cheb" Alakhin with Chief Inspector Susan Marshall as second in command. The ops room was run by DS Cameron Sinclair in a portakabin which they set up on a strip of waste ground at the corner of Luscan Embankment and Fairlie Street.'

A hand alighted on Corinne's thigh. A garnet signet ring slowly rubbed against her stocking. 'Talking loses time for fucking,' a voice said.

Emmet, who had been listening carefully to Corinne's account, not least because he knew for certain the first corpse was that of Little Sammy Tyrell, who had been eliminated in the fallout after the Minty Wallace, Ute Manoko and Joe May fiasco, looked up with a baleful stare. 'Fuck yourself,' he said, as he checked Walter was still okay. 'It's rude to interrupt. I'm talking with the lady here.'

'She's paid to screw,' Antoine Viall sneered, 'not to listen to the tired reminiscences of a clapped-out gangster.'

Corinne stirred to get to her feet. Emmet motioned to her to stay put. 'It's simple. I won't repeat it. Move away or I'll kill you. Well, what's it to be, brother?' he said, heavily accenting the last word.

Viall flushed then turned pale.

'Just walk away. It's easy.'

'Be sweet. Not like this, please,' Corinne whispered to Emmet.

'There's no other way to be. Right, Antoine?'

'Right.' In spite of himself Viall's finger and thumb started to pull at his ring, twisting it up and down. Fear was drying up his saliva. An acid taste filled his mouth. He turned away abruptly, then, from a safer distance, offered his parting shot, 'There's plenty others. They're all the same in the dark. Meat's meat, pussy pussy.'

'Go on,' said Emmet. 'You were talking about the portakabin.'

Corinne sighed. Her hand slid back in his pocket. 'From its southern window,' she continued, 'they had an uninterrupted view of the river. Its varied noises filled each silence and hiatus in their work routine. I often used to play there, staying out until the gloaming when the older kids chased us younger ones away. That very piece of wasteland had been one of our favourite dens. Runners used to speed from it in our game of hares and hounds, laying as many false trails of blatantly chalked arrows as they could, while their true course was camouflaged with tiny ones posted high and low. Then, after counting to a hundred, or, more likely, ninety-seven, the chasers set off in pursuit.

'So, although expressly forbidden by my mother to go down there after the murders, the lure of the place was too strong to be denied. One afternoon, coming out of school, I slipped away on my own and walked down the hill to the river. A woman in a black trouser suit was standing with her back to the water, dragging on a cigarette in short, sharp inhalations. She watched me mooch about for a few minutes then she came over and introduced herself as DI Susan Marshall. She found my Veldar accent strange and, to begin with, I had to repeat my answers to her questions. Her eyes were tired but kind, and I liked the look of her soft bob of strawberry-blonde hair curling over her ears. DS Cameron Sinclair, whom she called Cammy, came out of the portakabin and joined us chatting for a while.

'Over the next weeks, I saw one or both of them on most schooldays. Sometimes we bumped into them when I was out in town with my mother or sisters. They often talked about Superintendent Alakhin's fearsome reputation, his ruthlessness and the political jiggery-pokery he had used to advance his career. I began to look on them as a kind of second family. I imagined they were in love with each other and that one day they would have a child who would look like me. I spoke of them more and more at home which eventually led my mother, who secretly longed for juicy tidbits about the murders, to invite them round for tea.

'Susan came alone. Cammy was on duty. After a polite chat about me, our health, the town and the weather, she readily brought us up to date on police progress. She believed they were getting close to a breakthrough. It all turned on the testimony of one Wesley Ganrich, aka Joe Harmonica, a former one-man-band busker and now alcoholic vagrant, who had been arrested and charged with demanding money with menaces in Luscanpool, a nearby village.

'Once in the cells, Ganrich claimed that he possessed information concerning the Veldar inquiries, but he would only divulge it to Cheb in person. To Susan's surprise, Alakhin dropped what he was doing and immediately arranged an interview.

'On his return, he summoned her and Cammy to his office and told them what Ganrich had said. According to the vagrant, the key factor in the whole mysterious affair was a conspiracy plot to murder Ambilene and place his death in the middle of a concocted sequence of bizarre discoveries. Whether the first victim had been an accident, a suicide or a murder, he could not say, but the body had been stage-managed to gain maximum publicity. The same held good for the reappearance of the unfortunate Michaels child.

'Ganrich, prior to his arrest, had consorted off and on with Mary Langlands. She had attached herself again to him during a recent drinking bout with Con Green, "Peaches" and "Lazy Hambone" outside the car park of the DIY store on the Luscanpool road. When their grog had run out, a fight developed. Among shouted threats and sporadic fisticuffs, Lazy Hambone attacked Mary. With a cry of triumph, he waved a wad of banknotes, which he had managed to wrest from her within her layers of wrapping. Goaded, Ganrich stabbed him in the arm and continued to do so until the pain registered and he dropped the bundle. Ganrich then took charge of the money, peeling off enough for a further serious intake, which would see them through the rest of the afternoon. Over the following few hours, he pieced together, as best he could, what had happened to Mary.

'As he told it, her story began when she was waylaid by two

men whom she supposed were plain-clothes detectives. They bundled her into a car and drove her to a destination she now only dimly remembered. At first, she sensed they had left her in a police cell, but its lack of WC and the sheet of plain glass in the window did not tally with her previous experience. In spite of that she was not unduly frightened. After all, passivity and fatalism were day-to-day necessities in her struggle for survival. However, as time wore on, the dawning, dreadful realisation that she had no drink about her made her flesh crawl and soon she entered the clammy horror of the shakes. The gradual transformation of first the walls, and then the ceiling and the floor, into the squirming mass of her "little friends", as she called them, steadily engulfed her into her own private hell. Time stood still as the room yielded more and more of their swelling bodies.

'Then a voice spoke. She heard it clearly. It was a woman's voice. A figure appeared with a woman's shape. The figure stroked her hair and said something she did not understand. Afterwards, they took her outside and shoved her in the back of a van. Who they were she could not say. There was something else riding alongside her. It had lain face upward, rolled in a frayed brown carpet. The weave of the fabric kept mutating in front of her bleary eyes as she held on, trying not to be thrown about too much on the jolting journey. The face staring up at her looked like her old pal, "Soldier" Mike Hobart. She thought he had been dead for the past twenty years.

'In the middle of another room, she saw the body again, but it no longer looked like Mike. The carpet now was a gold and green affair. People were very kind. A tall woman called her Mary and patted her hand. Her bags were returned to her. The woman pushed money held by an elastic band into her pocket. "Tell them this," the woman said gently. A man helped her repeat the words, whatever they were. Finally, in another room, he was joined by a second man who listened to her story then let her go. Before her next salvation drink passed her lips, she vowed to leave Veldar forever.

'Susan Marshall openly and persistently expressed her doubts about Ganrich's credibility, but, in the end, her chief cut her short. "I knew him when he was a different person," Alakhin said. "His word is good for me."

'As by this time we were all agog, Susan went on to tell us about the follow up. Two local officers, who had taken Mary Langlands' statement, were interviewed and suspended from duty. They continued to protest their innocence. Alakhin intensified the investigation into Ambilene's background and all those involved in the running of My Friend Felicia's. Vera Sowenwell and George Aarons were arrested, but nothing stuck and they were released without charge. Any connection with the Michaels family proved fruitless.

'Although we later tried to cajole Susan, and also Cammy, for further information, neither of them volunteered any more details. Meanwhile, the road extension was finished on time, fulfilling the contract stipulations. The workers left. My Friend Felicia's resumed its old routine. Vera Sowenwell and George Aarons continued to be seen about the place as though nothing had happened. There was no sign anywhere of Mary Langlands. Ganrich was released by the Luscanpool police and the charges against him dropped. Susan and Cammy no longer came to our house and I lost the urge to visit the corner of Luscan Embankment and Fairlie Street. The river ceased to yield any more corpses.

'Then early November came and with it the arrest of Larry Kambilski, a neighbourhood acquaintance of the Michaels. After two days of intensive interrogation, he broke down and confessed to the murder of their daughter. Traces of her presence were confirmed in his house. He admitted confining her, sedating her and drowning her in the river, "so that she wouldn't have to bear another minute of this terrible life." He denied leaving her body where it was eventually found.

'The media rushed to praise Alakhin for the result. Within the week, he was assigned other duties and his team disbanded. The remaining two deaths stayed on file. Several years later, after his retirement from the force, he failed to make any reference to them in his bestseller memoir, *Fallen Among Thieves*.

'A local primitive-religion nut claimed in a letter to the *Veldar Argosy* that the spirit of the River Luscan had been desecrated and that seven years of abnormal flooding would result, but instead water levels were low.

'I remember all these strange events so clearly, as if they had occurred yesterday, because, on the night of eleventh November, my mother ran away with Cammy Sinclair and was never seen by us again. My eldest sister, June, took responsibility for me, and my life entered a new and troubled phase.'

Corinne had come to the end of her tale. She eased her hand slowly from Emmet's pocket. 'Thank you,' she said. 'You're a very good listener.'

'What's that? What's he good at?' Walter stood at their side.

'I must go. Perhaps I'll see you,' Corinne said to Emmet.

'Come and lunch with us today,' Walter said, checking his watch. 'Let me give you the details. Emmet will be there and his good wife. Have you met our confrère, Antoine? He's the one with an eye for the ladies.'

Corinne said nothing. She took the card Walter handed her and walked away.

'Start on the top four on the easy list,' Walter said when she had gone. 'There's no time like the present. The first two are playing poker at,' he passed Emmet an address. 'The others will be at home. Prosecute, brother, prosecute! I'll be okay here. It's the hour to prosecute.'

'Do you need me?' Antoine moved towards them from the doorway.

'No, my boy, no. For you, pleasure is the order of the moment. Indulge yourself fully while you've got the chance. I'm sure Emmet's friend will oblige. Emmet, I'll see you at the restaurant.'

Outside in the car, after he had turned on the ignition, Emmet saw the image of Minty Wallace's henchmen wading chest deep in Corinne's river. Why hadn't they weighted Little Sammy's body down? Had they really intended it to be fished out and used in some obscure collusion? The truth was he didn't know. Little Sammy had been an unfortunate burglar, who on the wrong night had wandered onto forbidden turf. Perfunctory questioning had shown him to be without allegiance and far from home. As Wallace was technically host to Manoko and May, his fate was sealed. The whole *pas de deux* had taken place with no one waiting around for the morning reviews. Mouths at the time had been zipped tighter than a teddy bear's arse. Silence and indifference had shrouded the incident ever since.

He drove into Argonne Boulevard and accelerated towards the climb to the bridge and the loop of the northern bypass. A couple of phone calls at this hour would suffice to disturb the sleepers and let them know a well-wisher had them firmly in mind. The poker game was different. It would depend on who was there and what they had with them. He looked over the rim of the flyover to the lighted office blocks beneath. Hallie would be well into her second shift by now, dressed in her god-awful grey overalls, lugging a vacuum cleaner from floor to floor. Money drifted. Money drifted away from him. It was always out of reach. As for the nice things, the good things, the stylish clothes he had bought her, the fancy perfumes, the not-so-good jewels she had pawned in the end, he might as well have opened the car window and watched his banknotes glide off in the slipstream before they spiralled down to rest with those below who already had, who always would have.

'Go back home and live like a lord,' Minty Wallace had said, after the doctors had explained his condition to him, as though the crumbs he carelessly swept from his table would sustain lesser mortals for life. Emmet adjusted the mirror for a better rear view. Go back home. That dream had died a long time ago, and now Sembele dangled the same bait. No. Greenlea was his home and he had the tools of his trade at hand. Keep on hammering. That was his motto. Keep on hammering, yet somewhere in the unsmiling, creased visage he had inadvertently glimpsed a second ago, when tilting the mirror, lurked a remnant of the boy he had once been, the child he himself had buried. The cold, deep waters of Corinne's River Luscan and the body of Little Sammy Tyrell receded from his mind to be replaced by the vista of a very different river, where the languorous, enervating heat of a summer mid-morning bloomed against his cheek. He relaxed his grip on the steering wheel, and, as he cruised past and beyond a slower vehicle, he let the boy he had been scramble down the gully and stand once more on top of the overhanging bluff to stare at the house across the scant water patches of the dried-up riverbed.

The construction of the house had been started by one Roscoe Syminton, an expatriate, who, it was rumoured, had made it big in Minneapolis. His haulage business there provided enough cash for him to consider building a dream showplace back home. So, he commissioned an agent to find a site near Stop 42, where he had spent happy boyhood years in the countryside, and, when that was done, he hired an architect. The foundations had no sooner been dug when he was killed in an automobile accident, with the further unfortunate result being that the fraudulent nature of his business was exposed, leaving his inheritors and creditors nothing but tax bills, lawsuits and grief. All work on the house stopped.

Five years on, the Levallois brothers, Jean and Loulou, from town, purchased the site and erected, bit by bit, the completed edifice. Emmet, slightly younger than Corinne in her story, latched on to them and their various helpers like a limpet. He obediently fetched and carried as they put on the roof and painted the outer walls. Slowly, a weird notion formed in his head that one day he would live there, one day the whole place would be his. How this would come about he did not know. Perhaps Loulou will give it to me, he thought, for all my work. He was less certain about Jean, who had a quick temper and a fearsome trajectory of spit.

At home, Granma said, 'Don't go there, foolish. They're not

proper men.' Whatever that meant. But go there he persisted in doing, and as often as he could. When he was told that the man who had initially started building the house was dead, it occurred to him that those there now might also die. He pictured himself coming across their bodies somewhere well away from the road, off the path, somewhere deep down in the tangle of the gully, lying prone underneath the bluff. Jean's face still looked hard and fierce set. Loulou's was sweet and round, his features untroubled by the flies that swarmed about his head. Death, he realised, could open doors, especially if someone was brave enough to hurry it along. Singing to himself contentedly, he ran along the track down to the property, which now for certain was destined to be his.

Fitting his hammer in the inside pocket of his coat, Emmet left his younger self, who had dreamed foolish dreams, and the car at the western edge of the Sander Housing project. He located Afton House on the estate map and strolled through the arch in the outer block to the courtyard beyond. The night air was chilly and damp. A faint precipitation graced his shoulders and the tips of his shoes. He sighted a phone box and made his two calls.

Entering Afton House, he passed by the lift and climbed the stairs to the third level. He turned right along the walkway. A car alarm went off somewhere below, followed by a medley of barking dogs. He rapped lightly on the frosted-glass pane of a door then repeated it loudly three times. A single dog continued to bark. A light came on in the hallway. The door opened a fraction. Behind it stood the figure of an elderly black woman, gingerly clutching the chain.

'I've come to play,' Emmet said gently. 'I'm sorry I'm late. I guess they've started without me.'

'Do I know you? You haven't been here before.'

'No, that's true.'

Emmet shoved the door open violently, bursting the chain. He propped the woman against the wall as she toppled back away from him. He strode quickly into the room at the end of the passage.

Voices halted suddenly. Cards stayed stuck in hands. Hammer at the ready, Emmet motioned to one of the five men seated at the table to get up. A couple of swift left jabs to his guts dropped him to his knees. He began sobbing softly. The others began swearing.

'Let's get acquainted,' Emmet said. 'Do right. Heed my message and I'll be gone like a bad dream.'

Their faces told him, as their eyes kept focused on the hammer, that he would not have any further trouble.

***

Hallie dreamed of respite. She imagined herself stretching out on the carpet at her feet, which was now transformed into a perfumed meadow where the prickle of the grass itched between her toes and softly chafed against her legs. Scents of wild flowers assailed her nostrils until she felt her very being begin to dissolve in the shimmering heat haze. On my own, she thought. By myself, just like the ads but without the camera crew hovering at a discreet distance.

Frankie Ramirez, the minibus driver on Wednesdays, was late. The majority of the cleaning gang, who had ventured out for the expected pick up, had come back in, colonising the atrium as best they could.

Ruby was busy settling into the receptionist's domain. One by one, she spread the contents of her bag onto the oak-veneer counter top: a tissue box, a sachet of painkillers, the folder of holiday photos sent a day ago by her daughter-in-law, a thermos of tomato soup, the little crucifix she had bought when Willie was sick and it seemed they might lose him forever, the case for her contact lenses.

Across the other side, Hubert Penley stretched out on the fake-leather chesterfield, his body poised between wakefulness and fitful sleep, a moist dribble of saliva lurking at the corner of his mouth.

Mohammed, Riz and Vladi, the Ukrainian, played three-card brag at the glass table beside the circular wall of the meditation area where a plaque in four languages informed visitors of its purpose.

The rest grumbled about lost time. They fidgeted unhappily, sitting then standing, smoking then deciding not to, watching the seconds creep onwards on the giant digital clock, then decamping to stare at their reflections in the long mirrors of the toilets, which Amelie had sprayed and wiped half an hour ago.

'Every floor timed to the second. Every building timed to the minute. They lay the figures on you and they say figure it out. You do as the contract says or you don't get the work. But they don't pay down time. Oh no! That's down to you. That's your loss. So Frankie's sick or something and the new man's lost. You ain't cleaning, you ain't earning. You get home late. But that's not part of their deal. It's down to you. Dead time. No account time. I tell you!' Amelie's raised voice made the card players look round and gave Hubert's frame an involuntary twitch.

'Take it easy,' Hallie said. 'After all, we could walk away. Get lost. Two less on the bus. Miss the next building. Show them it sucks.'

'And go where?'

'Oh, I don't know. Anywhere. Somewhere. I think there's still a club around here on Loret Street. In the old days, it was The Blue Papaya. I used to go there off and on. You could dance, get a cocktail, meet a stranger if you wanted. It had a certain allure all of its own. I liked it. Then Manny The Pilot got stiffed there and things changed. Two out-of-town tourists wedged his body in the broom cupboard. Poor guy was still alive when the ambulance arrived, but he died before they got to the hospital gates. Emmet went to the funeral. They closed the club for a while. That was the time Minty Wallace was ill, terminally it turned out. Jimmy Massoura, his possible successor, and Lenny Hovitz, the number one rival, were both inside on long stretches. Jimmy for conspiracy to murder and Lenny for armed robbery. So, in the circumstances, Manny The Pilot was just one of those things. Emmet stopped working regularly. I guess you could say the law prevailed in the end. Well, on the surface at least. Anyway, fashions changed. People began to do things openly that they once kept hidden. There wasn't any cause for shills and dives and clubs like The Busted Flush, Midnight Eve's and The Blue Papaya. You want to gamble? Go to the casino. You want to fuck on the q.t.? Go to a private suite or an Eros Hotel. You want to be dominated or just watch? Pick up the phone book and dial personal services.' She laughed. 'I'm showing my age. It's a club for young folks nowadays.'

'Don't worry about that, man. But dressed like this. Uh huh!' Amelie shook her head. 'When baby goes, she's gonna go all glittered up.'

'Anyhow, at least I got some good news before I left home. A courier came. Emmet's been offered a job driving round a woman called Emily Brown. It starts later today if he wants it. It's not for long,' Hallie shrugged, 'but what can you do?'

'When did Hubert say the bus left?'

'About twenty minutes. Something's up. Shouldn't someone ring again?'

'I'll do it. No one else will.'

Amelie walked off to the line of pay phones near the tall entrance doors. She called the operator and reversed charges.

Left on her own, Hallie wondered where Emmet would be right now, still at the party or back at home getting some rest. She did not like the sound of the night visits he had said were a possibility. 'The hours have nothing to do with it,' he had answered to her questions. 'It would be the same in daylight.'

'Who are these people?' she had persisted. He had given her the dead-lizard treatment, eked out with snips of Sembele's spiel about how inclusive the Old Man was determined to be nowadays, stuff about different peoples in one nation. 'Do we know them?' she had asked. 'No,' he replied. 'We don't.' It was the same old story. Ever since she had met him he had kept himself apart from his fellow countrymen. 'I left,' was all he would say with a shrug. Yet this Sembele knew him. They all knew him, imputing terrible deeds to him, deeds whose ruthlessness went beyond any crime

72

he had actually committed. In their eyes he had done it for the big whites—that was what set him on his own. He had not done it for himself and certainly not for them. He had sold himself to the man and had exulted in the power of his chains. 'Jest followin' orders, capt'n,' as she had heard the braver souls mutter out of his earshot. God knows he had never been a thinker. 'Get ready and do it and drop the "get ready"' was his motto. Now here he was, working with people he loathed, poking his nose into politics he did not understand. This Emily Brown thing could be a saver, a way out, if only he would take the chance, because he had ended up just like her, she realised ruefully, cleaning up other people's messes, handling other people's shit.

One of the other pay phones rang. Amelie, cradling the receiver to her breasts, gestured towards Hallie to pick it up. 'Thank you for answering,' a woman's voice said when she reached it. 'This is Elizabeth Kerry on behalf of the executors of the Amadeo Cresci Foundation. I have a message for you. The message is—' Hallie was on the verge of hanging up, but she held on as the voice continued '—Ute Manoko thought he had a deal, an opening in Europe as well as Japan. The trouble lay behind the scenes betraying the seller. If Ute had found them they would have died a dog's death. Instead, a one-time "block of wood" from the internment camp recognised Ute in the street and did away with him.

'Social news is Ms Emily Brown is visiting Greenlea. Her well-wishers hope she has a happy stay and that she is soon reunited with her errant father.

'Don't trust Chance Company. They don't trust you.

'Meanwhile, Kraus Fraternity are trying to package the old, sordid, dirty little secret. Get in touch with Vera Sowenwell. She knows the score.

'Thank you for listening to this short bulletin. This is Elizabeth Kerry.' The line went dead.

Hallie was still mulling over the astonishing call when the phone rang at reception. She watched Ruby reluctantly put down the photo she was engrossed in and answer it. Ruby spoke, then spoke again more forcefully, before firmly replacing the receiver. It trilled again. Ruby ignored it. Hallie felt the urge to go over and pick it up herself, but Amelie was at her side. The phone had given its last spasm by the time they reached reception.

'Who was it?' Hallie asked. 'What did they want?'

Ruby had a safari photo in her hand. 'They go all over the place. Africa. This is Africa.'

Hallie took the photo obligingly.

'Nobody really. Gobbledegook. Could have been a pervert or an insomniac with nothing to do. Though come to think of it, it was a woman, so forget that. Probably wrong number. She didn't say who she wanted. What company is this, by the way? I never know.'

'Insurance,' Hallie said. 'It's the Steady Drift Insurance Company headquarters. What did she say?'

'Some country out east, Asia I think. It was a kind of jingle. It rhymed with coffee and tea. Java. That was it. Javanee.'

'No names?'

'Names?'

'Yes. Who the caller was. Other names.'

Ruby shook her head. Amelie said, 'There's been a breakdown. Frankie phoned head office. He isn't sick. He's on his way in another minibus. He'll be here any minute now. Ten they said when I called. I'll let the rest know.'

Ruby started to re-confine her bits and pieces in her bag. Mohammed and Vladi pocketed the small amounts they had won from Riz. Amelie shook Hubert's shoulder. 'What you cooking, lover?' he said, as he stirred himself awake. Hallie went to the toilet to tell the others.

Frankie was all apologies when he pulled up at last. They piled past him into the bus, complaining of the cold as they hunched together inside. Hallie thought about Emily Brown. She tried to picture how she would look. A godsend or a threat? Nothing formed. She was too tired to think properly. No perfumed meadow awaited, just another building to clean. Beside her, Riz launched into a story about the TV actor and movie extra, Lucky Motion, who he had worked with once. 'Baby, I've heard it,' Hallie muttered softly, as she closed her eyes.

TWO

Although you become a fish
and throw yourself into the sea,
I shall search for you
in the most profound depths.
(Soleares of Romerillo)

Over recent months, haphazardly at first, fitting it in when time allowed, then more methodically with specific goals, Agnes Darshel had tried different ways to pick up her father's traces. Increasingly, they had left her with a heightened sense of his absence, his nothingness, which her imagined figure of him filled less and less.

The name that he had used, the name she and her mother had called him by, had proved, on investigation, to be false, and the history that accompanied it highly dubious. Foundation stones of family, date of birth and country of origin, crumbled under the weight of the repetitive bureaucratic stamp: NO RECORDED VALIDATION.

Surviving photographs in her possession likewise yielded scant tangible presence. The majority consisted of Sula, her mother, alone or in the company of relatives or friends. Fading notations in her mother's rounded script detailed the relevant background of dates, places and occasions, but revealed nothing of him. Presumably for some of them he had been there but always unseen, careful to be out of camera shot.

At times, when glancing at a particular group or solo portrait, Agnes sensed that it might have been his eye which had aligned the frame, his finger which had triggered the exposure, and none more so than the snaps where she, herself, made her entrance: Mom and Dad's beloved baby, their captivating infant, who crinkled up her face at the photographer with unconcealed glee.

In the few instances where he did show up, he had somehow

managed to turn away, right at the inapposite second, so that half his features were blurred or else he had surrounded himself with the only available shadow, in which he languished, barely discernible. Whilst everyone gazed good-naturedly or mockingly back at the camera, his eyes seemed deliberately averted in a conscious subversion of the normal rituals and mechanics of the process. None of these images took her any further forward. She had no clue as to how he would look twenty-five years on.

Her next step, taken somewhat reluctantly, had been to go back to Saint Callou, the town upstate where the three of them, father, mother and daughter, had once lived, contentedly it had seemed, to see if she could still locate some of his former friends, fellow musicians, workmates, casual acquaintances, anyone in fact, who remembered something about the enigma of René Darshel and could shed light on what had become of him.

One by one, she visited the places her mother had talked about so animatedly in the days before her death, only to discover time had obliterated the printing works where he had been an operative, and fashion had cancelled the music venues where he had played trombone. The bars and restaurants that remained now sported other names, different themes and changed clientele. Each night, on her return to her motel room, possibility after possibility whittled down under the thick, insistent black-marker stroke of a further deletion.

Then one morning, when she was on the verge of packing her bags and going, a breakthrough happened. A retired used-car salesman, who had traded with her father a couple of times, surfaced beside her at the counter of the Oak Leaf diner. He set her on the track of someone else. They, in turn, pointed her to other sources. New entries began to multiply in her notebook, and, because they ranged far and wide across several states, she left Saint Callou at the end of the week in revived spirits.

Back home in the city, she sent a blank tape to each of them requesting information. After a worrying gap of nothing arriving, her mailbox slowly began to contain the odd return. At first, they scarcely covered the bottom of the cardboard box—which had previously housed twelve one-litre cartons of Bethany's Grapefruit Juice—she kept in the hall cupboard, then they spread across her bedside table and eventually into another smaller cardboard box. More and more of her leisure time became disturbed by the compilation of cross references that she annotated from the dates they quoted, the places they had seen him in, the contexts of their relationship and the new leads they afforded. It slowly dawned on her that his pursuit was inexorably becoming her pursuit, and, if she continued in this vein, what she considered as her life was in danger of being taken over and relegated to the margins. She, therefore, resolutely put away the new arrivals unheard. After all, he could be dead, she told herself. Her enterprise could all have been a dreadful waste of time, but the recurrent image of her mother's last despairing, imploring looks and her outstretched fingers trying to people empty space would not allow the matter to be dropped so easily. The search for her father must continue. Whatever the result, it was her duty to persist.

The irony was, however, that just as the initial trickle of information had swelled into a gush, which threatened to sweep away her normal routine, now the flow began to dry up. No further tapes came. Decreased sightings of her father from 1963 onwards culminated in a total blank. No one in the network she had built up had seen or heard of him in the last nineteen to twenty years. In spite of her renewed efforts, another chapter had closed. She was left with a void.

In the following months, his name alone was all she possessed to plug the emptiness. She played with it, in odd moments, as though its constituent letters held his past and future. She pulled and pushed at them. She teased them out of sequence and reluctantly put them back as they were. René. René Darshel. People on the tapes uttered its syllables so easily, so smoothly, without hesitation, unaware that they were mouthing a lie, a camouflage, which he or others had constructed, leaving first Sula, and now herself, to disentangle its true significance. And what of her own name? He had surely robbed her of that in the same way that his abandonment of his wife and five-year old daughter had robbed her of her childhood.

Through the wearisome hours, at the end of what were turning out to be ever more humdrum and unsatisfying days, Agnes shuffled the variants, regrouping the letters of his name again and again. Where was or who had been Dan Shelere, Len Shradeer, Earl Henders, Red Lashreen, Ned Hersaler, Les Herrande, Sal Dreherne, Ran Shelrede? What would a 'share lender', a 'slender Lehar', a 'harden seller', a 'real H sender', a 'Dr Sen healer' do?

Needless to say, his name was only a surface. Its components, its globules of consonants and vowels, were nothing more than an echoing enigma. She sought refuge from the impasse in the embargoed collection of tapes, listening to them in repeated snippets as she drove to and from work, scavenging for anything that she might have missed in the first place.

They told her about his skinny arms, his hairline that had started to recede, the way he used to blink rapidly when he came out of shade into bright light, the murmur of his voice, like a monotone you had to strain to catch, as if he had only been voicing his own thoughts for his own hearing. They confirmed that he had stood over there, that he had sat in that particular chair, that he had gone out of that door into that yard, into that street, which, of course, was unrecognisable now, just like the neighbourhood, just like the city, just like life itself. He had been a person who had strayed into their lives when they, too, when all was said and done, had been someone else. Yet, for her sake and her enquiry, they had tried so hard to picture, to explain, to recover the basis of their encounters and transactions with the ghost they still thought of as René Darshel.

'Let me see, it must have been not long after I came out of the army. Spring 1961 . . . '

' . . . Mary had only just moved away that same September when he used to drop by. She didn't phone for a while and then we heard she was engaged to a boy in Lexboro.'

Once they had located the relevant time for themselves, the vestiges they then attributed to him embodied that time alone, a reconstructed past in which such things had been possible. Today, they averred, no one was like that. No one displayed that particular mix of sensibilities.

His presence flickered through their words, their silences, their different accents, like a will-o'-the-wisp, perceived briefly in the uncertain trajectory of their own memories. One thing, however, did stand out. She gleaned a common thread from her repeated listening, a minimally stated constant refrain: his habit of suddenly not being there, of departing without any prior hint or announcement.

'You'd look up and he'd be gone.'

'I'd see him again and off he'd go without a word.'

'At that time, he'd be with me sometimes. We'd sit and talk. He always told your mother he was somewhere else. I'm sorry 'bout that, but, anyway, I'd be frying him some food. We had a kind of a thing going, you understand, nothing deep. Or I'd get up to do something, brew the tea or coffee, see to my hair, fix myself. Most times he'd be gone. Now, let me see, one time he did hang around. On account of the weather, as I recall. Heavy rain and flooding, too. That time he stayed the afternoon. That was the only time. Reckon it could have been the last time I saw him.'

'You won't know this, but I remember seeing you when you were only a toddler. Sula brought you down to the works to meet him. Quite a crowd of us were there. René'd slipped off somewhere. Nobody picked it up to begin with. Mind you, he often talked about you. That's right. I'd say in his own way he was as proud of you as any father. He'd got something on his mind though and I don't think it was doing him any favours. Some days he never turned up and I know for a fact he wasn't always at your home. The boss wore it for a bit, 'cause René was a good worker, fast and skilful. The boss liked him. To tell the truth, most people did. He was an easy-going guy, but there was something that wasn't meat and potatoes like the rest of us. You'd never say he was settled down, not to the job, not to anything maybe. In the end, he just went. Before the inevitable happened, some said. Later, I learned the boss had told Lucas, Lucas Armitage that is, or was, he's been dead a couple of years, "If you ever see him again, or if he ever gets in touch, tell him I'll have him back." But nothing came of it. I think Lucas felt bitter towards your father for some reason . . .'

Hearing their halting testimonies for a second or third time, Agnes realised he had disappeared out of their lives exactly as he had gone from her mother's and her own. A secret, shameful relief nurtured itself within her consciousness as she grew more and more confident that none of them recalled him with lasting love. She stopped taking the tapes with her in the car, and then, one evening while looking at their disarray, the physical husks of her fruitless search, she scooped them up from the floor and sofa and consigned them back in their two cardboard boxes, whose flaps she sealed down with sticky tape. They fitted snugly into the space beside her shoes at the bottom of her bedroom cupboard.

Funnily, however, their voices would not stay there. When she poured a coffee during break-time, while she set out the papers for the day's boardroom meeting, when she dialled long distance and got an engaged tone, when she felt the sluice of a hot shower pummel against her skin on her return home, they whispered in her ear, 'I never knew he had a daughter.' 'You'll forgive me asking if you look like him or if you take after your mother, whom I never met.'

The wounds she had imagined healed long ago now started to pulse and reopen. It was all so unfair. She felt hot tears scald her eyelids and her hands would shake at stupid moments. Colleagues looked gingerly at her and asked if she was okay. She shook her head in reply but said, 'It'll pass. You know what it's like when someone leaves. I'll get over it. Thanks for asking.' Oh God, she thought,

I'm treating him as though he were my lover. Anger against his renewed power spilled over when she was alone, causing her to curse him to hell and to decide to have nothing to do with him, but the litany of voices she had thoughtlessly unearthed linked them both irrevocably together: René, Sula, Agnes, an unbroken circle. There was no real escape. Her search would have to go on. Where or how she did not know, but if she were to regain peace of mind she would have to find him and bring him to book for his countless derelictions because, above all others, she was his most legitimate accuser.

Yet it had not always been so. The voices also stirred her own vague memories, which mingled with theirs as the tapes slowly turned on their spindles. Memories where, rather than seeing him clearly, she sensed his omnipresence, his gigantism of being, the shapeless, all encompassing, nearness of his face, the smell that did not belong to either herself or her mother.

There had been a window seat somewhere. She had been hoisted up in his arms, laid down, then hoisted up again. His strength had wrested open a door at the end of a corridor, a door so huge, so anchored by a heavy spring, that no one else could make it budge. She felt the grasp of his hand round hers. It guided her. It gently drew her back and gathered her to his side. The hand which opened, after she had closed her eyes at his command, to reveal . . . what? Whatever it had been, a sweet, a trinket, it would not manifest itself, but the sensation of promise, the magic spell of waiting, remained.

When he had left their home for good and she had half understood what it meant, she had created a special nest for herself behind an old green velour sofa. She tried to talk to him there, rubbing her cheek against the fabric and counting up to forty-five, and then to fifty, in an attempt to bring him back through the open door. It did not work. No number, however varied, produced the desired effect.

She was aware, of course, that her mother's adult chronology had already disputed these childish glimpses of past events.

Moving from apartment to apartment, the layout of one compared to another, had all fitted schematically in Sula's recollection of circumstances, reasons and dates. The corridor Agnes spoke of had existed, but not the door with the heavy spring. The colour of the sofa was brown, and the upholstery imitation leather. They never lived in a room that had a window seat and, most telling of all, she had been a few weeks short of her fifth birthday, not her fourth, as she had imagined, when he finally disappeared. What, therefore, could she possibly gain in replaying these flawed and dim phantasms, which her mother had been at such pains to dispel? They might as well belong to the little girl of Earl Henders or Les Herrande for all the good they did.

The shameful truth was she had used her father's departure, together with the terrible mystery it had created, as a potent weapon throughout her childhood, and into her young adolescence, against the pettiness of her mother's daily expectations. The stultifying rules of acceptable behaviour, which bound Sula and with which she sought to bind her daughter, were there to be broken. He had done it. He had walked away regardless and he had not skulked back. If he cared, he had chosen to ignore it. If he loved, he had deliberately set it aside. His example opened up the wide, exciting world of freedom and indifference, which she had seized on in a thousand ways to prick and deflate her mother's certainties and circumvent her dearest hopes. When she had been deliberately late in getting up in the morning, when she had refused to go to school, when she had picked at the food her mother had prepared, pushing it dismissively to the side of her plate, when she had dawdled on the way home and would not come in at night, he had been at her side mouthing softly so that only she could hear, 'no, no, no, you needn't.'

Given time, however, her defiant 'no' had changed into a hesitant and then resolute 'yes'. As adulthood and independence approached, his influence steadily waned, until he became merely an unwanted remnant of her consciousness, no more important

83

than the outmoded clothes she used to wear or the playthings which had long since been banished to yard-sale boxes.

In contrast to his wilful egotism, she began to appreciate her mother's selflessness over the years in its true light. Sula had lived and worked uncomplainingly without a man, firmly shutting out the chance of a lover interfering in their lives. When Agnes had thrown René back in her face, she had borne it with good grace, free from bitter rejoinders. The reality was Sula had been her citadel, within whose walls, in spite of her repeated attempts to breach them, she had found a constant and loving refuge.

Separated at first by a neighbourhood, then by hundreds of miles, she had drawn ever closer to her mother as the years progressed. Every time they met, no matter how great the interval, they found themselves quickly in tune, playing to a score they instinctively understood. Agnes, invariably, arrived with the current man in tow, whom she teased and cajoled into paying court to Sula, while she sat watching her mother's dormant coquettishness get the better of her matronly reserve with ill-concealed relish.

Most of the men had left when she had asked them to, and Sula seemed not to mind every time a new Harry replaced a former Ivan. The few who persisted in sticking around both received and inflicted pain. A pain which proved to be only a passing discomfort when one terrible, never to be forgotten night the phone rang at her bedside, and, as she answered it through growing chills of apprehension, the bluest of blue Mondays with a vengeance came to call. Sula had cancer. She had told nobody. The emergency operation had been too late. The doctors wanted to talk.

Agnes showered, too shocked to weep. She dressed, packed a bag with a new emptiness filling the pit of her stomach and drove until the feeble light of dawn stretched through the sun-drenched morning to the oppressive heat of an airless July afternoon.

Throughout the ensuing days, days without hope according to the doctors' prognosis, she kept vigil at her mother's hospital bed, watching the morphine levels mount in the attempt to ease and cradle her frail and pain-racked body, which only a short time ago had felt so vibrant to the touch, so solid in the parting embrace.

As for Sula, it seemed she filled her remaining days with him. She implored Agnes to join him, repeating endlessly the times when the three of them had gone to Eithe ponds, the times on the shore when the light would not fade and they had no money, no money at all, but it had not mattered because, dear God, they had been together in time. Time draining away, Agnes thought, days, weeks at most, and here he was intervening at the last gasp, an absentee whose name her mother had not spoken for years, blundering in to spoil what she was desperate to say and feel.

Something was missing, something dreadful. It agitated Sula's hands and arms in spite of the ice which numbed her bones. She felt too weak to rise, too weary to do what she had to do. René had vanished. She pointed to the very spot on the ceiling where a moment ago his face had been, but Agnes foolishly maintained it was only the moving shadow caused by the changes in cloud and sunlight. It was the same when she heard his voice calling to her so distinctly from the corridor. Agnes returned with a determined shake of her head. In the end, unable to do more, she had to make do with a promise that Agnes would faithfully rejoin him wherever he might be. Exhausted, she fell back on the pillow. Agnes's hand rested on hers. Its weight was almost too much to bear, yet she took comfort from the knowledge that his name had been on both their lips.

From then on the die was cast, cast forever. Some other hand Sula could not see had spilled the dice free from their shaker. Patiently, she waited for their roll to cease. Hands, she thought, hands that once might have been folded in prayer. A deck of cards fanned out before her on the green baize of the bedclothes. Surely, they must realise she lacked the power or concentration to pick them up; especially when the dice still rolled and rolled.

René's chuckle in her left eardrum made her laugh out loud.

How sweet and salty his lips felt on the dryness of her cheek! How calmly he recited the numbers that fitted the puzzle! Each one so cleverly fell into place. It turned out he had only ever existed so as to be here with her and share this one shining, separate, impervious moment. There was no need, after all, to pick up the heavy, burdensome cards. No need for the dice to stop tumbling.

Agnes at last was listening to his words. Pride overwhelmed her as she watched him stoop and stroke his daughter's hair. Everything was going to be okay now that she had listened to his explanation. A one impervious moment.

But another voice cut in, a hateful voice. It murmured about the everlasting arms. Something was missing, something dreadful. Sula struggled to summon the phlegm to shout it down, to find the strength to kick up her legs and haul her skirts up for one final show of defiance. Whatever she did, though, she must not disturb the two of them. Agnes must not turn away from René, nor he from her. Still, be still, she told her body, but the needling drone would not stop.

' . . . oh what a friend we have gathering in the sheaves we will rest contented by the bend of the river this I know because his factories tell me so his works look on this and despair for the old rugged cross in the morning we will go rejoicing bringing in the sheep one by one two by two there is a balm in Gilead amongst the alien corn little boy blue will turn Manhattan into a many mansioned house on the hill but I do Dindi without the castle walls seek and hide for you the fatted calf and the widow's mite insures a small hotel in the still chill of the night to cling together and face the unknown . . . '

Her René, her Agnes reconciled. She strove to sing their names in exultation, but the other would not give way. Nothing seemed to halt its utterance. Its flow was . . .

'The beat beat beat of the tam tam the drip drip drip of I hear and you are the one he was funny that way and she was on the seashore o Lorelei I hear you calling in the pines another day five shirts and collars smooching away with the dashing iron nor all your needles and pins your scents of Araby when luck was a lady and dice will never come to rest or snake eyes . . . '

⎯⎓⎯

Agnes, struggling to stay awake, tried to unravel her mother's mumblings. They were more sounds than words, more humming than singing. Sometimes she cried out in anguish, and Agnes was appalled by the look of fear in her eyes. She cursed her father for his continual absence, for this now was surely his greatest and final betrayal, his last act of heartless separation. A nurse appeared and asked Sula if she was in pain, but Sula shook her head and gave Agnes a baffled look.

Then, one morning, when Agnes had returned to the motel room she had rented, the inevitable happened. The phone rang and she knew the words before the sister at the hospital spoke. She cried often afterwards, after she had ceded Sula's body and the simple rites were over, after she had chosen to believe her father was still alive, and she had decided she really would search for him. She did not expect him to share her tears. She cared little about who he had been and less about who he was now. She only wanted to bear witness to her mother's life and death in his presence, so that he could never say he did not know, that it had happened without him hearing.

⎯⎓⎯

. . . 'Hombi Tadjko started up a co-operative. He wanted to explore what he called second wave new thing. Russ van Effs and Melvin Singer were in it. A couple of kids and me knew Hombi's brother, Danito. We used to hang around his place. One day, Danito put on one of Hombi's working tapes by mistake. He started fooling around, imitating the sound, putting his hands up to his throat as if he was being throttled. Then he wanked at his cock and moaned and groaned like he was about to ejaculate. The others burst out laughing and I joined in, but the sounds stayed with me and I knew I wanted to hear them again and find out how they were made.

87

So one evening I ducked away from the rest and plucked up the courage to talk to Hombi, who was visiting his old lady. It wasn't easy. At that time, he was a forbidding figure to us kids. He had a real solid local reputation and a fuck-you-first exterior to go with it. Anyhow, I managed to get it out as best I could about the music I'd heard and whatever. He stopped me right there and damn me if he didn't play me stuff for around an hour, stuff that came from different times and different countries and he said, "Do you want to just listen or do you want to play?" I was embarrassed. "Both," I said quietly, half hoping he wouldn't hear, but he heard me alright and he smiled. Well, from that moment we hit it off.

'Later, when we met again, I told him how I'd started on the drums, and he invited me some months on to the Tuesday rehearsal sessions they held in the basement of the Lutheran Society Hall. Russ van Effs arranged for me to study with Sam Richards, and, as my technique and understanding improved, he persuaded my parents to let me attend the erratic hours the co-operative played during school vacation.

'René joined us for a spell in . . . I'm not good with dates. I think it must have been around spring '67. That's me with him in the photo I've included. I guess you won't have seen it before. Who took it or exactly why escapes me now. Anyhow, to get back on the trail, René was a good reader and he played both valve and slide trombone. I wouldn't say his time with us was very happy because, when you come down to it, he didn't express the feeling, the feeling you've got to have, as Lennie Tristano said. That's my book, anyway. Added to that, he and Hombi didn't get on. Part of the trouble was René was friendly with Wilson Loumans, the pianist, had even recorded with him on some small label back east, Blat or something. I think it may have been taped originally by one of Loumans' fan club and issued later. Anyhow, the story was when Wilson had quit working for the studios and had woodshedded for six months, he went back on the club and college circuit. René was in Amminghurst, doing what I don't know, when he bumped into Wilson in a Cantonese restaurant. They got talking. He went to Wilson's gig. After, they walked round and round the town shooting the breeze for hours. Now, let me tell you, before he played, Wilson couldn't bear to have anyone in the same room as him, and after he'd finished he couldn't bear to be alone. So it made sense. Later they met up again in Shawnee and that was the time they played together in a pick-up quintet.

'Now Hombi detested Wilson's whole approach and especially the music his disciples produced. "Arid intellectual con trick" was how he described it. He kept saying that motherfucker not only didn't know shit from shinola, but he wouldn't recognise real shit if he had three lifetimes. He never lost an opportunity to dish it up to René. Believe me, your father didn't need it. It really got his goat. They came near to blows once, but Melvin told them, "Hey, we've all got to eat," and Hombi cooled it.

'The other thing, like I said, René wasn't really following the same song sheet, not committed to go with us, go where we were heading. I got the impression he was building himself up to leave the music altogether, to give up on the life. I can't place exactly where it all started to slip, but some days he wasn't there and then he let us down on one of our rare paid engagements and that was that.

'After a week or so, Hombi stopped cursing him and we found a replacement. The exciting thing was by the time I quit school Hombi had got us funding for a tour. He took me and seven others. We played his music and Liz Freuch's and some early Theo Wright. That's how I began to experience the wider world and become less inclined to head back home. On that tack, your dad was spot on with languages. I've heard him do them like it was second nature, and I want to tell you he was always straight with me. He never treated me like a kid the way some of the others did with their stupid errands and their go for this and fetch that. No, looking back we had some good chats. Trouble was, at heart I'd say, he didn't care too much about anything . . . '

For some time, Agnes had only been half listening to the tape which, accompanied by a small black and white photo of her correspondent and the man he claimed was her father, had arrived on its own, long after the others. The combination of driving an unfamiliar car and following her newly bought road map demanded the majority of her concentration. Besides, she could reel off most of what he said by heart, not that it shed any more light on her opaque quarry.

A sign for Greenlea North showed up ahead. She dropped her speed and eased into the traffic heading for the slip road. A sudden flicker of indecision caused her to look out for a place to stop. She was almost there, nearly ready to assume a part she still did not understand, but she needed time to collect her thoughts. Ahead, a curved arrow bent towards Bay Bush Services. She followed a blue transit van past a line of parked intercity coaches and drew up by the cafeteria entrance. Taking the papers contained in the dark-green folder from her attaché case, she locked the car and went in.

When her lukewarm coffee was partially drunk, she pushed it aside and extracted the first sheets she had received from Chance Company, which had so unexpectedly set her upon her present journey. She reread their introductory letter, feeling its texture beneath the light pressure of her thumbs, as if to verify it had not dematerialised during the plane flight.

> *Dear Agnes,*
>
> *Forgive me for addressing you so familiarly, but I feel I already know you as I am in a position to help you in your continuing life journey. Many others have found themselves in a similar situation. Some, by chance, have used it as a channel to deeper fulfilment. Everyday existence can take on a new meaning. You see, I'm talking about the wonderful opportunities offered and arranged by CHANCE COMPANY.*
>
> *Each of our packages comes with a finance plan to suit all pockets and purses. Our range of options is wide and com-*

prehensive. Why not pick up your pen today and start to chart your future? It's fun and easy to do. Just complete and return the enclosed questionnaire in the pre-paid envelope. I promise things will happen quickly.

Remember, CHANCE COMPANY commands the cutting edge. We have enjoyed two great decades of inspired innovation. You'll find details of our terms in Appendix One. Appendix Two features client experiences, which you, too, could soon share.

Yours in anticipation,

Harry Fulton (Field Manager)

P.S. Our product will be tailored to your individual needs. You could find that special someone, Agnes. In your case, there are strong indications that GREENLEA would be an excellent location. DUTY and DESIRE will unite there with REVELATION and REWARD!

Agnes slid the letter back. Her fingertips met the metal of her new apartment keys lodged at the bottom of the folder. It had been quick, she reflected. From her sudden caprice to fill in the questionnaire, as in what the hell, then her decision to actually drop it in the mailbox in front of the Lansing Building on Wilding and Providence, to getting a pay-later scheme under the auspices of Desey Finance Corporation, swiftly followed by airline tickets and a hired car booking, had all been accomplished in less than two weeks. Now, here she was on the outskirts of an unknown city, in a foreign country, with the keys to an apartment she had never seen, a briefing for a character who was a Chance Company fiction and the name of her sole contact, Mr Roberto Ayza. She tied the toggle on the folder and glanced at her watch. It was 8.47 a.m. Around her, people were coming and going, their clothes and looks only slightly different from those back home. An announcement over the fuzz of the tannoy repeated a request for Mr Perkins to cash till eleven immediately please. At the far end of the room the sporadic tremolo beeps and bells of fruit machines punctuated the hum of multiple conversations. Three children began to run ever faster between their table and the counter queue, watched blankly by wearied adults. It was a scene she had experienced many times. Here and now, she thought. This is as good a time and place as any to stop seeing the world through the eyes of Agnes Darshel and begin to drift into my new, imaginary being, my separate entity, Ms Emily Brown.

Once back in the car, she adjusted the rear-view mirror and inspected her reflection, reminding herself to relax her jaw muscles more. She took out the dark vermilion lipstick she had bought at the airport and smoothed it over her lips. Her new character outline was vague in the extreme. A blank page would have served as well. Its implication seemed to be do as you will. A standard issue, she guessed, leading to the conclusion that she was just one more in a stream of clients who had all been Emily Brown before. Think Emily thoughts and behave Emily behaviour, whatever that was, she told herself as she drove back to the main road and joined the tail of traffic heading towards the city. A fit of scarcely suppressed giggles gurgled up within her when she saw the Lagran cut-off and realised she was almost there. Emily Brown was on her way home from the airport after seeing off her friend, Agnes Darshel, on another hare-brained trip. The joke was she did not know how to get there. After asking several pedestrians, she was still in a cheery mood when she finally reached the lights at the top of Lagran Hill.

The apartment was on the second floor of a three-storey red-brick building, which, along with five others of identical construction, made up the designation Tara Village. Each block bore an Irish name. Maynooth was Agnes's.

The first key she tried opened the outer door. Turning the second one in the lock, she entered her new resting place. She noted the smallness of the entrance hall and brought in her luggage. The sitting room had a lived-in look. The same applied to the kitchen, bedroom and bathroom. Magazines, books, CDs, fresh flowers, ornaments, cupboards stocked with tins and foodstuffs, a cabinet shelf arrayed with cosmetics and medicines, all gave the impression of someone already in residence, someone who had only popped out for a moment or two.

There were no clothes in the built-in wardrobe, however, nor any pairs of shoes, but a partially open drawer revealed neat piles of underwear, tights, knickers and bras. Agnes felt the weight of the towelling on a white bathrobe, which was casually draped over the shower screen, and pressed it to her face. It gave off an unfamiliar perfume. She inspected the set of cases, far superior to her own, that she found in the recess of the hall. They were empty.

For the next half hour, as she settled in, she half expected to hear the sound of footsteps outside, followed by a key turning in the lock and culminating in the reappearance of . . . She paused and said it softly to herself, 'Emily Brown.'

Curious as to what she would find, she rewound the tape of the answering machine. In spite of herself, she shivered slightly while she listened to the succession of unknown voices say, 'Hi,' and proceed to discuss their plans, give accounts of what they were up to and pose questions awaiting an answer, 'See you soon.' 'I'll be in touch.' 'Ciao.' She still had time to walk away, to revoke Chance Company's contract, to abandon this foolish adventure, yet she knew she would not, not if she truly wanted to meet her father. The phone trilled, making her start. She leant over and picked it up, saying, in her own voice and her own way, 'Emily here.'

Sonny Ayza opened his eyes.

He blinked. Sleep had mired his lashes with its sticky residue. A clammy sweat chilled his thighs and torso. Through the thin green curtains, a wan light was filtering across the ceiling. Shifting his head, he caught sight of a tiny moth, its wings closed, clinging to the bottom rim of the paper lampshade. Unusually, he could not remember waking up once in the night. I've enjoyed a sleep fit for the dead, he thought with a sardonic grimace. Was this an omen for his future perhaps? His normal waking up every two hours or so a thing of the past? What had been will no longer be? An unlikely scenario, he concluded, as he got out of bed, drew back the curtains and glanced at the familiar rooftops farther down the hill.

He padded barefoot through to the bathroom. Leaning over the tap to begin running a hot bath, he farted twice, quietly the first time, more emphatically the second. His body, it seemed, was continuing its usual routine as if nothing untoward had happened. While the water ran and steam misted the mirror's face, he dawdled over the toilet bowl, holding his penis in a sporadic pee. Compared to his urination of last night, it lacked urgency. Climbing into the bath, he ran the cold tap until the temperature of the water was on the verge of bearable. Its heat prickled his skin and then eased through his supine limbs. The back of his legs, shoulder blades and neck relaxed in its therapeutic volume. Slowly, he slid his head backwards and down until he was completely submerged. He closed his eyes. To live through the body. To exist in the body alone, if only for a second. He broke the surface and reached for the soap and sponge. It was Wednesday, fifteenth of November. In spite of himself, he was alive. Why not accept it? He soaped his genitals and squeezed the sponge beside the inside of his big toe. A light film of scum floated round his arms. Why are there things in the world? Well, now he had given himself a breather, a little more time to try and figure it out. Pressing down on the side of the tub, he levered himself upright.

In the wiped mirror, his reflection stared steadily back at him when he switched on his electric razor: Roberto 'Sonny' Ayza, son of Manolo Ayza, schoolteacher, and Rosario Delfin, milliner's assistant, brother of Veronica Ayza, lawyer, now married and mother of three, stepson of Sebastian Marva, composer and musicologist, Roberto Ayza, one-time adherent of 'nothing for us', inured wanderer, inconstant lover, fritterer away of opportunities, accumulator of forty-seven years, half-hearted suicide, present employee of Chance Company and denizen of Greenlea. Finished shaving, he rubbed his chin to test its smoothness and packed the razor into its case.

Back in the bedroom, he put on a navy-blue dressing gown and a pair of espadrilles. His letter to Veri rested against the bole of the table lamp. Above it, the moth was still there, motionless on the rim of the shade.

I am writing to you. [How pitiful his words had been! How inadequate if she really had read them!] *This is by way of farewell. I'm sorry I haven't seen or been with you and yours for a long time, but now you are all very much in my thoughts. Of course, you have the right to know and not to speculate. My reasons are manifold—*

He tore it up carefully without taking it out of the envelope. Once downstairs, he dropped the pieces into the pedal bin on top of the wrapped wad of chewing gum. The scattered sheets of Elizabeth Kerry's message lay on the table alongside Monse's packet. He left them where they were and busied himself making tea. The time was already 9.12 a.m.

While he tested the warmth of the pot, cradling its brown earthenware between his cupped hands, prior to putting in the tea, he heard Pooley, the Jack Russell terrier from next door, set up yapping and yowling, no doubt at something which had strayed into its territory: a cat perhaps, like the one on the sugar lump paper. It brought to mind the deepening colour of Sylvia's eyes as she became more and more engrossed in the telling of her story. Savouring the image, he swilled out the water and tipped in two spoonfuls of Japanese 'ghost' tea. Pooley, after a diminuendo of querulous, half-stifled growls, stopped barking. The cat, black, warning or otherwise, had presumably departed. 'Happy,' was what Sylvia had said. 'Happy to be in Miranda. Happy to be in Greenlea.'

When the tea was brewed, he poured some out and sat down.

The choice of two paths confronted him. Miranda with its past, which he could not change, and Greenlea with its possible present and future. The one shrouded within Monse's large envelope lay to his left. The other, dispersed in cryptic references he did not understand, was spread before him. He picked up the nearest sheet. What if Elizabeth Kerry's phone call had really been intended for him and not for Harvard? After all, she had not stopped speaking when he gave her his name. 'So there is no misunderstanding between us,' she had clearly said. Between us. Surely that must mean something? And he in turn, for whatever reason, had chosen not to leave what he had written and drawn on Harvard's desk, but had carried it with him and brought it home: an action either fulfilling part of his 'tidying away' or else a subconscious reflex to provide divergence from his stated purpose, a possible self-betrayal through the vanity of needing to solve an inconsequential, chanced-upon mystery. Now, the invitation to puzzle was in his hand. Who was Fernando Cheto Simon, whose colleagues were looking forward to meeting him? Meeting where? Meeting when? He picked up another sheet. What was the significance of a Gallo Mart store in Panalquin? Their logo was a crowing cockerel. That much he knew, but he had never been inside one in all his time in Greenlea. In the pot, the ghost tea leaves had opened out in thick dark ribbons. There was ample liquid for another bowl. He set aside the Kerry sheets. Greenlea or Miranda? Neither or both? He lifted Monse's envelope. The verifiable truth was, if she had not unearthed this, she would not have phoned him, and, in that case, he would now be lying in unconscious solitude upstairs. In its stupid way, whatever it held, it had led to his drinking this particular bowl of tea, his listening to Pooley's whines, his seeing a moth clinging to the lampshade.

Typically, Monse's envelope was crammed to bursting point with no slack to poke a thumbnail in. He took a sip of tea, got up and rummaged in the kitchen cabinet drawer to find a pair of small scissors. The sound of a car horn, repeating itself insistently, started Pooley off again on a chorus of challenging barks. People called their dogs by names which were often incomprehensible to strangers, Rusty not Polka Dot. An attempt to restore a degree of stereotypical dogginess? He eased the smaller blade of the scissors into the stuffed corner of the envelope and slit along the edge, revealing the tops of the photocopied pages. A further tear set them free.

They comprised of an old sixties newspaper article written by a journalist under the by-line 'Man About Town' for the *Orias Sentinel*. Monse's handwritten addenda scrawled at the head of the first page identified the author as one Felix Guiterez Abarca. '*Especially interesting for you, given your personal connections and the fact that he was a regular attendee of Tian's circle at the Goldsmith Café.*' she had inserted in the margin. Sonny smiled. Monse's enthusiasm was so palpable in the rush of her large, flowing script that it would be churlish not to at least look through her discovery. After all, time did not matter. He had nowhere in particular to go. The ghost leaves, as their name implied, would still provide several pots of tea. He began to read.

Another January! Time to consult my diary for up and coming events. None amongst them stirred my sentiments more than the eagerly awaited visit of the celebrated singer, Forest Mushroom, to our town. Jimmy Pilgrim, his erstwhile guitarist, had kindly let drop that the great man would be staying at the Colonial, and, through his further auspices, I was fortunately granted an interview.

Keen anticipation mingled with, I confess, a touch of melancholy accompanied me as I set out on Wednesday past's cold, clear morning. For alas, as we all know, the Colonial nowadays wears a somewhat forlorn and dilapidated aspect. Largely shunned by our fellow citizens, it ekes out a precarious existence on the custom of a thin stream of travelling salesmen and market hucksters. Its human attractions, if truth be told, have also seen better days, but 'twas not always so. In happier times, the Museum Café across the street, now gutted and open to the elements after its disastrous fire, had been for three generations an outstanding venue for song. Musicians performing there always put up at the Colonial. This tradition was now nobly confirmed by Forest Mushroom.

I found him seated at a table, his back to the wall, in the farthest recess of the ground-floor room. A young person of female gender sat beside him on the bench. He was wrapped in a sombre black overcoat of a distinctly foreign cut with a silk paisley scarf protecting his throat. His hands were clad in grey woollen mittens. His companion blew into a tumbler of brandy steaming with hot water as I respectfully introduced myself. After testing the glass gingerly with her fingertips, she indicated that I should sit opposite them. She then passed Forest Mushroom the drink and watched as he drained it in two hearty gulps, clapping for another as soon as he had set it down.

I ventured to enquire how the maestro was, speaking warmly of his rich and lasting contribution to our national culture. Then, seeing my effusions elicit no response, I changed tack and essayed various snippets of gossip I had gleaned from hither and yon. To my chagrin, exactly the same ritual was enacted when the waiter arrived with the second tumbler. Readers, for an unsettling moment, in the ever-stretching silence that ensued, I began to feel myself the hapless victim of the hundred and one little noises that threatened to overtake my carefully prepared questions with their insidious creakings and susurrations. In the face of Forest Mushroom's taciturnity and his companion's total lack of concern, my mind slid perilously close to straining to identify their locus and purpose. Hurried footsteps, cries, the rasping of files, a ring of keys dropped and dropped again, a lorry rumbling past, all began to disturb me to such an extent that I nearly missed it when the great man finally spoke.

God, this gadfly was tiresome and at the same time obdurately faceless. Sonny stopped reading and tried to visualise the very few occasions on which he had been commanded to join Tian Marva's famous circle. According to Monse, 'Man About Town' had been contributing to the *Sentinel* for over a decade and would have been there at the Goldsmith. Closing his eyes, he concentrated on trying to feel his hand resting on the bar of the double doors on his way into the café. Was it PUSH or PULL? PUSH. Now he could see the word in front of him, embossed in bronze curlicues.

The table, their reserved table, occupied the centre of the already crowded room, its position befitting their acknowledged status. A series of gilded rococo mirrors over on the far wall retained and multiplied their reflections while they leant back in their upright chairs, shoulders shaking with laughter at some new manifestation of local eccentricity or misguided idealism.

An elderly, wizened waiter—the Goldsmith did not seem to employ anyone under fifty—repeated and took his muttered order. 'A privileged visit thanks to the courtesy of you gentlemen.' Tian's voice, urbane as usual, purged of any trace of Llomeran accent, drew him a round of welcomes. Mouths opened in his direction, releasing breaths sanitised by eucalyptus and peppermint lozenges. He stammered out his acknowledgements. How gauche he sensed he was under their appraising gaze! The steady assault of acrid cigar smoke made his nostrils twitch, adding to his embarrassment. He tried desperately not to sneeze because he had forgotten to put a freshly laundered handkerchief in his pocket.

They were all men together; men of a certain class and age. There were no women or girls. It was not that sort of place. Schoolboy tales persisted, however, tales he had heard, of a legendary upstairs room in whose confines the more lurid sexual practices occurred. Therefore, while he sat and endured the inevitable questions about school, Rosario, Veri and what he was going to make of himself, he darted several surreptitious glances towards the staircase to the left of the bar, only to feel his cheeks burn and redden under Tian's enquiring and ironic stare.

Now some recognisable features and body shapes were beginning to form in his memory as he pinpointed their individual gestures and heard again their pet phrases being confidentially declaimed: Luis Man something, the chemist, one of his schoolteachers, Enrique Perez, Oscar Ferrer, the little hunchback, who had an antiquarian bookshop on La Doctrina Street, Pepe Nuñez, bald with a prominent broken nose, renowned skirt chaser and cuckold, Blas Sanz, elderly and bespectacled, a local landowner reputed to have anarchist sympathies, but no 'Man About Town', no Felix Guiterez Abarca. He was not at the table. His image refused to put in an appearance. Come to that, now that he thought about it, he did not retain a clear mental picture of Forest Mushroom either. What he had read so far was too vague. It lacked physical detail. It would need another effort on his part to render flesh back on the singer's ghost. Perhaps he would find a starting point further in the text. He returned to the article.

A soft crooning, a murmured snatch of song, joined my disconcerting noises. 'Under the bridge, the laundresses are working, Amparo, ay Amparo! I am sick for you.' His right hand moved in front of me. His fingers turned to the rhythm of the couplet. Encouraged, I reopened my notebook. Then, as if I had given him a prearranged cue, he looked me straight in the eye and said . . .

'Young master, let me lean on you.'

Sonny sipped his lukewarm tea. Blas Sanz, of course, that was it, that was the link he had been looking for. It had been on a night at one of Sanz's farms, a night when he was seventeen.

Guiterez was there with Tian and a crowd of others to carouse and listen to the singing. He had gone outside to take a breath of fresh air and be by himself in order to gaze at the shooting stars high in the clear sky over the fields. The Plough, the Little Bear, the

Pleiades, his inventory had only begun when he heard the sound of someone retching, followed quickly by the splash of vomit on the ground. A few grunts relenting into a low whistle provided a brief descant to the muffled cries emanating from the farmhouse. He watched a figure emerge out of the darkness of the courtyard beyond the outline of a fig tree. The man, on catching sight of him, lurched determinedly in his direction, pausing to spit copiously and rub the resultant dribble from his jaws with his sleeve as he staggered and pitched onwards.

'Young master, let me lean on you.'

Booze seeped out of every pore. Its powerful stench made his head swim as the man's weight on his torso and shoulders forced him ever backwards. After an ungainly, shuffling dance, they both ended up hard against the stable wall; Forest Mushroom, for indeed it had been him, once loosened from his tenuous grasp, crumpled and slid to the earth. On an impulse, he joined him.

What had made him do it? He could so easily have left him there. He could have slipped back inside unnoticed and, he realised now, chatted to 'Man About Town' and got his perception of the famous singer, no doubt imbued with phrases of the 'magic other' which Tian hymned so constantly. The thought made him laugh out loud. Luck had truly been on his side that night.

After they had lain for what seemed like an age, he had reverted to his study of the heavens, unsure whether his companion had fallen asleep or not.

'Little master.'

'Don't call me that.'

A keen glance scrutinised him. 'Okay, young man. Will you be so kind to go inside and bring me some food? Drink as well. Tell,' he paused as though searching for a name and not finding it, 'the old woman to give me some of her stew. I wonder if she's any tripe left. You,' using the familiar, 'have you eaten? Was it good? What did you have?'

'Blood sausage, oxtail and beans.'

'Some of those whores can cook when the spirit takes them, but, remember, be sure to get what the old woman prepared. Fuck it! We've got to get the best of things when we venture out into the world. Now I feel I'm going to be able to sing. I always wait till I've had a good spew at these shindigs. Then my body's free, I can do justice to our art. Go on! Go inside. Get what you can and bring me some of the boss's wine and a bottle of brandy while you're at it.'

By the time he returned, Forest Mushroom had found a stool and was seated by the covered well shaft. 'Food's coming,' he said as he passed over a flask of wine and laid a brandy bottle on the ground beside him. A sustained trajectory of liquid flowed downwards into the singer's open gullet. When his turn came, he swigged as long a pull as he could muster.

Once the flask had switched between them several times, Forest Mushroom belched and said, 'You don't talk much, young man, unlike your papa, the professor.'

'He's not my father.'

'Ah, you tell me.' The singer's attention turned to the brandy bottle, which he opened, sniffed and raised to his lips in an exploratory gulp. 'You can never be sure it hasn't been got at. This one, thanks to our host, is alright.'

'He's not solely a professor. He's a composer, a famous one.'

Forest Mushroom laughed. 'Tell me. Which one has he brought here tonight to hear me and Paco? The one to steal our music or the one to explain our own history to us? You see, I know how things work. For example, in the old days when the masters ordered our prison doors to be opened so that they could parade their holy pictures and relics in front of our eyes, some poor devil sang out, possessed by his misery. And every year after they came to expect the same, as if it were their due and at their decree. Listen, put yourself there! What do you do, lying there in your rags and chains, blinded by the unaccustomed light? Well, I'll tell you what happens. Some sing in hope of amnesty. Others join in, but believe me the doors soon stay shut again. Your professor and others like to call it tradition, noble folklore. Bloody hell! How they'd love to know the name of that first poor wretch. They'd swear he was the greatest and purest of them all. Now today when I smell and see shit, I know it's shit. I don't try and make it something purely Mirandan.'

At that stage, he remembered he had begun to feel queasily light-headed. The wine and a couple of brandies on top of it had proved to be a dangerous alliance. He had tentatively asked, 'Are you one of "nothing for us"?'

'No, son, that's for others to be. I am I. Where is your father? You see, I haven't forgotten what you said.'

'Dead. He died in France. Is it true that you only really sing for your own people, your own clan? That this, these dos where you're paid, is just . . . ?'

'Just what? A way of passing the time so I can haggle over money with lords or our host tonight and fuck impressionable girls? Who told you this? Ah, of course, I guess the professor. You think of your relatives. I'll think of mine. You non-gypsies always want to believe we have something hidden, something we won't show you. So you're quick to devalue what I do give and, believe me, most of the time it is my all.'

Their conversation was interrupted by the advent of an old woman dressed in black, carrying a bowl of chickpea stew and half a round of bread. Forest Mushroom extricated his knife and clumsily hacked off two slices. 'Eat! Eat!' he said, not beginning himself until he saw Sonny scoop up a mouthful.

'I'm going to leave Miranda.'

Forest Mushroom grinned and shook his head. 'You won't be able to. Sure you can wake up in Buenos Aires, explore foreign cunt, walk down the Boulevard des Italiens in Paris, get pissed on from above in Santiago do Chile, but none of us can leave, not even me, who didn't ask to be born here. You're too young, but you'll learn, sooner or later, that Miranda is actually our paradise and we are lost and sad without it.' He tipped up the bowl, wiped it clean with his last morsel of bread, got to his feet and swallowed a draught of wine. 'Enough. Come inside now. I'm ready to sing. These other things are of little importance.'

It was time for a break. The memories of his own encounter with Forest Mushroom had intruded into the tittle-tattle of the article. Sonny boiled fresh water for a second pot of tea and, while it was infusing, went back upstairs and dressed. Miranda as paradise. Now there was a thought, but what then was Greenlea for an unsuccessful escapee like himself, the inner or outer circles of hell? I am I. Easy to say, yet every day people were paying Chance Company good money to be, at least for a short time, someone else, and he was paid to abet them.

When he returned to the kitchen, the tea had kept its flavour, smoky and herbaceous, ghost leaves brewed and consumed by a living ghost who, for the moment, was free to go where he wanted to go, do what he wanted to do. Follow what is at hand, he told himself. Go where they lead. Elizabeth Kerry and Forest Mushroom can be my guides. They both arrived by chance. Their interpretation is down to me. He slurped another sip of tea and resumed reading 'Man About Town' from the top of the uppermost page.

> I need to say something I have avoided so far: namely the critical evaluation of Forest Mushroom's career, especially the years '59 to '62. I bow to no one in avowing that, at the height of his powers, he was capable of transforming the art of the golden era into a heart-stopping directness allied to a beguiling sense of rhythm. He could rekindle the most primitive songs into spluttering fire. Prisoners lamenting their fate were stones of rage and grief he unleashed into his audience's midst, yet he also could convey the grace of a girl's seductive hips, swaying down the street or parading by the river bank, with the teasing out of his ever more fragile vocal line, culminating in attenuated sobs. The variations of 'Curro Loran' and 'The Kid from Cenaul' are only remembered today because he is their living exemplar. No palms, laurels or encomiums were denied him whenever initiates met, but the

perplexing truth, which must be faced, is he has progressively squandered his talent on banal pastiches, pseudo-Latin imports and disastrous forays into light operettas. In consequence, his once-loyal supporters became dismayed, disorientated and, alas, ultimately disinterested. His name on a billboard nowadays no longer affords a guarantee as to the nature of his offering.

This was not what Forest Mushroom had said. Somehow he had missed out the relevant pages. He leafed backwards until he found what he was looking for.

. . . looked me straight in the eye and said, 'Uncle Antonio and I shared the first prize at the Pomegranate Festival. At that time, he was an elder of seventy-one, and I was only a lad of twelve. On the night before our turns came round, he sat me down at the back of the stage they had set up in Caidero Square and told me how he had walked there all the way from the mountains of his home village of Lazorca, a distance of some hundred and thirty kilometres. He had left a good three weeks beforehand, journeying only in the hours immediately after dawn.

'Antonio was truly a country person. He had worked as a goatherd, a tanner, a farrier of mules, a singer for a few coppers and a turned away day labourer. Like ourselves, he was used to picking up what he could, sleeping in the open if he had to, watching his balls freeze and his cock shrivel in the moonlight frost. He knew well the trails through the high mountain defiles, the rocky paths to shepherds' refuges, the way across the boulder-strewn, dried-up river beds, the lonely lookout of the hermit's cell. All our caves and resting places, the springs of each valley were known to him, and he ate and drank with whosoever he met, gypsies and muleteers, wood gatherers and policemen, singing for himself and others when the great Debla moved him. At the Cajal forge, he tarried blotto for two nights and two days during the celebrated piss-up you may have heard about, though it was years ago.

'Needless to say, news of his travelling and where he was going soon spread. Wherever he went, locals turned out to warn him of strangers, the perils in the road ahead, the persistence of witches at unmarked boundaries. In Eloyga, a talking cockerel flapped its wings on a midden heap and gave him sound advice. That very night, a red-scaled fish, which he caught and gutted by the bank of a ditch, bore him a trove of coins mixed up in its roe. A hare next morning, nestling in the grass, shrieked his name as, ears trembling, nose quivering, it sprang away from his approaching tread. These portents foretold success.

'So it was with an easy heart, having gained more fertile lands, he set his snares at dusk for partridges and quails, bedding down on straw for the night in high-roofed barns, where the hoot of the hunting owl brought him wisdom and the scurry of the fleeing rat tenacity. Later, when he passed the walls of Count Muñoz y Sintero's estate, the gardeners and servants all came out to greet him at the eastern gate. They filled his canteen with wine and gave him pasties and sweetmeats of honey and almonds to eat.

'On his seventeenth day of travel, members of my clan encamped by his bivouac on the outskirts of Rasinel. They knew the city where he was heading, so were able to tell him where he would find good lodgings. This was the first time he heard speak of my name and that he realised our fates were linked.

'On the following morning, he dallied with some washerwomen farther down the reaches of the river, and to this day they still swear that he brought one of them with child in spite of his venerable age. A sickly child, by all accounts, which died before it had the chance to count three Verbenas of Saint John.'

Here the singer paused and, raising his tumbler in a toast, declared, 'Strength to our pricks, those of us that have them! Now, where was I? Ah, yes. Uncle Antonio finally reached the tramlines to the north of the city on the morning of the twelfth. There he shared a handful of onions with men from the nearby brickworks. As he was still nervous of entering such a bustling and unknown place, he asked them what he should do. They advised him to stop where he was while they sent a message to the president of the jury, who, in turn, sent Vincent Uriguer's son to collect the wayfarer and bring him to the inn by the church of Saint Nicholas. The young man guided him through the streets as though he was leading a blind man, for Antonio was loath to look any inhabitant in the eye and kept his eyes tightly shut out of caution. In the same manner, he was delivered to the stage of the competition on the appointed hour of the designated night.

'In the event, he proved to be an untutored singer. After all, there was no one in his family to help him. He, therefore, relied on hawker's cries, threshing songs and personal variations on miners' laments he had picked up in his youth.

'When the prize-giving was over, he rested one more day, playing cards with the occupants of the inn and losing money, before setting off, this time in the company of Luis Canaver. They said their farewells on the far side of Saint Jerome Bridge. Antonio was happy to go. He never looked back. Soon his road became a country road, and from it he retraced his steps until he gained his home in Lazorca, a home that he never left again in his remaining lifetime.

'Years later, after his death, I met one of his great-nieces. She was amazed when I told her all of this.'

With these words and a brusque flip of his right wrist, Forest Mushroom indicated that my interview was at an end. All I could do was to give my bemused thanks, with as much civility as I could muster, and take my leave.

At the bottom of the page, Monse had interjected another flurry of footnotes. *'I am writing to you because.'* The persistent memory of his own words to Veri would not easily go away. They repeated themselves shamefully as he resolutely tried to bury himself in the significance of the Museum Café, the historical importance of the Colonial and the spider's web genealogy of Forest Mushroom's talented forebears and descendants.

Uncle Antonio, he learned, was one Antonio Escobar, long considered an unsophisticated representative of country singing, but now, thanks to modern scholarship and Professor Paul Fexon's seminal work, *Myths of the Golden Age*, identified as a forgotten semi-professional who, at the height of his career, had appeared with such notables as Toni Fortune and Isabella of the Geraniums. Following a prison term for vagrancy, he had returned to his native village where he continued to sing at local festivities and annual pilgrimages.

As to the young person coyly referred to by 'Man About Town', she was, in all probability, either Marie Semenova, who was often at Forest Mushroom's side after his second Paris triumph, or Lola Martin, who subsequently scandalised *'tout le monde'* by threatening to urinate on his open grave, a deep affront to gypsy custom and manners.

Monse's final gloss overleaf confirmed what Sonny had been thinking for some time. *'What you are reading is the full text of Guiterez's submission. The paper merely printed a note confirming the singer's temporary presence in Orias and reminded readers of a once-celebrated career. Other articles signed by him, however, continued to appear at regular monthly intervals.'*

He cleared away the teapot and bowl. Feeling hungry, he heated a pan, wiped it with oil, broke three eggs, beat them a little and then, off the heat, cooked an omelette. If I can never leave Miranda, he thought, I might as well summon the grace to bear it lightly. He finished eating and slid the empty plate under the running tap. There was no way his memories would wash away so easily. His mind was already made up what to do next. He would start at Gallo Mart, Old Station Yard, and look for Antonio Escobar's talking cockerel.

He picked up the Elizabeth Kerry jottings and put them in his pocket. *'Dearest darling ones, I am writing to you, as you have written to me, to ask how our cause is going at home.'* No, that was another letter which had best been left unread. Let its memory rest on top of his torn-up letter to Veri, like the finally discarded piece of chewing gum. Greenlea was where he was and where he was about to go into. Now he was ready to journey through it and take the ferry to Panalquin.

Immediately greeted as an old friend, recognised amongst the crowd as a former work colleague, introduced in sequence by different people as a one-time student at Thomas Malone, a graduate of Walker University, a recent participant in the Brightholme Seminar, kissed and hugged by strangers, her arm lightly touched by passing couples, her hand held a moment too long by an obsequious man dressed in a mulberry jerkin and dilapidated green corduroys and brown scuffed shoes, Agnes floated completely adrift in the uncertainty of being Emily Brown.

Emily certainly seemed popular. She appeared to be known by most people at the gallery opening. Their initial greetings quickly rippled out into invitations to meet after work, to do lunch next Tuesday, to join an outing to a concert on Friday, to attend Fred Jameson's new show at the Pelican, to roller-blade in the park sometime or to enjoy a dinner party, with a few special friends, this coming Saturday. Ever since she had given her name to the elaborately coiffured woman inside the entrance, she had been swept along by their chit-chat, a wary recipient of their ingratiating smiles.

'I don't mind admitting I had a thing about you in those days,' a young man said, looking mockingly into her eyes, 'but I was too gauche to ever think I stood a chance. You were so self-assured, so more worldly wise and sophisticated than anyone I had come across. Believe me, I hung on your every word and gesture. I don't suppose you even noticed I was there.'

'My dear,' a sylph-like blonde cut in, 'at first I wasn't sure it was you. Then I just had to come over. I was only saying to Bryony the other day, we never see any of the old gang and now here you are in the flesh and looking wonderful. Tell me,' she drew Agnes aside conspiratorially, leaving the young man to switch his attention to a maquette of a pubescent girl holding a pineapple to her bosom, 'have you managed to get over Martin yet? I heard he behaved like the real swine he always threatened to be. I could have warned you, it's true, but in affairs of the heart or downright lust, for that matter, it's best to stay,' she raised an elegant finger to her coral lips, 'don't you think?'

Agnes forced a smile and said, 'I'm terribly sorry. You'll think this is awful, but for the life of me I don't know who you are.'

'Julia. Julia Cyrone. Why, Emily, are you sure you're quite well? This is such an uncivilised hour, so early in the morning, for one of these launchings. PR, I expect, trying to give a new twist to an old refrain. But look, you must excuse me. I've just spotted Timothy Cozzens over there by the video installation. Frank and I are so keen on his recent work. Now are you sure you're going to be alright? I must dash. Lovely to bump into you.'

Left temporarily on her own, Agnes toured the exhibits. Porous Leaf Gallery, Castle Street, Lagran, had been the sole entry for today in the Emily Brown diary she had found on the bedside table. She had eagerly skimmed through its previous pages, crammed with names and places, restaurants and meetings, without coming across the one name which interested her. All forward dates had been blank.

As she stood in front of a gouache of a boy holding the reins of a rearing palomino, she became aware of a bald-headed man to her right, who was studying her with more than casual interest. Seeing her catch his eye, he slipped what looked like a small photograph into the inside pocket of his black and white houndstooth jacket, smiled at her and enquired hesitantly, 'Ms Brown?'

Agnes nodded, stifling the urge to delve in his pocket and

retrieve what she suspected was a likeness of herself. 'Mr . . . ?'

'Leo Manners. You probably won't remember me. I was with Hunt, Gransky and Liebfield at the time of your secondment.'

'On the contrary, Leo,' Agnes decided to play along, 'I remember you perfectly well. You were working on the René Darshel account, weren't you? Or was it the deal with Chance Company?'

'I see you haven't lost your sense of humour, Ms Brown. We all need a sideline to help us buy our artworks, don't we, and Chance Company, though it pays a pittance, keeps us amused. Who was the French gentleman you mentioned? Perhaps you could give me a lead, and we can see where it takes us.'

'Mid to late forties. US resident, urban nomad, valve-trombone player, serial disappearing act, now possibly living in Greenlea.'

Leo Manners shook his head. 'No. He's not fertile ground for me. I'm afraid financial services, the importation of exotic fish, autumns by Lake Ambret, the history of the Lombard family of Eltville, these are my rather threadbare specialities. At a push, I can trim through great cinematographers or the rudiments of beekeeping. Maybe there's someone here,' he paused and looked around at the thinning crowd, 'but most seem to be moving off already. It's piece work, you see.'

'Well thanks for being straight with me, Leo.'

'My pleasure.' He bowed slightly.

'Talking of Chance Company, have you come across one of their employees, Roberto Ayza?'

'Sorry to disappoint you.'

Agnes smiled. 'It doesn't seem to be my morning. By the way, what do you think of this?'

Leo looked at the gouache. 'Appealing subject matter to many, I'd think, but derivative, poorly executed and a tad over-priced. It was nice meeting you, Ms Brown. I'm afraid the office calls. Please have a pleasant stay in Greenlea.'

Agnes watched him leave then made her way back to the woman at the entrance. 'Is there a phone I may use,' she said, 'and have you a local directory?'

'You can use this one as long as it's a Greenlea call,' the woman said, indicating the telephone on her table and passing Agnes a phone book. 'Did you see anything that interested you?'

Agnes found Chance Company's number and dialled. 'Nothing grabbed me, I'm afraid.'

The woman smiled. 'Next time perhaps. You've got our card?'

'I'd like to speak to Mr Ayza, please. Roberto Ayza.'

'Putting you through. Please hold,' a woman's voice replied on the line.

'Yes, I've got your card, thanks,' Agnes said, waiting for the connection.

A tall, heavily built black man, clad in a russet overcoat belted at the waist with a matching pork-pie hat pushed through the outer door. Agnes turned her back to him as a new voice answered. 'Mary Appleby. How may I help you?'

'I need to speak to Mr Ayza. He's,' Agnes paused, searching for the correct job title, 'my file manager.'

'Mr Ayza is on leave for a week starting today. May I take your name? Is there a problem or an additional service you would like?'

'Ms Brown,' the woman at the table was speaking to her. 'This gentleman has come to meet you.'

Agnes turned round to see the man who had just entered. She replaced the receiver. 'Hi!' he said. 'I'm Emmet Briggs. I've been asked to bring you this from Chance Company.' He handed her a sealed envelope.

'Let's sit down. There are things I want to ask you. Over there'll do.' Agnes led the way to a bench in the middle of the gallery. She sat down, opened the envelope and took out its contents. It was a typed letter bearing Roberto Ayza's name and signature. Emmet Briggs, who had remained standing, joined her on the bench.

'Are you a friend, Emmet?'

'I don't understand.'

'Are you going to tell me about my history? How you previously met Emily Brown. How you don't know René Darshel. How this is part of the service, part of the paid charade.'

'Look, this is something I only started today. It's a real departure for me. Friendship doesn't come into it. It's simple. I've been hired to take you to the Berengaria Hotel this evening and to drive you to see a Mr Alakhin tomorrow. You don't want to go or you want to go by yourself, that's your business. If there's nothing else I'll be on my way.' He stood up.

'You know Greenlea, Mr Briggs?'

'I know it and, as it happens, I've also heard of Mr Alakhin when he was a policeman or so-called detective.'

Agnes took a decision. After all, she was the one paying the money. She might as well follow, for the time being, the route Chance Company was outlining, in spite of this morning's disappointment. 'Okay, we'll go then,' she said. 'Have you got where I'm staying?'

Emmet nodded. 'One thing I will tell you. When you're with me you'll be secure. It's my guarantee.'

'But what'll we find when we get there, wherever it is?'

'I don't know. Same as always, I guess. Just be ready because the dice are always loaded and sure as shit someone's lying, that's my advice. I'll be at your place at 8.30.'

Agnes laughed, drawing the looks of the few remaining visitors. She watched Emmet stride purposefully past them to the exit. Before he pulled the door open, he raised the flat of his right hand behind his hat, then he was gone.

Apart from the cautious tread and the occasional whispered comment of a couple still doing the rounds of the exhibits, silence dominated the gallery's space. Its subdued lighting seemed imperceptibly to echo the dank cloudiness outside. Roberto Ayza in the flesh is proving to be as elusive as my father, Agnes thought, as she picked up the envelope and got to her feet. She wondered if, like herself and Emily Brown, there was someone other hiding behind his name. She passed the woman at the entrance, who was now deep in a thick paperback book, and went out unnoticed into the street.

Bunches of white heather, leather belts naïvely decorated with supposed Egyptian pictographs and small mirrors tilted to show his features, were thrust in front of Sonny Ayza as he jostled with the crowd waiting to cross Roosevelt Way into the pedestrianised expanse of Constitutional Square, colloquially known as Aphrodite Park.

Young men and women with eager hands and eager tones wondered if he were interested in handyman services, minicab services, 24-hour dry-cleaning services, personal services, religious experiences, sharing a moment, if not now then perhaps later, if he would only agree to take their card.

On the far side of the road, three further straggling lines of similar hucksters and beggars waited for the lights to change so that they, too, could harangue and net the fresh shoal borne their way by the WALK NOW sign.

Sonny was in no particular hurry. He, therefore, let himself return the ingratiating eye contact of a random handful of his new importuners in order to hear at least the beginnings of their spiels in the vague hope of picking up something out of the ordinary, something that, however fanciful it might seem, could relate to the nebulous words he carried in his pocket. Nothing of the kind transpired, of course. Their patter and proffered cards merely confirmed the well-worn pitches he already knew.

Beyond this stratum of modern enterprise in the square itself, more traditional activities attracted the ebb and flow of passing spectators. During the hours of daylight, fire-eaters, a sword swallower, several statues, a unicyclist, two drunken mimes and a mimer of drunks, plus an ageing escapologist, festooned with heavy chains and immersed in a water tank every twenty minutes, plied their arcane skills by licence and custom. When dusk fell they stopped, gratefully relinquishing their poses and massaging their weary limbs. They collected their equipment and became simply another citizen comparing the day's takings with better times in the past, before departing, some to their cars and vans, others to the nearest tram stop, railway station or ferry terminal.

Love held sway after dark. Each night, the confines of the square trembled with anticipated assignations. The air sighed with crushed hopes and abject despairs, only to be freshened in new liaisons and grow chill again amid further betrayals and farewells. Enfolded in this myriad of intimacies, couplings and blessed ecstasies, everyone in Greenlea, it was said, had been here at some time in their lives. They came usually to pay their respects to the goddess and humbly or proudly lay their tributes at her feet then go, whereas those lucky or benighted few who had truly felt her hot breath upon their cheek or glimpsed her rounded thigh, found themselves transformed into permanent acolytes, returning come what may, fair weather or foul, to her venerated shrine.

Conscious of this erotic counterbalance, Sonny passed by the intent circles of gapers, dawdlers and pickpockets and reached the curve of the estuary embankment wall, which formed the square's southern boundary. In its lee, a line of pavement artists were chalking industriously, adding the final considered touches to their work: a practice which was their *sine qua non* ever since market research had shown that more people stopped to watch live action, and, once engaged in seeing the finish of a picture, the likelier they were to part with a donation. When they judged themselves unobserved, therefore, they hurriedly deleted aspects of their portrait or landscape, which they restored vigorously when an onlooker drew near.

A pitch displaying images of clowns holding balloons juxtaposed with matadors holding roses was the first on Sonny's route. Their long, angular figures had been constructed by a series of crude black outlines, which presumably were intended to evoke a sense of melancholic ennui. The two archetypes, to Sonny's eyes, appeared to be strikingly similar in pose and execution. The only difference being that the clowns were distinguished by their red, bulbous noses and exploded hats, whilst the matadors wore garish suits of light. The clowns held a purple balloon aloft in their right hands. The matadors brandished a red rose in theirs. In contrast to the overall technique, the balloons and roses had been depicted in meticulous detail.

The incongruity of these tall knights of the bullring compared to the fired-up, lithe, stocky, little men of reality made Sonny smile. Stray bits of theme that Tian had been commissioned to write for Mirandan TV came into his head and, without thinking, he found himself humming a few bars. Before his eyes, the images that accompanied them gradually supplanted the artists' inventions: the rolling terrains of the bull ranches intermingled with shots of empty stadia awaiting their public, moon-haunted nights over plains and cities, fighters praying in their hotel rooms giving way to festive crowds in procession, the first flutters of handkerchiefs in the arena spreading into an erupting snowstorm of white until the president signalled his permission for the band to play the triumphal march and two ears were held aloft while the slain, transfigured beast was dragged from the ring.

He was back once more in the Café Goldsmith. This time it was late at night after supper. A television set blared from the shelf in the corner as loudly as any in the more disreputable bars of the town. Veri switched her excited gaze back and forward from it, keen to interrogate Tian's impassive face. A thin column of smoke rose from the cigar, still glowing beneath its cone of ash, balanced on the ashtray in front of him. At last, he picked it up, patted her hand in encouragement, then leant over to kiss Rosario's cheek and, in so doing, dislodged the jacket, which was draped across his shoulders. Smiling, Rosario straightened it, and turning to him said, while her fingers smoothed his hair . . . what? He saw her lips move, but her words were lost, lost amongst the unwanted, intrusive memories of the TV's flickering images: Jimmy Bones poised between the bull's horns, ready for the attempted kill, Little Michael's dancing run as he planted his final banderillas, Frankie Street inching forward into the sunlight, his progress so breathtakingly slow that the crowd did not know how to react before he made them gasp with the grave opening pass of his capework. Funny how all this trivia returned, while his mother's words remained obstinately and, it seemed, irretrievably lost in the domain of ghosts, leaving only a wounded sense that they had been important, that they had meant something heartfelt. He ran his fingers through his hair in a token of her gesture. She would not do it anymore, nor rest her eyes upon his face. Day one of my new life, he thought ruefully, where the chance things I look at guide me back into a past I cannot alter.

The TV credits rolled. Music by Sebastian Marva. The whole company rose in sustained applause, 'Man About Town' probably amongst them. Cheers for the local composer. Cheers for the Mirandan way of life. Oblivion for 'nothing for us'. Then, judging the moment, Tian got to his feet and bent his head in an ironic bow. Someone stretched up and switched off the set, returning the Goldsmith to an animated normalcy.

It was time to move on, yet the fragment of the theme hung in his mind. He hummed a few more bars, realising it was a setting of a traditional threshing song, hardly fitting for the subject matter of the documentary. So, unknown at the time, the spirit of Antonio Escobar, Uncle Antonio, the country singer, had been there as well. The rest of the score, like Rosario's words, was gone, escaped, as though one of the balloons in front of him, aided by a sudden gust of wind, had broken free from the clown's grasp and was now hovering, somewhere unseen, outside the perimeter of its picture.

The first work of the second artist he came to exhibited a quietist domestic scene. In a brick-lined room, a young woman sat at a scrubbed pine table, holding a letter in her outstretched hand. A tear trickled down her right cheek. The title of the picture was *Bad News*. Behind her stood a kitchen dresser, stacked with blue delft storage jars. The last jar on the top shelf bore the inscription 'Vermeer'.

Next to it was a candlelit scene of a group of card players. Five men, dressed in workmen's blues, hunched round a table, their faces illuminated by a yellowish candle set in a green sconce. Its flame was their only source of light. Gradual shadow plunging to impenetrable darkness in both the foreground and the background completed the picture. The cards they were using were of the cups, clubs, swords and rounds variety. Around the base of the candle holder, the artist had chalked the letters, 'De La Tour'. The bathetic title he had given the piece was *Power Cut*.

Seeing Sonny and another passer-by study his work, the artist, a bearded giant of a man, stopped his labours on his third offering, got up, stretched himself and said, 'I've put in a black cat. See if you can spot it.'

Both of them obeyed, but neither could discern any catlike shape in the pervading gloom. Good-naturedly, the artist pointed towards the leg and feet of one of the card players. The passer-by said tentatively that she thought she could make out an arched back but could see no eyes or tail. Sonny confessed he was at a loss.

The artist, once they had dropped some change into his enamel mug, offered no further explanation, but instead returned to his final tableau, which showed the upper storeys of two large buildings. Framed in the window of one of them, a young man, dressed stiffly in a charcoal-grey suit, gazed across the divide to a window on the same level of the other building where, partially obscured by the swag of a red curtain, was the figure of a middle-aged woman. She stared downwards, as if her attention had been excited by something awful happening in the undepicted street below.

Sonny lingered while the artist tinkered ineffectively with the already filled in cloudy skyscape, then moved on, wondering what the given title would prove to be and who would be named as the inspiration behind the subject matter. The adjacent pitch was empty, and the subsequent four so uniformly banal that he scarcely gave them a cursory glance.

He was now at the top of the monumental cascade of the Port

Steps, which had been repeatedly drawn, painted and reproduced over centuries. Their flights, landings and quay had provided the setting for a flotilla of regal and aristocratic embarkations and disembarkations. Banqueting suite walls in municipal buildings still gloried in the solemn gatherings of merchants tallying the cornucopia of their off-loaded cargos, which painters had so carelessly strewn across their expanse. They formed the foreground to cityscapes and the background to river scenes. Mobs raced down them, dodging in vain shot and shell. Orators at their summit proclaimed lustily the rebirth of national identity, while below demonstrators unfurled red and black flags. According to fashion, they had been suffused in light, half obliterated in rain, metamorphosed in fog and romanticised by moonbeam. Their gradients graced sentimental genre paintings and particularised melodramatic engravings and prints. Lovers kissed and parted in their shadows. Rivals duelled with swords or pistols in their opalescent dawns. Assassins dropped bloodstained knives into the water from their quay. Suicides knelt on their unforgiving stones in their last bereft moments of despair, only for the scene to change as poodles, attired in military bandsmen garb, struck up a lively polka and young women *à la turque* assumed decorative poses at the river's edge.

Sonny paused and looked over the balustrade. Immediately below him, concealed in a bay to the left of the steps' first flight, a young man was bent over the last uncompleted panel of a large chalked triptych. A square piece of cardboard, wedged behind his collection pail and supported by the legs of a folding chair, informed the onlooker that the theme of his work was 'The Founding of the City' and that it was 'An Original by Jacob Kemmer'.

'Jacob Kemmer, at your service,' the young man said, standing up and seeing Sonny observe him. 'Please feel free to come down and have a closer look.'

Sonny checked his watch. The next ferry to Panalquin did not leave for fifty minutes. Twelve minutes walk would get him to the terminal. He had plenty of time to kill.

'I don't think I recognise your sources,' he said on joining Jacob Kemmer.

'I change them virtually every day,' Jacob replied, avoiding the implied question. 'Am I right in thinking that like so many others who stop here you weren't born and bred in Greenlea?'

Sonny nodded.

'Okay then, let me guide you through today's myths,' Jacob continued. 'In this one for example,' he pointed to the left of his triptych, 'I show the pursuit and mating of the Nereid, Huicraor, by Anchamam, the spirit of the river we see below us. As you can see, he finds her first in the depths of the ocean where she slumbers in the guise of a smooth Venus Shell. Pressing a giant conch to his lips, he awakens her and she slowly attains her rightful form, but, at the same time, her ever-watchful father, the god Nereus, spying danger, redraws the boundary of the sea and leaves Anchamam stranded on a hilltop. Undismayed, our hero changes himself into a heron and takes flight. Gliding over our estuary, he dives and seizes the magic fish, Lanooan, who, as a price for his freedom to perpetuate his never-ending cycle of migration and return, tells him to fly to the northern skerries, where, on the third night, he will find Huicraor resting in the shallows in the form of a black seal. The skerries gained, Anchamam lies in wait, making his hair into a swathe of seaweed. He sings of the joys of his home, his river, its reaches, rapids, pools and banks. He praises beguilingly the known and the yet to be known, until Huicraor, accompanied by the safeguard of a hundred similar black seals provided by her father, hears his seductive song. Trembling, she understands her future weird is to leave Nereus' kingdom forever. The seals submerge and rise, their heads sleek in the black water, blending into the darkness of the starless night. In order to see, Anchamam releases from his drifting hair tiny shoals of phosphorescent fish. They stick to Huicraor's muzzle and flanks. With a sudden powerful lunge, Anchamam binds her in his tangle of weed and speeds her south, while Nereus, in revenge, lashes our shores with tempests and engulfs our forests and glades with a tidal wave. Yet none of his rage or protestation is able to penetrate the cave where, as you can finally see, Anchamam and Huicraor consort. This sacred place in time becomes a Christian saint's cell, a pilgrimage for monks. Greenlea springs up on its site.'

Sonny, try as he might, could not reconcile the images at his feet with Kemmer's fanciful explanation. 'I'm afraid these concepts are quite alien to me,' he said, turning his attention to the larger centrepiece.

'Ah well,' said Kemmer, certain now that his audience would not walk away without leaving a reasonable contribution, 'this one I'm sure will appeal to you more. It has wider connotations. It illustrates the story of Odysseus and meta-Odysseus.'

'Like most of us I've heard of Odysseus but not, what did you call him, meta-Odysseus? Who was he?'

Jacob Kemmer smiled. 'As I've shown, one of them returns to Ithaca, the other is washed ashore on the very spot where we are standing. But forget the picture for a moment, and let me tell you the story. It's purely apocryphal, of course. By the way, who do I have the honour of addressing?'

'Roberto Ayza.' Immediately he had answered, Sonny wondered if he should have chanced Fernando Cheto Simon, Conrad Terence or, for that matter, Ute Manoko, to see if it provoked any reaction. There was something about Kemmer, something in his eyes and the sardonic way he gave his overblown descriptions. Skerries he had said, instead of isles or rocks. Was there some arcane hint of Elizabeth Kerry and the Cresci Foundation in his tour-guide patter?

'Smoke?' Jacob proffered a cigarette from the packet he had pulled out of his anorak pocket.

'No thanks.' Sonny shook his head and watched as Kemmer's fingers trembled slightly before tightening round the stem of a mauve throwaway lighter. Something was getting to him apart from the brisk wind he was trying to shield away from his cigarette. At his third attempt the light took. He inhaled sharply. The smoke drifted quickly across the images they had begun to discuss.

'Names in this case were a matter of life and death,' Jacob resumed. 'During the long voyage Odysseus' companions became increasingly uneasy about his intentions. Many of them harboured suspicions that he was deliberately and persistently avoiding setting a true course for home. In the beginning, his protestations about the malignity of the gods and the need to expatiate spilt blood by incurring a wandering fate had overridden any doubts, and, as time went by, he had deflected any criticism of his leadership by using his famed resourcefulness and cunning. So-and-so just happened unfortunately to have been crushed by the rock hurled by the enraged Polyphemus. Thingamajig hadn't plugged his ears properly when the sirens sang. Bugger-lugs had disobeyed orders and had stayed goat-like on Calypso's island. Jack-the-lad had lost his footing as they rolled and yawed between Scylla and Charybdis, his cries unheard by the straining helmsman.

'This unhappy state of affairs, however, could not be indefinitely sustained. The meagre level of booty they seized came nowhere near compensating for the danger and hardship they suffered. To a man, they wanted nothing more than to put into their home port and be reunited with their hearths, their kin, their families and their animals. They salivated in anticipation of the goat slaughtered in their honour. In their imagination, they ate and drank the hero's portion, while elders and children hung on their every word and their momentous exploits were declaimed in panegyrics. Yet here they were, denied those just rewards, buffeted by storms, half-starved, led hither and yon by a capricious commander, who, day by day, divested himself of Ithacan ties. The word never even passed his lips. Instead, he frowned and waved his fingers dismissively whenever someone mentioned it in reverent terms.

'So secretly, they began to plot against him. Their plan was simple: capture Odysseus and set him adrift. In the presence of their most potent fetish, they propitiated the gods for the success of their enterprise and found favour with Aeolus and Hebe. The auguries being fair, they set the appointed time and drew lots for the leading roles, but Linnaeus, who could not bear to betray his old companion in arms, stole to Odysseus' side and whispered in his ear two words, "Treachery, exile."

'Odysseus wept. His body shrank and aged. Then he embraced Linnaeus tenderly and said, "Fear not. I will go to them. I'll submit to them, but first they will hear me out."

'He duly mustered the company and, laying his sword and shield on the deck, proclaimed, "Whatever my fate is, I accept it. Wherever my lot leads, I follow it. You all know the man who inhabits this aging carcase. You all loved him once. You profited by his invention. You saw the light of another day by his cunning and martial skill. This man you see before you will surely die, but the name Odysseus will not. For I have it on the authority of Pallas Athene that my name will be translated into every tongue. Wherever she holds sway, the goatherd in his hut, the wine trader in the market, the prince surrounded by his warriors, all will know the name Odysseus. Therefore, I propose to you, as my final counsel, that you keep and nourish this god-given treasure, my name. One of you will become meta-Odysseus. Yes, he will lie with his queen, Penelope. He will hunt with his son, Telemachus, and bring his kingdom wisdom. The men who set out all those years ago are not the same as those who will return to Ithaca. Each one of you knows me and what I have done. Each of you carries the memory of past and home. Whomever you choose to be meta-Odysseus, I will tell him my inmost secrets. He will know all that is known to me. He will recall what I recall. What you choose to do with me is your concern, for I vow that henceforth I will never return to what was once my own."

'Hurriedly confiscating his weapons, they agreed his strategy and, within the hour, nominated Thalessos, who belonged to Ithaca's weakest sept, for they were confident they could manipulate him, even though he held the trappings of power.

'Odysseus, true to his word, imparted the necessary details of his life to the soon to be meta-Odysseus. When all had been revealed, including the dirty little secrets, and Thalessos moved freely and comfortably through the rooms and fields of his captain's childhood and youth, recognising friend and foe, ardent with the knowledge of the marriage bed and wary of thwarted rivals, they granted Odysseus the consolation of a raft stocked with a week's frugal provisions. Solemnly, and for some tearfully, they watched him disappear to larboard in the run of the wine-dark sea.

'Now, at last, the wind veered round. The sail bellied full, and to their ringing cheers the prow sped homewards like a leaping porpoise. Within the month they sighted the Ithacan roads. Joyfully, they waited for the tide and toasted their good fortune. In their exultation, they forgot the arbitrary wrath and cruelty of the gods, who had nurtured one Odysseus and one alone. It was Zeus, himself, who unleashed the thunderbolt out of a yellow dawn, which, heralding their doom, sundered their frail ship from bow to stern. Only one man survived the cataclysm. Clinging half-dead to the wreckage, gigantic waves hurled him to the shore.

'Next day, barely recovered, Thalessos rose unsteadily to his feet. Dragging himself off the cove where he had been swept, he came to a fork in the track. One way he knew led to the palace and kingship, the other to family and home. He fell to his knees and wept. Then, in a fateful moment, his mind was made up. No man can escape his own mortality, he reasoned. His path ahead was clear. He chose to wear the crown.

'They brought the stranger before the queen at her command. Her suitors hemmed him in with imprecations and pushing hands. "Who are you?" asked Penelope.

'"I am Odysseus," he replied.

'"You are not the Odysseus known to me," she said sadly, looking him up and down.

'"I am indeed your Odysseus and to prove it I will tell you of the talisman you gave me when we last embraced."

'His description of the brooch and the pin was so vivid that Penelope, to her surprise, saw it again in the instant it had left her hand for that of her long-lost husband's. "Where is it now," she murmured, "and where are your companions and ship?"

'"Alas, they are lost! You'll find their bodies and the mast broken on the rocks, but you will not find Odysseus because I am standing here before you." He then uttered the words he had said to her on their parting, followed by the words she had said to him.

'Astounded, Penelope felt ready to acclaim the returned wanderer, but her native caution stilled her heart, and she questioned him again. "If you were Odysseus would you not remember your favourite dog, Argos?"

'"Aye," he said, "I knew him from a pup. He had white sides, a russet back and a tail with a black tip."

'"Then send out the groom and bring him in," cried Penelope joyfully, "for I have fed him the broth of life, whose secret was bestowed to me by Pallas Athene. He still lives after all these decades of war and separation. Apart from me, he will go to no one but Odysseus."'

Jacob Kemmer paused and pointed to his depiction of the bloody consequence of the deceit, which culminated in the slaughter of meta-Odysseus. In total contrast, a small panel to the left of the carnage portrayed an Arcadian scene of harmony and richness. A venerable man clad in animal skins, his hair bedecked with the flowers of the wood and field, presided over a happy band of followers.

'As you can see,' Jacob continued, dropping his pseudo-Homeric style, 'Odysseus reached our shore. Humbled by his travails and in a new-found spirit of generosity, he shared his knowledge of the world, his patient arts and strategies, with the people he met along the banks of this very river. Under his tutelage, our city was born. He is its patron and to this day we still partake of his vices and virtues.'

Sonny had stared for a long time at the scene beneath their feet, losing and regaining Kemmer's narrative as he tried to reconcile the naïvely drawn rag-bag of figures, seascapes and landscapes with the elements of the story he already knew and the parts that were unfamiliar. Like the painting *The Fall of Icarus*, the stated theme, the foundation of Greenlea, occurred peripherally, almost unnoticed in the background.

'Have we met somewhere before?'

'I don't think so. Why do you ask?' Jacob stubbed out his second cigarette.

'No reason. My work brings me into contact with people you might describe as meta-Odysseuses.'

Jacob waited for him to expand, but Sonny did not say anything as he leant over and dropped a handful of coins into the collection pail.

'Let me give you this. It might interest you.' Jacob fished out a card. 'Several of my works have been photographed. They're in this exhibition. It's on tonight if you've got the time to spare.'

Sonny glanced at it out of politeness. He had all the time, if not in the world, at least from the moment last evening when he had put down the phone after Monse's call and had listened to the clock's unhurried tick. The imperative choice is to look and hear, he thought, rather than to ignore and pass by.

HIDDEN GREENLEA/ TRANSITORY IMAGES
Melo
4 Lavell Place
Sponsored by Amadeo Cresci Foundation

'Is there something amusing?'

'Only the beauty of chance coincidence. Seek and ye shall find as the scriptures say. Do you know anything about the sponsors? They interest me.'

Jacob shook his head. 'The public's my only patron. A photographer came up one day and asked if she could take me working. She returned last week and told me I was in the exhibition. I went to see it yesterday. That's all I know.'

Sonny said goodbye and resumed walking. The card nestled against the sheets of Elizabeth Kerry's message in his pocket. Pieces of whatever it was were coming together at random. He got the feeling they were going to continue to accrete one by one no matter where he went: now on his walk to the ferry terminal, later on his trip to Panalquin, this evening on his visit to hidden Greenlea.

Gusts of wind pummelled his chest and pinned back his trouser legs as he rounded the final bend of the embankment. The low concrete building of the ferry terminal lay ahead. Images of meta-Odysseus crawling crab-like on the beach came to him as he squinted into the blast, his eyes filling with moisture. Which ghost really haunts me? he wondered. Was it his real father who he had dragged from his untimely grave and transported back, time and time again, to Llomera and Paca Ceret's wine shop, or was it a meta-Manolo, his own creation, a figment of his wish for revenge, who, like his father, was really someone else, someone unknown, someone unreachable? 'He never thought of Ithaca. He frowned and snapped his fingers dismissively when anyone mentioned it and the ties of home.' Jacob Kemmer's words replayed in his ear, but where had he heard the words he so facilely put in the mouths of Paca, Vincenz, Tony Pigeon and My Son, his witnesses to his wanderer's return? Who had told him the gist of the tales they would tell, the thoughts they would express? Tian Marva, of course, their contemporary, the weaver of the sirens' song, his mother's lover and his future stepfather.

Inside the echoing booking hall, he joined a short queue to buy a return ticket to Panalquin. The departure board showed that the next ferry was running fifteen minutes late. Pushing the exit door open, his face battered by the even more robust and insistent blasts of wind, he watched as the incoming boat, dwarfed by the bulk of a rusting tanker behind it in the roads, beat its way towards the end of the mole and the shelter of the quay. No ancient gods were likely to impede its progress. Satisfied that he would soon be on board, he turned away from the water's edge and went back to the terminal. At the entrance, on the other side of the glass, he glimpsed a woman's face staring out. She looked sad. Her eyes were fixed on some point beyond him, her features immobile, as if forever set in repose. Monica Randell, he thought, always fated to journey home. While at the same time in his mind's eye he saw Victor Larries pull open his desk drawer and take a long swig from the bottle he had secreted there for such a day of rain and dull, grey winter sameness, when incipient despair insinuated itself into each impulse, gesture and fantasy, dampening and muting them down to the point of extinction. Sylvia's eyes, he told himself, rather remember Sylvia's eyes. Youth was on their side. They recognised the reality of hurt but were not daunted by it. Her stories merely helped her pass her working time. Today she would have a new one, the previous ones forgotten.

Inside, he entered the warm fug of the bar where the server's enquiring look dispelled his reverie. He ordered a shot of Demerara rum to go with his coffee. Around him, the narrow room reverberated with the noise of strangers breaking into unaccustomed conversations over the lateness of the ferry, the volume steadily heightening as each vied to make themselves heard above the others. An elbow jabbed his arm as he took a swallow. Carefully, he poured the rest of the rum into his cup and threaded his way to the seating area at the back. One chair alone was vacant at a small table for two. A man sat opposite, his face shielded by the open spread of the *Sportsman's Gazette*.

'Is it taken?'

The man lowered his paper. 'No.'

It was too late to withdraw. Sonny recognised one of his recent clients, a 'sticky' in the jargon, indicating a serial buyer of Chance Company packages, whom he had met on his arrival at the Tara Village apartment. 'Hello again. This is truly by chance. I'm catching the ferry.'

'And I'm meeting someone off it.' Antoine Viall folded his paper and put it down on the table. 'You look preoccupied, Mr Ayza. The cares of business no doubt. One might think you'd really have preferred not bumping into me.'

Sonny forced a smile. The affected vapidity of Viall's tone of voice, the mock pursing of his lips after each enunciated syllable, coupled with the languorous tilt of his head, irritated him. *Narcissus looking at me as though I were his mirror*, he thought. *A replica 'Man About Town' rehearsing his bon mots.*

'Antoine Viall,' Antoine continued. 'I meant to ask you. Did he ever exist?'

'Like all our products, as I'm sure you know, Antoine Viall is the intellectual copyright of the company. You've leased the file with the adjuncts you specified. When the lease ends another client can be offered the contract.'

'And if I held onto it, if I persisted in being Antoine Viall, what would the company do?'

'Take legal action. A tiresome matter for you. I guess at the very least it would bore you to tears.'

Viall laughed. '*Touché*. I'm tempted, you see. This is the best excursion I've taken. Mr Sembele has quite become my mentor. Only last night, he said to me, "The keys of the kingdom, Antoine. I can give you the keys of the kingdom." Well, that gave me succour. I swear he looks on me as a surrogate son. It makes you think. "They're jangling, baby," he said. "Don't you hear them? They're jangling just for you."' He laughed again then paused and looked round as the strains of an accordion started up in the doorway.

An elderly woman with untidy ginger hair, dressed in a grubby fawn raincoat, grimaced at the ceiling while her fingers stabbed its buttons and her arm extended its bellows. In spite of an ill-executed rendition, Sonny made out the strains of 'Naomi's Waltz', a tune which was currently popular with the buskers who went back and forwards on the ferries. 'You've only a week left,' he said. 'I'd say it was time for you to come back to reality and plan for the future.'

Viall turned back round to him and flexing his right hand gloomily studied his fingernails. 'My trouble is.' He fell silent as the music stopped and another tune started. 'My trouble is I want to go on being Antoine Viall, but I'm afraid I'm beginning to be caught up in violence. Perhaps even be implicated in a crime. Walter has employed this man, Emmet Briggs, a thug, an old-time hoodlum in the protection rackets here, ridiculous in his way, but I think capable of,' he paused then spelt it out softly for effect, 'm - u - r - d - e - r. My suspicion is Walter and he are planning to kill someone and it's going to happen very soon. Briggs bought a gun last night. I was there. I saw it handed over.'

Damn it, Sonny thought. Was this real or simply another part of the client's fantasy, a route to increased self-dramatisation? It was difficult to decide. 'For your own safety, you should get out immediately,' he advised. 'Tell the police what you know. I'll alert the company to handle things our end.'

Viall shook his head. 'You don't understand. It excites me, Mr Ayza. It excites me so much. It's the most thrilling thing that has happened to me since I witnessed a shooting in the Bronx. I was on a different contract then with your New York set up. Right outside Blatteriblax Records. I was standing there and suddenly blaam, pop pop. Do you know Emmet Briggs?'

'No.'

The accordion player pushed against their table, handing a mauve card to Sonny before he could question Viall further. It read, 'I am a deaf and dumb mute from birth. Help me sustain myself. Thanks for your generous giving.' She widened the opening of her canvas bag. Sonny passed her card to Viall and fumbled in his pocket for change. To his surprise, Viall turned the card over, took out a pen and began to write on it. The woman, emitting a high-pitched hum of alarm, tried desperately to wrest it from him. After a brief tussle, Antoine relinquished it and watched nonchalantly as, with a shaking hand, she smoothed at its surface in a vain attempt to efface whatever it was he had written. She pulled away from them in anger, still uttering panted signals of distress. All eyes in the bar had swivelled in their direction. A murmur of disapproval swelled. Antoine got to his feet. Sonny caught his sleeve and motioned to him to sit down again, which he reluctantly did. The hooter sounded outside. The awaited ferry had finally docked.

'I'm staying with it. You won't change my mind. Forget what I said. I didn't really intend to tell anyone. After all, we met purely by accident. It's just my feeling and I could easily be mistaken. Now I've someone to meet.'

'Tell me about Blatteriblax. We can walk together.'

Without replying, Viall rose from the table and pushed his way through the press of people making for the door. Sonny tried to follow him, but in the crush it was impossible to get past the intervening bodies. He watched Viall's head bob and disappear.

The last file of passengers were descending the gangway when he finally managed to get outside. A young blonde woman reached the quay and waved to Viall who was standing by a bollard at the stern. She joined him and took his arm. They spoke and began to walk away. Sonny eased through the crowd and hurried in their direction. The woman looked inquiringly at Viall as, breaking into a trot, he caught them up. 'Don't worry, Corinne,' Viall said, before Sonny could speak, 'Mr Ayza and I have finished our business.' He raised his right index finger to his lips. They walked off together. If Sonny wanted to go to Panalquin he had to go now. He turned back. Blatteriblax for the moment remained a name on a piece of paper.

Tired of walking by herself in the damp chill of Greenlea's suburbs, Agnes retraced her steps round the perimeter of the castle, which disappointingly had turned out to be an ersatz gothic pile of stained yellow and rose bricks erected in the mid-nineteenth century by a local sugar magnate.

Two dogs scampered towards her up the path. She hunched her shoulders and pushed her hands deeper into her parka pockets. The larger one, male she noted by its stiffening prick, worried persistently at the other's neck and flank. A man with their coiled choke leads about his arm came into view. He spoke to her as she passed, but his words were merely sound, unintelligible to her ears.

This lack of light, she thought as she reached the park exit and crossed the road. Everywhere there is this oppressive grey. More days of this and I surely will have the blues. She wanted to feel the velvet soft skin of a ripe peach in the cup of her hand, to have the trickle of juice squeezed from its flesh fill her mouth, to bask in the warm current of air when she stepped on to her back porch, shielding her eyes from the glare of the sun glinting off the car roofs in the road below. Instead, she was enveloped in grey murk. Everything around was muted and dull, from the flow of the traffic to the lacklustre displays in shop windows and the averted faces of passers-by. The search for René Darshel, she hardly thought of him as her father anymore, was leading her away from all that she knew, all that she liked. He was turning her into a stranger to herself, forcing her along streets she did not want to go along, isolating her in a city she need never have known, whose only attraction was the possibility that he might be somewhere in its midst.

She decided to buy some fruit and go back to the apartment. Ahead round the next corner, she spotted a yellow and black illuminated sign saying Gallo Mart, which she recognised from her visit to the gallery. The 'o' after 'Gall' was malfunctioning, switching itself off and on. Inside the automatic door, her nostrils breathed a waft of recycled heated air. Soft muzak filtered between the shelves and round the gondolas. Following the signs suspended from the ceiling, she moved to the right and back of the store where she quickly located a packet of instant soup. On her way back to the checkout, she picked up a net of clementines from a special offer bin. The yellow and black striped plastic carrier bag she put them in informed her that Gallo Mart cared for local people.

In Tara Village, once she had finished a bowl of the soup and had eaten two of the clementines, she felt better. She picked her way through the rack of CDs that she had already christened 'Emily Brown music'. Selecting one from the middle, she loaded it into the cheap hi-fi on the occasional table by the window. Neither the singer nor any of the numbers were familiar. She scanned the contents on the reverse of its jewel box—'Forgotten Lips', 'Cuban Party Time', 'My Midnight Ghost', 'Rumba Nova', 'Mister Quitter', 'Angels In Ohio'—then programmed one and four.

While it was playing, she made herself a coffee and knelt in front of the low bookcase in the bedroom. Emily Brown's books consisted of well-thumbed second-hand paperbacks with a decidedly romantic fiction slant. *The Return to Manderley* stood next to *Judith Remington* followed by the fat tome of *Folly of the O'Regans* and its slimmer sequel *Madcap Mistress*. She pulled out *Fading Wisteria* from the bottom shelf and saw a thin hardback jammed against the wall. Extricating it, she went back into the sitting room and programmed another track of the CD.

The book she held had a bluish-purple cover. Its pages were edged in gilt. The title page informed her that *Encounters on a Mountain Road* by Werner von Clems (born Koblenz 1886 died Montevideo 1935) had been translated by Alexander McGillvary (Regius Professor of German, St Andres University). A photograph of the author, covered by a sheet of tissue paper, on the next page led on to one headed 'Encomia'. She read the first two entries.

'Often, partly in jest but yet with a degree of deep-seated seriousness, Robert Musil would say, "What I wouldn't give to have written von Clems's books. *Encounters On A Mountain Road* in particular. One could die happy with the attainment of that shining summit."' (Stefan Zweig, *My Conversation With Musil*)

'I would not be standing here today if Werner von Clems had not been my guide and inspiration.' (Knut Hamsun from his Nobel Prize acceptance speech)

Always preferring to start a book anywhere but the beginning, Agnes tucked her feet beneath her body on the sofa and spread the book open at page 43. She speed-read another three pages before settling down to join the narrative.

Matthias Lemmel had never felt truly happy until he arrived in Sweden in the spring of 1906. The realisation dawned on him as he sat in the midst of a crowded mail train carriage, somewhere between Alvesta and Karlskrona. A piercing shaft of joy lit up his very being. He was overcome by a delicious and ever-increasing tide of contentment, which, in spite of his normally reticent nature, set his feet to tapping, his pulses to racing and his mouth to alternate between an inane grin and a hearty chuckle. He felt quite as though he had taken leave of his senses, such was the passion with which he viewed his fellow travellers pressed around him. Gazing with delight at the passing landscape of meadow, forest and lake, he saw himself striding out down the track, momentarily framed in the window between the pines and silver birches to the road that wound afar to a dimly visible farmstead in the blue distance. He imagined the sweet, clear air suffusing his newly ruddy cheeks, while the breeze tugged at his burgeoning beard. His cap was set at a jaunty angle. He held an ash plant firmly in his right hand. Ready for the road, he thought. Oh yes, at last I am ready for the road. Matthias was so encouraged he began to talk excitedly with the man and woman sitting opposite. Soon, in an unaffected way, he had drawn in the elderly gentleman seated beside him and those others curious enough to give heed to his conversation. He told them of his plans, his hopes and his dreams. He painted the picture of his past sufferings and numerous privations, which had weighed so heavily upon his soul in his journey from youth to manhood. 'Now,' he declared, 'those chains of resentment, for so long forged in a gnawing, sullen fire, are nought but webs of gossamer, idly rent asunder and forgotten in the slanting rays of the sun. I've become myself, for the first time I believe I am finally I.' He was twenty-eight years old.

In the ensuing weeks and months, he carried all before him in the surge of his newfound euphoria. Townspeople were genuinely glad to make his acquaintance. Everywhere he went he was met with a wave of recognition and a smile. Shopkeepers addressed him by name after one perfunctory visit to their establishments. Business colleagues attended to his suggestions without ill feeling. Workmen good-naturedly followed his commands. His peers lauded him like the very devil, clapping him on the back as the soundest fellow they had come across for a very long time. Members of the board even spoke of Lemmel as a coming man, followed by no less a worthy than the Director himself.

'Young dog,' said Gunnar Lovestrom approvingly to the burly figure of Eric Johansson, the chairman of the company, who was in the act of parting his frock coat and warming his backside at the corner of the stove, when they had retired for French cognac and cigars. 'Young dog,' repeated Gunnar.

'Young Lemmel. New blood.'

'A chip off you and I, Gunnar,' replied Johansson, contentedly. 'In our youth, eh, in our not-forgotten youth.'

Nor was the interest shown in Matthias solely confined to the male sex. Young women noticed his appearance at church. Their eyes pursued, whenever possible, his daily comings and goings, his promenades, his courtly bows, his gracious leave-takings. No suspected casual dalliance or engineered *tête-à-tête* escaped their attention. Mothers and, if truth be told, some ladies of a certain age and reputation discreetly bade him leave his card in the unspoken understanding that they, as well as their daughters, would be at home should he chance to call.

Not surprisingly in view of this general approbation, Matthias began to regard himself as an exceptional person. He prided himself as an arbiter of taste for the town, a positive harbinger of the future age. Silver and lemon, he opined, were the new colours. Accordingly, he ordered them to be incorporated into the weave of his suits, the dots and stripes of his cravats and ties. Old Ventona Paraguayan railway stock, he decided, stood at a particularly advantageous entry point for substantial gains. He, therefore, boldly bought when others sold. Day by day, because he saw it flattered and amused both his coterie and his public, he contrived to become more and more Swedish. He felt, at root, that his patriotism was more heartfelt and touching than theirs, which he noted was always tempered by a degree of self-deprecating irony. Similarly the pride he professed in Swedish achievements, be they in science or industry and commerce, struck him as all the more genuine because its source was altruistic. The 'Little Swede', as he became known throughout the town, held an opinion on everything and deemed everyone had a right to share it. In other words, Matthias Lemmel was poised on the brink of settling down, buying a house and finding a wife.

No matter that in later years he glossed over this fugue, this charmed interlude between the struggles of his youth and the despairs and terrors of his maturity. No aquavit or soused herring, no waving of the yellow and blue, could resurrect these few carefree months. The malignity of his fate soon overwhelmed them, snuffing them out as unthinking fingers extinguish the guttering candle flame. Swedish Matthias Lemmel, the Little Swede, might never have existed.

As no further mention of Matthias Lemmel occurred on that or subsequent pages, Agnes riffled forward searching for his name. Two thin, folded pieces of paper were lodged in the middle of the book.

Smoothing them out, she saw that they consisted of six thumbnail sketches of differing sizes and irregular spacing. What two of them represented eluded her. The remaining four showed: an olive tree under whose laden branches a man and a woman rested with a sickle lying at their feet, a black cat with its paw raised in a street lined with Japanese-style houses, a steep bank of pebbles encased in protective netting and a window display of pails, hammers, hinges and door locks, which gave the impression of belonging to a hardware store, except that standing in the background was a tailor's dummy.

The two indecipherable sketches occupied the top left-hand corners on each page. Agnes held them up in front of her. She was convinced they were more than mere doodles. Reminded of Gestalt tests, where sooner or later the viewer constructed a recognisable face or image, she studied them close to and at arm's length, but the density of their marks, the whorls and ellipses of their shading and cross-hatching, defied all her attempts at synthesis. Were they by the same person as the others? It was difficult to say. Certainly the same pencil seemed to have been used throughout. A vague feeling arose in her that she had seen something tantalisingly like them before, but where or when it had been, or whether it had appertained to someone else, someone in a book she had read or in a film she had seen, she could not say.

She picked up *Encounters on a Mountain Road* again. It was the only hardback in the apartment. Its fustian style was completely at odds with the rest of Emily Brown's library. Had it slipped down behind the other books by accident, or had it been deliberately concealed in the hope that she would find it? The answer, she guessed, lay with Chance Company and the person who had stage-managed her surroundings. Roberto Ayza? He was absent from the scene for some reason, leaving Emmet Briggs, a newcomer like herself to their procedure, as the only link.

The intercom buzzer sounded in the hall. No one was expected. She put the book down.

'Emily Brown? I have a package for Emily Brown.'

'Come up. I'm on the second floor.' Agnes pressed the release button for the outer door and opened her own. She listened to the ascending footsteps clumping up the stairs. The sketch image of the cat with its paw raised came into her mind, then in its place appeared the head and shoulders of a young, helmetless motorcycle courier dressed in black leathers and long boots. He handed her a shallow box and a receipt form. 'Sign here,' he said, indicating the bottom of the slip.

'Do you have a pen?'

He shook his head. Agnes retreated inside. When she returned he had advanced into the doorway and was looking around with feigned indifference. She wrote Emily Brown on the form and handed it back. He met her eyes for a second then turned to go.

'Where did you pick it up?' she asked.

'Sender's on the back,' he called out, 'in Polygon.'

A moment later she heard the outer door slam and the revs of a bike. Turning the package over, she read, 'From Amadeo Cresci Foundation, 70 Westgate, The Polygon, Greenlea.'

The woman, who had called herself Elizabeth Kerry, met Harvard Smith for lunch. Da Giovanni on Rokler Street was the venue he had suggested.

Outside the swim of current fashion, it was a shabby, cavernous restaurant near Belvedere Station, which most Greenlea residents assumed had gone out of business years ago. Amid the continual surrounding upheaval of building sites and office conversions, its unchanging, reassuring menu of Parma ham and melon, spaghetti a la vongole, scallopine or bollito misto and zuppa inglese, washed down with a flask of Chianti Putto under the world-weary gaze of its waiters, whose whole existence seemed dependent on its confines, fostered a refuge of what used to be for an older, out-of-town clientele.

Harvard, the back of his head and shoulders reflected in the foxed glass of a rococo mirror, was waiting for her at a small banquette table through an archway when she arrived. He looked older and more careworn than at their last face-to-face encounter.

'Are you ill?'

'I think so, a little.' He got to his feet and kissed her cheek. 'It's nothing. The air we breathe. The life I lead. A debit against my account.'

The waiter hovered. They ordered and, without meaning to, after a bout of inconsequential gossip, began to eat their first course in a companionable silence reminiscent of their latter days as lovers. Neither spoke again until Evangeline Simpson Jnr had finished toying with her risotto Milanese and Harvard had spooned up his last mouthful of clam sauce. 'Tell me about our progress,' she said, as the waiter removed the plates.

'Emily Brown here and running. She'll be at the exhibition tonight. I've got her plugged in for Alakhin tomorrow, and, of course, there's Louman's concert.'

'Did you give her Ayza's name?'

Harvard nodded.

'I gave him a message yesterday at your office.'

'What kind of message? Evangeline, we didn't discuss that.'

'My kind of message. You don't need to know everything in advance.'

The waiter returned with their second course. He placed Evangeline's scallopine in front of her and uncovered the meats of the bollito misto on his trolley. Harvard pointed in turn at the beef, the tongue and the cotechino and, as he watched the waiter carve and dribble each slice with its own broth, said, 'A low-key approach, that's what we agreed. Sonny's peripheral, a bit of insurance. Keep him that way.'

'Mashed potato, sir?'

A creamy, yellow mound was transferred to his plate. Christ, Harvard thought irritably, she doesn't change. She's been busy tilting it her way. Anything to get herself noticed, indulging in God knows what. He leant over and refilled their glasses with water.

Evangeline laid down her fork, took a sip and squeezed more lemon across her veal. The waiter departed. 'Another hound to chase the hare,' she said. 'As a matter of fact I've been sending messages to other buildings in the city.'

Harvard faked a grimace, which then turned real as a stabbing pain throbbed above his left eye.

'I can play, can't I? Your strategy isn't sacrosanct. Mother, by now as I've told you, would have been heartedly ashamed of what Chance Company has become. Even Selly Rycart would have had doubts. Hit the company at every opportunity. You know that's always been my tactic. They started it in jest, so I'm going to go out and play ball in my own way whether you like it or not. To you, Joe May is only a name, just a figurehead, whereas to me . . . '

Her voice trailed away as her words were drowned by the sudden shouts and animated chatter of a group of people piling through the archway. Outbreaks of laughter accompanied their divesting of coat and headgear as they jostled amongst each other in the restricted space.

Harvard strove to control the annoying pulse he felt beating ominously over his eyelid. He swallowed hard and held his breath. The smell of his food was beginning to make him feel nauseous. Beads of sweat clustered at his hairline. He inclined his head towards Evangeline, who, for the moment, appeared completely absorbed in the bustle opposite where waiters were hurriedly pulling tables together and arranging chairs.

A dapper man, clad in an expensively tailored Prince of Wales check suit, detached himself from the *mêlée* and came over to their table. He executed an ironic half bow. 'I hope we're not disturbing your pleasant assignation.'

Harvard cleared his throat.

Evangeline smiled. 'I'm with an old flame in a public place. There's nothing to disturb.'

The man laughed. 'Feel free to come and join us if you like after your meal. We'd be pleased to see you.' He gave another slight bow and rejoined his companions.

'Whatever happens you can't restore Joe May,' Harvard said. The waves of nausea were retreating. He felt sufficiently restored to try a mouthful of mash.

Evangeline did not reply. She stopped eating. Her eyes were fixed on the two white people in the group opposite. One of them, a somewhat podgy young man, was licking the neck of the thin ash-blonde beside him. She, meanwhile, was talking lethargically to the thickset man on her other side. The man who had come over to their table called out, 'Emmet, I wonder,' while a renewed barrage of laughter greeted someone else's remark. The blonde's hand by now was under the table feeling the young man's groin. She turned back towards Harvard. He looked pale, even paler than when she had entered. 'Why did you pursue me? Why did you bother? Even now you're hardly at the centre of things.'

A wrenching knot twisted then untwisted in Harvard's stomach. Emmet, could there be another person in Greenlea called Emmet? Another black person? The man's back, infuriatingly, was towards him. It was impossible to identify him for sure as Emmet Briggs. My God, what have I done? he thought. A flutter of panic assailed him. Here he was in the presence of his contact at last. Time was running out. Soon he would have to give his decision, and now there was a possible administrative error. The centre of things Evangeline had said, without knowing what it meant for him. Money or violence, either another disappearance in a long line of disappearances, or the final settlement; the choice was his. If money fails then fatality must occur, this had been the bottom-line instruction. Betray Evangeline's trust and erase the demi-god she had fabricated in the image of her putative father or betray the company; either way there was no going back. But Emmet Briggs. Was it possible that, whilst he had recruited him to squire Emily Brown and make sure she was safe, Walter Sembele had hired him to do what the contract stipulated? Stories we tell ourselves, he thought sourly. Future stories others will tell about me.

'I believe nowadays your wife is quite mad,' Evangeline continued. 'That at least is something you've managed on your own.'

Harvard pushed his plate to the side. 'She's heavily sedated, yes. We live each day as it comes.'

Evangeline rested her hand on his and said in a softer tone,

'Tell me how she is. What does she find to do all day? You haven't abandoned her. You've been faithful in your fashion.'

'Six bottles of spumante and a bottle of scotch. It's no time to stop the party. Not the Old Man's good thing.' Walter Sembele's voice carried beyond the waiter and the company. The man he had addressed as Emmet still had not moved round.

'They're enjoying themselves.' Evangeline slid her hand away from Harvard's. She ordered a coffee as the waiter passed.

'People exaggerate. She isn't that sick. It's really when we move that we get problems. Then she goes out and buys ten washing machines, dishwashers, a freezer in every other store. She worries we won't be equipped. We won't have the right goods. She comes home. I sort it out. Most people are kind once I explain. Afterwards, they phone me when she orders. With her medication, it's generally okay. She settles down.'

Evangeline's body tautened beside him. Her hazel-green eyes stared into his. The centre of her pupils looked topaz-tinged. As she bent her face to sip her coffee, a wisp of auburn hair strayed across her temple. The scent she was wearing, a faint trace of mimosa and crushed violets, reminded him of their time together. Her body was so close to him now, her body to which, in its youthful form, she had granted him access, her body, which in the past he had repeatedly abstracted, breaking it down into each component part, eroticising its curves and orifices, fetishising each indent and tiny blemish, it caused him a sudden, intense pang of separation and loss. Things were not manageable, far from it. His penis hardened against his thigh. He felt the urge to tell her he hadn't loved her before. He hadn't shown her the love she deserved. Blame it on youth, he could say; it didn't comprehend how I would lose you.

'This coffee's too bitter,' Evangeline said. 'I'm going to order some vino santo and those almond biscuits, whatever they're called.' She summoned the waiter. 'Do you want anything?'

Harvard shook his head. He was trapped in his desire to ask her forgiveness. If only he could kiss her full on the lips and hold her tight and abandon his scheming plans for her betrayal. It could happen, he tried telling himself. I could ignore Sembele. We could go together to a hotel room. I could play the percentages in her favour.

'Did I ever tell you,' she said, 'about the time I met him downtown in the Christmas shopping season? I was nearly eight years old with my birthday less than a month away. It was such a gloomy winter afternoon. Mother had taken me round the stores in what she thought was a treat. André, her man of the moment, drove us. Well, on our way back to the parking lot, I started playing up. I was in some kind of childish pet or other. I don't know why. Anyway, mother got angry. She grabbed me by the arm but suddenly let me go as if I no longer existed. I looked up. She stood transfixed. "Joe," she said, "Joe, is it you?" I'd never seen that kind of look on her face before. Her eyes were shining. She was truly beautiful. You could have put up her picture among the stills of movie stars and it wouldn't have been out of place. Naturally, I wanted to see who had produced this magical transformation. The guy was about medium height. He had on a black, beltless raincoat and a battered brown felt hat. A thin fairish moustache and beard fringed his mouth and chin. He was holding what I later learned was an instrument case. Mother leant her cheek towards him. He kissed it and looked at me. She said, "Joe, this is my daughter, Evangeline." The funny thing was she definitely hesitated before saying Joe and again before my daughter. He shook my hand. I felt the lightness of his grip through the damp of my gloves. They were red with white pom-poms. At the time I guess I was glad he hadn't tried to kiss me. He said something, something I only partially caught because an ambulance siren was wailing. "Unfortunate . . . better if . . . me again." Something like that. Mother touched his sleeve. She had tears in her eyes. Then he left. We watched him go until he disappeared into the subway entrance. Mother wouldn't talk about him, say who he was. She said I had a rich imagination whenever I tried to bring him up. From that day, however, her interest in André faded and soon he rounded up his sports stuff, packed his bags and went.' She dipped the tip of her biscuit into her glass of wine and held it out for Harvard to nibble. He demurred.

The party opposite was growing increasingly boisterous. Most of them had changed their seats. Walter Sembele now had his arm draped round the shoulder of the white girl, while he talked loudly up the table to a black woman at its head.

'Evangeline, have you faced up to the fact that we might not find him? He might no longer be in Greenlea.'

'Alakhin knows. He's certain.'

'Alakhin's retired. He's old. He lives in the back of beyond.'

'But he's still got his touts. A key informer, someone close to the source, that's what he said, remember. If he'd left, Alakhin would have sent word.'

Never go back, Harvard thought. It can't be done. Always go onwards. Whatever happens now, whatever I choose, at least I swear I'll never return to Greenlea. I refuse to haunt the scene of the crime, unlike her desired possible father. Across the way, Sembele's Emmet still had not budged from his seat.

Evangeline finished her wine and pushed out the table. 'Leave the tab,' she said. 'I'll pick it up.'

Harvard waited for her to go through the door of the toilet, then he beckoned the waiter and, as well as ordering the bill, asked for a couple of leaves from his pad. Quickly writing on one of them and folding it over, he pointed to Walter Sembele. The waiter delivered it. Sembele took it carelessly, read it and put it in his pocket. He waved in acknowledgement. The waiter asked, 'Is there a reply, sir?'

'Give the gentleman my card.'

At that point Emmet Briggs looked round. Harvard recognised the face he had studied the previous night when he had set up the Emily Brown file.

Evangeline sang while she puckered up her mouth and applied

lipstick in front of the long mirror in the restaurant ladies room. She had good reason to feel pleased with herself. Things were going well. Amadeo Cresci himself, if he had lived, would have been proud of her determined campaign against Chance Company, the organisation which had ruined him and driven him to suicide, and Harvard, well he did not need to know the extent of her plans. She capped the lipstick and put it back in her bag. 'Lovable, huggable Emily Brown,' she sang more loudly, moving her feet to the rhythm and shaking her hips.

A cistern flushed. One of the cubicle doors opened and a smallish black woman, whom Evangeline had seen at the other table, emerged. Feeling rather self-conscious, Evangeline said, 'Hi.'

The woman washed her hands and, looking at Evangeline's reflection in the mirror, said, 'That song you were singing, what's it called?'

'"Miss Brown to You". My friend I'm lunching with introduced it to me. It's an old song Billie Holiday used to sing. You know, the lady with the white gardenia.'

'Are you a singer?'

'Oh no,' Evangeline laughed. 'Can't you tell? I'm not musical. My father is, but I guess in that respect I take after my mother.'

The woman looked at her curiously. 'Do you mind if I ask your name?'

'No, not at all. I'm Evangeline Simpson. Why do you want to know?'

'There was something familiar about your voice. This morning my husband started work with an Emily Brown and someone I'd never heard of spoke about her arrival in Greenlea. Now you're singing a song with the same name in it. It seems everywhere I go her name crops up.'

'I just know the song. That's it.' Evangeline pushed the door open. She experienced an enjoyable frisson of pleasure. Things were getting better all the time. The recipient of one of her calls was walking right at her side. 'How did your husband get the job?

I've only recently come here and if you know a good employment agency it would help.'

'He's only on a short-term contract. The company's called Chance Company. They hire people for specific jobs or retain them on standby. They're worldwide.'

'Yes, I've heard of them. They're big in the States. They fake experiences for their clients. It's the way to go, according to them. Your crowd seem happy.'

'They're not my crowd, or Emmet's. They're full of false spirit, bad people mostly. They laugh easy and wait for others to cry.'

'Is Emmet your husband?'

'Yeah, that's him over there. Mr Sembele down the end runs the show.'

'And the blonde?'

'A local whore they've got in tow. Sembele's got money to spend. Well, so long. I must hear the whole of that Emily Brown song sometime.'

A scribbled note awaited Evangeline's return. She read it, crumpled it up and handed her credit card to the waiter. Harvard had gone. On her way to reclaim her coat, the ash blonde at the other table smiled in her direction, half raising her wine glass in mock salutation. Evangeline ignored her. Some people would never fit the big picture.

Walter Sembele watched Harvard Smith's companion leave. Never one thing to do at a time, he thought, there are always four or five. Now when the Old Man was struggling to secure his final term in office, powerful friends were calling in their markers.

At the beginning, his brief had been straightforward enough. The Old Man had warmly embraced him the night before he was due to leave. 'One more time, Walter,' he had said. 'Bring them home, good friend. Bring the votes of our diaspora back to us, both the living and the dead. I know how to encourage the living, and, on election day, you know how to raise the dead.'

They had parted on good terms, and he had nearly reached the east *porte-cochère* of the presidential palace, thinking that was that, when a voice from the shadows addressed him by name and requested a light. As he flicked his lighter, a slim young man appeared, leant forward and pressed his cigarette to the flame. He took the opportunity to cast a quick, surreptitious glance at the man's shoes. They were tan loafers, decorated with a fussy buckle. Catching his reaction, the young man smiled and said, 'Times change, Mr Sembele. I'm Ignacio Williams, Commercial Attaché. Shall we go somewhere more private?' He indicated a corridor to the right. Part way along he opened a door. Walter followed.

They had entered a kind of pantry dominated by a large open cupboard stacked with glasses of various types and sizes. A primitive, dirt-stained sink with one high tap stood underneath a barred window. He had waited while Williams extracted a file from his briefcase then passed him the top three sheets. 'As you see, a standard Chance Company contract. The client is Antoine Viall. He's ready to go with you. Follow the usual procedures.'

Out of diplomacy, he had read the details, careful to mask his annoyance. 'There's also another connection here,' Williams had continued more slowly. 'Our friends want to honour someone. I can tell you the Company thought he was dead some time ago, but it turns out the service was inappropriate. Inadequate might be a better word. We've agreed to provide a lasting memorial. When you get to Greenlea on your itinerary, hire someone suitable, someone expendable. I leave it to you. You've got the experience. But he needs to be a professional. Your liaison with the Company is in the papers I'll give you. He'll contact you in Greenlea, let you know the target's name, and the place and time. Jesus! There's a mouse.'

A tiny rodent had emerged from under the sink. Aware of danger, it scampered past their feet and climbed into the cupboard. Enjoying the Attaché's obvious discomfort, he had started asking questions, while Williams kept darting uneasy glances about the room. Barely concealing his relief, he had handed over the rest of the documentation and had declared their business completed.

Leaving in a foul mood, Walter had driven several blocks, parked his car and made a call from a public phone. He had hung on, waiting for the search to take its course. 'As you know, there is no such person listed,' the voice at the other end had told him. The 'as you know' indicated that Ignacio Williams was who he suspected him to be.

Now, here he was in Greenlea, fulfilling his obligations. He had never really had a choice. Emmet Briggs was hired. He had met Harvard Smith. Antoine Viall was noisily declaring his allegiance to the Old Man. 'Expendable' he kept hearing Williams say. Probably he, too, was expendable, either on his return or even before he got there. He looked around at the flushed, grinning faces of the freeloaders. Antoine's hand was descending again to fondle Corinne's thigh. Only Emmet and Hallie, sitting together for the first time and deep in conversation, seemed, like him, momentarily withdrawn from the festivity. They did not approve of him. He was well aware of that, but it did not matter. It was what people were prepared to do that counted. Greenlea, like the other places he had visited, did not care about them. It hardly saw them as they mingled in its streets. It identified only their functions: the garage mechanic, the garbage collector, the ticket inspector, the cleaning woman. It was not interested in their politics or their homeland. Like them he was invisible as he finagled the votes and arranged for someone, as yet unknown, to be eradicated. Emmet and Hallie, friends or foes, his task was to send them both to perdition.

___

Sonny Ayza looked back towards the quay. His eye surmounted the line of cranes marshalled on the dock to the grid of the city, spreading in its blocks, defiles and excrescences up and beyond its slopes. The damp of the rail seeped into the palms of his hands. A windblown spray numbed his cheeks and spattered against his shoulders and chest. Would he, he wondered, have felt a similar stinging spray standing at the stern of the ancients' ferry on its journey to the underworld if he had continued swallowing the pills according to his original intent? Still alive today, the throb of the ferry engines, the dip and push of its bow through the choppy waves of the estuary, were carrying him prosaically to Panalquin on a wild goose chase where, no doubt, as in Greenlea, the shades of those departed mingled constantly with the living as well as those who, like himself, perpetuated a sort of living death.

Watching the cityscape recede, he tried to banish the thought. Over the wake, scavenging seagulls planed in the air currents and dived for jettisoned scraps. Ahead, the rusty hulls of tankers and container ships rode at anchor in the roads. The biting edge of the wind in the more open water made him shiver. He moved away from the rail and sought shelter at the foot of the companionway.

The Cock, El Gallo, he recalled, had been a deadly dull Mirandan weekly devoted to ecclesiastical appointments and provincial tittle-tattle. It had existed precariously on the revenue garnered from pious notices of deaths and funeral masses, sequestered in black-outlined squares, which had covered its five to ten back pages. Increasing deaths among its dwindling bands of readers and subscribers had hastened its own demise. Gallo Mart, on the other hand, although ailing, remained an altogether healthier supermarket bird. Its crows still resounded throughout Greenlea and the surrounding region. Elizabeth Kerry's message gave its outlet in Panalquin a most curious significance that was hard to fathom. Whatever was there, or not, he was going to find out within the hour.

Tired of standing in the force of the elements, he climbed up the stairs to the smoke-wreathed warmth of the saloon where the bulk of the passengers were congregated. Removing a copy of yesterday's paper, he sat down in the only available seat. Next to him four men were playing what he guessed was canasta. Their concentrated silence was only broken by the occasional grunt as they picked up, retained or rejected cards. An image of Monica Randell's son fiddling with the controls of his Game Boy console, allied to the downy hairs on Sylvia's arm, abruptly vanished, however, as a triumphant shout, followed by an emphatic thump of a fist on the tabletop, indicated that the game had come to an end. The winner, in acknowledgement, briefly doffed his brown leather cap, revealing a mop of tow-coloured hair before he lowered it once again.

Batiste! Batiste . . . Cheto! Fernando Cheto Simon! The name on Elizabeth Kerry's list!

How, among all his father's contemporaries in Llomera, could he have forgotten Batiste's surname, the man who had been with Manolo and Iusebio at the front? The man who had been at their side during the retreat and who had been encamped close by when Manolo had finally succumbed to pneumonia across the border. God knows he had continued to populate Paca's with a throng of vaguely remembered characters he, himself, hardly knew, yet he had omitted Batiste, a stalwart of 'nothing for us', Batiste with his lick of straw-coloured hair spilling over his eyes as he chucked down his winning hand and pounded the table in celebration then, with a satisfied belch, scooped up the coins into his outstretched hand.

Gradually, this freshly recaptured scene of the nightly Llomeran card players, forever studying their cups, rounds, clubs and swords in the gloom of Paca's wine shop, interweaving with the actual shuffling and dealing taking place beside him in the bright lights of the ferry saloon, dissolved into the softer light of dancing shadows on the wall of the kitchen in Orias. Once again, he heard the sound of voices erupting in the passageway from all those years ago when he was ten years old, almost as distinct as if they had emanated from the wind-scoured deck below, and with a chill of recognition he knew why he had repressed a little bit of history and had expunged Batiste Cheto so effectively from his memory.

He had been disturbed, at first, by a low murmur he could not quite make out. Its persistence drew him up from the floor where he had been lying with the open pages of *The Brothers Sanchez and the Lost Tribe* cradled in the crook of his arm. Putting his ear to the door pane, he had tried to isolate the individual voices, but then, after a bout of increased fervour and still indistinguishable noise, silence followed and he had quietly returned to his book.

The black and white illustration on page 34 in front of him showed Raul, the younger Sanchez brother, pointing in terror into the interior of a gigantic cave from which he had fled. Behind him, a raging sea hurled spume over the guano-stained rocks. In one of its troughs, a bumboat, manned by straining oarsmen, beat its way tenaciously to his rescue. Outside, the voices restarted with an added intensity. Unable to contain his curiosity any longer, he closed this, his favourite book, opened the door and, finding no one around, ran to the salon.

Overall, it had already been a strange day. Rosario and Veri had been caught that morning in an unexpected downpour on their return from the Tuesday market. Forced to scamper off the road, they had sought shelter in the disused chapel of the Little Hermitess of Salaca, whose interior was mournfully dilapidated and filthy with grime. Veri had told him later that recent human excrement had been shat where the altar once was and that the air had been so stinking and horrible that it had driven them back to the crumbling threshold where they were spattered with the teeming rain. First the hills and then their view of the road itself disappeared in the unrelenting torrent. Thunder and lightning rolled, crashed and flared over their forced stopping place. Veri kept wanting to dash in and out, but Rosario pinched her arm tightly and, in an attempt to divert her attention no doubt, started to relate the story of the Little Hermitess.

Eventually, the storm lessened, and, when only a few drops of rain splashed and dripped from the broken coping above, the two of them set off again. On their way back, the road and its verges were strewn with snails. They were so abundant that Veri was able to crush many of them under her feet without being admonished. For several days afterwards, at the slightest pretext, she had grinningly tried to imitate their crunching, cracking, squelching sound.

Tian, for his part, it turned out, had risen with the dawn. After drinking a glass of the previous night's coffee, he had shut himself in his workroom, intending to continue the notation he had begun the week before. A frustrating hour of inactivity later, he was seized by an ungovernable rage which culminated in him wrestling over his chair, hurling the empty glass at the wall and exiting to pace agitatedly up and down the narrow field behind the house.

When he calmed down sufficiently to return indoors, he took a bottle of brandy from the kitchen shelf and ensconced himself in the bay of the yard where the logs were stored. His curses and shouted obscenities continued to reach the house for some time until they gradually tailed off as the contents of the bottle decreased. His mood then plateaued out with the few remaining snifters, inspiring him to lusty renditions of the sentimental songs that had been popular in his student days. Drowsiness overtook him by noon.

Their meal together, in spite of Veri pulling funny faces and trying to chatter about snails, was fraught and otherwise virtually silent. After it, Tian went back to work with no more success. He chose not to join his circle of friends at the Café Goldsmith at the customary time, but instead fitfully studied a score for trio of clarinet, cello and piano, recently submitted by one of his final year composition students. Rosario, some time after five, coaxed him to sit with her during the dead hours while she mended one of Veri's nightgowns.

Towards six o'clock, this restored but fragile domesticity was interrupted by the sudden, flustered arrival of Adelaida, who lived in the cottage at the top of the road. Breathlessly, she told them all that a stranger had been spotted twice; firstly standing in the olive grove farther up the hill by Josep when he had gone out to inspect his tomatoes after the storm, and secondly by old Domingo as he unharnessed his mule at the foot of Alberca Lane. Because of the many visitors, 'those unknowns' in her words, who came to see the professor, she at once thought of his house. The descriptions given, however, fitted a workingman. 'Not one of them,' she admitted, meaning gypsy, 'not by complexion anyway,' and as most of Sebastian's acquaintances were either 'ladies, gentlemen or bohemians,' she thought it best to check and bring a warning.

Adelaida had scarcely departed when the boots of an extra patrol were heard outside in the yard. Two of them presented themselves at the door. By their accents they were young Southerners whose rifles seemed too big for their bodies. Tightened vigilance was now in operation following the reports of an unauthorised person who had been seen acting suspiciously. If sighted, the barracks should be phoned right away. Their message delivered, they saluted again and rejoined their detail. Soon after they had gone, the murmuring began.

For whatever reason, Sonny did not go through the closed salon door immediately. Fear, whether fear of being sent away, or fear of some kind of disappointment, he could not say now looking back from such a distance. Instead, he had retreated to the kitchen where he picked up his book again, this time without opening it. The ticking of the clock seemed louder than before. The minutes dragged by in leaden fashion. Indecisively, he put down and lifted up the battered green covers of *The Brothers Sanchez*, the normal spell of their contents devoid of interest beneath the weight of what he sensed was about to be.

His self-imposed exile ended at last when Rosario poked her head round the doorway and said, 'There's someone here to see us.' Her tone was even, but her eyes betrayed a mixture of watchfulness and grief. Part of him wanted desperately to stay where he was, not to go with her, yet in the pull of his love for her, and her love for him, he knew there was no other choice but to go.

The shutters in the salon were closed. The lamps were lit. Tian, clearly annoyed, looked up when they entered. Opposite him, a man was sitting uneasily on the sofa. A fake leather and fur cap lay beside him. Veri stood behind, her fingers draped around his neck. She drummed them on his shoulders then giggled and tugged at his hair.

The man smiled. 'Don't you know me, Sonny?'

He could not answer. In the soft lamplight, the man's face, despite the deep lines and creases on his brow and cheeks, still retained a boyish air. His thick, unkempt golden hair curled around his ears. Veri intensified her tugging and fidgeting with it and the inside of his grubby-looking collar. She whispered a name over and over.

Rosario said, 'It's been a long time. He's shy. He's grown so used to Orias, he's forgotten Llomera.'

Hot tears smarted in his eyes. Tian muttered disapprovingly. Of course, it was Batistet. How could he have failed to recognise him? The colour of his hair alone had always set him apart and made him distinct. 'The Blond', people for miles around had called him, and he had always been proud of his golden mop. His comb came out at every chance to set it to rights, to sculpt it as befitted a ladykiller. Here in the salon, though, it had lost its lustre. All his clothes looked as though he had slept in them for days. The bottoms of his black trousers and shoes were caked in dried mud. His whole appearance exuded fatigue and an air of neglect.

'You used to come everywhere with me. Everyday you came looking for me, remember? You rode with me upon our tractor. I had to faithfully promise Manolo and your mother here that no harm would come to you. I was there to protect you.'

'And take him places he shouldn't have gone,' Rosario chided.

Batiste grinned. 'Only to the mill, to see the millers underground. Just to Ligac, to see the horses and the farrier. What if the carters and gypsies told stories, and the girls at The Crystals used language only known to Christians? They all knew who he was, your and Manolo's son, my little shadow.'

'It's a lie! It's a lie!' he shouted out, taken aback by the vehemence of his own voice.

An embarrassed silence fell until Tian said, 'Excuse Sonny's behaviour. You must be tired, Batiste. We'll let you rest now. You'll be alright here. We'll talk again later tonight. If you want to be alone with Rosario I'll make myself scarce.'

Batiste swivelled his head and tenderly kissed Veri's fingertips. He nodded to Tian. Then, as he wearily got to his feet, he pulled out a thin, brown paper parcel from inside his jerkin and laid it beside his cap on the sofa. An almost imperceptible sigh escaped his lips. He stared at Rosario. Everyone else's eyes fixed on the packet with its crumpled and partly torn paper and its frayed string. Without speaking, Rosario advanced towards it with the gait of a sleepwalker. She lifted it tentatively, as though it might disintegrate under her slightest touch, then she pressed it to her bosom. 'Thank you, Batiste.'

He did not reply. She began to weep softly. Veri dashed round from behind the sofa and clutched at her skirt, her own eyes filling with sympathetic tears. Tian led the way to the daybed in the cubbyhole where he, himself, sometimes dozed if he had been working during the night. Batiste sat down on the edge of the bed and took off his shoes. He stretched back and closed his eyes. 'Since I crossed the border,' he said, 'sleep and I have been strangers.'

Neither he nor Veri felt able to ask about the parcel, although they both sensed it had to with their father. When they were alone together, Veri said, 'It's probably Daddy's bones. They've been ground down and mixed with his hair. Mummy will burn them and bury the ashes. Then Tian can write music about it. We mustn't tell the teacher or anyone. You must promise never ever to tell.' Her face puckered up with grief and she shoved her clenched fists against his chest, rocking him back. He was overwhelmed with hatred for Batiste.

'I hate him! I hate him! We don't want him here,' he cried.

At supper, Batiste ate sparingly, declining a second helping of garlic soup. When Tian quizzed him about his life over the border, he explained that he managed to get by with working in the fields or taking the occasional factory job. He was a good mechanic, but steady work in that line was hard to find, and, although he spoke a variant of the local dialect, his knowledge of proper French had not progressed beyond the rudimentary. The papers he carried gave him a French identity that was okay for a casual scrutiny. Anything else and he would be in trouble. His accent would let him down. He asked Tian about the possibility of a genuine amnesty.

'It depends who you listen to. Some say they could come back, but in my opinion it won't be safe for a long time. Anyway, who is ready to forgive and forget? That's the unpalatable truth.'

'Have you been home?' Rosario asked.

Batiste shifted awkwardly in his chair and shook his head. 'Too dangerous. But perhaps if you ever went there you could speak to my mother. I know she's still alive.'

'Who knows? One day we might. It might be possible.' She glanced at Tian.

He shrugged. 'I've been thinking about the present situation. If anyone asks I'll tell them a French colleague came to consult me. Tomorrow I'll drive Batiste nearer to the frontier. After all, there's nothing remarkable about two musicologists on a field trip. We've got some suitable clothes, haven't we, Rosario? No, don't worry. It's the least I can do after the risk you've taken. My name anyway should squash any suspicions. Don't forget, Manolo himself asked Rosario and the kids to depend upon it.'

Now, as the card players at his side were well into their second game, Sonny realised that they had all laid an imaginary place for Manolo at that table. His absence had seemed more real, had carried more weight, than their own presence. It had been as if none of them could avoid looking over from time to time to see how he was doing, how he was dying invisibly once again among their company. Rosario especially had tended to the void, pushing her knife and bread ever closer to it, unnecessarily lifting the ladle from the soup tureen to fill the non-existent plate.

Batiste, he now was sure, had disliked being in the house, and he suspected, for her part, Rosario had wished that someone else had come, someone, who in life and thought, had been closer to her dead husband, rather than this one-time gadabout Lothario, whose drunken sprees and on–off courtships had been a perennial source of gossip in Llomera. As for Tian, there had been no mistake. He had made it plain in a hundred little ways that he found the intrusion tiresome and unwelcome.

The meal finished, they were sent to bed. He was glad to go, but Veri protested and wriggled more than usual. Only the threat of a slap and confinement in their room made her reluctantly comply. When at last they were tucked in and Rosario had kissed them, Veri asked, 'Will we see what's under the brown paper?'

'Yes. Yes, you will tomorrow. It's only some letters and things of Daddy's. Photos he had of us, identification papers, things like that. Don't you remember? We talked about it after we knew he had died. We knew some day we would get more news and see the things that were with him in the days we were apart.'

'Don't believe Batiste,' Sonny exclaimed. 'He tells lies. He makes up stories. He once told me there were ghosts in the cemetery when I was little and that when you ate the last scrapings of the pot you turned into a dog or a pig depending on how big the moon was.'

'And rub your belly on the ground,' Veri squealed, imitating a snuffling pig.

'Hush! This isn't about stories. Batiste was with Daddy when they crossed into France. Then he was sent to another place where he heard Daddy had died. His funeral had been held by the time he was able to get there, so he collected what there was and hung on to it. Iusebio hadn't made it to the frontier and Daddy had told Batiste where we'd be. Anyway, he's known Tian from their schooldays. He waited until he could find someone he could trust the things with, but the news for a long time was bad. People who had returned were arrested and put in prison. Now he's come in person. He's put himself in a lot of danger. So we must all agree never to mention his being here to anyone else. We'll play a game, shall we? We'll call him Monsieur Pierre. You can both say hello and goodbye in French, so it will be easy.'

He spent the rest of the night in jumbled dreams. In them a cat roamed about in a glade. While it swam across a stream, the water made it grow bigger and bigger. He struggled to get up and free it from the kitchen where it mewed piteously and scratched against the door, but the blanket was too tight around his body, and when he did manage to get it off he found that his legs had lost all their strength. They absolutely refused to carry him over the floor. He was Raul Sanchez and he was drowning. His head forced itself above the surface. He cried out to his rescuers, whose boat he saw perched on the crest of the next huge wave, but no sound escaped from his despairing lips. His body was exhausted. They only cared for gold. The horrible realisation made his flesh creep. Even his brother, Ernesto, was prepared to leave him here unmourned rather than lose time to pursue the heap of treasure, that was why they rowed so lustily, so fixated were they on rounding the headland and finding the cove where at the top of the cliff trail there was . . .

At last, the white light of dawn suffused the wall opposite. In the adjoining bed, Veri breathed softly in little rounded sighs, her mouth half open on the pillow. He pulled on a pair of blue shorts and edged the door ajar. The house was still and closed in on itself. He tiptoed down the stairs, halting at each creak before continuing his wary progress. No sounds of anyone waking disturbed his opening of the outer door to the courtyard. He shivered as the heavy dew wet his bare feet. He crossed the yard and went into the road.

Below the verge, the outskirts of Orias were stirring to the indignant crowing of cocks patrolling their territorial dung heaps. The braying of donkeys and the whinnying of mules joined the chorus as they were led out, pulled and coaxed between the shafts of their carts. The first mail train of the day was already on its way. Plumes of its smoke hung by the river's edge then drifted out over the valley.

Turning the corner, he saw the figure of a man sitting on his heels, his back pressed against the far side of the courtyard wall. He joined him. He stretched out on the earth at his side. Batiste took off his jerkin and wrapped it round Sonny's naked shoulders then, cupping his hands, he lifted Sonny's feet and rubbed them vigorously until the numbness went and they tingled. Slowly, Sonny's tiny shivers ceased and, as the feeble warmth of the sun increased, he began unselfconsciously to chatter about this and that, telling about school, his playmates, Veri, his mother, Tian and the journey he remembered from Llomera.

While he prattled on, Batiste fished out a tobacco pouch and cigarette paper from the jerkin pocket. He rolled a thin cigarette and said, 'There's a lighter in there as well.'

The wheel would not spark to begin with, but with the help of Batiste's steadying grip he produced a flame. Prolonged, exasperated curses at some recalcitrant beast rose from below. Batiste took a drag and blew out two expanding smoke rings into the air. It was then he had told him about the mule, the one with the lopsided star on its head, which last month had kicked back at him, narrowly missing his thigh.

'Climb these little hills! Climb! With my Mariana, I'll make my living,' Batiste sang softly.

Looking earnestly into Batiste's face, he said fiercely, 'I'll always be "nothing for us". Forever and ever!'

Batiste chucked away the butt of his cigarette and lifted him to his feet. 'It's cold,' he said. 'It's time to go in. I must leave and the sooner the better.'

The ferry bell clanged twice, interrupting Sonny's reverie. Beside him, the canasta school began sorting the cards into their separated packs. Most of the people in the saloon were already pressing towards the companionway, although the dock at Panalquin was still a few minutes distant. Sonny rose and tagged on behind a group in the middle of the room.

He had read his father's letter, perhaps that was the real reason he had expunged Batiste from his recollected Llomeran childhood. It had been among the bits and pieces of the mysterious parcel. He had read it surreptitiously. Later, Rosario had burned it along with

159

some others in an enactment of Veri's preposterous suggestion.

It had been Veri who had first actively dared to rummage about in Tian and Rosario's bedroom in search of the tantalising contents. She had announced her discovery of the treasure, concealed under a layer of sheets and pillowcases in the bottom drawer of the wardrobe, with a whoop of unrestrained excitement. Snatching out a thin bundle of unsent letters and some photos of family and friends, which Manolo had kept with him, she defiantly stuffed them in her knickers as she dodged past him at the door.

She had them spread out on the low stone shelf under the lean-to behind the washing tub when he caught up with her outside. While she carefully studied one of the photos, he saw his chance and grabbed several pages of the letters. Slapping at him and trying to pull his hair, she angrily fought to make him give them back to her, but he lowered his head and butted her hard in the ribs and midriff until she gave up. Temporarily winded, she watched him retreat with his prize to the log pile. 'We've got to put them back,' she wailed. 'You'll spoil it all. Mummy and Tian will be home soon and they'll know we've taken them.'

Ignoring her continued entreaties, he arranged the pages as best he could and began reading. It was not easy. Manolo's writing was crabbed and small and the paper was blotched and yellow with age. He had to guess at many words. Veri by now had joined him. She perched above him, looking down resentfully but no longer trying to recapture her haul.

> *My dearest darling one,*
>
> *I am writing to you, as you have often written to me in the past, to ask how our own particular, private cause is going?*
>
> *Well, I hope, especially as the common cause now goes so badly. I fear, in truth, we and our generation will not be able to see it out. Indeed, yesterday, a recently arrived comrade told me that*

our last front was broken and in retreat.

It's three weeks now since we and another platoon crossed the border, Rosario. Not surprisingly, the mountains weren't any different. The rocks and stones still cut my feet in the same way they had on Mirandan soil. The ridges were just as painful to surmount as those back home and the goat tracks just as steep.

At last, we made the descent into the bowl of an upland valley. There we forded an icy river and regrouped on a grassy escarpment above the water, waiting for our stragglers. As we pitched our remaining supplies, we saw a flock of sheep skitter away from a shepherd in the distance. He didn't approach. That evening, four gendarmes and a lieutenant from a French infantry battalion, who spoke Mirandan, arrived and ordered us to rendezvous next morning at the nearest road. Only a few hours remained for us to be ourselves, in charge of ourselves, before we surrendered to the wishes and dictates of others, yet we were all strangely silent and apart, as if the bonds that had bound us so tightly together were now loosening and dissolving with each successive sheep bleat we heard and each identifiable star we saw shimmering in the chill night air.

Beloved, I must tell you that Iusebio is dead. I've been trying to put it off. I wasn't there myself. The commander identified his body among twenty-three others at a field hospital near Camprodon before it too was shelled and abandoned.

The fact is none of us can come to terms with death, in spite of it being with us from the start.

My relief at not being killed is mocked by the

bodies I leave behind. Death rips our fragile equality to tatters—a baker, a schoolteacher, a lathe turner, a day labourer—united one moment, the next three dead and me alive, set apart through no merit or fault of my own. I fear I've lost my grip of what was the desired state, because, sooner or later, even the toughest among us has found the shell they'd grown to face the world with smashed to smithereens when they twitched and moaned under bombardment, like the fellow they had secretly despised, who retched up on his tunic each time he pulled the trigger. I, too, have become changed, my love. The ordinary things of the world and life now pierce me to the quick. I have no defences. It's as if my skin and the protective membrane of my retina have been winnowed away like chaff, and anything and everything lodges permanently with me, writes itself upon me, buries itself within me, and, I was on the point of saying, becomes me.

The memory of fucking, and nothing but the memory of fucking, has been my only antidote. You and I have always been honest with one another, so I won't lie and say I've only thought of your opening thighs, your bush, your slit into which I've slid my cock and fucked until you—it's always predominately you—experienced the feel, the existence of my flesh in your flesh. Only then, in our imagined repeated comes, does a little of my fear and desperation seep away.

I've talked with Batiste, to return to more mundane things. In common with a few others, he believes we'll soon re-mobilise and go on fighting. It isn't feasible. Day by day, the French authorities are *extending their jurisdiction. Inevitably, we chatted about Llomera. Now he's away from it, Batiste has decided there's only one girl there he's really struck on. For some reason, given his usual boasting, he refused to tell me her name. Whatever she's called, she'll be married to someone else long before she sees him again.*

Ironically, after all that has happened, I'm ill with possible pneumonia. A French doctor examined me. They talk of transferring me to a hospital in Pau. I'll write again from there if they take me.

Rosario, one thing is good. You see, I've got there in the end. It's the knowledge that you and the children are with Tian. I'd known for a long time that he was in love with you, and, although you denied it, I always felt deep down I only had you on sufferance until you recognised your own love for him. That's why I proposed what I did. I could not have borne you seeing me as an obstacle to your happiness, a husband whose absence tied you to a duty from which you would only be freed by his death. As I said to you at the time, though you called me cruel and unfeeling, being with Tian guaranteed safety. Both sides of the conflict are amenable to his gifts. Musical folklore dressed in a certain garb plays just as well with the mistress of the house as with the skivvy.

I'm too tired to write more. I've got the feeling I won't return to Miranda. Our life together is over. Enjoy your days and nights. Watch over Sonny and Veri. If you can, forget me.

Embraces,
Manolo

'I'm going to put them back.' Something in the tone of his voice and the determined look in his eye must have made Veri hesitate because she did not ask what was in the letter. She followed him meekly indoors and watched as he replaced the letters and then the photographs back in their place in the drawer. Putting her arms up round his shoulders, she kissed his cheek. Something icy cold in his innards gave him the first stirring that from now on he would never again be totally at home in his own country.

Four days on, he watched Rosario light a fire in an old bucket with holes in it from his bedroom window. When the flame took hold, blackened fragments of paper swirled gently upwards in the breeze.

The ferry had come alongside. Down below, they were tethering it to the bollards on the dock. Coming down the stairs and onto the gangway, Sonny almost felt physically sick at the memory of his guilt in reading the letter and his dismay at the extent of his father's betrayal. His skin felt cold and clammy. A man behind him elbowed past. Batiste Cheto. Fernando Cheto Simon. Elizabeth Kerry, whether she intended it or not, was sending him as much backwards as forwards.

Agnes Darshel replaced the receiver. Intermittent calls from so-called Emily Brown acquaintances had littered the early afternoon. Each time the phone rang, she had taken the opportunity to carefully insert the names of René Darshel and Roberto Ayza into the casual flow of chit-chat, and, each time, they had failed to elicit any positive response. After the third meandering and meaningless recital of Emily's supposed history and relationships, she had been tempted to ignore the next persistent ring. The possibility, however, that the caller might be the one she was waiting for, the one who might shed some light on her goal, had kept her dutifully getting up and down to answer, what again turned out to be, mere froth, gossip and distraction.

Dispiritedly, she slumped back on the sofa and closed her eyes.

Sequential images of her mother and father, as she visualised them, at their first meeting, then during their courtship days, then caught in the heat of their initial sexual encounters, segued across her mind. Why could they not have stayed like that? Why had he, above all, consented to set up house and play families when it was clear he would never be faithful, never settle down? Anger against him tightened in her stomach. Unthinking or callous, his motives no longer mattered. His going, her mother's life without him, her death, these were the incontrovertible facts she had to face, but what if Chance Company proved to be a blind alley down which she was squandering her hard-earned savings? What if she was, in reality, as far away from finding him as she had been before she decided to bite their come on and fly to Greenlea? No, the thought was too bitter. She refused to be reconciled with failure. Somehow, somewhere here, it had to happen. Nothing would stop her confronting him with his crimes.

She shifted her position. The packet, which the motorcyclist had delivered, rumpled and creased under the pressure of her thigh. Lifting her weight, she drew it out and idly glanced again through the covering letter addressed to Emily Brown.

As a valued subscriber to Contemporary Lives, *the Amadeo Cresci Foundation is pleased to enclose a preview taster from the forthcoming oral biography of one of the most fascinating and least known movers and shakers of the business world.*

We are confident that, after experiencing for yourself the story of his humble but colourful background, you will definitely want to be among the specially selected group of our readers to receive a copy of the complete work at a limited period bargain price.

Yours in sisterhood,
Elizabeth Kerry.

Why sisterhood? Agnes thought. There did not appear to be any feminist connection. The subject of the biography was male and the title of the work, *The Life and Transformations of Fernando Cheto Simon*, did not hint at gender politics.

When she had originally opened up the packet, she had looked down the list of oral sources given at the front of the thin bound manuscript. All the names were foreign. None of them were in any way familiar or interesting, so, disinclined to spend more time reading after her ineffectual browse in *Encounters on a Mountain Road*, she had set it aside. Now, however, with the manuscript in her hand, she leafed forward to the first page of the narrative. Forget the previous cul-de-sac, she counselled herself. Follow the Emily Brown trail. Let's see where it leads. She punched the cushion behind her into a more comfortable shape and, focusing her attention, began to read.

The names they gave him were Fernando Cheto Simon.

He yowled and puked like any good Christian when the priest dabbed the holy water on his undefended, upturned gob— Fernando Cheto Simon, his own bestowed trinity. Father Robles proclaimed them with the same solemnity he reserved for the Father, the Son and the Holy Ghost.

In time, the child would come to prefer the third in each case—Simon, his maternal surname and the Holy Ghost, mysterious, spooky, all pervasive, yet at the same time unknowable and unseen. Unseen like his absent father, Batiste, a disgrace, a scandal, but I'm getting ahead of myself.

Of course, that little shit, Toto Felipe, tried to prevent the christening. He used his official position, as keeper of historic monuments to warn that a child born out of wedlock was bad enough, but a girl who brazenly and emphatically declared to all and sundry that the father was Batiste Cheto, a proscribed ne'er-do-well, who, if he had dared to be present, would surely and rightly have been arrested and carted off to jail for a long and demanding rehabilitation, was not only a liar but a dirty whore, the daughter of a whore, determined to throw ordure and sin in the face of law-abiding, right-minded folk.

To everyone's surprise, the priest, Father Francisco Robles, that severe and ascetic man, who only ever wanted to quit his presbytery for the sanctuary of his church, who, it was whispered, suffered the agonies and torments of the damned when his duties forced him out into the world to administer the last rites, who had never spared, and never would, a kindly word, or look for that matter, to his dwindling flock, held firm. He ignored the village's moral strictures and conducted the service in spite of his hierarchy's disapproval and subsequent censure.

This stand on behalf of Antonetta Simon, I can tell you, was all the more unexpected because, over the years, he hadn't even had the decency to exchange the customary pleasantries with Angelica, his housekeeper. A finger laid upon his fleshy lips had abjured her to silence on the rare occasions when she had been emboldened to try and relay what you really must know, Father. 'I swear I've never even heard him loose a fart,' she gossiped to us. 'His bowels move without noise their wonders to perform. O God, preserve us! What terrible sins have we committed to deserve such an outcast, such an example, as a priest?'

Antonetta retrieved her baby and said to her elder sister, Gloria, who was standing beside her at the font, 'Well at least that's done. Whatever happens he'll be with the company of the angels.' Then she murmured a little prayer to St Ann, whose face she had always liked, asking her to look out for her son and give him a coat and shelter if all else failed.

The truth was she had been afraid Father Robles would choke when he got to the name Cheto, but in the event it had seemed to give him no pause, although he had quickly decked it out and surrounded it with a brief homily on the infinite grace of

God, which bloweth where it listeth, and the reflection that we are all sinners in a sinful world.

Outside, the neighbours from St Roch were gathered in the western porch, some of them out of genuine kindliness, others because, when all was said and done, Antonetta was one of their own. Needless to say, none of Batiste's family were there. Church desecrators to a man and woman, they obdurately stayed put on their holding, pruning and hoeing on their slopes. True, Rafael, the head of the clan, had offered comfort as he saw it, but Tonetta had refused. 'Let the boy come to us if he's a Cheto,' he had said. 'We'll look after him until Batiste returns. You can come as well,' he had added as an afterthought. 'You're strong enough. You can work.'

So she carried the baby back to number 48 at the top of St Roch and laid him in the cradle Iusebio had made for Gloria in anticipation of the arrival of their own child—the cradle that Gloria had taken down and shown to her sister when she heard her news. Tonetta had wept on seeing it and had begged her sister to keep it for the day when she found herself another man, but Gloria had only smiled bitterly and said, 'Two fucks and you're ready to produce. Two years and . . . ' She hadn't finished what she was going to say but instead had asked, 'Anyway, where am I going to find a man? There's nobody here and just think about the ones who wander in from outside.' On that note, they'd laughed and kissed. Tonetta accepted Gloria's gift. It strengthened the complicity between them.

At the celebration, there was wine and some blood sausage left over from the pig Vincenz had slaughtered the previous November. Gloria put a dish of sugared almonds on the table. Maria from 34 brought a pot of spicy potatoes and old Luisa slipped out an apronful of cauliflower fritters. The Sobradiel girls and little Jaumet deposited a bucket of snails they'd gathered that morning. It was an auspicious start.

Later that evening, Tony Pigeon dropped by and, once he had

had a few more drinks, began to sing, just for the child, 'with my horse out on the road.' He accompanied it with a little jig and caper to show how the horse stepped out, and how the cart bumped and swayed from side to side.

No one mentioned Batiste, but he was in their thoughts as were the others who, unlike him, would never return. Joaquin told them that the guards were watching the comings and goings from the other side of the cinema, but Paco, the baker, said he had shared a cigarette with them and they were simply killing time until they patrolled the south road.

As the days and weeks and months passed, Fernando felt the air and sun on his face and eyes when Antonetta placed the cradle on the doorstep. The unfocused shapes he came to know as her and his aunt Gloria were joined by things that appeared, moved and were gone—a fly, a drop of rain, the paw of a marauding cat, a moth that alighted on his coverlet.

The sounds and smells of St Roch slowly canoodled him from his universe of self to an awareness of the other, the things beyond his immediate touch and grasp—a cock crowing, the rumble of a cart, the protests of a donkey forced into a narrow alley, the false starts of Remigio's lorry, its repeated backfires, the clack of the treadle and the whirr of the sewing machine as Tonetta bent forwards over the cloth, Gloria running water for the pot, the drip, sizzle and splutter of hot oil, the deep bell from the church, the cracked toot of the crier's trumpet before he yelled out his announcements, then fainter as he rounded the corner, Tonetta's breast, his sick, his shit, his blanket, his suck of fingers and toes, the odour of Tonetta's bed, the smell of the glass on the picture of the Sacred Heart, the wax polish Gloria used, the feel of the oilcloth on the backs of his legs when they sat him on the table, the heaviness of the air before a thunderstorm, its lightness and freshness after—in a word, all the things that were later lost to him, yet, when randomly encountered, never

169

ceased to prick at his heart, for, like all of us, he had been in paradise without recognising it.

Soon, he grew into a sturdy and inquisitive little rascal. There was not a pot or a bucket or a heap in the street that was not molested by his prying fingers. If something stood he tried to push it over. If something was above he clambered up until he could knock it down. If it was dirty yeuch he crammed it in his mouth or smeared it on his face. His aunt threatened him with a beating, but when Antonetta finally put him across her lap, fully intending to spank him, she ended up only tapping him on the rump then righting him and giving him a kiss and a hug, to Gloria's despair. 'He's no worse than the others,' his mother said. 'He's alive. What do you want?'

Alive was what Fernando was. He quickly added the length and breadth of Gatar Street as far as the butcher's shop, then on to the corner of St Bartholomew, to his explored kingdom. True, some he met on his toddle spat and talked darkly about his father, but to him that was all the same as glug, glug, glug or chew, chew, chew. His grinning mug soon made them relent.

Passers-by, during the day, gave his mother a progress report on his travels as she soaked the chickpeas or stitched a hem. 'He's at Victor's.' 'He's with the cousins.' 'He's tormenting Augustinetta.' 'He's peed himself.' 'He's been on Auntie Luisa's roof feeding the rabbits.' 'Dammit! He's more of a Simon than anything else. He's got your eyes. The eyes of your pa. You can see it when he laughs. Right at home in Llomera that's what he is.'

He wailed and cried though when they took him to the fields. His bellows and sobs contorted his screwed up face. They convulsed his little frame. Tonetta and Gloria took it in turn to drag then carry him, kicking and screaming, along the ridge past Orange Miguel's hives and down the path on the far side of the hill. The sight of the open sky seemed to send him into paroxysms of rage, nor was he pacified by their hoeing of the red earth between the drills of potatoes, or the pointed out butterflies flapping their mottled wings among the rows of tomatoes and beans. The drone of a hornet, which if it had ventured into the confines of St Roch would have been a wonder to behold, a prize to try and capture, here only provoked whimpers of fear followed by shrieks of torment. He girned and sulked and bawled all through the morning till Gloria, at the end of her patience, told him to either shut it for the love of Christ or they would leave him there for good. His hands and eyes said it all as he clutched piteously at her skirt. The sisters laughed. 'Son,' Gloria said, 'you're not going to be a countryman, are you?' Then, realising what she had uttered, she stopped watering the plants and touched Tonetta's arm, for Iusebio and Batiste had fought under the commander whose *nom de guerre* had been 'The Countryman'—a courageous and wily captain or a ruthless and bloodthirsty destroyer, depending on whether you shared the empty plate of 'nothing for us' or marched with the bound up rods over your shoulder for the greater glory of the fatherland.

Restored to his own midden, however, Nando was his old self. His chubby legs carried him from one blether about his doings to another. He was never shy in company, no matter what their age or size. Everyone was his pal, yet none more so than Paca, who kept the wine shop in Molino Street. Right from the beginning they had hit it off with a deep and mutual fascination. 'Paca, apaca, apaca' were among the first words he managed to form.

The pair of them, oblivious to time, sat for hours together at her door while she waited for customers. Perched beside her on a chair, Fernando grinned contentedly up at her wrinkled, dark-brown face as she exhaled smoke from her cigarillo above his head or shelled peanuts for him to chew. Each morning, at eleven, she toasted his continued well-being with a glass of her 'mixture', a ferocious blend of dry anis and muscatel, which she drank, according to her, to keep herself right.

A passing stranger would reasonably have wondered what it was they found to discuss so earnestly, for in Paca's company Fernando took on the gravitas of a middle-aged man. One minute, while he listened to her with his head cocked to the side, he resembled a much travelled wanderer, who knows he still has far to roam, the next, nodding sagely at her observations, he assumed the guise of a learned friar, who had poked his nose into a thousand arcane and forgotten tomes.

Day by day Paca guided him through the tongue-trippery of the '*Three Sad Tigers*'. She saddled him up so he could ride the western range with '*Fast Draw Jim*'. She told him Tarzan was an American because she had seen him dive off the Brooklyn Bridge, and that Nanook lived in a country without a name. Nearer to home, she explained why St Teresa had suffered so, poor creature, and how what's-his-name had become St John of God, who wasn't the same as St John of the Cross, whose dark night of the soul she described as though it had been a particularly bad bout of indigestion. 'There are a multitude of Johns in the world,' she averred, 'that's why the fair on the eve of their name is such a wonder to behold.'

Almost as if they had happened last night, she related the trials and tribulations of that cunning rascal, Lazarillo, born with his feet in a river, whose exploits and sayings she knew by heart. 'Just like that other sensible fellow, Sancho, Belly by name,' she said, as she rubbed his and then her own, 'who had the great misfortune to be in the service of a crackbrained fool who never noticed if vittles were on the table or not.'

Gradually, Fernando learned through her gossip the foibles and peccadilloes of the menfolk who frequented her tavern. He knew which were the misers and which were the spendthrifts, those who could hold their drink and those who were not quite right in the head. He knew the exact day each month the barber came back from the whorehouse in the city and that Uncle Carlos wasn't really the father of the girl in the grocery store. What it all

172

meant he did not know, but it confirmed what he had immediately sensed. Paca knew everything; everything there was to know in the whole of the world.

Strangers, as well as neighbours, paraded through her tales. She opened up the lives and trades of pedlars, itinerant bricklayers and carpenters, cuckolded Pepe with his vanloads of second-hand clothes, tubercular Martin with his poor quality shoes displayed in expensive boxes, Toni, the gypsy, with his battered guitar, so that the possibility of lives spent beyond Llomera dangled beguilingly in front of her entranced listener.

'I'd let a gypsy in,' she said, 'if he came and asked me first. It's alright if they are expected, but it's no good if they barge in unannounced. That way plenty trouble's guaranteed. They find their way at night by the stars. They all love St Barbara and say that Christ was a black man. They'll journey from all over to join a procession, but you won't catch them inside a church. Never say "I'm off for a pee" in their presence, for to them that's a dirty insult and a horrible blasphemy. Now, as I've often told you, I've only to hear someone tune up a guitar, others to clap and someone to sing the couplets, and next day I remember them all word for word.'

As good as her word and straight from her heart, Paca passed on the couplets of songs to such effect that, in later years, whenever Fernando heard the clap and beat of palms, he could fit a dozen couplets to the tune. She sang them according to her mood. When she was happy and a light mountain breeze filtered its grace along the dark alleyway, she would tilt her head back and sway her ample hips to 'When you come with me, where will I take you? For a walk along the royal ramparts.' Conversely, when she was sad or money was tight she preferred the miner's lament, 'You told me your name was Laura, Laura by name, by name Laura. But the laurels are faithful by nature and you are not to me.' The one that stirred Nando most, however, was 'Two hearts were placed on the scales. One begged for justice, the other vengeance.' The bloody image of hearts torn from their bodies intrigued him, as did the thrill of justice and vengeance, but then Paca spoilt it by winking at him and laughingly taking a slurp of her habitual 'mixture'.

One day, as he grew older, Fernando made an important discovery. Words that were written down at home stayed the same. When Gloria or his mother read the items from a shopping list or said the title of the film shown on the poster tacked to the cinema door, they said the same thing, whereas Paca, when she saw the balloon rising above Fast Draw Jim's head, said one time, 'Two down and one to go,' but later, when looking at the same balloon, changed it to, 'Tonight, my friend, you'll sleep with the devils.' Studying the movement of Paca's lips, an idea buzzed in Nando's brain box. Paca could not read. Therefore, he must learn as soon as possible so he could show her. Reading, with what she knew already, would place her on a par with the saints. The thought frightened him a little because, as far as he could make out, saints went to special places, beside the Pope perhaps, and he did not want Paca to go away. 'I won't tell anyone,' he whispered, to her bemusement.

Now it was Paca's custom to flesh out her tales and homilies by occasionally adopting a variety of voices, and this practice began to issue from her listener's mouth with the same unconscious ease with which he picked up a stone in the street, inspected it for a second, then casually chucked it away.

Back at home, Antonetta, busy with ironing and the stepping stones of her own thoughts, let her son chatter on about Paca and the doings of the day, when she suddenly realised she was hearing Paca say, 'Dirty scoundrels, they ought to be whipped. Lazy good-for-nothings!' Followed by what could only be Luisa at the washing trough, 'scrub, young man. Give me a pela and I'll scrub you clean' and then Remigio's hoarse mutter, 'Whore's shit! What a fucking mess! Must I do it all myself?' The words were piped in a child's voice, but the intonation and the individual mannerisms were so curiously adult that, instead of rebuking him for swearing, she joined in his chuckles of delight. Like her, Fernando clearly believed the world about them was all the better for being pulled by its nose.

This talent remained with him as he grew older. He sharpened and refined it, even after he reckoned that Paca was only another old woman, who, like many others, clung to the sayings and superstitions of the past which, when you really thought about them, made little sense.

He still continued to say hello to her, of course, and hang around long enough to answer her questions out of politeness. Yes, he could read and write and add and subtract and multiply and divide many columns of figures. He knew what a pyramid was and how many centilitres made a litre. Yes, he was nine now. It was very different from when he was just a kid.

Paca looked at him and saw his impatience to be gone. She was wise enough to know how things are and must be for the young, yet she wanted to give him her blessing while there was still time. 'Listen, my king,' she said, taking his hand. 'Your mother's a good woman, a brave girl, and your father's a good man, too. Don't heed what anyone says. Keep him in your heart. Tonetta does. I do.' She let go of him, and then, as she had no host to offer him, she unscrewed the top of the jar beside her and poured out a faltering stream of peanuts into his cupped hands.

Fernando repeated, 'Keep him in your heart,' using Paca's voice as he strolled off. He pressed the dry shells away from the nuts and stuffed them in his mouth. Turning the corner, he narrowly missed bumping into Vincenz and Tony Pigeon, who had stopped to argue over the run of last night's cards. A moment later, safely out of earshot, he counterpointed Vincenz's guttural boasts with the high-pitched squeaks of Tony's bad luck. It seemed as though he only needed to be with someone a second to catch their way of talking, their particular turn of phrase, like a germ. Under the intuition of his tongue he was able to unlock the communal wardrobe of Llomera and slip on and off, according to his whim, someone else's old jacket, best Sunday trousers, black mourning dress or white confirmation suit, all of which conveniently shrank to fit his diminutive frame. The one person he never sought to imitate, however, was his mother. The thought of doing it never even crossed his mind.

This talent for mimicry naturally endeared him to his schoolmates. They repeatedly asked for his rendition of the rising and coaxing tones of their own Miss Lopez as she sought in vain for the answer to the next line of long division chalked up on the blackboard. When freed for the afternoon, while they shoved, straggled and hopped their way home, he rebuked them in the saddened voice of Mrs Vico from the big class, but then absolved their threatened punishment by reverting to his own carefree lilt.

In the presence of adults he was much more circumspect. It was clear a part of them enjoyed his cheekiness, but the way they looked at him sideways contained an undercurrent of disapproval. Therefore, in school, when his classmates pointed at him and tugged at his arm or stabbed a pencil into the back of his neck, in the hope of getting him to take someone off, he feigned ignorance and continued to stare straight ahead with a look of benign innocence. On top of arithmetic and spelling, like the rest of us, he had begun to learn how to dissimulate successfully.

Nor, when he went to the fields, did he dare mimic his aunt behind her back. These days they worked together happily enough: he pulling up potatoes, she watering the tomatoes and lettuces. Later, climbing up into the fork of an olive tree, he watched her sturdy, stooping figure gather up the fruit he had dislodged. From his height through the branches, he could see over the valley to the three tall chimneys of the brickworks. Gloria glanced up at him as the fall of olives stopped. 'Work, child,' she said. 'Dreams are the same over there as they are here.' Fernando obediently resumed tugging his hooked stick among the silver-green leaves. No doubt, beyond the chimneys other olive trees grew in a similar valley. Close by, another olive tree awaited him. The valley floor was covered in olive trees. As far as his aunt was concerned, when it was time to harvest olives then that was what she did without question. It was immutable. He could see the logic, yet beyond the beyond he guessed there was something else, something totally different, unconnected with the repetitive chain of what they did, having nothing in common with olive trees and brickwork chimneys, something that was not a dream but a reality. The thrill of the glimmer of escape from what he loved troubled his psyche. He redoubled his efforts. The olives rained down beneath him. 'That's the way,' Gloria said approvingly. 'A bit more and we'll rest and eat.'

When he was around eleven years old, Fernando's growing curiosity about his father's relations began to trouble the equilibrium of his daily life. Unlike the families close at hand with whom he made friends or temporary enemies, they were a complete mystery. None of them ever appeared in Llomera, as far as he could make out.

He badgered his mother for details, but beyond the listing of their names, Rafael, his grandfather, Guillermina, his grandmother, Jacinta, his aunt, and his two cousins, Lupe and Milagra, both of whom went to school in Cirit, her information was scant and unsatisfactory.

'But why don't they come to see us?' he put to her.

'They bide where they are. They're a law unto themselves.'

'Don't they like me if they're my grandparents?'

'I'm the one they don't like. They would have taken you in if I'd given you up to them. Something I'd never do.'

The scary thought of that having actually happened, of an

alternative life where he grew up among strangers without the comfort of his mother beside him, disturbed yet intrigued his inquisitive mind. Accordingly, he pressed on with repeated questions about them until one day, for the sake of peace, Antonetta announced that they would beard the famous Chetos in their lair.

Three mornings later, Remigio, on his run to Cantellos, dropped them off at the foot of the stony track, which wound uphill to the smallholding.

Guillermina, sitting on a stool in the yard, was busy skinning a rabbit when they finally appeared in view over the crest. Without returning their greeting, she completed her work and then stared long and hard at Antonetta before turning her gaze to Fernando, who returned it with a hesitant smile. 'You've brought him I see,' she muttered.

'Only on a visit. It was his wish.'

Guillermina laughed bitterly, 'What good's a visit? We're not ones for visits here. A son who comes home and chooses to screw a wanton girl but can't spare the time to find his way here and see his own mother, that's a visit.'

'You know it was too dangerous. If he had been picked up here, Rafael would have been arrested as well. Anyhow, it's not your grandson's fault.'

'There's nothing for you here. If you intend to keep the boy then do it. He's no part of us. You've wasted your journey.' The old lady brushed the rabbit skin from her lap and, gripping the dark-red carcase, got to her feet.

Fernando, for once tongue-tied, looked perplexedly at his mother. Antonetta, her face flushed, took his hand and turned to go.

'No. Wait.' A woman's voice came from inside the kitchen. Batiste's sister, Jacinta, emerged into the doorway. 'Let the boy stay, mother, if he wants to. Do you want to stay, son?'

Fernando shifted his weight from one leg to the other. Jacinta smiled at him, but Guillermina's face was unrelenting. He sensed the throb of his mother's suppressed anger beating within her. 'I need a pee,' he whispered. Antonetta pointed behind the fig tree in the corner. Guillermina took the rabbit indoors as he scurried off. The dribble and then the stream of his urine splashed up and down the twisted bark. Peering round, he saw the two women talking.

'Have you heard from him?'

Antonetta nodded.

'Is he well?'

'Yes, well enough. I haven't heard for a while, and it's only rarely. Someone else forwards news.'

'Whore's shit! We'll both be old before Batiste comes back again. None of us will be the same. Why don't you find a new man? I wouldn't blame you.'

Antonetta shook her head. 'Where's Rafael?'

'Up top with Lupe and Milagra. I'll be taking them some food soon. Want to come? You'd like to see your cousins, wouldn't you?' she said, as Fernando rejoined them.

Now his mind was made up. It had not been before. He had not known whether he wanted to go or to stay. 'No,' he said firmly. 'I want to go home. I'm not a Cheto. I'm a Simon.'

Fernando remained unnaturally quiet on the long trudge back to Llomera. He wandered its streets alone as he slowly munched at the thick slice of bread rubbed with oil and tomato, which his aunt had given him on their return. 'Keep him in your heart,' Paca's words from all that time ago would not leave his brain. He tried imitating Guillermina's scowl and Jacinta's sing-song modulation, but neither dispelled his hurt. Coming back round into St Bartholomew, he scuffed away the little circle of marbles two younger kids were playing with. 'I'm Fernando Simon,' he said, bunching up his fists as he looked from one frightened face to the other. 'Remember that!' It did not help.

Later that night at the supper table he continued to scratch at his invisible itch. 'Why can't I have my own grandparents?' he said querulously.

'Don't be silly. I've told you when they died. You've seen their graves in the cemetery often enough,' his mother replied.

'But why? Why?' A glob of egg yolk dribbled down his chin as he struggled to get out the words. 'Why is Batiste Cheto my father?'

'I've explained it to you many times. Batiste and I love each other even though we can't be together.' Antonetta took his hand, which trembled in hers. Gloria was on the verge of saying something. Antonetta's eyes entreated her to stay silent. 'Listen,' she said, after kissing Fernando's eyelids. 'Batiste's in France. He works there. He's never committed a crime. In war one side loses the other wins. We have to stay here and wait for things to change.'

'He's never asked you to join him—thought about that?' Gloria spat out, unable to contain herself. 'You kid yourself with that philanderer. It's better the boy knows.'

'Hush!' Antonetta dabbed her handkerchief around her son's mouth. He jerked away from her ministrations and gazed fascinatedly at the dark-puce blotch spreading on his aunt's cheek.

'Let me tell you,' Gloria continued remorselessly, 'the very morning after you persuaded me, against all my advice, to leave you alone with him, even while he was telling me about how he'd heard about Iusebio's death and that Manolo Ayza had also died and that he and others had erected a cairn to the fallen on the French side of the border, even then, not content with having you, the greatest love of his life, he tried it on with me. These black clothes didn't stop him trying to grope me while you were upstairs and the names of his dead comrades were tumbling from his lips. Yes, a real man you've found yourself. One to stand by you at every turn.'

Stung by her sister's words, Antonetta rose from the table

and went into her bedroom where she tugged open the middle drawer of the chest by the bed and took out a battered oblong tin surmounted by the partially worn away image of two bluebirds pecking at each other affectionately on the lid. On her own, listening to the heated voices of Gloria and Fernando, she raised it momentarily to her lips then dropped it to her side and resolutely carried it through to the light. 'There,' she said, as she put it down on the table and lifted the lid. 'There you are. Your father thinks of you and me. He lets us know where he is and how he's doing and when he can he sends us money.'

The letters came from Orias. They were written by Rosario Marva.

In the beginning, she simply forwarded the skimpy and erratic news Batiste sent from over the border, changing the two or three French republic notes into Mirandan green. What Sebastian Marva, her husband, made of it was anyone's guess. In any case, he could not have interfered because soon an independent correspondence began to flourish between Rosario and Antonetta irrespective of Batiste's letters.

Rosario asked about things in Llomera and wrote about her children, Roberto and Veronica, both of whom were fathered by our own Manuel Ayza, who taught school here before the outbreak of war. Antonetta replied with general gossip and tales of Nando and how hard it was for Gloria to live without Iusebio. She . . .

Agnes put the pages down and closed her eyes. Roberto Ayza again. His name was turning up too often to be a coincidence. Someone was definitely pointing her in his direction. Firstly, there was his involvement with Chance Company and her stay in Greenlea, and now, in addition, there was his appearance as a child in an unsolicited manuscript sent to Emily Brown by the Amadeo Cresci Foundation, whoever they were. Did he know her father, know where he was? Could he, himself, she paused on the brink of daring to think the impossible, be her father in a so far unrevealed identity?

She opened her eyes. They flitted distractedly over the shabby utilitarian furnishings and fittings of the nondescript room. Here she was, stuck in a brief transit area designed for someone who did not exist, thinking crazy thoughts. A succession of Emily Browns, or their equivalents, she guessed, had sat on the same sofa and were likely to continue doing so when, successful in her search or not, she had left the city. Nothing here belonged to her. Everything that surrounded her was someone else's accessory, including Roberto Ayza. A gnawing sense of loneliness, which she had not felt in years, began to unzip her customary resolve. For the first time since she was a child, she had abandoned rational thought and had put herself completely in the hands of others whose motives, apart from making money, were obscure to say the least. She had let Chance Company, a nebulous outfit, entice her to a city she instinctively disliked, in the outside hope of finding the man she had long banished to a permanent exile or an unvisited grave. 'I left him,' she said softly then repeated it. 'It was me who also left him.'

'Yours in sisterhood, Elizabeth Kerry.' The phrase kept troubling her. She picked up the pages again and flicked through them, looking for any further mention of Roberto Ayza. There was none she could immediately see; yet there was something wrong with the text, something that had bothered her earlier. It did not make sense. It purported to be a kind of oral history, but none of the contributors, listed or not, could have known the innermost thoughts, or recalled in such detail the long-past conversations, of the main protagonists. Who was the real author? Why give it to her if not to point her in a particular direction? Do something, she told herself. The trouble was, there was no routine to follow, no busyness, which normally filled her life, only the gap between being Agnes Darshel and being Emily Brown, and it was beset by unanswered questions.

She went into the bathroom, lowered the plug and turned on

the hot tap. As she studied herself in the mirror, the phone rang. She lessened the water flow and moved back into the hallway. 'Emily Brown.'

There was a pause. She heard the muffled sound of voices, then one voice, deeper over the line than when they had talked at the gallery.

'Emmet Briggs. I'll be a little late this evening. There's another business I must see to. Don't worry. Wait for me.'

I'm not completely on my own. There is someone else, Agnes thought. His voice was calm and steady. The look in his eyes, she recalled, had been different from the shifty looks of others or the apologetic glances of Leo Manners. He was prepared to meet things head on, no matter what. She had sensed it then. Careful, don't be sucked in, she reminded herself. Remember he's being paid by Chance Company.

'Do you know the Polygon district?' she asked, when he had finished speaking.

'Sure, though it's not on my usual round. The local joke is you only end up there if you've given up on life. Death's waiting room, they call it.'

'I want to go there. Will you take me?'

'Leave it till tomorrow. We'll stop off on our way to Alakhin. I've got to go. See you tonight.'

The sight of the orange-coloured Greenlea directory beside the phone when he rang off made up her mind. She opened it at the residential section. Ayza R. There it was, the single entry, 2 Charlock Rd. She dialled the number. After a moment, a pre-recorded tape came on. 'Sorry, I'm not available just now. If you wish to leave a message please speak after the tone.' His voice was light and modulated, without a trace of what she imagined a Mirandan accent might be. She spoke firmly, carefully choosing her words over her increased heartbeat.

'This is Emily Brown. I'm a client of yours. I know you're on leave from work, Mr Ayza, but I'd very much like to discuss my stay in Greenlea with you in person. I've been reading about you when you were a boy. Please call my number. It's 81164 if you don't already know it. I look forward to hearing from you very soon. My real name is Agnes Darshel.'

She had done it. Whether for good or ill, time would show. She put down the phone, went into the bedroom and undressed. What would he look like, this so far elusive Roberto Ayza? Slight build, jaunty step, pencil moustache, slicked back black hair? She continued parading a motley collection of masculine features when she immersed herself in the just bearable heat of the bathwater and shut her eyes: paunchy with dark jowls and brown eyes, clean shaven, taller than expected with some feature or characteristic that resembled a certain photograph a drummer had sent her. She stopped imagining. No, don't start to think that, but, it was too late, she already had. Would there be something in his make-up, in his physiognomy, which would betray the connection she was looking for? How old would he be? She tried to recall if there had been any dates or events she could place in the text she had been reading. None came to mind. He was older than the other boy, the subject of the biography, Fernando Cheto Simon, of that she was sure. Her imagined picture of Matthias Lemmel from the *Mountain Road* book flitted into her mind. She watched as her composite, shifting image of Roberto Ayza solidified into the hazel-eyed, open-featured, smiling Matthias, who, for a second, turned his rapturous gaze away from the undulating Swedish countryside outside the carriage window to stare directly into her, his reader's, eyes.

'Forgive him,' her mother had whispered when she had leant over the hospital bed to gently brush her hair for what turned out to be the last time. She had nodded, of course, and had said yes several times, but forgiveness had been, and still was, beyond her powers. Let him exist in the world at the same time as me, she had thought. It was as far as she could go. A single meeting, then end it, remained her goal.

Stepping out of the cooling water, she wrapped the white,

towelled bathrobe around her and wiped some of the steam from the mirror glass. Emily Brown—Agnes Darshel. Roberto Ayza—René Darshel? Was that how he had begun? How he was again? A man from a country her mother had never mentioned, an employee of Chance Company, who, in his spare time, might still play some trombone? She wiped the mirror edges and made up her mind. If Mr Ayza did not ring back then she would visit him at home.

'Aha, look how fortune throws us together even on the other side!'

Sonny heard the words coming from somewhere behind him, but, because he did not connect them in any way with himself, he continued pushing through the straggling lines of people waiting at the bus station, towards the taxi rank beyond, until a hand touched his sleeve and a voice spoke his name. Surprised, he stopped and turned to be greeted by the beaming face of Albert, visibly out of breath with the exertion of catching him up.

'Didn't you recognise me back there? You looked so preoccupied when I called out. You were quite lost in your own world, but you see, my friend, no matter where you go you're sure to bump into a fellow Mirandan. You're not rushing to meet a client are you? I'm not holding you up?'

Sonny shook his head. 'No. I'm on leave, remember? I'm only wandering around passing the time.' His real reason for coming to Panalquin struck him as so ridiculous and arbitrary that it was best left unsaid. The tantalising opacity of Elizabeth Kerry's message was in danger of turning him into a spurious detective, a snapper up of foolish and inconsequential connections, who lacked the fundamental knowledge of what it was that had to be detected.

'What a waste!' Albert exclaimed. 'Don't you get tired of this northern greyness and murk? You could be somewhere in the sun.'

'The sun shining in the sky doesn't change what's on the ground or in people's hearts. Lyon, Yokohama, Greenlea, the next place I move to, they all have their weather. I adapt.' He shrugged, and then, regretting the stern note which had crept unwanted into his voice, he suddenly embraced the startled Albert and patted him twice on the back. 'Thanks for the meal last night and thank Monse for thinking about me.'

Albert returned his embrace. Heads swivelled in their direction, intrigued by the sight of two middle-aged men, incongruous in their respective heights, one short and dumpy, the other wiry and thin, greeting each other in such a conspicuously effusive manner.

Without realising it, Sonny thought, you and Monse prolonged my life. If she had not stumbled across the Forest Mushroom article I would not be standing here with you today. He regarded Albert with a warmth and affection he rarely showed. 'And where are you off to, man?'

'The ferry. I've finished my bit of business here. I was seeing an old customer, Vic Larries, on Marine Drive. To tell you the truth . . . '

'Electrical goods,' Sonny interrupted. 'He runs electrical goods shops.'

'No. What gave you that idea? He's an insurance broker. You seem very carefree this morning. I must tell Monse how much better you look.'

'Oh, it's only a story someone told me. Obviously a different Victor Larries was in it, but what was the truth you were going to tell me?'

'Well, to be honest, it's the prospect of getting back on the ferry. It's silly, I know, but it makes me feel quite queasy. Drowning, you see. I have this stupid fear I might drown. I get on board and I think what if we went down with all hands or what if the rail suddenly gave way and no one saw me as I plunged into the water, no one was there to shout man overboard or throw me a lifeline. Crazy, I know, completely irrational. The estuary is sheltered for God's sake, and accidents virtually never occur. After all, I got here safely. Nothing dire happened and yet while I was on board, I tell you.' He hunched his shoulders apologetically. 'I didn't know where to put myself. The constant throb of the engines, the weight of the water moving under the hull, they're like the quickened beat of my own pulse, the oppressive coursing of my own blood through my veins. I wanted to be sick, but there was nothing to retch up. No sooner was I on deck to try and grab some air than I thought no, this is worse, so I ended up back in the saloon with my eyes tight shut, willing myself to think about anything rather than the sensations of the journey. Truly a hopeless case.'

'Why put yourself through it? Couldn't you have sent someone else?'

'It's a rare occurrence, thank goodness, but Mr Larries demands the personal touch. He could easily go to one of our local competitors who are quoting cheaper rates. Anyway, now you've seen the uncertainties that plague me whenever I step beyond my set routine. The gods are jealous of my unflustered domesticity, the everyday pleasures I find in my little loves. It doesn't matter how I try to propitiate them, they prefer to see me undone by fear, sweating under the anguish of impending loss.' The ferry hooter signalled the five minutes departure time as if in accordance with Albert's presentiments. He turned and looked towards its berth. 'I must go. I don't want to miss it.'

They embraced again. 'I'm sorry I'm not travelling with you,' Sonny said.

'I didn't expect you to. I'll live. Didn't your Sebastian Marva once boast that one day he would possess the powers of Orpheus, that he would charm the rocks and mountains into song, that he would be afforded safe passage wherever he went? A youthful folly, of course, and who, apart from us, mentions him or his music today?' With these parting words, Albert hurried off, raising his right arm in a brief backward wave as he threaded his way through the crowd.

Sonny watched him disappear, then, when the hooter had sounded for the final time, he crossed the road to the first taxi in the line, gave the direction, Old Station Yard, and settled into the back seat. The driver nodded, dropped the newspaper he was reading and started the engine. He took the continuation of the dock road in preference to the east town intersection. A possibly longer route, Sonny guessed without saying it.

Blurted messages of future pickups filtered through the crackle of the intercom as the chassis bumped its way over the increasingly dilapidated road surface. Sonny half expected Elizabeth Kerry to come through it next with an update of information, but that only happened in the movies, not here on a grey, drear day in Panalquin.

'Ah putain, c'est du cinéma!' He could hear Mado's voice snort dismissively, just as she had in the past whenever he had instinctively put forward a romantic interpretation of events. 'L'abri, la bouffe, baiser bien, le fric, le pouvoir.' The spoken litany of her materialism rang in his ears. 'Shelter, grub, good fucking, that's what we need. Money and power. Who's got it? Who wields it? That's what we need to know, my poor dreamer. The rest is for the movies.'

The strictures of her words remained clear across the intervening time and space, yet he realised, with a sense of shame, he could not picture her face in its full details. It was blurred, like the distorted noise still coming over the intercom. Certain features and characteristics surfaced alright, like the addresses and names the office controller was dispatching to other cabs: her auburn hair twisted in a chignon or later radically shortened in a bob cut, the dark-chestnut colour of her eyes grown soft and translucent as he eased his fingers up between her thighs, the wry down turn of her mouth when she tentatively bit into something she instinctively knew she would not enjoy, were retained, but her totality escaped him. The real separate her was missing, unconnected from its constituent parts, as perhaps it had always been. She was like Lyon itself, he thought. If he did go back, in truth, he would soon be lost. The connections between places would be other than he remembered, and the new would have replaced many of them. He let her go. Like himself and Lyon she was now someone he did not know. There were enough ghosts he hauled around.

He looked out the window. The berths along the quayside were empty. Apart from himself and the driver, the only signs of life were the seagulls perched on the bollards and timbers by the water's edge. Out in the estuary, through a spreading rift in the gunmetal clouds, slanting weak sunlight caught the line of container ships waiting for high tide. Somewhere beyond them, no doubt, was the ferry and Albert's confessed voyage of unease. In sympathy for his friend's plight, Sonny mentally sketched the bell of a buoy in mid-channel, its tongue clanging mournfully, while the waves uplifted, pitched, then lowered it once more. There was sufficient space for him to encapsulate it in a few quick strokes and shadings on the margin of one of the Elizabeth Kerry papers, but he allowed the bell to drift away undepicted, as he had jettisoned Mado's fugitive presence, and instead turned his attention to the driver, a seemingly taciturn man, who had not spoken a word since the beginning of the journey.

By now, having left the waterfront, they were traversing a series of narrow lanes which bisected blocks of semi-derelict import-export warehouses. On a brick wall, beneath high, boarded-up windows, Sonny made out the acid-lime and orange letters of the entreaty 'EXECUTE LUTHER WENDE!' The driver squinted his eyes and checked his passenger in the mirror. 'Rat City,' he said in a heavy Panalquin accent. 'They've bust a gut to get human life back round here, business start-ups, loft conversions, artists' studios, new-age crafts, psychic jamborees, you name it, but all they've got is rats. It's a wonder we're not stricken with the plague. You know Panalquin?'

'Not really. I don't often come over.'

The driver nodded. 'Well, see over there,' his arm indicated a swathe of waste ground pitted with broken up foundations and studded with truncated reinforced concrete pillars, 'that's where Minty Wallace was born and brought up, the so-called "King of the Southside" or "The Boss of the Waterfront". Now look at it. Zilch. Zero. At one time he had his mitts on all the outfits, all the enterprises. You couldn't wipe your arse or flush the toilet without a tribute going to him. They say he even tried to go international at the height of his reach. Think of it. The criminals saw ahead how things were working out. It was rumoured he had a Japanese partner. Charlie Vesseps, who used to bankroll a speiler in Carson Street, we just passed it back there, told me he had seen them with his own eyes. I forget the word. They cut each other's fingers off or something. Anyway, Charlie said in the end it didn't come to anything and then before you knew it Minty had had his day. You can't do business if there's no business, right? Nowadays, if there was a new Minty Wallace no one would know their name. They wouldn't show themselves. It would all be done with computers. Only figures scrolling on a screen. No need for people. No need to rebuild this shithouse.' He swung out to pass an articulated truck, which had drawn up alongside the sagging wire fence of an abandoned machine shop. The factory floor was open to the sky. Everything of value had been stripped. 'A lot of them stop here for a quickie,' the driver went on. 'It's quiet and there's no hassle. Love among the ruins and the rats, huh.'

Catching the red light at the junction with the inner ring road, the driver took the opportunity to load and switch on a tape, as his passenger seemed disinclined to enter into conversation. The soft, sibilant strains of the languorous bossa nova accompanied him as he moved off and accelerated up the incline. Under the lilt of the whispered, caressing tones of the male vocalist, he began to tap his fingers on the rim of the steering wheel and dream himself on board his own oft imagined pleasure boat, setting the course for deeper waters. He changed lanes and dropped behind a large Mercedes. In the tack and yaw of the elusive beat, which the singer seemed to lose only to stress again more insistently, he cut through the waves away from the harbour. The craft's wheel responded to his lightest touch as he changed down and braked for a slow up in the traffic ahead. A black retriever, long since dead, sat by his side as he admired the mast, the sail, the trim of the deck. The sea, now green, now white spuming, then aquamarine, was ever changing like the names he gave to his precious boat: Swallow, Happiness,

Sea Mew, Future, but they could wait. The fine line of paint from the sign writer's brush could wait. More important was the feel of the polished timbers beneath the soles of his feet and the sight of the sail billowing out and the land disappearing to the stern. Escape. Escape and *'ao vento que passa meu coração'* as long as the song kept playing.

A Japanese yakuza, Ute Manoko? Sonny had heard more than his fill of local stories about Minty Wallace and his notorious organisation. Most of them could be attributed to the teller's need for self-aggrandisement or their desire to flirt with the thrill of the illicit, the overtly antisocial, enticing reverse of the daily coin, where naked greed and ruthlessness shone forth for all to see. In their yarns, Wallace's stature became embellished, his power exaggerated, so that each of his mythologisers could feast once more on their scraps of recounted terror, their personal moments of danger, the raw violence they had witnessed at first hand. A possible Japanese connection, however, was a new and different slant. Did Panalquin combine both the mysterious Gallo Mart building and traces of Manoko? Was Wallace the common denominator? Who really was Elizabeth Kerry? In a strange way, like Monse, he was beginning to charge her with the responsibility for prolonging his recently unwanted life. In his head, bits of the scant recalled refrain of 'The Kerry Dancing', if that was its right title, blended into the music from the driver's tape. 'Gone too soon,' he murmured out loud.

'You say something?'

'Not really. I was listening to your music. Do you understand Portuguese?'

The driver shook his head. 'My lady friend got me the tape. She likes to dance Latin American style. We go to classes Sunday afternoons.' He slowed into a roundabout, took the second exit and proceeded downhill.

Larches, interspersed with the occasional silver birch, on either side of the road indicated that they were finally leaving the rawness of industrial Panalquin for the douce confines of the suburb of

Massard. Here, spread through this elongated wooded dell, were the dreams made realities of the town's wealthier citizens.

Their substantial properties lay concealed behind high walls or lengthy fences. Access to them was gained by winding drives shielded by rhododendrons and azaleas. A prevailing mist shrouded their lawns, punctured here and there by the stiff outstretched branches of a monkey-puzzle tree. Gazebo windows, moist with condensation, overlooked mossy steps leading down to sunken gardens, where only the rasping croaks of frogs revealed the presence of ornamental ponds under whose thin carapace of lily pads glided expensive and exotic fish.

Each residence had originally been custom built to its owner's specifications. Thus Swiss and Austrian style chalets intermingled with sandstone baronial mini-castles, whose towers, in turn, afforded glimpses of vernacular mock-Tudor halls. Neoclassical façades bordered the grounds of low, extensive haciendas. Displaced French Riviera villas adjoined baroque hunting lodges. All of them proclaimed: 'This is somewhere else in some other time.'

'You've got the celebrated Tree House over there,' the driver said, pointing to a red gravel driveway, which quickly disappeared from sight. 'I bet you've heard of it.'

'Yes, I have.' People always want me to look, Sonny thought. They never tire of things to show me. His suspicion that the driver was following his own idiosyncratic route rather than the fastest way to their destination was being confirmed.

'It's still a *cause célèbre* round here. They never solved it. The police . . . '

Sonny stopped listening. He had come across the so-called Tree House years before in Yokohama when he was still a fitful student of architectural developments. Initiated by the soon to be disbanded Alsor Partnership, then modified structurally and aesthetically by Louise Vanderenden of Son Quy Associates, it had been erected in 1969. Vanderenden had swept away its original conception as a dialectic of inside and outside, the laboriously concocted *trompe l'oeil*, the primacy of water and foliage within the walls, the fake garden without, to create a serene open space cradled by curtain walls and personalised by the moving of paper screens. Against her advice, the clients, Mr and Mrs George Balsemeth, had insisted on floodlighting the grounds so that they and their guests might contemplate nocturnal nature whilst remaining invisible within the darkened house. Bit by bit, in order to facilitate their viewing areas, they began to modify the internal design, up to the point where Vanderenden finally declared the structure could no longer be considered as her work. Interviewed by the Maoist tendency magazine, *The North Will Also Be Red*, she stated, 'My former clients have elevated the contemplation of an elm tree above the harmonious functioning of the efficient synthesis I provided.'

These arcane and long-forgotten aesthetic skirmishes, of course, as Sonny knew well, were not the reason why the driver had drawn his attention to the property. The cause was much more direct and salacious. The Massard Tree House had been home to a sensational mystery. Sonny had heard about it from work colleagues soon after his arrival in Greenlea. The phrase, 'like the Massard Bird Woman', he learnt, was a local way of conveying something intangible and unresolved.

The sordid affair had begun, as so many of them do, with the discovery of a dead body. It had been found in the Balsemeth house, lodged in the bizarre setting of a ripped up car seat, surrounded by cardboard boxes, household rubbish, ferns, branches and twigs, which quickly fed in to the public imagination as a form of nest.

The post-mortem revealed that the deceased was a woman in her early forties who displayed many traits of a sixty-year-old. Severe malnutrition and dehydration were contributory adjuncts to the primary cause of death, namely myocardial infarction.

Throughout the subsequent investigation, the corpse stubbornly remained known as Female X, even though many suggestions and theories proliferated as to her real identity. What was clear was that she was not part of the known fluctuating population of local or regional bag ladies, vagrants or beggars, nor could she be traced back to mental asylums, reception centres, prisons or religious or secular charities dealing with the detritus of modern society.

Frenzied news coverage immediately blazoned sensational headlines across the country: 'BIRD WOMAN AT MASSARD', 'CUCKOO IN THE NEST', 'DEATH ROOST'. They boosted circulation and stoked the public appetite for seeing the rich being dragged towards the gutter, their well-manicured fingers stained with the most depraved and sordid acts. Hints of abduction, forcible confinement, torture, perverse sex rituals and recently verified acts of Satanism further titillated the public mood and increasingly pressurised the police.

Overwhelmed by the media hullabaloo, George and Vivienne Balsemeth constantly maintained their utter bewilderment at the extraordinary turn of events that had engulfed them. 'It is inconceivable that this tragedy could have happened in our house. We were only absent for half a day,' George was reported as saying.

His wife had concurred. 'There is no part of the house that goes unsupervised for more than a day. Our West Highlands, Scotty and Leviticus, would have detected the presence of an intruder at once. The poor dears would have been besides themselves.'

The investigators, for their part, attacked the problem diligently and systematically. They grilled the Balsemeths, their prime suspects, separately for hours during repeated periods of custody. They interviewed their relatives, friends and anyone who had floated in their circle of influence. They threw the dirt they had gathered, but all to no avail. At the end of the day, they were unable to tie the enigmatic body either directly to them through physical evidence or to any of their blood relations or the wider grouping of business colleagues, workers or ex-employees. Postmen, utility service men, meter readers, odd-job men, gardeners, door-to-door knockers, anyone who could have had some knowledge of the property were tracked down and their statements filed. Local burglars, plus a raft of general low-lifes, were continuously chivvied.

The kites they flew in response to the questioning of sex rings and drug connections proved to be simply fantasies in line with the already well-fuelled rumour mill. Nothing stuck. All was conjecture. The identity of Female X remained an impasse.

Interior Ministry officials discreetly sanctioned approaches to the underworld for help. Minty Wallace, among others, was contacted. The word, however, was final in each case. 'This isn't one of ours. You are on your own.'

As the pressure intensified and leaks embarrassed the Ministry, the cops started praying for a suicide they could close the whole thing on, but the Balsemeths were made of stern stuff. Shocked to the core by the invasion of all they held sacrosanct, bent and bloodied by the vile accusations that had been put to them, they nevertheless maintained their indefatigable self-esteem and their undoubted love for one another, no matter what the smear or calumny. Moved by their pained aura of patrician disdain and their visible stoicism, powerful friends and Massard neighbours slowly rallied to their aid muttering, 'There but for the grace of God, I suppose.'

Eventually, as always, interest waned and the media decamped. Police resources were withdrawn. Several false leads kept emerging in a by now apathetic world. The affair shrank back to purely parochial dimensions; though the file stayed technically open. It provided a useful depository, over the years, for the attention of those who had taken a wrong turn, misjudged advancement or simply failed to read the signs. The Bird Woman and her nest transmuted into apocryphal tales and local jokes through which Sonny had absent-mindedly pieced together the varied threads of wildly disparate accounts.

' . . . I remember Cheb Alakhin saying on television, "Some things we just don't know. From time to time we need an unsolved mystery like the corpse at Massard."' The driver, having finished his spiel, gave a satisfied grin and checked his passenger's reaction in the mirror. 'We're nearly there.'

Sonny grunted, feeling certain that he had been taken for a ride. They were out of Massard and approaching the crest of a hill. At its summit, the cab turned left and pulled up.

'Old Station Yard. This is what you asked for.'

Sonny paid with ill-concealed bad grace, halving his intended tip. A bad beginning, he thought, as he got out, stretched his legs and looked around him. The taxi drove off. A mistaken journey, he repeated to himself. Indeed, the mistake was only too palpable, for nowhere in his field of vision was there a supermarket sign or anything like a Gallo Mart depot. Instead, immediately in front of him were an empty showroom, three boarded-up shop windows and, on the corner, a smallish two-storey building. A tawdry rough cast bungalow guarded by an old-fashioned petrol pump lay to his right, while on his left was a high, blackened yellow brick wall sealing the yard's boundary. The situation was ridiculous. He had let a woman, who he had never met, entice him to this depressing and completely uninteresting spot purely by his chance interception of her vague hints of mystery and conundrums to be solved. By chance, he paused on the words, thinking back to the virtually deserted office and the timing of the call. Had it really been by chance? As much chance, say, as Chance Company process, which was less haphazard than its users supposed. Harvard Smith—Chance Company—Elizabeth Kerry—Amadeo Cresci Foundation—himself as chance presence or chosen recipient? Still wondering, he walked over to the two-storey building.

Inside the narrow doorway, a metal plate held the typed and handwritten list of inhabitants from top to bottom: A Freer, Fur Importers, Lions Inc, Financial Advisors, Zenia Ropotski, Clairvoyant, the next slot was vacant, Happy Landings Carpets. Tracing the indent of the empty space with his forefinger, Sonny leant forward and pressed the attached buzzer. No one answered. He pressed again and waited. Somewhere above, its rasp disturbed the silence of a place whose threshold he might or might not cross.

He stepped back and studied the grimy and weather-streaked

windows in turn. Behind one of them, he envisaged a poky office leading to a dowdy hallway. A worn brown carpet, no doubt provided at a special discount by Happy Landings, covered the floor. Against the wall stood a rickety table holding a kettle and two mugs, one of which Zenia Ropotski delicately raised to her over-lipsticked mouth when she slipped in to pay a social call between client consultations. 'The fates, my dear,' she whispered, before letting the mug rim rest briefly against her bottom lip, 'have ravaged us all.' Nothing could be seen through the dirty glass. He pressed the buzzer one last time. No answer. The office was most likely empty, denuded of furniture and fittings, or else someone still sat or stood there, someone of unknown name and gender, someone who had lost the inclination to advertise their presence or answer the irrelevant pressing of a buzzer.

Sonny moved away. He had no desire to try the others. Across the yard, the petrol pump, on closer inspection, proved to be disused. The bungalow awaited demolition. Keep out skull and crossbones signs were nailed to its door and windows. It was time to leave and cut his losses. There was nothing here that fitted with Elizabeth Kerry's message. He was tempted to crumple up the sheets of paper and throw them away. His hand slid towards his pocket *'C'est du cinéma!'* He repeated Mado's contemptuous phrase, but then what would life be worth without those moments in the dark when our eyes were fixed on the absurdly blown-up image of things we normally would not see? He dropped his hand. The message stayed where it was, then, after one last look, he rejoined the pavement outside the yard entrance to find a bus to take him back to Panalquin quayside.

However, he had not gone thirty paces before his progress was blocked by two women and a man, who was clasping a large terracotta jardinière to his chest. Sidestepping out of their way, Sonny caught a glimpse of an opening leading to a patch of waste ground, and what looked like a temporary car park lined with makeshift stalls. The space, he realised, lay immediately to the rear of the building in Old Station Yard. Four giggling young women coming towards him looked him up and down and turned into the entrance. He tagged along behind.

The stalls dealt either in plants or garden accoutrements. He quickly passed those with pot plants and packets of seeds and headed to those up against the back of the building that he had half-heartedly sought to enter. The windows on this side were small and barred. One at the top bore the inscription: Lions Inc. The rest were frosted.

Business in the corner was concentrated on the sale of jardinières of different sizes and pieces of ornamental sculpture, ranging from cats, dogs, turtles and one startled fawn, to truncated classical columns chiselled with acanthus leaves. As none of these items interested him and none of the windows afforded a view into their interiors, he was about to leave when, at the far side of the car park, he spied the familiar black and red striped colours of Sunrise Tea & Coffee being lowered on an awning above a white wagon. The attendant slid the pole out of the ring and disappeared round the side. With a sense of routine resumed, Sonny left the shadows he had been chasing for the certainty of an espresso.

The man at the counter was a raw-boned, skinny individual with a prominent hooked nose and a slight squint in his right eye. He was considerably older than any of the Sunrise employees Sonny had come across in Greenlea. His name tab identified him as Joseph.

'Cold day,' he said, putting down Sonny's cup.

Sonny nodded and unwrapped his Black Cat sugar oblong before upending it into the hot liquid.

'Not unusual for this time of year.' Joseph seemed inclined to talk. Sonny, at the moment, was his solitary customer.

'I didn't expect to see you here,' Sonny said. 'I'm a regular at your stalls in Greenlea. I didn't realise the company covered Panalquin as well.'

'Oh, yeah. This site's temporary, but in the old days they had a franchise in the railway station itself. Of course, it was closed down. Then they demolished the lot, tore up the track and all.'

'It seems an out of the way place to have a station. I mean, it wasn't connected to the centre or the docks.'

'No, you're right. There were only two lines south: one to Veldar, the other to Lake Ambret. That's where I'm from myself. Now there's a godforsaken hole. Hear a dog bark or a chicken fart and they'd yack about it for days. I couldn't wait to get on that train.'

'And where we are? What used to be here?'

'Warehouses, I think. Stuff like that,' Joseph shrugged. 'Nothing much.'

'A Gallo Mart depot?'

'Might have been, but nowadays it's all just in time and central haulage.' Sonny looked surprised. Joseph smiled. 'I follow the markets and trends. A few careful investments. You never know. Hopefully, everyone can find their niche, or, failing that, their resting place. Excuse me.' He took the order of two of the young women Sonny had followed earlier.

Sonny sipped his coffee. He scrunched the sugar wrapper and dropped it into the small waste-paper receptacle affixed to the ledge below. The Black Cat logo was out of sight, but he fancied that its raised warning paw hovered fleetingly somewhere between the garden statuary and the wall of the nondescript office building.

'*Mmmum en sus aguas cristillinas aaaahmm la playa donde esta vez mmmumm,*' Antoine Viall jauntily hummed and sang the opening bars of 'La Isla Encantada', the rumba that had been insistently reprised at the previous night's party. Swaying his shoulders to its beat under the feeble wattage of the light on the landing, he grinned as Walter Sembele flourished the bunch of keys in his direction before inserting the one that locked the door of their campaign headquarters.

'The keys, Antoine, the keys of our kingdom.' Walter slipped them back in his jacket pocket and patted them reassuringly. 'And now we've earned a rest. I'm tired and I must be active soon enough again.'

They descended the narrow staircase in Indian file, the bare boards creaking under Walter's light tread, then once more with Antoine's heavier footfall. 'You let him go off on his own again,' Antoine said. 'Is it wise? Shouldn't one of us check whether Emmet is actually carrying out your instructions?'

'Each to his own speciality, Antoine. Granted, none of us has clean hands. We are all guilty sinners, but we don't have to witness everything with our own eyes. Emmet has a list of people to pacify. In front of their families, if it helps. Oh, I know he's not a believer in the Old Man, yet he follows his code. He'll do it, rest assured, and when it's over and we all go our separate ways. Well, I don't need to draw a picture.'

Outside, they stood for a moment together on the pavement. Walter winced at the overcoat-piercing stream of cold air blowing down Salonika Street. He pulled up his collar. 'All these ironmongers,' he said, burrowing his neck and head deeper into its protective warmth. 'I don't understand them.' He shivered. His gaze took in the identical window displays on either side of them. In the face of their studied duplication and the assault of Greenlea's rigorous climate, his normal sprightliness seemed to ebb away. He reached out and held on to Antoine's sleeve, gripping the flesh beneath. 'You're right to play the game, my friend, whoever you really are. Pay the money and choose to be Antoine Viall or someone else invented for you. Business with the living grows wearisome sometimes.' A melancholy smile stilled his usually mobile features until it vanished and a chuckle rose from his lips. 'Ghosts, now them, I can handle. There's enough of them to clear these handyman necessities. See you back here.'

Antoine watched him walk away. His stop-go, push-pull rolling gait marked him out from the surrounding pedestrians. His hands swept gently in front of his chest, clearing his path as though he were parting the waters, while his head was tilted attentively towards his left shoulder. The whole body movement incorporated his oft repeated boast, 'Now I'll get things a-moovering. You see, brother, I really am the seventh son of the seventh son.'

Once Walter was out of sight, Antoine turned and made off in the opposite direction. He had decided he, too, would rest for a few hours in the flat provided by Chance Company at Tara Village. 'Whoever you really are.' Walter's words pricked him as he strode along. They had taken him by surprise. In truth, they had done more than that. They had jolted him. It was the first time Walter had openly acknowledged he knew that Antoine Viall was not his true identity. His true identity. Did he have one anymore? He certainly preferred those that had been tailored for him rather than the accidental properties of birth. Their banks of memories especially, and Antoine Viall's in particular, were much more intriguing and redolent than his own, fading into oblivion, patchwork of now scarcely comprehensible pleasures and muted pains. Riffling through Chance Company's Appendix 3: Past Situations, in its dark bottle-green folder, before assuming a new role, remained stronger and more satisfying meat than any tepid offering of his own memory. Some of the contents the Company detailed. Others were left deliberately vague so that the client could fill in the details and bridge the gaps for themselves. Like Antoine's dining table, he thought with satisfaction as, regaining his equilibrium, he reached Annunciation Square.

He had placed its existence in Viall's one-time family home at 30· Rue des Houx. A name which Antoine, as a small child, had confused with 'hibou', resulting in his father, Pierre, dubbing him thereafter Master Owl though, in fact, neither owls nor holly bushes were anywhere in evidence.

In those early days, he conjectured, the dining room itself and its most precious object, the mahogany table, exerted a strong fascination on the impressionable boy. A fascination deepened by the fact that the room was usually locked and only opened up for special meals prepared on family anniversaries or favoured saints' days. The surrounding ritual was always precise. On the preceding morning, his mother, Francine, went to the dresser drawer in the kitchen and obtained the all-important key. He followed her eagerly, clutching at her skirt, ready to dash into the released space when she turned it in the lock. If fortune held, he was allowed to stay and play inside while the room was aired and its dusting and cleaning commenced. The preparations completed, he stood on guard outside when his mother re-locked the door. Next day, they kept him away until the table was laid and fresh flowers were placed in the two ornamental Chinese vases on either side of the mantelpiece.

How he waited with growing excitement for the guests to arrive: aunts, uncles, cousins, in-laws or, on other occasions, business friends of his father with their wives and children. At last, the magic moment drew near. Francine signalled to Pierre that all was ready and the company were ushered through to their allotted places. Extra cushions were piled on selected chairs for himself and the younger kids.

From this elevated vantage point, the room exuded an exotic mixture of women's perfumes, men's unguents, hibiscus blossoms and grown-up food. Half hidden among the arms and elbows of this genial throng, undisturbed by the shifting of cutlery and plates, he dropped his cheek against the white starched tablecloth and dreamed he was in his own true kingdom, whose crown he wore in his ever-expanding beatific smile.

By evening, teetering on the brink of sleep, Francine led him away, while the company dallied, smoked and drank, chatted and played hands of cards on the still festive table. Behind him, before his eyelids finally drooped and sleep completely overcame him, he heard the drifting strains of a habañera, popular at the time, sung by one of the aunts, 'How many walls will your family build to stop me seeing you again?'

When the last guest had said their goodnight and the front door was closed and bolted, fast asleep in his bed, he dreamed he stood once more at his mother's side, watching her lock the dining room door and return the key to its dresser drawer.

On the eve of his next birthday, he plucked up courage and, unobserved, opened the drawer himself. There was no key inside. Only odds and ends and discarded pieces of bric-a-brac got in the way of his fumbling fingers. He rummaged in the adjoining drawer but found nothing. Years later, after they had moved to another town where his father had opened a dry goods store, he asked his mother about the all-important key. Francine stared at him in surprise. 'The old dining room was never locked,' she said. 'Why on earth would it have been? You're surely confusing it with something elsewhere. Maybe you remembered some of the silly tales they used to tell at the time of the food riots. Poor people believed then that the rich and the bourgeoisie had every scrap of their food under lock and key and that they kept a savage dog tethered to the fridge for good measure.'

The entrance to the Rag Market loomed ahead. The last twist of not finding the key had been another of his own ironic additions to the Chance Company memory blueprint. Thinking about it now helped ease the sting from Walter's parting remarks. Neither a 4 nor an 11 tram, the two he needed, were waiting. A coffee stall this side of the lines proffered a more congenial waiting place than the exposed stop beyond, and, more interestingly, there was a young woman with very short brunette hair, dressed in a black leather blouson and black ski-pants tucked into calf-length black boots, drinking at the counter. As she turned her back, he took in her high apple-cheeked behind with approval. Approaching closer, he imagined how he would feel cupping each buttock in turn in the palms of his hands. Different from holding Corinne's. Hers were tapered pear. He had entered her persistently fore, and once, with her consent, aft, his psyche still smarting from Emmet's snub. Her pudendum was shaved. Her eyes were dead. He knew they had stayed dead even when she summoned the fake sense of pleasure her trade demanded. No doubt, she had thought of something else, someone else, the moment when she would be rid of him, perhaps even she had escaped into false scenes and memories parallel to his as Antoine Viall. The difference was he had money. And a gun, he reminded himself. She lacked both.

His target was conversing with an older man, who stood slightly apart at the corner of the counter. She probably knows him, Antoine guessed by her body posture, but they are not together. He stepped up and ordered a cappuccino. When it arrived, he edged his saucer nearer to hers. She was still talking in a low voice to the man on her right. While she kept her back to him, he studied her short, on the verge of being cropped, hair. It invoked in him a series of coalescing images both erotic and ambivalent: a young supplicant in an enclosed religious order spreadeagling herself in abnegation on a tiled floor, a Japanese woman with wet hair, he had seen in a movie, kneeling obediently before her master's crotch, women's heads being forcibly shorn like suspected collaborators in old Second World War newsreels. As always, to the victor the spoils.

He eavesdropped on her conversation as he drank the coffee. Her accent did not sound local. The vowels were evenly stressed, the consonants harder. The man she was speaking to wore a tightly belted, oatmeal-coloured heavy winter coat. A grey astrakhan Russian-style hat covered his head down to his temples. A blue patterned silk scarf was knotted carelessly around his throat. 'I know what you mean,' she was saying. 'When I first arrived I often had the feeling you've just described. I'd turn a corner, and, instead of the busy streets I'd walked along, I'd find myself in a gloomy backwater with nobody else around.'

'These are the gifts given to youth, Sylvia. A recognition of the unexpected. At my age, everything has already happened.'

Her name was Sylvia. Antoine repeated it silently to himself, anticipating the possible moment when she might let him undress her and he could whisper her name in the revealed reality of her nakedness. He finished the cappuccino and wiped away any lingering froth with the corner of a paper napkin. If her acquaintance, he did not want to describe him as her friend, expected a rebuttal of his remark, such as 'You are not old', it was not forthcoming. Instead, she moved over to him and said something Antoine was unable to catch.

'There's no need,' the man said audibly. His hand alighted on her shoulder. She spoke again. Once more it was too soft to be made out. The man removed his hand, nodded briefly, said goodbye to the woman serving behind the counter then walked away.

Sylvia returned to her cup. A satisfied smile turned up the corner of her mouth. They were complicit. There was complicity between them. Antoine forced himself to calm down. What did it matter? Many men, many young men, must have been attracted to her in the same way as himself. He ordered another cappuccino.

'Too much coffee is bad for you.' She looked straight at him for the first time, and in that second he was lost. He was undone. Everything that had protected him before, everything he had accumulated or perceived, was swept away in the serene power of her casual gaze. Her face, he realised, was 'The Face'; the face he was fated to contemplate in wonderment and humility. She spoke again. 'Although I wouldn't have said it a moment ago when Mr Guthrie, the owner, was here.'

He was staring at her like an idiot, a gauche out-of-town rubbernecker. He prayed she did not need words; that they did not need to start with words. Her nose, he could see now, was a little too long and straight in the overall alignment of her features. Her forehead and cheeks were pale with slight freckles. Her ears were small and delicate, their rims reddened in the cold. She wore no earrings. The only make-up she had applied was lipstick in the shade of pomegranate rind, which moistened her lips as she pursed them in an amused moue. But her eyes! Their gaze was so direct, so beautiful. What colour were they? Greeny-brown? He could not tell for sure. Their colour was immaterial. In their core, they transmit light, he thought. Everything they see becomes transparent, including me.

She moved her head and began chatting to the server who

brought his second coffee. Accept me, he willed. Accept me as you see me. 'Your name is Sylvia,' he said. 'I heard the man who left call you that.'

'Mr Guthrie.' She turned to face him again. 'Yes, I'm Sylvia Manjon. Like Marta here, I work for Sunrise.'

'Lucas Jones,' he heard himself say. 'I only arrived in Greenlea yesterday.'

She shook him by the hand. He deliberately let go of it.

'What brings you to the city?' she asked. 'Business?'

'Chance,' he replied, breaking out into an unforeseen laugh. 'Sheer, wonderful chance.'

<hr>

From time to time, Rosario included a page of her son's drawings so that Antonetta could follow the progress he was making. Once her little daughter, Veronica, also scribbled a note of her own to accompany her mother's tidings, although her memories of her birthplace must have been well forgotten. Tonetta kept them and put them in the tin with Batiste's now largely discontinued correspondence; the tin, with its emblem of enamoured bluebirds, into which Fernando delved surreptitiously one morning when Gloria was at the fields and his mother was visiting her ailing neighbour, Auntie Luisa.

First he took out all of the contents and, after memorising which was the top and which was the bottom, spread them carefully across the blanket on his mother's bed. His father's stubby pencilled scrawl was written on thin sheets of paper lined with tiny squares. A date was entered in the top left-hand corner, but without a place name to the right, unlike the way he had been taught at school. Each of them began '*My Darlingest Tonetta*' and finished with an initial '*B*' under the expression '*one day we will see.*' They were disappointing. Fernando felt cheated. How much better if they had been postcards with interesting stamps still attached! They bore no trace of what it was like to be abroad. There were no pictures of what their houses, streets and towns looked like. Poorer than here in Llomera, obviously, uglier in every way, he imagined, because every day Miss Lopez reminded them how fortunate they were to live in the best of all possible lands, the truest to God's purpose, the noblest in fulfilling its historic destiny.

The letters from the woman in Orias, by contrast, were on proper writing paper and were written in a neat, easily legible black ink. He read the last two and stopped. They were boring, full of stuff women went on about: children, school and other women. He was about to put them all back, aware that his mother might return at any time, when the corner of an irregular shaped page caught his eye. It was crammed with small sketches, fitted in higgledy-piggledy. Sifting through the rest, he discovered three more. They were unlike anything he had ever seen before. Turning them this way and that, miniature leaping frogs and apples and men in doorways coexisted with bicycle wheels and donkeys and open chests spilling coins. They were fascinating. How, he wondered, could someone get this detail into such a tiny space? Almost in a daze, he selected two of the pages, folded them slowly, trying not to get them too creased, and put them in his shirt pocket. He then replaced all the rest in reverse order back in the tin and shut it in its drawer.

When Monday morning came, he could hardly wait to get to school. Right away, outside in the yard, he waved them proudly in front of his best pals, Domingo Arneis and Joaquin Torres, promising them adventures to come. His first impulse had been to claim they were his own work, but he realised, if he did, that they might, not unnaturally, ask him to draw more and his lie would be easily exposed. He, therefore, simply said, when they had gathered round him at break, 'I found them. They're a secret code. With their help we can . . . ' He paused. He had been going to say, 'Find our gold in Russia,' as he had heard grown-ups say, but Russia, wherever it was, was out of reach for them, so he simply added, 'solve the mystery.'

Three days later, they and, if truth be told, Fernando were weary of studying the supposed clues and hurtling off to the four points of Llomera's compass without coming across anything out of the ordinary. Fernando began to nurse a growing feeling of resentment towards them and the boy, smart aleck Sonny Ayza, who had drawn them. Sonny, he thought contemptuously, what kind of name was that? Fit only for a little kid, yet this one he knew was older than himself. He screwed up the drawings into a tight ball and grasped them in his fist. By the time he reached Molino Street, he had his mind made up. Tearing them into fragments, he threw them into the open doorway of Paca's wine shop. A hoarse male voice, he recognised as My Son's, boomed out an expletive. He quickly took to his heels and was safely round the corner before anyone stirred to find the culprit.

Two sheets destroyed. The remaining two presumably left in Antonetta's bluebird tin. Two similar sheets she had discovered earlier today secreted in a book placed in her bedroom. The work of Roberto 'Sonny' Ayza. They had to be his. The description fitted them to a T. Agnes now felt certain he had been in the apartment prior to her arrival, that he had looked around before slipping his telltale signature, his clue, between the pages of an obscure book. And yet she might never have picked it up, unlike this stuff in front of her concerning Fernando Cheto Simon. It did not have a read me, read me, on its cover. Chance, she thought. They work by chance. Emily Brown might not have a time-obsessed white rabbit as her guide, but her, so far elusive, Chance Company contact seemed to be pointing her in some, as yet, unfathomable direction. Why had his sketches triggered off an accord with a place or a moment she could not remember or in any way visualise? She felt the skin of her scalp begin to crawl. A weird, light-headed feeling made her close her eyes. Again, suppose Mr Ayza was not only a Chance Company employee. Suppose he was . . .

Agnes opened her eyes. Read on, she told herself. Seek and

ye shall find. She was now more and more convinced that this fake biography was either a disguised autobiography or the work of someone who delighted in assuming other voices, a trait which was attributed to the young Fernando.

So, as no one yet has found a way to stop it, time passed. The sun rose. Its warmth dispersed the morning mists. Its heat suffused the tended fields and terraces, the wild ravines and bare outcrops of mountain rock alike. Clouds formed, slow moving or scudding, and vanished. The moon divided up her quarters then did them over again, just as though she had followed her own diagram in an almanac. Faint rain turned heavy and the wind blew in the wrong direction until it remembered where it was and desisted altogether.

The black-lined boxes, beseeching prayers for the souls of the dead, covered, as always, the twelve back pages of the regional newspaper. Their replacements, newly arrived Mirandans notified under Births, would have been heartened to read, if they had possessed that accomplishment, that the Minister for High Days and Holidays had visited X, Y and Z, in all of which he had received a rapturous acclaim. 'Our tomatoes contain all the proteins and vitamins necessary for a healthy and active life,' he had declared to an enthusiastic public which, on the evidence put before them, united professors of medicine with illiterate day labourers, village watchmen with heads of government departments, carers of souls with country girls who serviced lorry drivers.

Unceasing vigilance and steely resolution ushered in a new dawn of economic and spiritual regeneration. Miranda once again found friends abroad who opened factories so that her workers could make a living, who maintained airbases in order to protect her freedom and who ventured increasingly across her borders to soak up and marvel at her unique, unrivalled folklore. Shutting one eye, she forgave her malcontents and, if on opening it, those who had been foolhardy enough to return ended up in internment camps and prison, well the leopard does not change overnight, nor does the dog stop whining without a dose of correction.

Fernando, of course, remained oblivious to his context. He continued to live each moment for its singularity before loosening the hours into his personal cargo of long clinging days and quickly expiring nights. Llomera existed for his eyes only. He drank in its streets and alleys. He ate its crannies and squares. He spat out and pissed away its cul-de-sacs, its outskirts and its vacant lots. Its inhabitants grumbled, chirruped, moaned, blasphemed and squawked from his stomach, throat and mouth, until one day, when he was twelve years old, their chatter ceased, and he painfully learned that they and his surroundings were entirely separate entities, both of which bore scant cognizance of his existence. The idyll, within which he had sheltered, turned out to be no more than a tissue of frayed gauze, easily rent asunder. The Llomera, which he had so avidly consumed, became one-dimensional before his gaze, like a painted flat in the theatre waiting to be hauled up into the flies. Deserted by scenery, scriptless and devoid of stage business, fear stepped up to its mark to fill the gap. It poked behind his eyes. It tightened his belly and scrotum, numbing his lips and legs. Silence was its watchword. Despair was its only promise. Antonetta was ill. Gravely so was the doctors' verdict and prognosis.

She had felt unwell for several months. After a couple of indecisive visits to the local medical assistant, she had gone on the bus to Cantellos, first to the doctor and pharmacy, then to the clinic. Their diagnoses to begin with were uncertain. Her symptoms seemed contradictory, but then her face became puffy and swollen and her eyes looked as though they had been blackened in a fight. She was in great pain when she urinated.

In desperation, Gloria wrote to Rosario Marva, who at once forwarded money with the news that she and her husband,

Sebastian, had contacted Professor Maino, a music-loving friend and specialist in women's diseases. He promised to come to Llomera, but it was too late. Before he was able to make the journey, Antonetta collapsed on the kitchen floor and was ferried to the clinic in Cantellos in an ambulance. Within two days, she was dead. Uraemia had claimed her life. Her kidneys had failed, it transpired. Urine had mingled with her blood.

At the burial ceremony, Fernando stared down past the lowering coffin into the meaningless space beneath, the patch of earth, which had been dug to make a grave, the space where, from now on, his mother would always be. A part of him remained there at the graveside, even when he preceded the others and walked away. The best part? He could not tell, but he sensed deep inside him he would never be able to retrieve it. A fragment of iron, wrested from somewhere in the impoverished earth, had pierced and collapsed his vision of the world and had lodged itself irredeemably in his being. He was alone, enclosed in a ravine without escape, surrounded by walls of rock too sheer for any man, let alone a boy, to climb. The knowledge that he was condemned to live in a new existence where he would never see his mother again made him shudder with cold, even though the sky was blue above him, the sun hot on his prickling neck and grasshoppers sang in the verge at his feet.

Damn the Chetos, he thought. Fuck them all! His grandfather stayed at home because of Father Robles. All of them would rather run up the blood-red flag of 'nothing for us' from their measly shithole than acknowledge Antonetta's death, and the worst of them was his own father. Blinding tears stung his eyes. He began to run, leaving the dallying knot of male mourners to straggle out beyond the cemetery wall.

He ran and ran full tilt all the way up the hill as far as St Bartholomew, where a stitch in his side made him stop and double up. Out of nowhere, Paca's words came back to him, 'And your father's a good man. Keep him in your heart.' Angrily, he threw them from his mind. His breath came in short gulps. He felt his heart or his lungs, he was not sure which, flutter despairingly against his ribcage like a bird denied flight. 'Stupid old arsehole,' he muttered out loud. 'What does she know about him?'

The open doorway of the baker's caught his attention as he continued upwards to St Roch. He entered on an impulse, looked quickly about, and, on seeing a small tray of madeleines on the near counter, grabbed three of them, crammed two into his mouth and scuttled out with the other one before Paco had the time to shout out that he had not paid. Their taste was bland. He shoved his finger along his gums to dislodge the crumbs. The cakes did not help. He got rid of the third by dropping it into the already filled lap of Elizabeta, Vincenz's youngest daughter, who was sitting on her doorstep shelling broad beans. She stared up in surprise, but Fernando did not stop. He was now into the short stretch of St Roch. Soon he would inevitably be at his own door, behind which his aunt and the rest of the women were gathered waiting for the men to return. The street had not changed. It rose for a bit and then levelled off as it always had done. Within its houses, on either side, and from its flat roofs, querulous questions and shouted replies assailed his eardrums. He scuffed his feet and carelessly grazed the back of his swinging hand against a wall. It had not even drawn blood. Only a short time ago, this had been his unthinking home, the place from which he started out and to which he unerringly returned. Now, as he went over what he would say to Gloria, he realised it was his prison to which, because of his youth, he was consigned.

Another different voice, more astringent than its predecessors, yet perhaps still the fabrication of a single author. A mother's death and an absent husband. '*Yours in sisterhood, Elizabeth Kerry.*' A girl called Elizabeta who had received an unexpected cake. Clearly Antonetta was not Sula, nor was Batiste Cheto René Darshel, her missing father, but the parallels were too marked to be coincidental.

Either that or I'm going crazy, Agnes laughed. I'm starting to submit to the Emily Brown in me. Hold on until tomorrow, she told herself. The scheduled programme is guiding me to the ex-detective, Alakhin. Emily Brown will meet him, but Agnes Darshel will also confront her so-called sister and the thumbnail sketch artist, Mr Sonny Ayza. Satisfied with the future plan, she picked up the final extract, wriggled herself into a more comfortable position and read on.

⊏══▷

Two months later, a stranger called. Before she even attempted the ascent of St Roch, the available female population had her in their sights. Observations and opinions quickly formed: on her own, a foreigner by dress and complexion, of a certain age, heavy-hipped, sashaying behind, heels too high for the cobbles, fulsome make-up, extravagant rings, a whore? No, abroad they all looked like that and besides she did not have the telltale stare, the yes I'm truly here glint in her eye, instead just a gentle inclination of her head, her auburn hair tied up under her white and gold patterned headscarf. Where was she going? Was this a chance tourist wandering through, a sign of things to come perhaps, or had she a purpose, some connection she was waiting to make?

In answer, she finally stopped in front of the closed door of number 48 and knocked. Old Luisa looked up from her chair across the street and called out, 'Wait! She's out. Wait!'

She motioned downwards with her shaking hands, but the woman understood and said in halting Mirandan, 'How long time?'

'A little. Ten minutes.' Again the old woman signalled, showing ten raised fingers.

The news of the arrival reached Gloria before she turned the corner on her way back from the grocery store. She laid her pannier down against the wall and scrutinised the visitor from top to toe. 'You're looking for something?'

The woman nodded and smiled. 'Someone. You are Gloria?' she struggled with the surname then gave up. 'I have,' she pointed to her handbag, 'a thing for her.'

'I'm Gloria. You'd better come inside. Too many people can see you here. The whole place is busy trying to work out who you are.'

They sat awkwardly across from one another at the table. The visitor handed over a sealed envelope, which Gloria, keeping her eyes on her, slowly opened. She took out the twenty green notes it contained.

'My name is Thérèse. I'm a friend of Batiste. He's broken heart he's not here in that time. He is at the farm.'

'Jesus Christ!' Gloria said furiously, slinging down the money. 'That disgrace will get us all killed with his stupid games. He doesn't keep in contact. He provides nothing for years and when it's too late he does this. He's not a man. Just because he can get it up he thinks he can do what he likes, but he's not a proper man. Oh, bloody hell!' Gloria began to cry softly, then, remembering she had a guest in the house, said brusquely, 'Would you like something? Something to eat or drink?'

Thérèse was about to say no, but thinking it might ease the situation she said, 'Yes. Whatever you have. Thank you.'

Gloria rose and put out a plate of almond biscuits which had been overlooked after the funeral. 'Are you his woman?'

Thérèse shook her head. 'No. It's not that. It's safer for him to travel with me. You understand?'

It was Gloria's turn to shake her head. 'People are dead. My husband died. Now Antonetta's dead. No. I don't understand. What is it he wants?'

'To see his son.'

As dusk seeped swiftly down the street, Gloria and Fernando accompanied Thérèse to the Simca she had parked by the wall at the foot of the oval steps. The local guards were still at the barracks and it was too early for any night patrols on the road.

Thérèse followed the Urtela signpost. Fernando said, 'You're going the wrong way,' but was silenced as his aunt's fingers dug into his wrist. Her skin was sweating slightly and he noticed that her breathing was irregular. He would have preferred to have sat in front with the foreign woman. It was the first time he had met a foreigner, never mind riding in a foreign car. When he had arrived home, Gloria, after his astonishment at seeing a female stranger in the house, had taken him aside and had explained that they were going to see his father and that, no matter what happened, he must not tell a soul. Part of him then had not wanted to go. He had even considered running off. The rest of him, however, had thrilled with an intensity he had found disturbing. Anyway, he had known by the implacable look in his aunt's eyes that running away was not going to work. It seemed he was destined to meet his father.

Now in front of him, Thérèse's hair smelt nice. He saw, as she shifted her head to look in the mirror, there was a tiny mole below the lobe of her right ear. Unlike his aunt, she was not used to the open air. He imagined her skin as pale and cool, yet warm at the same time. The interior of the car had its own smell: a mixture of unfamiliar tobacco, gasoline and plastic-covered seating. He laid his cheek against the back of the seat. A word bubbled in his mind: clandestine. He was on a clandestine journey, like the time when he had stolen into his mother's room, opened the drawer and felt about, aware of the smell of her clothes, the memory of which now filled him with shame, to find his father's ill-written notes in the bluebird tin. That smell of her clothes, which was not the smell of the seat sticking to his ear, or of Gloria, or of himself or Thérèse, lingered in his nostrils now, in spite of the finality of the grave, in spite of the hole he had watched them covering over. The car tyres drummed loudly on a change of road surface. Beside him, Gloria's lips were moving silently. No, he would never tell anyone what he alone knew.

Before they came to Ligac, Thérèse took a right turn. A bridge and a dried-up riverbed showed in their headlights. She changed down and began the twisting ascent round the shoulder of a mountain, sounding her horn to warn any oncoming traffic as she swung the vehicle into the hairpin bends. Gloria's body stiffened at each shrill toot, but they were alone on the road. On the other side, they dropped down towards Cirit and started their westerly route back.

Fernando was glad of the lengthy detour. Travelling in this car appealed to him. He was going along roads he had never gone along before, passing places he had never been, seeing trees, slopes and rocks picked out in a beam of light, while all around in the darkness lay an unknown landscape whose configuration he could only guess at as being more of the same. It was the same way he had thought about his father, when he had bothered to give him a thought, not as a man like others he knew, Remigio or Tony Pigeon for example, or even his grandfather, Rafael. They were all solid and filled in, whereas Batiste was only a name, a word people said, a being, but a being without flesh, without hands, teeth or legs, reduced to a sound like a sigh, the banging of a door, the rattle of a stick trailed against the railings, the sound you wished was not there when you closed your eyes in bed.

Thérèse checked twice in the rear-view mirror before she braked to enter the dirt track that led to the farm. Ahead of them, the house lay in darkness, all its windows tightly shuttered. When Thérèse stopped the engine and they got out in the same silence that had enwrapped them during their journey, part of the Plough shone through the ragged cover of cloud. A familiar whiff of wood smoke and wet sacks greeted them as Lupe unbolted the door in answer to Thérèse's repeated, intermittent knock. Fernando wriggled away from Gloria's restraining hand and shot down the passage and into the room where the whole Cheto family were gathered. Milagra was standing inside the doorway.

She bent clumsily to kiss his cheek as he brushed past her. Three empty chairs were placed round the corner of the table. His heart was beating fast. Where was Batiste? His brain seemed unable to take in what his eyes were seeing. He felt his cheeks grow red hot. They must look scarlet, but now he knew where his father was. He was the unfamiliar man sitting between Rafael and Guillermina and Thérèse.

Behind him, Gloria muttered a hello to the company. The figure, who he was now seeing for the first time, spoke to her and to Thérèse. Fernando waited. Time seemed to abate. He felt the pressure of his aunt's hand guiding him forward, but his legs did not want to comply. He was transfixed by the eyes of a face, which regarded him without curiosity, almost as if they did not see him at all, almost as if his presence was down to someone else, someone with no connection to the family. Then the eyes turned away and the lips spoke to Rafael, and he found he was sitting down beside his aunt.

As if on cue, Guillermina ordered the two girls to bring in the supper. Jacinta went with them. Rafael, ignoring the guests, discussed loudly how much diesel he needed to buy with Batiste, as though the night was like any other. Lupe brought him a cartwheel of bread, which he clasped to his chest and sawed into chunks with his knife. Gloria sat upright and rigid, staring in front of her, gathering every particle of resolve for the battle she sensed ahead.

Jacinta and Milagra returned with a tureen of chickpeas, a pile of plates, a bundle of assorted forks and a goatskin of wine for the men. Batiste asked for a glass for Thérèse. When it was fetched, he poured her some wine. He spoke with the accent of a native Llomeran. Fernando saw he handled the goatskin with ease, tilting it up and squeezing a thin stream of red wine into his upturned mouth, as if he had drunk from it every day with Rafael out in the fields.

He was smaller than Fernando had expected. The famous

blond hair seemed darker than in other people's descriptions, but that could be down to the shadows from the oil lamp. His eyes were greyish-green, like his mother's. The cast of his jaw and the length of his face, though, were his father's through and through. There was something boyish in his gestures as he ate, the way he glanced sideways at his parents for approval that he was eating all of his food without spilling any.

'I'm Fernando Simon.' At last, Fernando felt emboldened to speak.

All the other voices stilled. Milagra giggled and set Lupe off. Batiste gazed at him alone. 'I know who you are. I am your father, and, as you say, you are your mother's son. No one understands that better than I.'

Gloria shoved her plate aside, unable to contain herself any longer. She was on the verge of getting up and attacking Batiste physically. 'You think you can come back after thirteen years, home to roost and have the fatted calf served up to you. But this child isn't the fatted calf.' She chewed on each word and spat them out in gobbets, as though she was priming hand grenades and lobbing them across the table. 'Don't worry. Don't be frightened, darling,' she whispered to Fernando. 'I'm here to protect you.'

Batiste translated what she had said for Thérèse's benefit. Gloria continued glowering at him, daring him to mention Antonetta or Iusebio, her late husband.

'Have you had enough to eat?' Batiste asked Fernando, then, looking straight at Gloria, went on, 'Your aunt is an admirable woman. You can stay with her if that is what you want. I'll give you some money before I go.'

'For God's sake, say what you've got to say,' Gloria re-erupted. 'We came here. We gave you that. Now get it over. The sooner we can leave.'

Rafael began to curse. Batiste said, 'Don't upset yourself, father. Gloria has right on her side. The thing is, Fernando, if you prefer, you can come with me to France. We'll be gone tomorrow, early. There's some danger in it. I won't pretend there's not.'

'Your mad scheme will get the boy killed,' Gloria shrieked. 'Do you dare to say you love him more than I do? Everything he knows and holds dear is here.'

Thérèse shifted uncomfortably in her seat. She said something in French to Batiste. He shook his head. 'They won't hurt the boy, even if the worst happened. He'll travel as Thérèse's son. We've got the documents and a photo of a boy taken some years ago. I've got French papers and they've little reason to stop tourists.'

Gloria still looked aghast. 'He'll be taken to a reformatory. Is that what you want? If you love him at all as a father.' She broke off.

'Man, she's right,' Jacinta said, looking beseechingly at her brother. 'Let him be for Tonetta's sake.'

Batiste shrugged.

'I'll go,' Fernando's voice was clear and confident. Amid the vituperation and hubbub that greeted his declaration, he felt himself transported to a still, open space. He understood what his words meant. He understood that he was in the process of abandoning his home, abandoning all he knew and was familiar with, and that he was dealing his aunt's love for him a blow from which it might never recover.

'Batiste,' she said quietly, 'Batistet, I know Tonetta loved you and in your way you loved her. Enough people have died for your cause. Don't you think by now any human life is worth a hundred times more than some futile dream that has slipped away, never mind your own son's? I am asking you, on behalf of Iusebio and the others who won't return, leave Fernando here.'

'There'll be strikes and demonstrations, you'll see. When the time is right the workers and peasants will resist, but that's not why I have come. Fernando, you've heard your aunt. I have nothing but respect for her and the memory of her husband. What do you want to do?'

'Go with you.'

The die was irredeemably cast in spite of Gloria's repeated entreaties. It would have been so easy to retract those three simple words, but the moment had passed. The chance had evaporated. The future now lay otherwise. In the years ahead, when questioned about his decision, Fernando either stated baldly, 'I said, I'll go' or occasionally, when afflicted by a twinge of doubt or regret, 'alas, I said, I'll go.'

Agnes dropped the pages onto the carpet and closed her eyes. Llomera, Orias, Miranda. She resolved to buy a map to pinpoint their location, as well as one of Greenlea and its regions. She needed to find her own bearings.

Take your time.

Rest there, high up at the curve of the wall, and look at the night sky. Above you, the clouds are slow drifting. They reveal, pocket by pocket, stars which have gone from light to extinction and birth to light.

A swathe of the valley below appears under the moon's faltering guidance. Its olive trees, unlike you, have aged unaffected by the virulent mishmash of history. Beyond them, the invisible mountain slopes, locked in their imperceptible geological shift, lead by their defiles and goat tracks to the cave where you, Vincenz and Tian sheltered in the oft repeated tale, the tale your son here begged for, over and over, until his childish sleep unpicked Rosario's words, like Penelope's stitches, in anticipation of the following night, when she retold them once again.

'Really, I don't remember it.'

Not your voice, but Sebastian's, snipping through the threads of what you must have told your wife in your bygone days of intimacy.

'Sure we roamed about as kids do. But we never went as far as the caves. As you know, they were a good half-day's journey from Llomera, and we didn't have transport. Anyway, the truth was

Manolo was always timid and hanging back as a boy. He had to be coaxed along.'

A renewed flurry of snow stuck, then melted, on the outside of the tram window. Sonny returned from placing his father in a mythical Llomera to the reality of a winter's evening in Greenlea. Why had he resurrected Tian's jibe? What could it matter now? He raised his eyes as people began to file on board. Around those still waiting, the pavement glistened in reflected green and red neon splotches. A woman sat beside him. He leant over to give her room. After a perfunctory glance, she took out a newish-looking paperback from the small knapsack on her lap, opened it at the protruding bookmark and began to read.

There will always be another version, he thought, even if I wished it were mine alone. Copying his neighbour's example, he slipped away from the here and now and returned to the imagined figure of his dead father whom he had deserted a moment ago.

Look down there on your left.

The approaching headlights of a car lit up the stretch of road that runs past the Cheto farm. It's the road perhaps Batiste whispered about when he knelt beside you on the grassy escarpment over the border. The road whose every dip and bend and straight you once knew well, and, as he told about his tryst with his unnamed girl, you recognised the patch he meant at the twin pines and the slope between the rocks where the ground was sandy and dry. Words he whispered to you. Unknown words he whispered to his new-found love along this very road. Were they, 'Wait for me, I will return?' So different from the words you must have whispered in Rosario's ear here in the village; 'Go to Tian if the worst comes to the worst, he has always loved you.' How did you rationalise it? Was it because, in the event of calamity, defeat and death, he was better placed to weather the storm? Was it because he had shown already, in his student days, how adeptly he could play the bohemian nihilist at night, whilst after lunch faking the romance of Mirandan soulfulness amid the Romeo y Julieta haze of those who appreciated a good cigar, but knew that foreign imports were only suited to the discerning few? Why did she not protest? Why did she not tell you your idea was monstrous, or was there some part of her, tired of your life together, which was eager to join her real lover under the camouflage of your approval? Confidences shared in other places. Batiste and you. Later, he would pick up your scraps of home, your family gleanings, and keep them for years before finally handing them over, each of you in turn a custodian of the other's desires.

Bats swoop around your head and sheer away over the new Llomera spreading out beyond the old outskirts.

Listen, hesitant footsteps come your way. A slight, bowed figure rounds the bend. He pauses to catch his breath and, like you, gazes outwards over the wall into the night. A pungent whiff of antiseptic and ether assails your nostrils as he draws close. His wounds, however, are quite healed up. His face and limbs have been righted. His mind put at rest.

'Nolo.'

'Iusebio.'

'What's happening?'

'Things, as ever.'

You walk together, as best you can, down the incline and through the archway into St Roch and then St Bartholomew. Some of the houses look familiar, almost as if they contained some connection with yourselves. Their doors and shutters are closed. Their inhabitants presumably asleep. A skinny black and white tomcat sprays before increasing its lope to flee your presence. Linger a moment. Iusebio turns and waits. Two old friends reunited on a night stroll. Two ghosts forced by one who persists into the prison of existence.

Paam! Ptock, Ptock. Paaam!

Round the corner, My Son is banging desultorily at a water pipe. His grey nightwatchman's cap with its dirty-yellow band is tilted back on his grey, close-cropped hair. A quarter of a loaf of bread, a cold omelette and four anchovies in a tin lie on a bit of paper at his side. He drops his spanner and spits out the remnants of red wine he was swilling in his cheeks.

'What?'

'We're on our way down.'

'Eat!'

'We have.' Iusebio is eager to be off.

'Wait a minute. You've time to spare. There's no one else around and the night goes slowly. What do say, my sons?'

You say, 'Why bother with this? Surely, there's no need any more?'

My Son winks and picks up his spanner. Paam! Ptock. Ptock. 'The old ways are the best, my son. It gives me something to do.'

The woman beside Sonny sighed, moved her bookmark forward, closed the book, returned it to her knapsack and got up. Her retreating figure balanced expertly with the lurches of the tram as it swayed round the corner then accelerated again. When it slowed at the next stop and she descended, he thought incongruously, for they were in no way alike, of his final glimpses of the woman he had spoken to at the office last evening before the lift door shut. He had felt then she might be the last person he would talk with in his whole life. 'Hallie Briggs,' he muttered to himself, Hallie Briggs who had only been aware of his existence by the state of his desk.

'Where are you on the Wende affair?' The man behind him cleared his throat and spoke for the first time.

'It's the same old rigmarole,' another deeper male voice replied. 'People are fed up with it. We should send them back to Benin, or whatever it's called nowadays. Why should we get involved? Their politics are antediluvian and all TV does is show the same old footage over and over.'

Sonny blocked out the continued drone of their conversation. The clamour surrounding the detention of the fleeing warlord and his brother would no doubt subside and be forgotten. Wende's name would disappear from the city's graffiti lexicon. Greenlea, always on the verge of catching up with the cusp of fashion, was ceaselessly intent on reinventing its and others lapsed traditions while guilelessly effacing what only last year were its burning concerns. No sooner had the amusing bamboo wallpapers and lei-strewn dark pools of chic bars and night haunts gained the cultural ascendancy than they were judged quite Tikied-out, and those in the know moved on to *faux-austere* canteens designed for multi-tasking stakhanovites. Businessmen pinned ironic Soviet badges to the lapels of their safari suits. Ersatz *Komolskaya Pravda* posters, festooned with beaming youngsters in white shirts and red neckerchiefs, rejuvenated ailing brands of washing powder with new cleaning power. The 'in word' was 'uncomfortable'. 'Secluded' and 'busy' were out. Choice was paramount everywhere, and, like Chance Company 'identities', everything was for sale that possibly could be for sale.

The snow was falling more heavily when the tram reached his stop. Sonny, with already tingling fingers, dragged his black leather cap out of his overcoat pocket and pulled it down hard over his head. In spite of the filthy weather, he remained set on going where he had been invited to go, seeing whatever it was that Jacob Kemmer had provided, being ineluctably present with the things of the world and walking along the necessary streets to get there.

They were different from Llomeran streets. There was no nightwatchman round this corner hitting an exposed water pipe and singing, 'I don't know how to understand the hearts of women'; the beginning of the second chorus of the ballad Albert had sung the previous evening. No familiar ghosts hove into sight when he glanced up and checked the name.

He was in Kefoin Street. A long street on the city map which he had never entered before. Lavell Place, the site of the Melo Gallery, lay off it. On either side, three-storey buildings converted into offices with steep steps down to basements stretched in front of him. Their ground-floor lighted windows revealed an assortment of empty, cramped workspaces, tables laden with computer screens and faded posters of Goan beaches and the Manhattan skyline by night affixed to the walls above rows of grey filing cabinets. Arrays of door plaques indicated a preponderance of solicitors, travel bureaux and insurance brokers interspersed with the occasional administrator of oaths, osteopath, dentist or chiropodist. Darkened windows were veiled in Venetian blinds or, in one case, by drawn curtains. Sonny let his gaze transfer freely amongst them, but in none of them was there a figure looking back nor a cleaner going unconcernedly about their task.

The snow was beginning to settle. It clung to the soles of his shoes as he walked. The offices now gave way to a parade of shops: a dry cleaner's, a kosher butcher, a newsagent and a bicycle retailer. At the next corner, high up on a red-brick wall, a yellow neon arrow pointed to the right. Underneath it was the illuminated legend: Berengaria Hotel. So this was where it was, he thought. No doubt, Harvard would be already there, busily involved in meeting and greeting, puffing and pushing Chance Company products, yet unaware of Elizabeth Kerry's message, which should have come his way.

Sonny crossed the intersection. Traffic was intermittent and he seemed the only pedestrian foolish enough to be abroad. The Rainbow Bar, Izzy's Salt Beef, Autumn Moon Rendezvous, Casimir's Kebabs, Keos Taverna, as he passed, all of them bore the forlorn air of enduring a long, unremitting evening of scant customers and too many counted moments.

The yellow sofa in their tiny seventh-floor flat on Rue Gasparin had been a kind of Dijon mustard yellow. The Berengaria Hotel arrow must have acted as a midwife, releasing its memory back to him. Mado lay on it with her feet tucked up beneath her haunches, while he paced the room, stopping from time to time to gaze out of the window at the early spring evening below.

'Ah putain! Que sont tristes ces Mirandiens hors de leurs pays!'

A sofa, he thought, I can see a sofa, yet still I cannot reconstitute her face to my satisfaction. How he had clung to her independent being during those first months of exile! He had striven again and again to absorb her body into his. At times, he had penetrated her with an anger and fury he could not control; an anger and fury which later he had attempted clumsily to soften with tender endearments.

This street seemed to go on forever. He suddenly wanted to get off it and have a drink. Should he turn back to the Rainbow Bar or continue? He decided to carry on, but the block did not look promising. Apartment buildings now were shabbier than those before. They were no longer fronted by shops or restaurants. He was resigned in going straight to the gallery, as he had originally planned, when his eye caught a sign on the other side of the road saying DEMEL in black letters on a battleship-grey fascia. He crossed over to investigate. The front of the establishment gave no clue as to whether it was a bar, a restaurant or something else entirely. The window to the left of the doorway was curtained, betraying nothing of its interior. The one to the right was blind and covered in stone. He pulled the door open to get a better idea of the activity within. Three threadbare-carpeted steps at the end of the short hallway took him into an open room to his left, where he unexpectedly found himself back in Yokohama.

A small oak bar curved round the far corner. A hefty brunette in her late forties or early fifties stood behind it, the back of her head reflected in a tilted oblong mirror fringed with fairy lights. The glass display shelves held nothing but bottles of Scotch whisky. Sonny pointed to one at bar level and perched himself on a high stool. The woman set a small drinks mat in front of him and picked up the bottle.

'Single or double?'

'Double.'

She filled a measure and poured it out into a tumbler then reached for some ice, but Sonny shook his head. 'Straight's fine.' He took a mouthful and set the glass down. A burning sensation in his throat was followed by the taste of liquorice. He looked about him. A leathern shaker for poker dice stood at the end of the counter. Above it, fixed in a bracket, a small black and white TV set soundlessly relayed a boxing match.

The brunette said, 'Would you like to play or have the sound turned on?'

'No thanks. They're not my style.'

The walls of the room were decorated in a kind of tartan wallpaper. The carpet, likewise, continued the motif of blues, reds and browns. 'Mama Whisky! Hai!' In these surroundings, it was easy to envisage other whisky glasses eagerly raised in an oh so similar mirror in a bar in downtown Yokohama during the days when the Company thought the future was Japanese and their traditional moon was multinational over the business parks and alleyways. Nights of toasting 'us and us' and 'just in time' in the more and more drunken unravelling of East and West until one night, on a TV set just like this one, a one-time surviving 'block of wood' shouted, 'I recognise this man. It's Dr Fukido. He was in charge of C Laboratory where they tested the vaccine in the camp.' A regrettable incident in a no doubt blameless life of enterprise and philanthropy, but enough to turn his host for the evening's spirits sour and render the rest of the de rigueur gaiety distinctly melancholy.

'For we've lost our dear old momma and must have whisky or we'll die.' The words of the Brecht/Weill tune rang in his brain. And Ute Manoko? Certainly, he was unlikely to have been 'a block of wood'—much more likely to have owned, or at least terrorised, dozens of whisky bars like Demel.

'Similar please, Margie.'

The deep voice took Sonny by surprise. He had imagined himself her solitary customer.

'I'll bring it over, Emmet.'

'Fetch some fresh water, too.'

She let the tap run for a moment, swilled out a small brown jug and partially filled it. Sonny watched her reflection carry it over, with a whisky bottle in her other hand, towards a booth at the other side of the room. Its occupant was screened from view by a smoked-glass partition, one of three, which gave a touch of privacy to the otherwise open space.

'I've never known you take it,' she said, as presumably the man added the water to his drink.

'Indulge me, Margie. There's always a first time and hopefully never a last one. Sit down and talk awhile. I'm sure the gentleman won't mind. He can always yell out if he wants something. You've got a tongue in your head, haven't you?' he said more loudly.

As the last remark was clearly aimed at him, Sonny swivelled round. Margie remained standing, her head visible above the partition. 'Yes, I've got a tongue,' he said evenly.

'You see,' the Emmet person said, 'everything's going to be just fine. This man's no trouble. He's only popped in for a quiet drink. Isn't that so, citizen?'

Something in the man's tone alerted Sonny to a degree of edge and danger. The brunette, Margie, looked nervous, as though she would be far happier behind the bar than keeping her unseen customer company. She sat down. The man spoke in a lowered voice. Sonny turned to face the mirror, making sure he was not seen to eavesdrop.

While he paused over his drink, deeming it right that he should depart in his own good time, he heard the faint ghostlike ring of a telephone in another bar in yet another city. What was it Rosario had said to him on the morning he was due to leave Miranda? 'You can't escape from this world, Roberto.' Then she had embraced him, 'You might, however, escape within it.' Tears had filled her eyes, her mouth half undecided between regret and a kind of resigned mockery.

'*C'est pour toi. Une femme.*'

He took hold of the receiver from Georges, *le patron*, 6th October, 1954, Bar des Indes, Passage Habert, Lyon.

'*Allo, dites!*'

'Why, oh why, won't you come? What will it take?'

She knew his childish secrets. She loved him as a sister should an elder brother, but to Veri his actions were incomprehensible. He was so near the frontier, only a matter of a few hundred kilometres from Orias itself.

'You don't know what you're doing to me. Mother is going to pieces. After his stroke, Tian is like a child. Your place is here to help us. What gives you the right to punish everyone who loves you?'

'*Jolie voix, un peu comme,*' Georges hesitated, searching for the comparison, '*comme la juliette de Jean-Christophe. Mirandienne?*'

'*Bahoui, ma sœur, Veronica.*'

The space. The intervening, unbroachable space between. The roads, the railway tracks, the air corridors leading eventually to the customs posts where the police uniforms changed, and although, at first glance, the earth, the fields, the trees looked the same, everything was different; the everything that was in the bone and beyond redemption or, at least, his redemption. He swallowed the rest of the whisky and got to his feet. His perfunctory goodnight went unacknowledged.

Outside it was still snowing. He waited for a caped cyclist to pass before recrossing the road. Two men came towards him; the first in a navy-blue parka with the hood up, the second, younger, with a thin khaki jerkin, his short fair hair glistening with drops of snow. Both of them afforded him a quick glance before striding purposefully on. What had they seen? Sonny wondered. A Greenlea citizen, as he had been recently called, on his way home, or a living ghost whose body happened to be in Kefoin Street, but whose emanation displaced in others strode down the streets of his long-deserted birthplace. Manolo, Iusebio, My Son, Paca. Why could he not let them rest as they deserved? They belonged to a past, a past which the present ignored, a past which long ago he should have cut adrift in the same way as Raul Sanchez (illustration p136), leaning over the gunwale, had hacked and sawed with his knife in his frozen and bloodied hands, at the rope which towed the filthy sack of booty, whose promise of untold wealth had destroyed his brother and rendered his shipmates mad. Even now, he thought ruefully, I drag up some spurious, half-remembered childhood book. Don't fill these gaps, he told himself. Walk to the gallery and nothing more. Think of Elizabeth Kerry's message if you must think.

He had reached the penultimate block of Kefoin Street. Lavell Place was on the right. A few strides down it, the Melo Gallery lay in darkness. No light shone behind its plate glass window. A notice was affixed to the door. It read, 'Owing to end of temporary lease Transitory Images now at Cynara Room Berengaria Hotel.'

Sonny turned away and retraced his steps. This was the Old Station Yard all over again. If Kefoin Street had been served with any form of public transport, he would have called it quits and waited for a bus or tram. As it was, he kept a look out for a stray taxi, determined to hail it if it arrived before he regained the yellow arrow, but only an occasional private car went by. He trudged on. Nobody entered or came out of Demel when he passed it on the other side. Now the arrow was only a block distant. It seemed he was fated to persist and go. Where arrows pointed people were meant to follow, and he could use the opportunity to have a quick word with Harvard. He increased his pace, his eyes squinting into the blown flurries of slanting snow, and turned the indicated corner.

The lights of the Berengaria Hotel appeared blearily at the foot of the short cul-de-sac. In the foyer, people stopped their conversations and regarded his wet and snow encrusted figure, unaware till then of how heavy the fall had recently become. Still dripping, Sonny studied the board listing the day's events. 'Transitory Images' was stated as now housed in the Cynara Room, which was situated in the basement. The Lorelei Suite on the second floor hosted Chance Company's Twenty Years Exhibition.

After depositing his coat and cap with the cloakroom attendant, he made his way to the concierge desk. 'Harvey Smith. Chance Company. Will you ring him please? He'll be in the Lorelei Suite. I'm Mr Ayza from the same company.'

The man obliged then handed him the phone. Sonny said quickly, 'Good evening, Harvard. I trust things are going well. As I happen to be here, I thought we might have a chat.'

The sound of other voices, cut off as though a hand had been put over the mouthpiece, gave way to momentary silence before Harvard's even tones replied. 'You surprised me. Can't you stay away from work? I hadn't expected to see you until next week. What brings you here?'

'Chance. A chance meeting earlier today and then a chance change of venue. I want to talk to you about the Albert Cresci Foundation. I'm on my way up.'

'Hold on.' There was another pause. Sonny was on the verge of adding Elizabeth Kerry's name, but Harvard resumed. 'Come up by all means. Better if we meet in hospitality though. I can give you five minutes. It's room 274.' The phone went down.

Sonny thanked the concierge and took the stairs. When he found room 274 the door was ajar. Harvard was alone. He gave Sonny a lugubrious stare. 'I'm worried about you,' he said. 'It's been very noticeable lately. If I didn't know you better I'd say you were letting some of the details of our work prey on your mind. My advice is to take another week off. Do other things, Sonny. See other people. Drink?'

Sonny shook his head. Harvard replaced the cognac bottle he had picked up from the service table and subsided into an easy chair.

'I'm not here to hold you up, Harvard. I just dropped in on my way somewhere else. Tell me about Cresci and I'll be gone. We don't need to get sociable.'

Harvard laughed. 'You've got the damnest way of shoving your pecker into Christ knows what. Okay. Cresci was just a crackpot in a long line of crackpots trying to shaft the company. It's old news, but some people can't ever get enough snake oil. There was a lawsuit. He failed. End of story. Now, if you'll forgive me, I have things to attend to. Think about what I said about taking more time off.'

'I will, but what was Cresci's petition?'

Harvard stood over him, shifting back on his heels. 'Cresci

claimed he had purchased Chance Company rights that covered the Midwest, if I've got it straight. Said it had been parcelled out, signed and authorised by Joe May. Of course, it collapsed in court. May had already been dead for several weeks by the time the so-called franchise exercise took place.'

'And the Amadeo Cresci Foundation?'

'Search me. A charitable organisation? Another guy called Amadeo Cresci? Names are names. We both know that. Now duty calls.' He stepped past Sonny into the corridor. 'Phone me in a week's time. We'll really talk then.'

In the lift going down to the basement, Sonny tried to pinpoint the reason for his boss's unease. Was it simply the fact of him turning up uninvited or was it his questions about Cresci and the Foundation? Perhaps it had been an amalgam of the two. Anyhow, he felt justified in keeping the knowledge of Elizabeth Kerry's connection to himself. There was no doubt Harvard was off balance about something, and he instinctively felt her message held the key.

When the lift doors opened, Sonny was surprised to find the entrance to the Cynara Room thronged with people. Some were energetically pressing their way inwards, while others protestingly shoved their way out. He edged his way to gain the inward stream, but as he did so a greater concerted outward push forced him back towards the lifts.

'Been done before, of course, but invigorating nevertheless don't you think?'

Sonny screwed his neck round to get a view of the speaker, whose voice sounded familiar. Elbows jabbed in his side. He gave up trying to compete against the prevailing tide and drifted rightwards until he finally managed to extricate himself from the crowd, which was now heading for the stairs. His body pressed uncomfortably against the wall, his eyes encountered the glistening bald head of Leo Manners. Manners' mouth was fixed in a self-satisfied smirk. A young woman, who appeared to be with him, stood at his side.

She was dressed in olive fatigue trousers with a similar coloured T-shirt covering her bra-free breasts. Her lightly freckled face was unadorned by make-up. Long dark hair swept back from her forehead was gathered in a plait.

'I've just arrived. I haven't had time to see anything.'

Manners' smile grew more unctuous. He was obviously enjoying himself enormously. 'That's the whole point. There's nothing in there to see. The walls are bare. Transitory images ha ha. I knew it would appeal to you, Mr Ayza, to your particular sense of fun.' He turned to his companion. 'Mr Ayza has kindly put some commissions my way from time to time. This is Emily Brown, Mr Ayza. We met earlier today. Another gallery as it happened.'

The young woman stared at Sonny with a curious expression. 'Do we know each other, Mr Ayza?'

'No, I'm sure we don't.'

'Emily's recently returned to Greenlea. She's been gallivanting all over the place. We thought she'd quite forgotten her dull old friends.' Leo's chirpiness continued unabated. 'But how did you know this was on?'

A fresh wave of either newly disgruntled or satisfied art lovers surged out of the Cynara Room, chattering noisily and causing Leo and Emily to be pushed closer to Sonny.

'I heard about it from a pavement artist at the Port Steps,' he replied when they were able to retrieve their individual space.

'Are they still there? How odd. Working from home these days I rarely get into the city centre.'

'You have an unusual name,' the young woman said. 'I'm trying to place its origin. There can't be many Ayzas here in Greenlea.'

'Nor Emilys I would imagine. It's not a first name you hear much nowadays. Miranda. I'm Mirandan.'

'And what exactly do you do, Mr Ayza, apart from giving Leo commissions and attending deeply uninteresting exhibitions?'

'I work for Chance Company.'

The aftermath of his statement sealed a momentary pocket of

complicity in which Emily regarded him with a barely concealed sardonic smile and Leo puffed audibly, 'Well. Well. There we are then.'

People by now were dispersing more freely. For the time being nobody else came down the stairs or out of the lifts. Leo took his cue and shook Emily's hand. 'I must dash. So nice to see you again, Mr Ayza.'

'I must go as well,' Sonny said, still wondering why Emily Brown was looking at him in such a strange manner.

'A name for you before you leave,' she said. 'It's Fernando Cheto Simon. A long time ago your mother sent his mother some of your drawings. Your given name is Roberto, isn't it? They were very detailed small sketches. I came across some very like them in the back of a book.'

Sonny was stunned. Was it possible he was talking to Elizabeth Kerry in person? He tried to remember the exact intonations of her speech on the phone. 'Which book? Where did you find it?' he managed to utter.

'In the flat you provided me with at Tara Village. Can we drop this pointless charade? Why do you think my father is here in Greenlea?'

'You are a client? Emily Brown is a name you've been given?'

She nodded exasperatedly. 'As you know, I'm Agnes Darshel and you are my Chance Company contact.'

'I assure you I am not. As a matter of fact, I'm on leave at the present. I've never handled your file or heard anybody mention it.'

She regarded him fiercely, then, adjudging by his expression he was being sincere, said, 'Until I met you just now I had a stupid thought,' she paused, 'a so ridiculous thought.' Her eyes were moist. 'What is happening?'

'I don't know. Why did you ask me about Fernando Cheto Simon?'

'He was a kid I was reading about from a place called Llomera in Miranda.'

'And he had something to do with a Batiste Cheto?'

'His father.'

'Where did you get this book? Was it there you saw my drawings?'

'That was different. It's not a book. It's a kind of script account from some organisation called the Amadeo Cresci Foundation.'

'We need to talk at length, Agnes. Somewhere else more private. Do you trust me?'

'Not entirely, if I'm honest. Listen, someone is waiting for me in the foyer. I'm already late. I wouldn't have come down here if I hadn't bumped into Leo. I must go. Give me a ring early tomorrow morning. No doubt you have the number.'

'Better if we meet in person. Do you know the Belvedere?'

'No, but I'll find it. It will have to be the afternoon. 3.30 say?'

'Meet me at the entrance. Don't tell anyone else you've seen me.'

They walked up the stairs together. Agnes said, 'My father's René Darshel. Chance Company wrote to me and suggested that he was here in Greenlea.'

'Sorry, I don't know anything about him, but I do know it was a very unusual and irregular approach. Look, let me go on and collect my coat and check if anyone from the company is around. They're holding a do upstairs.'

'Yes, I'm going to it. It's part of my mapped-out itinerary.'

Once in the foyer, Sonny scanned the sparse assembly: a man and a woman at reception, three women at a table having drinks, a thickset middle-aged black man sitting on a chesterfield, a knot of business types waiting at the lifts. Satisfied, he went to retrieve his coat and cap. 'Ticket 74.'

The attendant retreated to the racks. 'Three items,' she said. 'Coat, cap and a package.' She proffered a large manila envelope. It was addressed: 'Attention of Emily Brown.'

'I didn't leave this.'

'No, sir. A woman came after you had gone and said you would take care of it.'

'Is she still here?'

'No. She left. Is there a problem?'

'No problem.'

Sonny donned his coat, stuck his cap in the pocket and took the envelope across to Agnes who was standing beside the black man. She glanced at its front quickly, eased open the back flap and scanned the first two pages. 'More about the Simon kid,' she said. 'No accompanying letter this time. Let me introduce my friend, Emmet Briggs. No doubt you'll tell me you didn't hire him to show me around.'

'I didn't.' He extended his hand. 'Sonny Ayza.'

Emmet held it in a powerful squeeze before letting go. 'Citizen. We met briefly some moments ago,' he explained to Agnes. 'I said then this man's not going to cause any rumpus. I was right in that drift, wasn't I?'

Sonny ignored his threatening glare. 'Have you a wife called Hallie by any chance? I spoke to her yesterday.'

'Citizen, you've got things on file, I know that, but leave my wife out of your shit. This is something you should truly believe.'

'She works in my building. I don't know anything else about her or you. Agnes, I'll try to find out who set up your file and your stay here. By the way, you mentioned an accompanying letter. Did it have an individual signature apart from Cresci Foundation?'

'Elizabeth Kerry.'

Sonny nodded. 'I see. Till tomorrow then.'

<hr>

When he had gone, they moved towards the lifts. Emmet stuffed the envelope into his inside coat pocket for safe keeping. 'A touch of the rat about our recently departed,' he said. 'I'll keep an eye out for him.'

'I'm not sure, Emmet. I think he was telling the truth. I'll be okay.'

An empty lift descended. They got in. Agnes pressed the second-floor button. The door closed. 'People mention my wife at their peril,' Emmet said.

'You love her?'

'Yeah, like the sea loves the shore. She counts on that.'

The Lorelei Suite lay on their right farther down the corridor. The babble of animated chatter drifted towards them as their feet sank in the thick pile of the carpet. More from Cresci and Elizabeth Kerry possibly, Agnes thought, and now I've met the elusive Mr Ayza. Disappointing, but then she had been stretching credibility to have imagined he could have been connected in any way with her father.

Walking beside her, Emmet started to get the feeling the kid was somewhere near. On this carpet, his uneven gait would leave no footfalls. A door opened ahead. A man came out with a key in his hand. Over his stooping shoulder, Emmet had a vision of the room slowly filling with water. He saw it tumble over the rim of the bath, sluice mesmerically across the tiles and inundate the floor and bed coverings. The man turned towards them. His shoes and the bottoms of his trousers were perfectly dry. He muttered a good evening as he finished locking up.

'Can I help you? Do you have an invitation?' A young Chance Company greeter hailed them once they entered the suite. Agnes handed her the card she had been given. 'Miss Brown, of course, and Mr Briggs. Welcome. Please enjoy the evening. There are other guides who will help you if you require more information on your way round. Miss Brown, are you alright?'

Agnes had gone deathly pale. Her legs were wobbly. She leant on Emmet, unable to speak as the young woman fussed about her, for there in front of her, from a huge mounted photograph, staring beyond her into a distance she could not see, was the clear-cut image of her father's face, exactly as it had been in the drummer's snap.

Emmet's eye quickly travelled to the focus of her sudden consternation as he held her upright. Like Agnes, he, too, recognised the man whom he had met years ago off the Panalquin train at Veldar station. The same face had sat beside him as they drove to the secluded house where Minty Wallace and the Japanese contingent were patiently waiting.

THREE

No mother ever gave birth
to one as unfortunate as I am.
Along the road I am travelling
run two equal footpaths.
(Popular Alegrias)

A static grey mist confronted Lucas Jones when he drew back the bedroom curtains on the following morning. It had dissolved the contours of the hillside opposite and rendered the whole of Tara Village invisible.

He opened the window a fraction and sniffed the air. It smelt of seaweed and petrol faintly tinged with smoke, as if a bonfire smouldered somewhere in its opaque density.

Shutting the window carefully so as not to disturb Sylvia's continuing sleep, he checked the time on the bedside radio clock—6.11 a.m.—then slid his naked body next to hers under the sheet. He laid his hand gently on her haunch and tentatively pinched her gathered skin between his thumb and forefinger. She did not stir. Indeed, she seemed to be scarcely breathing, her mouth and nostrils cradled in the twisted indent of the pillow.

Lucas withdrew his massaging fingers and lay on his back. He felt his erection slowly loosen and shrink to flaccidity. Antoine Viall would not have resisted its urgings. He would have awakened Sylvia no matter what and put her still half-asleep body immediately to the question. Lying here, however, in the dark beside her, he did not need to be Antoine Viall. He had time. They both had time. Lucas Jones and Sylvia Manjon had time; time to have sex, time to be together, time even to be apart and yet to conjure up and dally in each other's existence.

In spite of the window being shut, the strange, pungent smell of the mist outside, which presumably still persisted, began to insinuate itself into his further thoughts of Sylvia. It brought back hints of the clammy feel of one of the rolling Atlantic mists he knew from his childhood, which had been partly spent on the desolate seaboard of northern Patagonia. The stronger rank odour of bracken after the rain joined the mix, and, with recovered clarity, he watched as a boy ran out of the family house into the faltering dawn whose uncertain arrival twitched and winked against the dim horizon. On the slippery ground of the cliff path, his feet splayed away from under him, sending him crashing down in a bracken clump. Its icy fronds brushed his face. Amid its entanglement, an acrid reek assailed his nostrils. The seat of his trousers and his shirt were soaking wet. Below him, as yet barely illuminated, lay the elongated sweep of Horseshoe Bay. Above, hidden from view, gulls, gannets and kittiwakes added their repeated cries to the muffled boom of the ocean breaking on the shingle bank. He got to his feet, a figure emerging silently from his fall.

Sunrise, Lucas reflected, a neglected stupid moment from his real past which had waywardly resurfaced. Sunrise Tea & Coffee and now Sylvia. He turned his eyes towards her sleeping head. What was in her sleep? He did not know. Leave it rest. It did not matter to him what dreams she had, neither what she let go nor what she retained. She was here with him. They lay together. He was Lucas Jones who now could come to grips with who he was.

Sylvia snuffled twice into the pillow. She jerked her knees up to her stomach and wriggled over. Lucas adjusted his legs to give her room and closed his eyes.

Lucky, his father's brindle German shepherd bitch, jumped up and licked his cheek with her rough tongue. Feeling the force of her paws on his chest, he struggled to push her away. She bounded on ahead, her tail wagging, this time to a clearer shore, where, with a single bark, she turned and waited for his arrival. Pebbles rocked and tilted beneath his sandaled feet. Buds of bladderwrack popped under his soles. He felt the wind buffet his face with the promise of more rain to come. Who had he been when, through half-shut bleary eyes, he had taken in the rocky confine of the bay? Who had he been when he listened to the hiss of the breaking, exhausted waves on the beach and saw the confident glimmers of light steadily banish the darkness from the sky? Who was it who, his body and brain permeated by the elements around him, finally stopped running, out of breath and with a stitch in his side, to stoop over Lucky as she obsessively rolled and rubbed her spine among the mounds of rotting seaweed? Had it been then, while disturbed sandflies hovered over her muzzle and flanks, while he scanned the sea for sight of a ship, that the possibility nagged him that he was destined, like everyone else, to be alone in the world, cut off from the pretended normal connections his parents and other adults espoused? If not then, then some time shortly after, certainly before he left school, well before his flight to Santiago and his subsequent ignominious return to the fold of the family shipping business in Valparaiso, a veritable lifetime before the few years later when his father and mother were killed in an automobile accident and he had the means to sever all so-called ties and leap into the endless liberties and variations afforded by Chance Company.

The magnetic pull of being someone else, the casual slipping on and slipping off of invented histories, the lure of acting in ways inimical to his upbringing, of consciously subverting and sabotaging his own predilections and moral scruples, had fed and sustained him from one set of acquaintances to another as he shuttled first across the Americas and then to Europe and Greenlea. Here and now, however, was the important thing: a place and time to hold firm and be himself in bed with Sylvia, who, without thinking, was herself, and who would continue to be herself, a continuance which, if he got it right, might include Lucas Jones as a permanent fixture.

He opened his eyes, knowing he was too wide awake to sleep, yet somehow he must have slept because he was alone. There was nobody beside him. The room was in darkness. The curtains pulled back, 7.05 showed on the clock. 'Sylvia?' he called out, fearing she had already left.

'In the kitchen,' she shouted back. 'You've nothing in the fridge. Don't you eat here? All I've found is coffee.' She appeared naked in the doorway and turned on the light.

'Come back to bed.'

She knelt beside him and kissed him. He kissed her breasts and began to pull her down. She moved away. 'The coffee's ready. I don't like sex in the morning. It's too predictable.'

'You didn't mind last night. Wasn't that more conventional?'

She got up. 'I'll bring the coffee. I'm going to shower and dress. You are not unhappy are you?'

'No, I'm not unhappy.'

She returned with two cups: one large, one small. She handed the small one to Lucas. 'I'll drink out of yours,' she said.

Lucas propped himself up. The liquid was lukewarm with no sugar. He drained his cup, set it down on the floor and took her free hand in his. 'Stay. It's still early. There's a thick mist outside.'

'For a little while, then I'm going. I want to go home before I start work in the Rag Market.'

'I'll drive you. Don't worry.'

'No. I'll catch a tram. I'd rather go by myself.' She removed the cups and went back through to the kitchen. A moment later, he heard the splatter of water on the floor of the shower cubicle. His instinct was to follow her in, but a sense of caution held him where he was. No sex in the morning—what kind of regulatory whim was that?

The flow of water ceased and Sylvia emerged, wrapped in a yellow bath towel. She dried herself, dropped it and began putting on her underwear. Neither of them spoke until she was fully dressed.

'I'm glad you came to Greenlea,' Lucas said. 'I count yesterday my lucky day when we met. Why go on with the coffee stall though? I'm sure you could do a lot better. I could help you.'

Sylvia sat down in the chair where her clothes had lain. The mist outside was as murky as before. 'It all started at the airport,' she said, as if he required an explanation. 'I was waiting for my luggage at the carousel when I noticed a weird person paying me exaggerated attention. She or he, it was difficult to tell which, was done up in a style I'd never seen before. A mishmash of fabrics had been stitched together to form a sort of waist-length tunic. Beneath it, what at first I had taken to be a cherry-red velour skirt proved to be, when the creature moved, a pair of culottes. Then a voice in my ear said, "We are all seen. Some, like our friend over there, however, decide to guarantee our gaze."

'The speaker was a stocky middle-aged man I remembered seeing on the flight. I asked if he knew him or her. "No," he replied. "A *rara avis*, yet see how quickly people look away. They soon take the originality in their stride and resume their own concerns. Talking of which, here comes our luggage."

'Alongside us, arms and bodies stretched out to pick up cases and bags, but there was no sign of mine. Purely to be polite, I asked him if he was from Greenlea. "Nowadays," he said, switching into Mirandan and handing me his card. "If you ever need assistance, please call. I've often been able to straighten out the little bumps and bends in the road which inevitably await someone like yourself who is trying to get acclimatised." We didn't speak anymore. He duly collected his belongings and left. Eventually, my cases arrived. I loaded them on a trolley and wheeled them to customs.

'Through the days and weeks that followed, I never imagined I would look at his card again, let alone take up his offer. I had interpreted his "straighten out" as at best ambiguous, at worst manipulative. If I thought of him at all it was as a shadow, a footnote, which went with my recollection of the strange person's exotic dress.

'Then two calamities hit me, one soon after the other. Both of them undermined my decision to stay in Greenlea. The relationship I was in turned cold and unresponsive. It became unbearable for the two of us to share the same space. We avoided each other as best we could, but in the end there was no point, so I moved out of his flat. I went to lodge in a succession of cheaper and cheaper dingy hotel rooms where, even in the poorest, I had difficulty in raising the rent. At the same time, the authorities turned down my application for a work permit. Before completely writing off the whole sorry episode as a disaster area and going back home, which I heartily didn't want to do, I rummaged among the odds and ends I had accumulated, dry cleaning tickets, discount offer vouchers, mini-cab firms' phone numbers, to unearth the card the man at the airport had given me. It said simply, "Andrew Guthrie, Sunrise Tea & Coffee Co." The telephone number below belonged to Panalquin.

'When I rang, a woman's voice answered. Eventually, he came to the phone. Yes, he did remember me. Yes, he was only too glad to help in any way he could. Plucking up courage, I suggested we might meet. No, it would not be possible. He was departing on business for the next few weeks, but, as my situation was urgent, he would take immediate steps to find a solution. I was not to worry. His colleague with whom I had already spoken would ring me back before the day was out.

'Two days later, I had an interview with the personnel manager of Sunrise. I started work the following morning. They advanced me a month's wages as a loan, which I could pay back interest free over a year. Three days into the job, the firm informed me that my work permit had come through.

'Mr Guthrie's assistant also found me an attic flat near the Belvedere. The owner was on a long secondment to Senegal, and, as she preferred spending her leave in Australasia or the Caribbean, I had the place to myself. I paid the bills and a nominal rent. Don't look like that, Lucas. I know what you're thinking, but until yesterday I hadn't seen him in the flesh since we crossed paths at the airport. Okay, occasionally I got small gifts, a box of chocolate truffles, a bunch of chrysanthemums, a set of wine glasses along with a short note of best wishes and encouragement, perhaps direct from him or issued on his instruction. He's helped others in the company in similar ways. They all say the same, men and women. He opens doors. He shows interest in a discreet way but never asks for anything in return. "We have him in our thoughts," Marta, my workmate, says, "that's his reward."'

Sylvia fell silent. She looked at Lucas pensively and gave him a melancholic smile.

'Screw him,' Lucas said. 'I don't want to hear or know anything more about him.'

Sylvia rose. 'I'm going. I enjoyed it. You gave me a bit of yourself. You didn't need to, but I'm glad you did.'

'No, hang on a minute,' Lucas slipped out of bed and retrieved his boxer shorts. 'Don't go yet. There's things we need to fix.'

'Say then.' She looked at her watch. 'What is it?'

'I want to see you. I want to go on seeing you.' He was interrupted by her giggles. 'What's so funny?'

'Nothing. It always amuses me the way men put on their socks. So earnestly, as if they'd never encountered them before. Don't pay me any heed. Yes I'll see you. Come to the Rag Market this evening.'

The telephone rang in the hallway. Lucas embraced her. She let him hug her, but her body did not respond. 'Aren't you going to answer? I will if you won't. It's not right to let it ring while you are here. Someone's waiting to get in touch.'

He let her go reluctantly, left the room and picked up the phone. 'Antoine.'

It was Walter. Annoyance mingled with relief that he had answered it and not Sylvia. 'Walter, this isn't a good time.'

Sylvia pecked his cheek as she went past. He called out to her, but she was already gone. He stared at the closed door.

'Sorry to intrude on your amours, but I won't be long. You'll be back in the sack in a twinkling. This is important, however. We're set to cast the ark adrift, brother. Our appointment in Greenlea is nearly over. Everything tells me the sheaves are going to be full and fat. They're gathering in for the Old Man's table. Most of the local philistines are now discomfited. One more attention to detail and we'll be there. Tomorrow you and I will be on our way. Now listen, brother, we never met Emmet. We didn't have any truck with him. He was just a bad dream, Antoine. A name they scare children with. He's no person. You know, the old Polyphemus hoodwink jive.' He cackled at his own joke.

'I'm not going. I'm staying here.'

There was a long pause at the other end of the line, then Walter continued in a measured tone, 'Of course, that's entirely up to you, but consider this particular place, Antoine. You've been jumpy ever since we arrived. It's only a façade for us. There's nothing here to sustain us. There's no life for us behind its doors or between its walls. Look at this fog now. Take it as an omen. You and I need some heat in our limbs. Leave before you're hurt by some imagined attachment. All right, you needn't come with me. That's not what I'm saying. Simply take the advice of an old percentage player.'

'My mind is made up. You go. Antoine Viall now is a thing of the past.'

'Very well then, if I can't persuade you I'd better say farewell for it's unlikely we'll meet again. Tell me your new name if Antoine Viall's no more. Give me that privilege at least.'

'My old name. Call me Lucas.'

'Lucas.'

The line went dead. In spite of the warmth indoors, Lucas sensed both the chill of the mist outside and that of his recovered Atlantic dawn. Lucky rolled over once again on the shingle at his feet. She yammered then bounded ahead to the water's edge, her paws and legs in and out of the receding tide. Above, the sea birds mewed and cawed in complaint and response, their wings tirelessly hovering as if they swooped forever over some perennial, gigantic rubbish dump. Only the ocean's distinctive beat and roll was missing. Its absence brought him a vague sense of unease.

He left the hall and let the hot tap run freely in the bathroom sink before inserting the plug. All he needed to do was concentrate on

Sylvia. Her image would fill the gaps. He decided to go earlier than he had planned to the Rag Market.

'Free,' he muttered as he soaped his hands. No Walter, no Emmet, no Chance Company, no Sylvia's benefactor, nor any present or past mists were going to disturb his inner resolve. While he brushed his teeth, his mouth grinned back at him in the mirror. He buried it in the nearest towel, thinking of the yellow towel Sylvia had used. 'Free,' he repeated when he switched off the light.

'De quoi s'agit il?'

The question floated up from the open window on the bottom left of the building's inner well. A man's voice answered from somewhere inside the same apartment, the exact nature of his reply too faint for Fernando to make out. Madame Vernon, however, seemed satisfied, for she did not repeat her query.

The uncertain whine and the whistling, crackling sound of Radio Toulouse came from above as unseen fingers fumbled with the tuning dial.

Halfway down a door slammed followed a moment later by the crack of two slaps and the ensuing wail of *le pauvre Emil.*

At the Morsom's directly opposite, plates were being taken from the dresser and deposited on the table, ready for the evening meal. Fernando hoped he might catch a glimpse of Juliette, but if she was already at home she lacked the generosity or the grace to appear in his line of vision.

Juliette. The truth was he should have been doing his homework, or at least practising his scales rather than idly sticking his head out of the kitchen window, eavesdropping on the neighbours. Juliette.

He imagined her in the white and black polka dot frock she had worn on the previous Sunday when she had come back from visiting her cousins in Lanemazan. He thought about the ascent his hand might make underneath that frock as it touched first the back of her knee and then encountered more warm flesh as it moved from her thigh to the curve of her buttock. He thought about the wonderful, entrancing moment when, while she picked up a bottle from the bottom of the cupboard, a shaft of sunlight had clearly picked out the shape of her bare legs and the outline of her pants. She had laughed and her face had reddened at his father's crude remarks until Madame Morsom had said, *'Tiens, tiens, sois le bienvenu, mais ça alors!'*

Juliette. What would his hand meet if, instead of having her back to him, she faced him eye to eye? He knew, of course, but what would it feel like? He unbuttoned his fly and placed his hand over the base of his balls. It would be . . . No words were needed, only the movement of his fingers and the image.

He finished masturbating in the toilet on the landing that they shared with the Darshels on the same floor. *'Les gogues,'* as Jacques Darshel, a carpenter from Paris, referred to it.

Agnes shuddered and dropped the page. She tried to visualise the boy's face during the solitary act, cooped up, his trousers at his feet, in what she imagined was the cramped space of the sordid lavatory. It had been early evening then, all those years ago, as opposed to early morning now. Had he put on the light to masturbate just as she, unable to sleep, her mind endlessly racing with images of her father transmuted into the guise of Joe May, the founder of Chance Company, had eventually turned on her bedside lamp and begun to read the further instalment of the life of Fernando Cheto Simon which Roberto Ayza had handed her at the Berengaria Hotel?

This time no list of 'witnesses' was appended. There was simply this abrupt start to presumably his new life in France. What did he look like? How different had he been from the large portrait which had unexpectedly stared down and beyond her at the entrance to the exhibition? She needed some kind of proof, something more tangible than the coincidence of a neighbour's name before she would accept that he, too, was in all probability her father, and yet her instinct told her he was, just as, when faced with the final bloated appearance of May, it had told her he might have died but René Darshel continued to live. Controlling her emotions, she located the subsequent passage and, steadying the rest of the pages against her upturned knees, read on.

Batiste now ate at French hours. He drank French drinks. At the moment his son dreamily relinquished the voluptuous image of Juliette in the realistic awareness that she was not likely to be interested in a younger kid, his father stood four-square at the zinc counter of Chez Alain, downing his first petit Ricard of the evening before bidding the company '*à demain*'.

A brisk two-minute walk took him to the Bar Zèbre where he had time for a couple more leisurely ones and a chat with *la patronne* about the day's PMU payouts and the forecast state of the going at Saint-Cloud next afternoon. Over at the Tabac, he purchased his habitual packet of Boyards and then it was one more, or maybe two, at the Café des Cygnes, which steadied him for his arrival home and the preparation of the customary soup.

Since Fernando had come with himself and Thérèse from Llomera, he had not returned to Miranda. His adventures or '*petites vacances*' as he called them were a thing of the past. He still kept his Party card, but, when someone asked him about the strength of the Workers' Commissions or mentioned a planned strike, he smiled apologetically and said he knew nothing about it. Even when he bumped into fellow Mirandans he distanced himself from their embraces, their hullabaloo, their nostalgic lists of food, wine and whores, making himself scarce at the earliest opportunity. He much preferred to drink on his own or to go up the narrow stairs to the top floor of the Hôtel Régence to visit Odile, Fanny or Clothilde.

The truth was he was wounded inside, only it had taken him time to recognise the fact. The black bull they all dreamt of and worshipped, the fallen god they bred wild and free so that they could sooner or later encumber it with barbs, bewilder it with trumpets, then plunge their sword through the folds of its flesh, guiding the curved blade past its muscles and tendons to sever its arteries and stop its heart, its juddering body, which they hitched up and dragged away to butcher and to turn into triumphal meat, had gored him secretly. It had twisted its horn deep in his gut, while the world, in which he thought he had a place, maintained its usual show and composure, its implacable surface of this will ever be. His wound was not susceptible to treatment. It could not be assuaged by meat or drink or the placing of his cock into any known or unknown vagina. Nor was it like the wounds of his dead companions, Iusebio and Manolo, who one day had simply ceased to exist.

'Not there' was its name. 'Condemned to be here' was its prognosis. Not there with Antonetta to feel his lust subside into day by day domesticity. Not there to await the birth of his son. Not there to settle down in the place where he had been born and had always known. Not there when she fell ill and needed him. Not there when she died. Not even there when others bore her aloft and stood at the edge of the hole into which he had never gazed, and never would gaze, though he knew every step of the way, every turn of the road, every peeling patch of the cemetery wall. Each time he closed his eyes, he tried to be there. The brief time they had been together—in particular the night when she had asked nothing of him and he had been alive, more truly alive and sentient than at any other time of his life—he relived while the alcohol kept him tossing and turning, unable to sleep. Yet the face he saw, the body he so eagerly uncovered, was not utterly hers. A part of her had vanished during his long absence, which, to his horror, he replaced with the glances of others, the nape of a fractionally longer neck, the small of a surely slimmer back. The rapturous moments they had stolen together dissolved in an unwanted montage of other women who had looked in his eyes and had liked what they had seen. Antonetta was gone. She had eluded his beholding. Her grave was forever closed. No futile scratching of his at the covering dirt could allay his loss and pain.

Fernando, meanwhile, had been shipwrecked by his father's increased moroseness. As the months went by, the vigour of Batiste's decision to bring him to France had evaporated in broken-off conversations and more and more impenetrable silences. He could have returned to Llomera. It was not entirely impossible. Indeed, his aunt begged him to do so in her weekly letters, and at times it was his dearest wish, yet an irrevocable stubbornness, a determination come what may to brave the fates, kept him where he was.

As a stab at his father, he had insisted on enrolling under the name of Fernando Simon at the Lycée Jean Moulin where he soon picked up French with an ease that Batiste and the neighbours could only marvel at. Naturally, he spoke with the local accent of the Languedoc, but he was soon able to soften his consonants into the '*langue d'oui*' when he went to his music lessons with Arsène Gil, a one-time inhabitant of Senlis in the Île de France. Within the building, Jacques Darshel introduced him to the strange utterances of '*Paname*', and a weekly reading of the raffish exploits of '*Les Pieds Nickelés*' completed his education.

'If a Breton were here or an Ougagalo,' declared Madame Morsom, 'Nando, within half an hour, would be gassing in Celtique or braying in Bargouine.' Juliette noticeably had not joined in the resultant laughter.

On this particular evening, however, Fernando encountered his father in a more expansive mood. They chatted amiably enough over their reheated chickpea soup. Batiste yarned about the hard times before the war and how Manolo Ayza's kid, Sonny, used to dog his footstep nearly every day. Fernando, for his part, chatted about Louis Roupier, his best friend at school, and M. Gil's squint, which made you think each eye was looking at the other.

After he had cleared away the plates, Batiste did not leave immediately for his nightly game of cards at Les Quatres Coins. Instead, he drank several more tumblers of red wine, and, as he watered a second one for his son, he began to curse at Sebastian Marva in what soon became a repetitive refrain. 'He always got it right, boasting that he was the greatest daredevil when we were boys, yelling that he was always the first to jump where others hesitated, the bravest to take the blows when others flinched. Always calculating, always sucking up to those with power and influence, positively oozing the impression that he was instinctively on their side though, of course, for him music was his excuse, his sole concern. Then he dares to set himself up as the protector of Manolo's wife and kids. The ideal family man. Everything he does tolerated and sanctioned by the state.'

Fernando tried to interrupt by asking about Marva's compositions and what they were like, but his father was not listening. 'Look at these,' he said. 'The kid's got talent.'

For the umpteenth time, he drew out the dirt-lined sheet of folded paper he kept in his wallet. Fernando, by now, knew each of the eight thumbnail sketches off by heart. He loathed them with the same intensity that Batiste reserved for Sebastian Marva. Without glancing at their grubby surface, he visibly sneered as his father's finger pointed in turn to a face at a window, top left, then three bottles, two squat and one long-necked, an oyster in a half-opened shell, an old woman's face, a skinny dog with its tail curled up, two empty peanut husks, a thumb and four fingers, laid side by side, and finally, bottom right, a bayonet stuck in the ground with a man's cap over the butt. If only they had been in the bluebird tin, he wished, they, too, would have been torn into shreds instead of being paraded for him to gawp at when Batiste got sentimental over young Sonny.

Refolding the paper carefully and putting it back in his wallet, Batiste rose from the table and went out. He was unlikely to return before the small hours. Fernando was left on his own again. 'It was the epoch of my long exile, my exile from myself,' he declared years later. Because I realised I was an exile like my father: he by circumstances, which were cruel, I by choice, which turned out to be my birthright.'

Music rescued him. It and the proximity of Juliette leavened his isolation during the otherwise flat and tedious daily round.

In the beginning, it had reached him from afar on the very first Sunday morning he had spent in Muret. A capricious wind, carrying now and then the faint sounds of a band, had ruffled his hair when he and Batiste had turned the corner and crossed the bridge over the railway tracks already shimmering in the heat towards Toulouse. The street ahead dipped then twisted and climbed. The strains of music came and went as they walked. All eyes and ears, Fernando drank in the Frenchness, the exciting foreignness of his new surroundings.

Together, they passed the shuttered shop fronts of first a bookshop, Librairie Éloise, among whose stacks he would later meet and get to know Louis Roupier; then an exotic fish emporium, Aquaia Variés; an outfitters, Les Modes D'Aujourd'hui, its twin display windows open to view; an ironmongers, S. Pepin Et Fils; a haberdashers, Au Coin Du Bon Tissu; and an electrical goods shop, P. Perez, which he pointed out to his father who said no, they weren't Mirandan.

Farther along, the only shop open was La Patisserie Béarnaise, in whose white and gold interior he was destined to lust over the brown-freckled cleavage of Mlle Becquot after Juliette had snubbed his silly chatter. The blare of a radio and the insistent clack and trill of a pinball machine from the opposite side of the street momentarily obliterated the sound of the still elusive music, but then they passed through an archway in the old town walls and gained, between high rose-brick buildings, the flank of an open square lined with plane trees.

The municipal band stood in a semicircle at its far end. They were clad in dark-brown uniforms with orange piping. Their ranks consisted of cornets, trumpets, trombone, flute and clarinet. A girl flautist and an older woman playing the clarinet broke up the otherwise solid male presence of sturdy patriarchs and sallow youths.

Fernando stopped where he was in wonder and growing delight because, although their timing was idiosyncratic, their intonation and pitch faltering, their grasp of harmonics rudimentary, their maintenance of the melody line erratic, something within him, which he had never experienced before, became vividly alive. He saw his own fingers dab the keys, his lips fit round a mouthpiece. He felt a reed vibrate with his own breath. A possible future opened up in front of him, and for that intense moment he was no longer in a strange and unfamiliar place. His mother had died, but he was alive. His father was a virtual stranger, but music existed in the world. One day, almost unimaginably, he, too, would die and be gone, but before that happened he would play music. These imperfect notes, cadences and flourishes that he was listening to could be transformed, of that he was certain, and, when the band stopped to indifferent, scattered handclaps, the music continued in his head. Out of nowhere, he grasped that music never really stopped even when its strains had faded and died. Its will to multiply, to replicate, to shift by half and quarter tones, to sustain and energise its crescendo, was too insistent. If it was written, others would play it. He had to be one of them.

After a pause, the band struck up another tune. Fernando ran towards them. He fixed his gaze on the clarinettist. Her individual face and body disappeared in his urge for knowledge and became solely the embouchure of her lips and the movement of her fingers opening and closing the keys.

Batiste regarded him with surprise. Fernando's attention was so rapt it was as though the boy were hearing music for the very first time. 'Come on, he said. 'Let's go. There's nothing here.'

'Can't we wait at least till they've finished. I'll be okay if you want to go and come back. I'll wait here. I promise. Don't worry.'

Batiste repressed a surge of annoyance. He felt like seizing his son's arm and dragging him away. Fernando had chosen to come with him to France, but he was still a Simon. He recognised sadly that the boy would never obey him in the unquestioning way he had obeyed his own father. 'Not there' demanded its price. He said, 'Ten minutes more and then we'll go.'

Fernando nodded contentedly. The musicians reached a wavering conclusion. Their conductor bowed and announced, 'To the inspiring memory of Fréderic Mistral.' People clapped politely. Looking around, as the players started to pack up their instruments, Fernando wondered who he could find to make his new dream come true. Who, among these faces, now busily discussing he knew not what, would have the insight to let him learn to play and one day join the band? 'A clarinet,' he whispered.

'What did you say?' Batiste asked.

'A clarinet. I'd like a clarinet.' Fernando searched for the words he needed to make his meaning clear and serious. 'More than the food I eat.'

Batiste laughed. 'Music'll get you a drink, a pretty girl's smile perhaps, but it won't pay the rent or guarantee a full belly.'

Fernando fell silent. He did not speak during the rest of their walk. In his heart, he accepted that his father would not help him. Out here in this new world of France, however, there was bound to be someone, as yet unknown, who he was fated to meet; someone who would open an attic door and retrieve a battered, disregarded case for him to unclasp and take out the half-forgotten clarinet that their grandfather used to play in the municipal band. 'Here's a photograph, they would say. 'You can make him out in the second row, third from the right.'

As things worked out over the ensuing weeks and months, he never did get his hands on a clarinet. Instead, he started to learn an instrument he had never heard of: namely a valve trombone.

The way it came into his possession caused him a lot of shame and guilt, so much so that for a long time he persisted in a series of lies and evasions, which gradually evolved into half-truths before years later becoming what truly happened.

The valve trombone had been deposited in the left luggage office of the Muret railway station by a certain Taji Mohammed, a one-time musician with the court orchestra of Rabat. He informed Julien Coras, the railway employee who gave him the receipt, that he would return in two hours' time to catch the mid-afternoon train to Montrejeau. Why he had alighted at Muret no one ever found out.

The meagre facts, as collected in the line of duty by Sergeant Rabotte of the local gendarmerie, confirmed that he paused underneath the station clock for a full five minutes prior to leaving. Once outside he turned right then, changing his mind, walked left down Stalingrad Avenue towards the industrial zone. Part way along, some kids, picking on his genial expression and somewhat rolling gait, began shouting abuse, followed by a few random stones hurled in his direction once he had passed. At that stage, he seemed to be on the point of approaching the gates of the abattoir, but an exiting van, Yves Préjean, Livestock, hooted at him, and Luxor, Préjean's Alsatian, thrust its muzzle out of the window, bared its teeth and snarled.

Half an hour later, he pushed open the door of the Café des Sports and ordered '*un petit express*.' Rèmy, who was fooling with the coffee machine, pretended not to hear him, so he repeated his request when Madame Opins herself came through to the bar. She looked him up and down in return and, not unkindly, according to her deposition and that of seven others present, suggested that he find somewhere else, somewhere '*plus convenable*' where they had, as she put it, '*plutôt le gout exotique, Marseille par exemple.*'

Odile spotted him as she came out of the back stairs at the

Régence. 'There was something about him,' she said. '*Vraiment un drôle de mec mais avec un petit air du gaillard*. He whistled that tune of Mischa Xavier's, "Le Printemps M'Accompagne".' She called out to him, '*Ohé, le gars!*' But he cocked a deaf one and went on his way. 'A religious type, *un Mussulman*,' she concluded, '*ou bien sans le fric*.'

Next he halted to buy some lemons from Béatrice in the Place des Laitiers. At the adjoining stall, he showed a keen interest in the girolles and chanterelles Loulou Gossard had picked that morning, but without making a purchase he turned into the Rue du Sénéchal.

Nobody it seemed had noticed him from then on until he paid for the room at the Hôtel Mimosa: room 15, off the second-floor stair turning. The notes he gave to Sévèrine were genuine and in crisp condition. His passport, also in order, and his completed Carte du Séjour were still in the desk drawer of her cubbyhole when the police arrived.

After entering the room, he had not wasted any time: time only to quarter the lemons and set them on the faded blue coverlet of the bed, to smoke half a pipe of kif and let the rest go cold, to remove all his clothes, to hang up his jacket and trousers in the wardrobe and drop his shirt, pants, socks and shoes in a pile beneath the shuttered window which overlooked the corner of Rue des Bonnes Eaux and the Passage Ducasse; time only to sit down and slit his wrists with an old-fashioned cut-throat razor, time to bleed towards unconsciousness and death in a town where no person knew him and where he had no discernible reason to be.

One death more, another body for the authorities to take away, some stubborn stains that could not be removed, yet, all in all, the regulars of the Mimosa were needfully a philosophical bunch. They knew only too well one could cop it anywhere, and who amongst them could truthfully say they had never given topping themselves the time of day. '*Un pauvre diable evidemment, mais ainsi gavotte tout le monde,*' was their envoi.

In due course, Sergeant Rabotte submitted his dossier. The town gossiped a little then grew bored. Within a week, the investigating magistrate from Toulouse signed the release papers for the body. Taji Mohammed's suicide was properly processed and his fleeting contacts soon forgotten.

As no next of kin had been identified, the valve trombone left at the railway station joined other found and uncollected items in a monthly sale. On Arsène Gil's advice, Batiste bought it for Fernando.

Getting over his initial astonishment, Fernando surreptitiously studied his father's face when, after opening the case, he took out the instrument and the mouthpiece. His recent awareness of Batiste's vulnerability made him try hard to disguise his disappointment that he was not holding a clarinet. Batiste, however, simply said, 'That's that' and disappeared into the kitchen.

In between his mouthfuls of rabbit stew when they were seated at the table, Fernando fingered the valves and spat experimentally into the mouthpiece, wondering what the sound would be like when he was able to control his breath flow. Batiste watched him indulgently without scolding. Across the plates, he appeared more at ease with himself, more the way he had been at the Cheto's farm when Gloria had confronted him, more ready to deal with whatever choices other people made. A clarinet can come later, Fernando decided. This is my beginning. He stood up and embraced Batiste. 'Thank you, father,' he said.

'It's yours, son. Do what you want with it. Arsène will give you some lessons. I can afford a few.' He hugged Fernando and let him go.

From that evening on, he showed no interest in the trombone or his son's playing progress. It seemed as far as he was concerned the transaction had ended and the matter, apart from paying for supplementary sessions with M. Gil, was outwith his control.

In the event, Fernando's first lessons went well. Within a few weeks, thanks to his ever-increasing appetite for practice and his copying of his teacher's embouchure and fingering, he secured the start of a basic technique. The trombone soon became his most treasured companion. He played it out in the open on the scrubland by the railway siding or under the bridge near the industrial zone when it rained.

As he grew more proficient, he began to play at home, listening with mixed apprehension and pleasure to his neighbours' comments, which accompanied his muffed, stilted, and eventually successfully sustained, melodic line. In the airless trap of the inner well, a few voices cursed him to hell, but the majority were encouraging, especially Jacques Darshel's, whose bass sallied through the partition wall with a '*Vas y le môme! On guinche ce soir.*' Fernando increased the volume in response, while in his mind's eye Juliette, dressed in a midnight-blue strapless gown, her hair pinned up, her breasts tremulous after the exertion of the dance, gazed up at him adoringly as he stood above her on the crescent of the bandstand.

His peers at school, however, took a different view. 'You know whose that was?' Laurent Pavier called out jeeringly after him when Fernando set off for another music lesson. 'I'll tell you whose it was. A dirty Arab who wiped his arse with his hand. He was so ashamed of himself he cut his throat, and now his donkey brays through you.'

'Perhaps you knew him,' Jacky Mermoz shouted. 'Perhaps he came here to see you. Maybe he's your real father,' he added with a sudden flash of inspiration. 'You're not Mirandan. You're Arab.'

Others took up the chant. Their stupid jibes lasted for days and nor did they stop when Fernando managed to corner one of his tormentors and land a punch. With an increasing sense of shame, he began to feel that Taji Mohammed's shade stood listening when he played, that he could hear it audibly sigh whenever he fumbled the notes, that it was permanently on the verge of ordering him to quit, to put away forever the instrument which he had unwittingly usurped. This ghost possessed an added, dreadful allure because in Fernando's imagination, given the nature of the death, all the blood must have flowed from Mohammed's body leaving the corpse unnaturally white like an albino's. The situation demanded an urgent resolution. A new history had to be found, a plausible alternative, which would convince and silence his classmates.

The first thing he invented was that M. Gil had really bought the trombone at a sale of old band stock in Toulouse after failing in his bid for Taji Mohammed's at the railway station. M. Gil had revealed the truth only when he, Fernando, had shown how troubled he was by owning something belonging to a suicide. Secondly, he made sure he talked about his father as much as he could. At every opportunity, he poured out tales of Batiste to anyone willing to listen. He was the best mechanic. There was nothing about tractor engines he did not know. He was a good shot. He had been a *'résistant'*. Why he had even met Jean Moulin.

'The Lycée Batiste Cheto,' Jacky Mermoz sneered derisively. 'Pull the other one.'

Fernando realised he had gone too far. He quickly tried to backtrack, but Lisette Daran piped up, 'How come you're called Simon when your father's name is Cheto?'

Fernando blushed. He felt like *pauvre Emil* awaiting another taunt, another blow. 'It's my mother's name,' he said. 'In Miranda we can choose which name we want.'

'*Arabe, Arabe, Arabe,*' they began to chant. The day was lost. He trailed home alone.

That night, Taji Mohammed awoke him with a smile. He took Fernando by the arm and led him down a corridor and then through an open doorway into a courtyard, where a trickle of water dripped from a pipe into a narrow stone trough. While he watched, Taji untwisted the ties of a sack which lay under a lemon tree. A pile of tiny dead birds dropped at his feet. The stone of the trough, which Fernando supposed would be cool and smooth, turned out be rough when he laid his cheek against it. It burnt his skin. Taji began playing a clarinet. Antonetta joined them. She danced as Taji played, laughing at her son. Her final peal was so piercing it released the bluebird from the cover of its tin. Fluttering over her head, its wings encouraged the other little birds to come alive. Drawings. There were ever more and more of those damned drawings for him to remember and destroy. With relief, he felt his hand rest on female flesh, his brow meet a rounded female belly. Juliette. He was about to reach up and kiss her when Paca spoke to him. It was her hand he was holding. It was her belly in front of him. The whole thing had been one of her tales about Moors and Christians. 'Work it out for yourself, Nando,' she said. 'Sometimes Moor, sometimes Christian. It depends on the times and how the wind is blowing.'

Similar confusing dreams involving Taji Mohammed, coupled with other playground confrontations, continued to bedevil his progress with the valve trombone until the day arrived when he met and talked at length to Louis Roupier, an older boy three years ahead of him at school, and through him heard for the first time the music he felt he had been born to play.

The chanced upon grail resided in a series of scratched and hissing second-hand 78s stacked in Louis's bedroom. Its inscription read 'Duke Ellington & His Orchestra', and its exemplar, Fernando's new-found guide and mentor, bore the name of Lawrence Brown. He listened over and over to Brown's trombone lead and solo on 'Rose of the Rio Grande', while Louis buried himself in the tome he had recently bought at the Librairie Éloise. At first, crudely blowing along to the record, then stabbing at the melody line, he at last managed one day to match his phrasing with some of the passages. The achievement of Brown's control and legato fluidity, however, was completely beyond him, and with a growing sense of humility he recognised that the way ahead was going to be long and demanding.

Louis, his new French pal, had always lived in Muret. His parents, Adèle and Gilles, worked for the Post Office: she behind the counter, he in the sorting office and on the mail run to and from Toulouse. In spite of this background, Louis in his imagination lived totally in the United States of America.

He transformed his narrow, cramped bedroom into an expanded, ever evolving transatlantic space whose location he notified by a sheet of paper tacked to the door. It shifted from a brownstone on Brooklyn Heights to a low-ceilinged cantina in Gallup, New Mexico, from a broken-down shack on the banks of the Missouri River to a drugstore on Hollywood Boulevard, where at any time of the day or night Lana Turner or John Garfield would drop in to check the latest *Variety* in-dope or picture gross. During the day, in the street and in school, he talked in French to French people, but at night, sequestered in his cold-water apartment, he hobnobbed in Yankee phrases with loggers and grease monkeys, Navajos and Seminoles, stockyard workers and soda-jerks, flophouse night clerks and the cute stenographer who had just moved in with the folks next door.

Louis garnered his know-how from Republic Pictures cowboys, Warner Brothers gangsters, M.G.M. musicals and the funnies section, which arrived intermittently from cousins settled in Montreal. Month by month, he unravelled the mysteries and tracked the adventures of Dick Tracy, Terry and the Pirates, Mandrake the Magician, Prince Valiant and the saucer-eyed, haunted face of Little Orphan Annie, while he listened to the swing and jazz records he had unearthed amidst the random detritus of M. Comenichi's Toulouse bargain shop.

Whenever he had more money to spend, he purchased translations of American books at the Librairie Éloise: James Fennimore Cooper's *The Last of the Mohicans*, read and reread,

Mark Twain's *The Adventures of Huckleberry Finn*, read, Edgar Allan Poe's *The Narrative of Arthur Gordon Pym of Nantucket*, read, Herman Melville's *Moby Dick*, five chapters read, John Dos Passos's *USA*, one volume read.

On one particularly lucky day during a weekend foray to M. Comenichi's, he rescued, from the dusty piles of miscellaneous junk, two battered boxes full of gold. One held the dilapidated and well-thumbed pages of a *Tumbleweed Tales* series, illustrated, when the front cover was intact, by a tall cowpoke spinning a lariat towards the reader. The other contained back numbers of *American Crime Magazine* and, joy of joys, their French version *Les Gens Du Milieu, USA*.

Later, through continuing research, he found to his chagrin that the authors of the Westerns were Europeans who, like himself, had never even seen the range, never mind having had to fight their way out of a box-canyon ambush. This unexpected blow, however, was more lightly borne because of his discovery of his true American hero, Jack London, at the same time. Through his treasured pages, Louis slid blissfully into the old pre-war USA of oyster pirates, night-time hobo jungles and the march of the tramp army with its own appointed generals to Washington DC. By torchlight, under the bedclothes, he experienced the delights and dangers of *John Barleycorn* and suffered the apprehension and terror of icy death in the Alaskan winter when, to no avail, the live-saving fire could not be lit.

Fernando, too, was intrigued and curious about the space and grandeur Louis described, but to him the books and comics were secondary. The stack of scratched records, which unfortunately added no further Lawrence Brown, remained his focus. '*Sont tous les nègres?*' he asked hesitantly one day.

'*En jazz oui, mais en swing il y ont des chefs blancs,*' Louis replied, leaving Fernando to ponder the situation with an uneasy feeling in the pit of his stomach.

At his next lesson, he put the matter tentatively to M. Gil

who told him, 'Music is music. Learn to read well. If you can play from notation, it doesn't matter whether it was written by a Negro or a White.'

Fernando was reassured by this to an extent, but he still wondered about the parts which were not written down. As he pressed the stops on the valves, he still sensed the ironic gaze and lingering presence of the trombone's erstwhile practitioner creep into the room and make his notes vanish as soon as he had imperfectly formed them.

Agnes put down the six remaining pages. The lists of books had bored her. She felt no need to read the rest. They could wait now she knew for certain her father's beginnings in the world. He was Fernando Cheto Simon, a Mirandan born in Llomera. He had journeyed to Muret in France and from there to America, where he had become René Darshel, Joe May and perhaps others in a sequence she had yet to determine. At the same time, she had gained a grandfather, a grandmother, a great-uncle and several great-aunts whose existence she had known nothing about.

The words she had read were his words, of this she was certain. Only he could have written them or vouchsafed them to another as yet unknown to write down on his behalf. At last, she knew the boy he had been. She now grasped a hint of the man he had become, but where he was and in what guise he would appear still eluded her. She could only hope that either Chance Company or the mysterious Elizabeth Kerry or the ex-policeman, Alakhin, held the answers, because the anger she bore him had not abated within her. She would not allow him to brush aside his disappearance as, no doubt, he had brushed aside the ghost of Taji Mohammed over the intervening years.

'I promise,' she said out loud.

Emmet inserted the jemmy into the crack of the doorframe and tugged. After a few concerted exertions, the wood began to splinter and buckle. In the old days, under Wallace's organisation, he would have stood back and waited while a specialist did the job, but these were different times. Now it was each man for himself. He applied one final wrench. The door gave. A burglar alarm went off. Behind the door, he found a utility room. The downward directed beam of his torch showed him the way through to the kitchen. The continuing noise of the alarm was all to the good. It added to the sense of impending mayhem. Rather than drag a sleeping man from his bed, the chances were the target would now come to him.

He opened the first door off the central corridor. The moving light pieced together a snug den, which no doubt was Lambert's personal hideaway. As yet, there were no voices to be heard above the unrelenting clamour of the alarm. He tried the second door. It revealed a spacious sitting room furnished with a giant TV, audio stack, wall cabinet and three-piece suite. Lambert lived well. Here in his suburban ranch-house, as Greenlea fund-raiser for the Socialist Regeneration Party, he was comfortably sheltered from the vicissitudes of his native land's cash-crop economy which guaranteed ever deepening poverty to his potential voters.

A light suddenly came on under the fourth door on the right. Emmet entered quickly. Lambert was sitting on the edge of the bed, trapped in the act of pulling on a pair of slacks over his underpants. His wife lay beside him, propped up against the pillows. Her mouth opened in a scream. Lambert tried to say something like, 'I've called the police,' but his words were garbled. Dropping his torch, Emmet hit him twice in the solar plexus. Lambert was a puny guy in his late-forties, incapable of much resistance. Emmet twisted his neck in an arm lock and sat down on the bed. Lambert's wife kept on screaming, her body now rigid. She watched in terror as Emmet took out a revolver from his pocket with his free hand and pressed it against her husband's temple. Her scream segued into broken, racking sobs.

'Life's precarious,' Emmet said. 'There's nothing you can plan for.'

He drew back the trigger. A warm stream of Lambert's urine spread through his underpants and onto Emmet's coat. Emmet put away the unloaded gun, let Lambert go, picked up his torch and got to his feet. 'Remember the Old Man's power is everywhere. Turn to other things else neither of you is safe.'

Once he had retrieved the jemmy, which he had left on the kitchen table, he looked in on the couple again before finally making his way to the front door. A vestige of light from the twin ornamental lamps outside reflected on its mullioned panes. He undid the chain, slid back the bolt and left the door ajar. A glance at his watch confirmed he had been inside for four minutes. He started down the gravelled drive.

Behind him lights steadily went on throughout the house. Down at the gateway, a man with a brindle greyhound on a leash stood as if rooted to the spot. Somewhere nearby a police siren wailed, followed by another. 'Misty morning to be out, citizen,' Emmet said pleasantly as he drew close. The dog sniffed at his shoes. Its owner did not answer. Brushing past him, Emmet strolled down the hill. At the first corner, he turned, crossed the road and climbed into the waiting car.

'Jesus Christ!' Walter Sembele was hunched in the passenger seat, his body still shaking with unwanted tremors. Emmet switched on the ignition, eased out from the pavement and drove slowly away, keeping his eye on the rear-view mirror.

'You didn't, did you?'

Emmet shook his head. 'The gun wasn't loaded.'

'From where I was the din was unbelievable. A shot could easily have gone unheard.'

'Show them you're not afraid or bothered and the rest follows smoothly. It gives their despair at their powerlessness time to deepen. I'm glad to see you stayed put because I wouldn't have forgiven you if you'd let me down. That's why I said no Antoine. I don't trust him. It had to be just you and I.'

They drove on in silence.

Due to the mist, Walter failed to distinguish where they were, never mind if they were following the route they had previously taken to Lambert's house. Somehow he desperately needed to regain the upper hand he had lost while Emmet carried out his thuggery. In truth, he had only assented to come along as a prelude to do what he now knew he must do. Emmet had placed him in potential danger during the break-in, testing whether he had the stomach to stick it out and wait, or the cowardice to cut and run.

'Thanks to your efforts the harvest is in the barns, brother. The Old Man will surely reap what we have so diligently sown. Now you can go home and rest contented.' His voice sounded shrill and unconvincing. The jauntiness he had intended in his tone felt flat. He detected a distinct lack of saliva in his mouth. With mounting unease, he realised he was still afraid.

Emmet, as if sensing his frailty with unerring timing, swung off the road into a car park and drew up alongside its boundary wall. Opening the glove compartment, he stowed away the torch, then, reaching into his deep inside pocket, he extracted the jemmy and dropped it behind his seat. When that was done, he took out the revolver.

Walter's heartbeat quickened. His feet twitched up from the floor. He felt the blood rush to his head. A clammy sweat attacked his constricting chest muscles. 'It's n-not loaded,' he stuttered.

'That's what I said.'

Emmet's face beside him was calm and impassive. Time suddenly seemed to relinquish its flow. The terrible now of this moment was obliterating all his time in Greenlea, all his time in service to The Old Man. It was swallowing whole the feeble illusion of any remaining future time. It was . . .

He tried not to look at the gun. He tried not to see Emmet's finger curled round its trigger. A nervous giggle, which he struggled to suppress, escaped and rose from the pit of his stomach. His guts rebelled. They were on the verge of something shameful. His hands desperately wanted to grip something tight. The steering wheel perhaps. Perhaps they could turn the key, start the car, grab the wheel or else wrench open the door and he could dive out and . . . Thought deserted him. Still Emmet did not speak. Time. Christ, time was impaling him devoid of any action. Do what you came to do, he pleaded with himself. He had nothing to lose. Anything was better than this terrible void. 'I've brought your money,' he managed to utter. 'It's what you're owed after this morning. Please, may I?' He gestured nervously towards his pocket.

There was no reply. Emmet appeared uninterested, as if any movement made was completely irrelevant. His eyes were shaded in the gloom. Walter, for an intoxicating second, wondered if they were actually closed, that he was simply taking a short nap with the gun in his hand for cover. Emboldened, he went on. 'I've got another amount. A substantial amount. It's yours now and the same again later. Please take it. I'm happy to talk terms with you.'

The eyes now were clearly locked on his own. The barrel of the gun jolted him in the ribs. 'Oh, please,' he whispered.

'You sought me out, Mr Sembele. You came to Greenlea and sought me out in my city, my territory. You hired me. I did as you instructed.' Emmet looked inquiringly into his face. Walter nodded hastily. 'So I'll take the money now and the whole of what you say you're ready to pay me.'

'I can't. The balance won't be sanctioned until,' he choked on the words, 'until your victim's death's confirmed. You'll get it in the old country along with a new life for yourself and your wife. The Old Man . . .'

'The time for foolishness is past, Mr Sembele,' Emmet interrupted. 'You should know that.' He waved the gun towards Walter's pocket.

Walter fumbled and extracted two packets. Emmet glanced inside, laid the revolver in his lap and riffled through the notes. 'Tell me about it as we go,' he said.

The engine purred into action. Emmet released the brake. The clock on the dashboard showed 7.49 a.m. Time slid tentatively forward.

Intellectually, Walter knew the psychology. He was supposed to feel some gratitude towards his tormentor and deliverer, but his body remained in a different place. It still wanted to thrust open the door, jump out and damn the consequences.

They filtered into a busy boulevard. Heavy lorries lumbered by on the other side, while their own lane began to reduce to a crawl. Walter surmised there was probably either a sequence of red lights ahead or road works of some kind. By now they were virtually stationary. It could be done. If he was going to run, this was it. But run where? To the airport and invented stories to satisfy Ignacio Williams and his superiors? To some unknown place out of town where eventually Emmet would track him down? No. He had to see it through as he had always done. They moved on. He was committed.

'It's not our thing,' he said. 'Not directly.'

Emmet grunted. 'It never is.'

'Call it a favour for friends of the Old Man. They want a certain person eliminated for sins of the past, which they haven't forgotten nor forgiven. He's here in Greenlea. They passed it to me before I left, you understand. Why do one thing when you can do two? That's their philosophy. I've met my contact. He's got a short time, preferably before I leave tomorrow, to supply the name, address and particulars.'

'What makes you think I'll do it if you're long gone?'

'The money. I can change things and arrange you get it here. Your self-pride. Our antagonism if you fail. The truth is I'm tired, Mr Briggs. I'm ready to go home. If the intelligence I've gathered is correct, the ballot will be in our favour and the same goes for most of the rest of our diaspora. This other matter is none of my making.'

'And Viall?'

'He's no longer in the equation. This is strictly between ourselves. You see I'm leaving you as a free agent. Where can I contact you if word comes through today?'

'Demel. It's a bar on Kefoin Street. I'll be there this evening. Give me the details of how I collect the balance. Else it's no go.'

Walter nodded. 'You have my assurance.' He looked out of the window. 'Even without this mist our people are invisible here. I can't fathom why you stick it. The only time they congregated joyfully was when Poppa here brought them something. Otherwise where are they? In the depot, that's where, cleaning and maintaining. That's no life, brother.'

'Aren't you forgetting it's the dead that turn up to post their votes.'

Walter laughed and tapped the dashboard. 'You see, there's no reason for us to fall out when we understand each other so well. Like your wife, a charming lady, now I'd say she is your mainstay, right? Well, in the same way, I'm your meal ticket to better things.'

Emmet stopped the car. 'Salonika Street is the second left,' he said. 'Remember this deal is purely business. I become very unsettled if someone tries to cross my personal boundary. Take the little fright I gave you as a possible down payment. Then you'll find we understand one another. Now, let's have it exactly how I collect my fee.'

⎯⎯⎯⎯⎯⎯⎯

Watching Walter's figure disappear in the thickening mist, Emmet put away the gun and rejoined the slow moving traffic.

Hallie was asleep, stretched out on his side of the bed, when he got home. Her cleaning overalls were draped over the back of the easy chair. He bundled them up with distaste and dropped them in the laundry basket. Once he had installed the revolver in the shoebox at the bottom of the wardrobe next to the carton of ammunition, he took off his coat, shoes and the rest of his clothes.

Under the shower, he increased then decreased the heat setting, targeting the pressure between his shoulder blades. Turning round, he soaped his torso. 'I've got my mojo workin',' he sang softly. Unlike the song, it worked alright on the woman sleeping in the next room. He held the proof a hundred times over, but the question was, would it work to get them both the crock of shit dangled in front of him. Scaring Lambert and Walter had been easy, but the forward game looked hazardous. Killing, as far as he was concerned, had always been a step too far. Encouraging the guy to get lost and never come back was well within his repertoire but getting his hands securely on the prize would not be easy. They wanted verification. The opposite of the Little Sammy Tyrell farrago. It remained a tantalising opportunity, however, to get himself and Hallie out of the dispiriting spiral of odd jobs, long hours and reduced pay packets. He could finally burn these demeaning overalls.

The colder water invigorated his skin. Strong boy for hire. Bad man when the money was down. That was the way it had always been. No talking. No mercy. Only the do. Always the do. But, at the same time, always the look in the eyes of those who hired him, Wallace included, even though he had professed friendship as the years progressed. It was a masturbatory look, waiting to come while he made the hit, thrilling to his violence as a surrogate dream of their own desires, and then when it was over and settled the same stare of barely concealed contempt. Some even had dared a 'hail fellow well met' touch at his arm. 'Good nigger. Nice nigger. Why don't you cool out for a while? Let things drift along. We'll be in touch.' To them he was a relic from the past, a curiosity they had paid a pittance to see in action. Aw shawnuff, man, but it sure don't work on me.

He felt thirsty. Stopping the shower, he stepped out of the cubicle and filled a glass with water. He drank it down in one gulp. As he lifted it from the running tap a second time, his bloodshot eyes confronted him in the mirror. Brushing away the smears of steam, he stroked his stubbly chin and jowls. They were in need of a shave before he met Agnes. He swallowed the rest of the water and replaced the glass on the shelf. When he had towelled himself, he plugged in his electric razor and sat on the bathroom stool. His continuing desire for yet more water irritated him. Two glasses were surely plenty. He got up and closed the door in case the sound of the razor wakened Hallie. On his way back, his fingers rested round the tap. Stop, he told himself, start shaving.

Olokun. The buzz of the razor deepened and whined the name as he moved it from his cheeks to his chin and above his mouth. Olokun. Other people's orisha, not his. Like those girls walking by the riverbank. One of them a skinny little girl whose daddy sent her to school in town, her uniform all pressed and neat, on her way to Stop 42 to catch the bus.

'Well, good mornin' little schoolgirl. Little schoolgirl, how do you do.' It was Olokun this and Olokun that. A spirit guide for girls. 'Well me Ogun shows the path. See over there the house on the bluff and the trees beyond.'

'I'll tell my daddy!'

No good. No use. But Granma'll fix it. It's just a little tear that can be mended. Just another tear to shed to join the other tears. 'Dry your eyes girl. It ain't no use. Can't you see the river's dry and Olokun's no good without water.'

When she had run off, a mangy dog he did not recognise lurked ahead of him on the trail, its muzzle distorted between a whimper and a snarl. Automatically, he had picked up the nearest stone with which to threaten it, but instead of fleeing, its tail between its legs, it had advanced towards him as though it alone held the right of way. As it drew near, he launched the stone. It smacked into its flank with a dull thud, yet without even a yelp it still came on. Trembling, he stood his ground and waited. The animal's growls reached a keening pitch. 'Ogun protect me now!' It slobbered around his feet. Don't look down! Stay still! he commanded himself. Look over there instead. See that bird! You can just make it out in the depths of the branches of the tree. A snarl. A snuffle. He had not looked down. The dog took one more sniff and moved on at its own steady pace. The bird was no longer visible.

Emmet switched off his razor and returned it to its case. He decided he would tell Agnes all he knew about the man in the photographs they had seen last night. Hallie already knew. She knew as much as he did about what had happened at Veldar.

Through in the bedroom, she was still fast asleep. In a little while, he would brew some coffee and see if she wanted any. He sat down in the easy chair. To load the gun and pull the trigger— would it matter so much at the end of the day? Whatever, that would be something, like the kid, that Hallie need never know. He lifted his head back and closed his eyes in order to gain a few moments devoid of thoughts. Soon, in spite of his intent to stay awake, he drifted off into a dream-laden slumber.

<hr>

The final plenum of the Pan-African Congress had scarcely had time to convene when two European-dressed, sober-suited delegates quit their seats and met each other at the rear exit of the hall. Recognising one another at first glance, they dispensed with both hand gestures and words as unnecessary to their purpose.

Together they waited for the arrival of the express lift to take them to the sixty-eighth floor.

On the wall, above the large mounted photographs of Lagos by night, tannoy speakers relayed the ongoing praise speech from the Chad delegation. The taller of the two switched off his pager and preceded his companion into the empty, mirrored compartment, which had silently arrived. The other limped across the threshold behind him, his swelling tool filling the black-pinstripe crotch of his trousers. His girlish voice giggled as the contraption gained speed. Oblivious of the watcher, he masturbated freely between floors thirty-four to fifty-seven. Gradually, his semen soaked through the cloth and splashed onto the carpet. First, it obliterated the background drone of muzak, then their reflected images in the glass, and finally it doused the sepulchral glow of the fluorescent light. His companion stood apart, patiently waiting until a hiatus was achieved in which the world and their surroundings would reinvent their solidity and once more be ordered into names.

They gained the roof through the open tinted doors of the

Heliotrope Lounge and squatted down beneath the struts of the funnel-shaped water tank. The honk and screech of rush hour traffic, sliced and spiced by the wails of ambulances and the sirens of police cars rose from below. The taller of the two punched numbers into his mobile phone. Messages flowed back: call and response, response and call. Satisfied, he extracted his personal organiser from his antelope-hide attaché case. Nothing could be left to chance. It was his duty now, as it had always been in the past, to foretell and uphold the ceaseless order of the future, so that justice might prevail and the name of God, which his companion had vouchsafed to him, might continue to be known to all mankind. The keys of the kingdom, he thought. They shall all regain the keys of the kingdom.

Meanwhile, their sleeper was about to awake. Until now Ogun had been his watchword. The heat of smelted iron, the trodden path through the forest and the hammer blows had been his emblems. Elegba, personally, had gone to show him other ways. Now he, Ifa, would rectify his mistaken spirit identity.

The faint hiccup of the water seller's cry in the street below overrode the din of the traffic. A jug of iced water juddered on a luncheon room's counter as an articulated lorry thundered by. Down by the river, the homeless and dispossessed left their shanties and bivouacs for a day's begging in the city. One woman alone stayed by the water's edge, watching the turgid flow seep and roll, brown in midstream, black under the railway bridge, sepia-yellow on the far mud shore. Turning seawards, she called out three times to her voyaging son.

Elegba laughed and jumbled the paths which led away to a multitude of destinations. Immovable at his side, Ifa strengthened the vertical and horizontal strokes and consolidated the circles which, even though they were written on water, contained the name for all future endeavours: Olokun.

Emmet awoke. His throat was parched. It felt raw when he

swallowed. Swivelling his head, his eyes met Hallie's gaze. 'Been awake long?' he said.

'Uhhuh. Since you came in I think.'

'No, you were fast asleep. I must have dropped off myself.'

'I'm not going to argue with you,' Hallie said wearily. 'You're back and not arrested or worse. That's what's important.'

'Want some coffee? I'm going to do some fresh.'

She shook her head. 'No. I'm going to try and sleep some more. Did you get paid? You made sure?'

'Yeah, I've got it. A final fee. Their election deal is over. I got Walter to come with me. It made it easier. He leaves tomorrow.'

'I'm glad. You might not care, but their politics stink. People won't forget this, you know. Lambert's got influence. Crime they shrug at, but this is different. And Antoine?'

'Not there. Not in the picture anymore according to the gospel-spouting brother, though I got him to choke on that shit. That's one pleasure I enjoyed at least.' He moved across and sat on the bed. 'Why don't we take a trip? We could go hot style. North Africa say. Give people time to forget.'

'What's brought this on? You haven't done something?' She reached for his hand. 'Tell me you haven't darling.'

He squeezed her flesh. 'Nothing's happened. All I've done is frighten people. I just reckon you need a break. Time away from the shitty routine. We've got enough to last a bit and then, well we're not kids, reality won't faze us. In a few days we could be off. Think about it.'

'I don't know, Emmet. We'll see if you're really serious. One thing is for sure though, I'll be glad when Walter Sembele is on that plane. I haven't forgotten the look he gave you at the restaurant. Pure malevolence. Malevolence with relish on the side.'

'He plays the manipulator. He lays on the superstitious jive, but underneath he's just another scared human being who knows his time is nearly up. Don't worry about him. He's a transient now.'

'A transient?'

'It's an old phrase of Minty's for someone who briefly gave us grief but wasn't important enough to have his name remembered. Go back to sleep. I'll try not to wake you.'

The illuminated figures of the digital clock above the glass door of the oven slid from 10.18 to 10.19. Outside, the possibility of light remained remote. Agnes dropped her breakfast plate and coffee cup into the plastic draining tray, dried her hands and went back to the bedroom, where she seated herself in front of the mirror and began applying her make-up. Emmet Briggs was due at half past.

Finished with her choice of lipstick, she picked up a bottle of her favourite scent and was about to dab some behind her ears and on the front of her wrists when she saw its removal had toppled over the typed envelope, addressed to Emily Brown, which had arrived in the morning post.

Momentarily interrupting her toilet, she spilled out its contents on the one still unencumbered patch of the dressing table, as if to verify with her own eyes the continuing existence of the concert ticket, the backstage pass and the accompanying explanatory note. It was true. This evening, Wilson Loumans was booked to play solo piano at the Veterinarian Hall. Thanks to her anonymous tape correspondent, she already knew of Loumans' link to her father in the past. Now, according to Chance Company, the pianist held recent information concerning his whereabouts. Their note was again signed R. Ayza, an enigmatic squiggle which either meant he had lied to her last night when he said he knew nothing of her presence in Greenlea, or someone else persisted in misusing his name. Whichever it was, she resolved, while re-stoppering the bottle, to treat him with caution when she caught up with him later today at the Belvedere.

Raising her head, she noticed, through the wing of the mirror, that several of the unread pages she had dropped from the latest instalment of the Fernando story had somehow ended up under the bed. With a sigh, she got up, knelt down and stuck her arm and head forward in order to retrieve them.

No sooner had her outstretched fingers managed to gather them together than she experienced a powerful sense of déjà vu. In the enclosed space between the bed and the carpet, the discreet odour of her newly sprinkled scent seemed to hover in her nostrils, coalesce, then metamorphose into the more pungent and insistent smells of musk and patchouli. In her mind's eye, her black low-heeled shoes grew into crimson sling backs many sizes too large for any feet. She sensed her fingers touch not these sheets of paper, but others, which she had randomly scribbled over and stuffed into an empty shoebox when she had heard her mother's voice outside the door. But where and when exactly and why had she hidden away, dragging the box with her under the bed?

An aroma of perfumes she would never use, papers whose details were lost, crimson shoes that clattered on the wooden surround. She tried to concentrate on each in turn. Dressing up in her mother's things had been one of her favourite games, games that Sula usually regarded with complicit amusement. Perhaps there had been an accident of some kind and she had clumsily spilled too much of her mother's perfumes. Perhaps that was why the sense of their smell now lingered in her memory. If it had occurred it must have happened when she was around four or five. He would still have been there. The bed under which she crouched would have been his as much as Sula's. What was it she had scribbled on and then concealed? If found out, it would surely have only earned her a mild rebuke. Was the uncertain shoebox her equivalent of her father's bluebird tin? Had he brought with him to America, for some reason, his hated Sonny Ayza drawings? Was that why she had sensed their familiarity when she had stumbled across them here in the flat?

There was nothing more. She had no inkling of what had happened next. Whether the memory was something she had partly imagined or a real episode she could not say. She straightened up and put the rescued pages on top of the rest of the text. The outer door buzzer sounded. She answered it and slipped on her coat.

Emmet Briggs was waiting for her, his back to the entrance, staring out into the surrounding murk. 'The car's over there,' he said, indicating the shrouded adjoining block.

'Do you mind if we go to Polygon first? There's someone I need to see at 70 Westgate and by then the weather might have lifted for the rest of the journey.'

Emmet nodded. 'Okay. This won't last. Sooner or later a wind'll spring up and shift it.'

Agnes fell in with his stride. He had on a long-peaked cap of brown leather and a short coat of the same material. A pair of plum-coloured slacks leading down to tan loafers adorned with acorn-shaped tassels completed his dress. There was no one else about. 'It doesn't look far on the map,' she said, 'but I'm still trying to find my way around.'

'It's a weird area. It's south-west from here. So we're going in the right direction towards the estuary bridge. I can't take too long though because I must be back in the city this afternoon.'

He unlocked the door of a grey saloon. Agnes climbed in beside him. She had expected to enter a part of his own particular space, but instead the interior was purely functional. She could spot nothing extraneous. There were no personal items on view.

'What's weird about Polygon?' she took up when they reached the main road and were following the blurred outline of a tram.

'It's a newish suburb. A planner's botched dream of alternative living, but the way things panned out it's become an enclave for people getting ready to die. We've got a local saying, opened in Panalquin, matured in Greenlea, closed in Polygon.'

He carried on explaining the analogy, but Agnes was no longer listening. She was thinking about the person she hoped to meet on her unannounced visit. They drove on in resumed silence until they entered the tunnel beneath Lagran Castle Bluff.

'I've got to tell you something,' Emmet said, 'something about the man whose photographs we saw last night and something about me. I don't want you to get upset. Remember I said I'd guarantee your safety. You have my word on that.'

Agnes turned towards him. His face was troubled. 'Go ahead,' she said. 'As you guessed, he means a lot to me.'

Emmet kept his eyes fixed on the road ahead. 'Okay, just hear me out. I was freelancing, like now, when I first arrived here. You see, I'd learned to look out for myself in the style I'd got into before I left back home. Understand I was still a kid. The adrenalin buzz hitched me up through my first individual hits and then I moved on bit by bit into a few experimental stick-ups. Naturally, my pickings were so-so, haphazard you could say, and soon gone. Sure they bought me a few good clothes and now and then a second-hand car and women, a cavalcade of women who called me Joe, Buck or Freddy, whichever name I told them. Lie up a little was my plan. Another hit. Another good time. Easy come, easy go, that's what I reckoned, but somehow deep inside I knew I was watching my time waste away. So when the Zamir brothers offered to put me on their payroll I was secretly relieved.'

He paused to check Agnes's reaction then, as she said nothing, he went on, 'The job was straightforward enough. I was always there to pick them up at the agreed places. After the heists, I guarded them in a sequence of furnished apartments and hotel rooms. I was careful not to listen when they discussed future plans, and when they indicated someone needed a spanking I took care of it. The thing is all the inevitable hanging about for days and days, weeks even, and then the operation is successfully carried out. Well, it's best shared in others' company. In truth, they were relatively small-time, but my percentage was okay, better than I'd grafted on my own. They gave me shape and, as it turned out a passport for the future.

'Then Minty Wallace came along. You won't have heard of him, but believe me at the time he was the guy, not just local but national too. One day he came up to me in the Pheasant Bar and said, "Listen son, I'm hearing about you. Good things, real good things. Maybe I could tolerate your company. Come in with me and your future's writ large."

'Well, join him and you'd joined for life. Going against him wasn't an option. I took his offer. Wallace's outfit before long became my life, THE LIFE we used to call it, until I met my future wife. Even then, if I'm honest, but that's maybe a word you don't want me to say. Anyway, nobody, least of all me, would have guessed that in the end I'd be the one to survive. Him and Jimmy Massoura and the rest of the troops. Now, here I'm back on my own again scrabbling up stray bits and pieces, while all Minty once had is fat zero, only to be reinvented and packaged as part of the Panalquin Experience Walk for visiting tourists.'

They emerged from the tunnel into the continuing swathe of mist. Agnes felt an emptiness gather and expand inside her. The man at her side for whom she had held an instinctive warmth was a gangster capable of terrible acts. 'What has this to do with my father?' she forced herself to say.

'Your father?'

'Yes. They were his photographs we saw last night.'

'I met him when I worked for Wallace. It was back in the sixties over on the south bank in a little country town called Veldar.'

Agnes's sense of apprehension increased. Her private feelings about her errant father were one thing, but the possibility that he had been involved with criminals was quite another. 'You'd better tell me about it,' she said, as she stared out the windscreen at the slowly enlarging stretch of dual carriageway emerging through the mist.

Emmet did not reply at once. Thoughts of Corinne, Alakhin, who he was due to meet very soon, and Little Sammy Tyrell bothered him. 'Always start with the corpse,' that had been one of Alakhin's watchwords, but he did not want to begin with one of Corinne's bodies nor, for that matter, Little Sammy Tyrell's. 'The detective resurrects the victim, lives with them and through them until the murderer resurfaces.' Alakhin again, philosophising during a TV reconstruction. Strange how he had never tangled with Minty or the organisation. It was as though all crime had been individual according to his remit.

'I was waiting on the platform at Veldar Station,' he said at last. 'Manny The Pilot was in the car, probably taking a few toots from his hip flask to pass the time. Wallace, Jimmy Massoura and the Japanese contingent were already in session back up at the villa we'd rented. Joe May, your father, was expected on the next down train from Panalquin. For some unknown reason, he had insisted on coming alone all the way from America.'

'Japanese? What Japanese? Why Japanese?'

'The head oriental was called Manoko. Ute or something like that. He had a henchman, whose name I don't remember, and four others. It was a balancing act between them and ourselves. Minty had chosen Veldar as a gesture away from Panalquin and Greenlea, but to tell the truth I always felt they held more clout during the negotiations even though we had the territorial advantage. What the deal really was or who brokered it I never knew, except your father fitted in the middle somehow. They were involved in sorting some franchise demarcation on a need to know basis and that didn't include me.

'Anyway, they finally closed the options. The Japanese departed. Your father, as far as I know, went back to the States. Minty had his lawyer and accountant work on the details, but after a month or so we heard that Manoko had died and the whole thing petered out. Minty drew in his horns and returned to business as usual.'

Agnes shivered slightly. A sign for the estuary bridge with a right turn to Polygon underneath appeared ahead. 'What was he like?' she whispered, swivelling her neck to watch Emmet as he filtered into the slip road. 'What did you make of him?'

Emmet tried to think back. 'A civilian. He struck me as a civilian. That was my immediate impression when he stepped off the train and walked towards me. He was younger than me, smaller and with a lazy stride. His clothes weren't proud. They looked as if he had

281

simply picked up the first things that came to hand: a houndstooth sports jacket and olive fatigue pants. Not right. Not right at all for the occasion. Either he was so naïve he didn't realise what he was getting himself into or he just didn't care a damn about his own safety or what people thought. I didn't know for sure. Later Manny said to me, "The kid's gone into the lions' den. Mark my words we'll be picking up the bones." I understood what he meant because nobody had said, "Take him back or see him on the train." In the event, he came on his own and he left on his own. Just opened the door and strolled down the road.'

'Did he say anything to you?'

'He chattered away in the car on the way up. I didn't pay him much mind. You see, I had him down as a lightweight. Manny said a few things. Manny was like that, an affable fellow, especially after he'd had a few drinks. When we got to the house and he was in the parleying, well I wasn't there most of the time.'

Tears came unbidden to Agnes's eyes. 'Did you ever see him again?'

'Last night was the first time. I hadn't thought much about Veldar. This is near enough to Polygon and where you want to go.'

Emmet's banal phrase cut through Agnes's remaining defences. No, she did not want to go. She did not want to be here, sitting beside him, asking him, of all people, what he thought of her father. Why try to drag a ghost from obscurity even if he were still alive? Why not ditch Emmet here and at the same time Emily Brown? There had to be a train or a coach, if not a taxi, back the city centre. Within the day, she could be gone, pick up a flight and ask her mother's forgiveness later.

They stopped in a parking lot. 'It's quicker on foot from here,' Emmet said. 'Most of Panalquin is pedestrianised.'

Agnes got out. The chill of the now rising wind made her cheekbones ache. Through bleary eyes, she saw they were high up on the exposed flank of a hillside. Over the crumbling stone balustrade in front of her, she made out a jumble of low-rise buildings descending to the bottom in the dispersing mist. Emmet strode out ahead, making for an opening which presumably led to the way down. Leave at once in the opposite direction or follow him and then go after the visit? Agnes remained undecided.

'The funicular's coming.' Emmet turned and, seeing her still standing near the car, called out, 'We don't have to go if you've changed your mind. We can drive straight to Alakhin's.' He moved back towards her. 'I knew I was taking a risk telling you what I used to do. You decide.'

'And your wife, what does she decide? How does she manage to stay with someone who does what you do? At least, whatever my father did he cut himself off from my mother and me beforehand.'

Emmet stood where he was. Her shoulders twitched and her face convulsed in a spasm of grief. 'My wife's changed,' he said softly, 'but she's never denied the thing we had, the thing I believe we have, the thing I hope we always will have. Your daddy wanted to make a killing, wanted to sell his soul maybe. I don't know exactly, but he was only playing at it. He didn't fool anybody who was in the life. Like I said, he was a civilian.'

Agnes watched his lips move. Some of his words escaped her because of the wind. Overtaken by anger, by the need to strike out at him, to beat at him with her fists, anything to dent his infuriating composure, she strode towards him. 'I don't want to live the hurt,' she blurted out. 'Since I've been here all I've done is magnify the hurt.'

'Life isn't good, Agnes Emily.'

The straggling drift of the mist bore a smell she only now realised, a strange smell. Her breath rose in shorter inhalations. She was up close to him, but unlike him she found she could not hit out so easily. Footsteps made her pause. A woman holding a child by the hand came through the opening and walked past them. 'The funicular's arrived,' Emmet said. 'Seventy Westgate wasn't it?'

They were the only passengers in the old-fashioned wooden cabin. Sweet wrappers and rounds of orange peel littered the floor.

Emmet positioned himself midway along the semicircular bench by the windows. Agnes sat opposite. 'I imagined something more up to date,' she said.

'It's deceptive. They're new, but they're designed old.'

A bell trilled twice. The doors came to. The cabin smoothly began its downward journey.

'You must know Alakhin as well,' Agnes said, looking over Emmet's shoulder at the scar of ochre earth, running like a faltering ribbon between the frosted humps of grass and tangled bramble bushes which separated one building lot from another. 'As an adversary, I mean.'

'We've never met. He was an established sideshow for a while, sounding off about his grasp of the criminal mind on TV shows and in newspaper articles. Then he retired and all sorts of crazy rumours followed. Give this place a name, even a name from the past like Alakhin's, and it spews out a hundred fantasists, networks of interpreters, droves of witnesses, all of whom claim chance encounters and first-hand knowledge of someone they've never met. Alakhin had gone blind. He was a recluse, a prisoner in his own house, drinking his own recycled piss. He frequented fortune-tellers. He was deranged and confined in a mental institution. He secretly owned a chain of massage parlours. Somebody saw him working in a petrol station mini-mart; another was served by him at the bar in the ferry terminus. You listen. They'll peddle it.'

The cabin glided alongside a narrow platform. Emmet stopped speaking, got up and moved to the door. Agnes followed him out a stride behind. On the other side of the exit, she caught up with him, and they walked along together down the curved slope of a deserted street lined by white two-storey houses, their scallop-shaped overhanging eaves lowering over doorways reached by three identical steps. Alternating green and brown shutters protected their ground-floor windows. Some were open, others still closed. Behind the panes of one of the open ones, Agnes noted a slumbering tortoiseshell cat, its body stretched between

284

a bowl of hyacinths and a pair of orange rubber gloves. Farther on, a front door was ajar, but there was neither sight nor sound of the inhabitants. The only sound to be heard was that of their own footsteps. Emmet, for the moment, appeared lost in thought as though he felt he had said too much and was regretting it. 'A place to come and die,' he had said to her, and looking round she could sense it was true. There was, in spite of the obvious newness of the surroundings, a curious tinge of incipient decay.

They rounded the curve. The street changed its name, but the houses remained similar. The angry gnat's whine of a moped from somewhere unseen began to torture the silence.

'Nothing's straight here,' Emmet said. 'One loop leads into another, crescent after crescent. All uniform buildings in four designs. A separate design for each four geographical divisions. Polygon's a white thing, man. It thinks it's Switzerland.'

Agnes was amused. Back home, how often had she been told such and such was a black thing? 'You've been there, I take it.'

'Nah. It's all mountains and skis and chocolate shit. You do it for me. I pass.'

'Just give a little yodel.'

'Yeah, sound it for me.'

The whine of the moped climbed into a strangulated throttle as it finally emerged into view and hurtled towards them. Emmet moved to his right, Agnes to her left. The driver, a youth in a metallic-blue helmet, yanked up the front wheel then lowered it, hunching down behind the fork of the handlebars.

Why had she said it? The two of them were hardly Pinocchio and Jiminy Cricket setting out on the road of life. Besides, she had always hated the movie. Emmet had done bad things and no doubt would do more, but after all he had said he would look out for her, and there were places she might have to go, places to which he might have the key as well as the knowledge of their unspoken rules.

'Westgate's somewhere round here. It's the only gate they

have. No East, North or South, only West. I'd ask a citizen if one was about.'

'Where is everybody apart from the kid on the bike?'

'Commuted or immured. They don't even twitch the curtains. Time to try that yodel.'

Agnes laughed. 'Eedeel-yel-eee-tee!' She broke off in a giggle. 'It's not my speciality.'

Unlike the Alps of Switzerland, the houses of Polygon did not provide an echo. Their walls snuffed out her brief and shrill cry. The street and its similar predecessor might as well have been elaborate *trompe l'oeils*, false perspectives of a model village designed for a redundant exhibition rather than the homes of living people.

'Here it is,' Emmet said, after they had rounded another curve. He pointed to an archway through which Agnes made out a cobbled court flanked by pollarded lime trees with iron railings ringing their trunks. 'Westgate.'

A second archway at the far end ceded into a mirror image of the court they had already crossed. Seventy was the tenth building on their right. They ascended the three steps to the front door.

'Strange place to have a business,' Emmet said.

'The Cresci Foundation.' Agnes pressed the intercom button. 'I'm not sure they are a business.' She pressed again. The designation below read 'Ronnie Khan, Ceramics'. She was about to try it when she heard a crackle followed by a woman's voice, 'Amadeo Cresci Foundation. I regret we do not deal with the public directly. If you are interested in our work please give your name and address. We will mail you information. Thank you for your introductory contact.'

'It's Emily Brown here. I'm sure you'll want to see me.'

There was a pause while the intercom sighed with the invisible answerer's breath then the voice spoke again, 'Come up, Emily. I'm on the first floor. Are you alone?'

'No, I've someone with me.'

'I would prefer to see just you. Tell them to wait outside.'

'That's not acceptable. Take it or leave it.'

The door catch was released. The intercom went dead.

'Want me to go with you?' Emmet said.

Agnes nodded. They entered a spacious hallway. A bicycle rested against the far wall. Three closed doors presumably contained the premises of Ronnie Khan, Ceramics. An uncarpeted staircase rose to the floor above. On the left of the landing, a light shone through the frosted glass pane of a door. Agnes turned the handle. Emmet followed behind.

An oblong room devoid of usual office furniture confronted them. A dark-haired woman, whom Agnes guessed was in her early to mid-twenties, stood facing them with her back to the window. Apart from her, the only contents were a canvas-backed film director's chair, a water cooler on a stand and a telephone lying on the biscuit-brown linoleum.

'I've been expecting you, Emily,' the woman said, staying where she was, 'though originally I had hoped we would not have had to meet. I'm Elizabeth Kerry. And your friend is?' She looked enquiringly at Emmet.

'Emmet Briggs.'

'I have seen you before, Mr Briggs, yesterday lunchtime at Da Giovanni. In fact, I may well have chatted to your wife. She was sitting beside you at your table. Our paths crossed in the ladies, and in a roundabout way we discussed you, Emily.'

'Why did you send me the supposed life of Fernando Cheto Simon?' Agnes's blunt question cut through the stilted politeness Elizabeth Kerry was showing to Emmet. 'How do you know who I am and where I'm staying?'

'Supposed life, is that what you think? I can assure you all the material has been scrupulously researched and verified. Surely you must have recognised the authentic,' she paused, choosing her words carefully, 'aroma of your father's origins and childhood. As to your second question, Chance Company's approach to you and the fact of you settling here in Greenlea are largely because of my instigations. I have an ally in their camp. Someone who, out of

287

regard for me, is committed to our cause.'

Agnes felt her bearings shift and tilt. The existing unreality of being Emily Brown was now sliding away in an unexpected direction. Either the woman in front of her, in this strangely bare room, was suffering from delusions or else she was merely stating what had actually taken place. The truth was difficult to judge. She glanced at Emmet for possible clarification, but he simply shrugged and said, 'I'm not in on this. I was hired by Chance Company to accompany you. That's all I know.'

'All I want to do is to find the man we are both searching for,' Elizabeth Kerry continued. 'The rest of my campaign, this Cresci Foundation, is only an irritant, an occasional mosquito bite that sometimes punctures the closed memory of those who destroyed and then forgot Amadeo Cresci and Fernando Cheto Simon. I am not naïve enough to think it does them lasting harm, but why do you look at me so guardedly, Emily? Do you not see? Do you not feel we are more than allies? We share more than a common cause.'

Emmet strolled to the cooler, detached a plastic cup and filled it with water. 'I'll be outside,' he said. 'Call if you need me.'

'Yours in sisterhood,' Agnes muttered as much to herself as to the woman facing her.

Elizabeth Kerry smiled. 'If you like. We are, we can be sisters, Agnes. You see I know your name. We share a father. You know him as René Darshel. I know him as Joe May.'

'While all the time he was really Fernando Cheto Simon.'

'A name he left behind when he came to America. Remember, our grandfather, Batiste, was a Mirandan CP member. His way in was to become M. Darshel's deceased son who died shortly after birth.'

'But how and why Joe May?'

'That is where my story begins, Agnes. Firstly, let me confess that Elizabeth Kerry is only a pseudonym, my mirror image of your Emily Brown and the rest of Chance Company's identities for hire. My given name is Evangeline Simpson. I bear, for my sins, exactly the same name as my mother. Imagine what a bequest that is to give a child. Is it any wonder I prefer to call myself something else? Why not sit down? The chair is comfortable enough. I will explain. Your Mr Briggs will wait, that is what he is paid to do.'

'No thanks. I'd sooner stand.'

'Do what you like.' A peremptory tone crept into the newly revealed Evangeline Simpson's voice. She stooped and picked up the telephone, seemingly on the point of prodding numbers with her outstretched index finger when she abruptly returned it to its rest. 'My mother, Joe May and a man called Selly Rycart founded Chance Company,' she declared, looking beyond Agnes to the outline of Emmet's shadow caught in the glass pane of the door. 'It got going in the early sixties. Joe was the ideas guy. Mother and Selly had contacts. Mother knew influential people and Selly was established in the business loop. He and Joe met by accident in New York City. Selly introduced him to my mother and that was that. They became lovers after a little time. For both of them it was their grand amour. Then I was born.' A wince of pain distorted her mouth. She paced slowly along the window to the corner of the room and back again.

'Tell me whatever it is that's troubling you. You say you think of me as a sister.'

'My mother had other lovers.' Evangeline stopped her patrol and looked at her visitor with a sardonic half smile. 'Oh, not only the casual sex of the times, but other persistent relationships. One of them was off and on with Selly Rycart, and in that lies another version concerning me.' She paused, took a steadying breath then continued, 'Rycart always maintained Joe May was nothing but a fiction, that in effect he was the first Chance Company prototype, File Zero, in a manner of speaking, a mythical founder invented by himself and my mother. They picked an obscure musician Rycart had come across at an East Village gig to flesh out their scenario in a series of staged tableaux photographs. When their myth-making had served its purpose and Chance Company had progressed to an expansion strategy, they closed the file. Joe May died a convenient death. Worse than this denial of Joe May's genius was what followed. I was eleven years old. I was home from school in our duplex on Third Avenue. Mother was out somewhere. Selly Rycart came. He confessed to me.' Evangeline stopped. She raised her hands up to her chin as if she wanted to wave away an image which tormented her. 'He confessed to me he was my father.'

Overcoming the tangle of her own emotions, Agnes said softly, 'I'm listening. Please go on.'

Evangeline sat down in the director's chair, drawing her knees together. 'Mother would never tell me who my father was, though I pleaded and pleaded with her. "You've got me, darling," she insisted. "You don't need a father. You'll learn one day men are better kept out of the house." Then she laughed. Selly, of course, said he would always provide for me and cherish me in his heart. Frankly, I was appalled. I tried to run away. I hung out with other disturbed kids and fell in with the crazies I saw on the street, but there were always Mafia guys about and they kept bringing me home. "We's watching out," they told me. "No trouble in the neighbourhood." I kept acting up until mother finally split from Selly for good. After a time, she pulled out of Chance Company as well. Selly for his part went his own way. After that he seemed to forget about our existence. He never called or brought up the father thing again.'

'He's?'

'Dead.' Evangeline smiled. 'Unlike Joe May, he truly died. They cremated his mortal remains in upstate New York in September '78. My life's work was clear. I had to attack the Company and vindicate my father.'

'Suppose,' Agnes tried to put it as diplomatically as she could, 'Suppose . . . '

'Rycart was right.' The sentence was finished for her.

'I've found out Joe May, as you call him, was involved in some highly dubious business dealings here with known mobsters and criminals. It looks like he was trying to sell something which fell

290

through in the end.'

Evangeline shrugged. 'It is the Cresci story, too. Joe sold him a Florida franchise of Chance Company's operation. They busted Cresci. The Company's lawyers wore him down in court and drove him to suicide. They played the Joe May death card. No, it is simple, Agnes. Leaving my feelings aside, I made a choice, a very conscious choice. Joe May is my father, not Selly Rycart. I am totally on his side, Agnes, as I trust you are. The day is near when we can be reunited. Alakhin knows he is here in Greenlea. Wilson Loumans is an old friend of his. Add your presence, and I am convinced he will show himself out in the open. My planning is coming to fruition. Wait and see.'

'But aren't you afraid?'

'Why on earth should I be? Meeting him, being together with him is what I dream about.'

Agnes lowered her voice. 'He could turn out,' she paused. 'He could tell you he wasn't your father.'

Evangeline got to her feet. Her voice rose, 'I told you my decision. Now you must choose to accept me as your sister or not.'

'That's meaningless. I loved my mother. René Darshel abandoned us. My only reason to see him is to bring him to account for that act. His other incarnations don't concern me. You though, it strikes me, hate your mother so you created a . . . ' Agnes searched for the word, 'a hagiography of someone who might or might not be your father. Someone who, as far as I am concerned, does not deserve your adulation.'

The doorknob turned. Emmet re-entered the room. 'We need to get going. We're falling behind schedule,' he said to Agnes.

'Ms Brown was leaving,' Evangeline said coldly. 'I have work to do.'

'Yes. There's nothing for me here. Some things you can't make choices about.'

Evangeline crossed to the phone and picked it up. She fingered the digits. 'Wherever you go I will follow,' she said. 'This is only the beginning, Emily Brown.'

Without looking back, Agnes went through the doorway. She and Emmet had gained the top of the stairs when they heard a voice distinctly enunciate, 'This is Elizabeth Kerry on behalf of . . . '

———

My second day, Sonny thought, as he at last managed to extricate himself from the resistant block and jostling push of the crowd in Constitution Square. My second day of supposed new life, yet, instead of achieving a clean break and being nothing more than a reflecting consciousness of the presence and now of Greenlea, here I am caught up in my habitual tics of memory, finding fugitive traces of those I've known in the random faces of those about me. It is impossible to avoid seeing and being seen, but why is it so hard to wear a neutral gaze free from interpretation and introspection?

An unexpected image of Tian's strong and supple hands insistently pulling out specimen trays of pinned down butterflies drifted from somewhere into his mind. Christ! he thought. I only have to think about memory and another one surfaces right away.

They had been together, for some reason that now escaped him, on the top floor of the Orias Natural History Museum, killing the residue of a typically unhappy afternoon. 'Look! Look at these!' Tian had kept saying—a command which he had obeyed with bad grace; surly to the last, grudgingly giving each subsequent variety his half-bored, half-repelled attention. 'Look at them! Bloody hell! Can't you see their beauty?' Sonny impatiently snuffed out the rest of the scene, and, without waiting for the WALK NOW signal, dodged through the traffic onto the pavement by the estuary wall.

Yesterday's trip to Panalquin had not helped. Elizabeth Kerry's message had turned out to be a blind alley. The reality of Old Station Yard had not fitted into what he had imagined he would discover, and on the way there his new future had slid treacherously back once more into the past. His memory of Batiste Cheto had arisen from the waters of the estuary and crept into the fug of the saloon and the hands of the card players, a forgotten and repressed name released by their gestures and the pieces of paper he carried. Cheto. Fernando Cheto Simon. Agnes Darshel, masquerading as Emily Brown, had later uttered that very name, pronouncing the maternal surname, Simon, American style with the accent on the 'i' and revealing, at the same time, two things unknown to him: her Chance Company identity and his mother's erstwhile letters to Batiste's mystery girl, the mother of his son, who lived in Llomera.

Below him, on the exposed ridge of the foreshore, he watched a hooded figure skim a metal detector over the washed-up debris left by the previous high tide, his arm advancing inch by inch as he repeated his short exploratory sweep. How absurd it had been, Sonny now realised, to suppose he could move around the city and perceive it as it really was, that he could absorb its surface with fresh eyes and from that surface somehow pierce its shielded depths. Walking down Kefoin Street last night, which at the time had seemed to be without end, or forcing his way through the Constitution Square crowds before his ferry journey, or riding on several trams, he had, amid the intermittent siren calls of snatches of overheard conversations, tried assiduously to concentrate his gaze on details: the graffito lurking underneath an apartment number, a half-finished shop front sign, a vista of an entry passage suddenly revealed by a van moving off, the floral pattern of the russet carpet in the over-heated corridor of the Berengaria Hotel. At each instant, his goal had been to turn himself into a simple pair of eyes and ears attached to a disinterested head, being propelled by an anonymous body. Instead, he had ended up merely distracted. The streets he traversed, the buildings he stared at, the nooks and crannies he selected, even the composite cityscape itself, kept reminding him, through their similarities and differences, of the places he had formerly inhabited: Orias, Lyon, Yokohama. Everything he saw projected a crooked mirror, which unerringly reflected back his own refracted and ambiguous memories.

The sound of running feet pattering behind him broke his reverie. A second later, a jogger eased by, his shoulders rotating as he moved purposefully ahead. Sonny saw him reach the Port Steps and forge onwards without a sideways glance. Down there, out of sight in his sheltered enclave, he hoped he would find Jacob Kemmer hard at work—Jacob Kemmer who might hold the answer to the previous night's exhibition without exhibits.

His crouching figure, assorted chalks strewn in front of him, was indeed there when he came to descend the initial flight. Beyond Kemmer's outstretched hand, Sonny spotted a variety of scenes separated by jagged black boundaries in the manner of a stained-glass window.

'You've forsaken the ancients I see,' he said.

Jacob Kemmer leant back on his heels and turned his head. 'Mr,' he paused, 'Ayza,' he completed with satisfaction. 'A second visit so soon. This qualifies you as an interested spectator. With luck, I may come to count you as one of my regulars. Yes, as you rightly observe, I have temporarily abandoned the city's founding fathers for some of its enticing *fin de siècle* melodramas, all pictured here in their notorious crime settings.'

'Minus the corpses it seems. Reminiscent of the style of an exhibition with only blank walls.'

Jacob Kemmer looked up enquiringly. 'I'm afraid you've lost me. What do you mean?'

'Don't you remember? You gave me a card yesterday. You told me photographs of your work were on show. Admittedly, the venue had been changed, but when I got there I found nothing. Just people staring at an empty space. Concept had defeated content.'

Jacob shrugged. 'It's nothing to do with me. The images weren't under my control. Photographers and gallery owners play fast and loose, but I hope you didn't have a totally wasted journey.'

'No, as it turned out. I learned something, and after all I followed your direction.'

Ignoring Sonny's last veiled remark, Jacob stood up and, with an open gesture of his hands, invited, 'Please, look.'

Sonny obeyed. Nothing straightforward would come his way,

of that he was sure, yet he still sensed Kemmer was some kind of messenger who was taking a particular interest in him.

A grey rotunda, topped by a white dome in a fold of green parkland dotted with hollow oaks, occupied the bottom left of the composition. Across its thick black dividing line, a cupboard door stood partly ajar in a dilapidated kitchen. On a dark-blue wall by its side hung a row of bells. Gorse bushes, licked by fire, on a railway embankment straggled upwards, bisecting other blocked off segments, to a red-brick signal box, numbered 94, below which the tracks disappeared into a tunnel mouth. In the middle right, a man holding a raised lantern illuminated the floor of a stationary brougham where a bunch of white heather lay. The remainder of the piece was as yet unfinished.

Jacob provided a clipped explanation while Sonny took it in. 'Scene of a lovers' suicide pact. The girl died. The man survived and was charged with a conspiracy to murder. The cupboard in the kitchen of Dr Alsop's suburban villa where the poison was found. The bells used by Alsop and his mother to summon their two victims, illiterate servant girls, to the upper rooms. Police, alerted by the burning scrub, stumble on the beginning of "The Case of the Mistaken Signalman". The so-called hermaphrodite corpse discovered by Peeps Monaghan at Number 8, Little Chapel Yard. All of them assembled from the annals of crime, greed and folly, which titillated and fortified public opinion in the 1890s. From the heart of old Greenlea to its ever widening margins . . .'

The sound of approaching footsteps halted Jacob's commentary. He turned away from Sonny, who had been waiting for an opportunity to press him further on the events of the preceding evening.

'Mr Guthrie, it's a pleasure to see you again,' Jacob said warmly.

The newcomer, scarcely acknowledging the greeting, immediately thrust his hand deep in his coat pocket and pulled out his wallet. He separated a note between his fingers then propped it in Jacob's collection tin. 'Important things first,' he said. 'The niceties can look after themselves.'

Jacob gave a mock bow. 'You have the priorities as ever.'

This ostentatious display grated on Sonny. He felt it was a show of my generosity outweighs whatever it is you have managed to produce. Silently, he studied the features of the new arrival. He had a well-fed, rounded face whose jowls and incipient double chin were tending to fat. His head stayed lowered on Jacob's work preventing a clear view of his eyes until, suddenly aware of being scrutinised, whilst the pavement artist enumerated his historical sources, they flashed across to stare at their beholder. Some quirk in their set and the high bridge of the nose separating them struck Sonny as somehow vaguely familiar. At the back of his mind, he recognised a characteristic look he had come across before in a context he could not quite place.

'I am remiss. Forgive me,' Jacob said, seeing their mutual curiosity. 'I should have introduced my new spectator. Since yesterday he's begun to include me in his daily routine. Mr Ayza. Andrew Guthrie.'

His words and his accompanying smile, however, failed to elicit any sign of polite enquiry. Instead, Andrew Guthrie frowned and shifted his feet, as if he were on the point of going there and then. He directed a long, sardonic glance at Sonny and said, 'Carry on, Jacob, I was listening.'

Disconcerted and sensing the growing tension between the two men, Jacob hesitantly continued, 'Executions followed, of course. It was an unbreakable pattern. Murder committed. The guilty identified, then tried and condemned to death to great public approval. True, they no longer had a cart to follow with celebrations on the way, but the initiates still gathered in force outside the prison walls at dawn.'

Damn him, Sonny thought. I am not going to go just because he snubs me. He dropped the change he was carrying beside Guthrie's note. 'When you've finished,' he said, 'I'd like a word with you, Jacob.'

'You bear an unusual name. Unusual, that is, in Greenlea,'

Guthrie intervened. 'Your first name wouldn't happen to be Roberto by any chance?'

'It is.' Sonny nodded curtly.

'In that case and taking a guess about your age, well, I'd say you'd netted a connoisseur, Jacob. Perhaps even a competitor.'

Jacob looked blank. He turned to Sonny for help.

'Mr Ayza, if I've got it right, is quite the skilled draughtsman,' Guthrie continued. 'Sketches of his wormed their way into my early life. 48 Saint Roch, Llomera, to be precise.' He stared directly at Sonny. 'Old Paca Ceret at the dram shop used to talk about your father and mother. She was a fount of gossip. You have a sister, I believe.'

'Veronica,' Sonny replied, completely taken aback.

'So you two know each other,' Jacob said. 'It's true what they say about Aphrodite Park and the Port Steps. People are bound to meet up again at least once in a lifetime.'

'Oh, I doubt Mr Ayza was even aware of my existence,' Guthrie went on, 'but for some reason my mother kept some of his youthful drawings, and, God knows, my father was forever praising them. He was an admirer of yours, Roberto. Many a night, especially when he had been drinking, he'd make sure I knew how gifted, how intelligent you were. "That's a boy with a future," he'd say. "A real future for one of our own."'

'Who are you?' Sonny's muttered question faltered and almost died in the air between them.

Guthrie smiled sarcastically. 'Why, Andrew Guthrie, of course. I am a businessman here in Greenlea. In fact, probably like Jacob you're one of my customers. I own the controlling interest in Sunrise Tea & Coffee. Once, I came from another country as you did. I was a different person then, in the same way we were all different people before. There's nothing else to tell.'

'Then I'll rephrase my question, as you insist on being semantically correct. Who were you? Llomera is a very small place. If your parents knew me I must have heard of them.'

'Easy. My mother was Antonetta Simon. My father, Batiste Cheto.'

Sonny fell silent at the enormity of this simple statement. Yesterday's fabrication of the appearance, deeds and words of Batiste Cheto, an exile, an 'unwanted' in official Mirandan parlance, had translated into living flesh and blood a morning later. He felt as though he had accidentally stumbled across the key to the hidden treasure chest thrown away by Raul Sanchez in his old childhood adventure book. What other ghosts waited in the wings to manifest themselves? The man regarding him mockingly a few feet away, however, bore no resemblance he could see to Batiste. His hair was dark. His mouth was small and tight. He did not share Batiste's aquiline nose. He had to be more of a Simon than a Cheto. Antonetta Simon. Batiste's abandoned girlfriend? It was not a name he could immediately recall from his brief days in Llomera. Was he truly in the presence of Fernando Cheto Simon? 'How?' he said.

'You're not making sense.'

Jacob, satisfied that they both had paid and realising that they were involved in their own private conversation, resumed his chalking. Sonny distractedly looked over at his initial energetic marking before replying. If this was Fernando, should he mention Elizabeth Kerry's message, and what should he say, if anything, about Agnes Darshel's presence? 'I mean you talk of being a boy in Llomera, but your father couldn't have gone back. It would have been far too dangerous.'

'Twice. He went twice. He was a Cheto don't forget. The first time to see my mother and impregnate her. The second when I saw him with my own eyes, but that's all in the past. Now, we live in other times. It's been interesting to meet you, Roberto Ayza. I even believe it has done me good, for you can't imagine how I used to hate you. How much I wanted to see you crushed and destroyed by misfortune. Now here you are, and in the end I wish you no harm. I must go. I have business to attend to. Goodbye, Mr Ayza. Until the next time, Jacob.'

Kemmer waved his hand without rising. Andrew Guthrie walked to the first step then stopped, paused and came back close to Sonny. 'On reflection,' he said, 'come and see me at home tomorrow if you can. Make it morning, around ten. I live in Massard. Here's the address. We'll disinter the bones and give our upbringings a proper funeral. By the way, what line of work are you in?'

Sonny took the address card. 'I'll be there. Chance Company, I work for Chance Company.'

Andrew Guthrie had already reached the top of the steps. Sonny did not catch the baleful expression that crossed his face.

'Why stop here? We can't be far away surely.' Agnes watched with irritation as Emmet pulled off the road and drew up on the verge of a narrow track which led into the woods.

'I've got to relieve myself. Besides, I feel like stretching my legs. You should take the time to do the same. The lake's through there. Enjoy the view now the mist's gone.'

Still annoyed at the delay, Agnes waited until his retreating figure finally disappeared amongst a clump of silver birches before opening her door and stepping out. The now prevailing chill breeze flicked across her face making her eyes water. Hunching her shoulders against it, she plunged her hands as deep as they would go into the pockets of her coat and walked down the rutted track, avoiding the scatter of icy puddles slowly melting in the faint, intermittent sunlight. A civilian—that had been Emmet's judgement of her father. In the eyes of a professional criminal, René Darshel's transgressions—she refused to think in terms of his other names— had been simply those of an overly greedy Joe Schmoe. Was there any comfort in that? Had his actions been for anyone else apart from himself? And suppose he had pulled off the deal, whatever it was, was it possible he would have reappeared, gone back to Sula and herself, continued his music, forgotten life as Joe May? Or, there was a thought, gone back to being Fernando Cheto Simon. Either way, it had not happened. He had evaded again, presumably

299

into a new identity.

The sullen, grey waters of Lake Ambret were now clearly visible through the trees. The track petered out, giving way to squelchy ground and the low line of the foreshore. Emmet stood a short distance away, his eyes fixed on some indeterminate point on the lake's surface. His concentration was so intense it gave Agnes the feeling he had deliberately come here in order to stare at something whose significance was hidden from her. 'Let's go,' she called out. 'We're wasting time. You said you had to be back in Greenlea, and I must meet someone there after I see Alakhin.'

He did not budge. 'Go back. I'll be with you in a minute,' he shouted. 'We won't lose anything.'

Blast him, Agnes thought. He is here to help me and now he is trying to order me about. She stopped where she was, determined not to give him satisfaction. 'How big is the lake?' she asked. 'I can't see the other side from here.'

Emmet ignored her question. His gaze remained fixed over the water, then he shrugged and moved towards her. 'Not that big. Travel ten miles and you'd be round the other side. You haven't bought me, you know, nor has Chance Company.' He fell silent and looked away. 'I needed a few moments alone, that's all. There are things I need to sort out.'

The gentle change in his tone encouraged her to ask a more personal question, 'You still got a family, Emmet? I mean back where you originally came from.'

'Hallie's my family. I don't hold no other. Family's overrated. You share a name or blood, so what.'

'Share a name.' Agnes grimaced. 'That's my problem. My father seems to have donned them off the peg whenever the fancy took him, but then neither of us has a real name. Women always have men's surnames and, no doubt, yours belongs to some dead slave owner.'

'I don't let that shit get to me. It's not worth perplexing yourself with it. What we do is what we do.'

'You got a photo of your Hallie with you?'

'Sure. Want to see it?'

Agnes nodded. 'Please.'

He fished out his wallet and handed her a colour snapshot. 'It's from six years ago. We were at a reunion at the Blue Papaya. I got someone to take Hallie on her own.'

Agnes studied the middle-aged black woman in front of her. She was wearing a silver evening gown and sitting on a midnight-blue banquette. Her head was tilted forward, her lips slightly parted. Her expression was one of amused seductiveness, as if she were teasing the photographer to delay his shot for as long as possible. By her looks, she must have been quite something in her youth. 'She's beautiful.'

'It goes beyond. She's changed. Things change.' He put the photo back in his wallet. 'You wanted to go. Let's do it.'

'Yes. Alakhin will be waiting.'

They turned away from the shore and walked together towards the car. The sense of her aloneness printed itself on each of Agnes's successive steps. Emmet had Hallie. He belonged here. It was the part of the world he inhabited, whereas she had no one. She had only strangers telling her things about a man who was proving himself more of a stranger. A twinge of apprehension tensed her shoulders. What would Alakhin reveal? Steady, she told herself. I've been through worse. The face on the photograph she would pull out if someone asked her, as she had asked Emmet, was, as yet, unknown and unformed, but one day, one day it would be there. 'Keep her safe,' she said, more for her own benefit than his.

Once on the road again, Emmet put his foot down. The speedometer climbed to 80mph and held there on the long, straight stretch ahead. Glimpses of the lake flashed by between the thinning clumps of birch and elm. On the other side, ploughed fields were interrupted by unmade roads leading to corrugated-iron roofed sheds and open hay-filled barns. A large sign promised a soon to be developed haven of executive housing.

'It's around here somewhere,' Emmet said, after he overtook a furniture removal van and braked sharply into a series of S bends. 'He's sure picked an isolated hole to end his days. I'm told it's a renovated gamekeeper's cottage. If we see a garage I'll stop and ask.'

'There,' Agnes said a few minutes later, 'just up ahead. It looks like a store of some kind. I'll go in.'

Emmet flashed the indicator lights and drew up alongside the cluttered display window of Lakeside Chandlers & Mini-Mart. Agnes got out. She pushed then pulled the door open. A bell above her head announced her arrival.

Five minutes later she re-emerged, waving a sheet of paper. 'They drew me a little map,' she said, easing back in her seat. 'They didn't recognise the name of the house, but once I mentioned Alakhin they said, "Oh, the detective's. Sure." See, we're here and there it is. We go through the next hamlet on the side road to our left and then it's first right into the woods and first right again down a private road. They've never seen Alakhin, but evidently he's the subject of a lot of gossip.'

Emmet started the engine. 'No wonder I couldn't find it. It's in nowhere surrounded by nowhere. I'll bet you made their day.'

'Country ways, country time,' Agnes joked. 'My popping in was a mini-event in the mini-mart.'

Their new directions proved simple to follow. A straggle of three houses led into a narrow road bordered with plantations of young firs, which turned into another one enclosed by old woods of beech, elm and holly bushes. Beyond lines of stacked timber, they arrived at a sign marked Private Road.

'Jesus! It's mournful here,' Emmet exclaimed. 'With the rake-offs Alakhin got I sure would be somewhere else.' He slowed as they bridged a tiny stream. Their destination lay around the bend.

Agnes had already pictured a venerable stone cottage with a kitchen garden at the back and nearby a field with hens and a goat and a dog roaming about somewhere. Instead, a cream-coloured, pebble-dash bungalow sat in a small clearing. Parked in front, on a tarmacked semicircle, stood a battered Second World War jeep. Emmet stopped beside it.

Agnes climbed out the car and went up the four steps to the front door. Her finger was poised to press the bell, but before she could do so the door opened, revealing the figure of a tall, gaunt man. His eyes were puffy and bloodshot.

'Chief Superintendent Alakhin?' she enquired.

The man shook his head, keeping the door tight to his body, barring any sight of what lay within.

'I'm Emily Brown. I have an appointment.'

'Yes that is quite right. I'm Cameron Sinclair. The chief will be ready soon.' He stepped back to let Agnes pass. The odour of peppermint on his breath failed to mask the pervasive smell of whisky on his clothes. 'Perhaps your driver might like a sandwich and a coffee later. I could bring them out.'

'Mr Briggs is a friend of mine. He'll come in with me.'

'As you wish, Miss Brown. Just as you wish.' An ironic smile accompanied Sinclair's mock politeness. 'The chief and I are entirely at your service this morning, or what remains of it. Please come this way.'

Agnes and Emmet followed him through the hallway and down a passage where first he paused briefly to restore a walking stick to a more upright position in its stand and then to tap his knuckles against the glass of a barometer. 'In here,' he said, opening a door on his left.

The room was in total darkness. Sinclair moved across it and switched on two large table lamps. Heavy green curtains shrouded the window. The fierceness of the heating made Agnes gasp involuntarily. Sinclair smiled, 'The chief is old, Miss Brown. He needs the warmth and he no longer cares for the distraction of the outside world. Please sit down. No, not there, that's the chief's. He will be with you in a moment.'

'Veldar,' Emmet said, blocking Sinclair's way as he was about to leave. 'You and I will have a chat about Veldar later.'

Sinclair brushed the brown suede panel of his cardigan with the back of his fingers as if he were dislodging a fly which had inadvertently dared to invade his personal space. 'I'm sure I don't know what you are referring to, but really this is none of your business. No offence. Now, if you stand aside, I'll fetch the chief. He's had his nap. He took it early today. He doesn't sleep much at night nowadays. You'll find he is good about the past, Miss Brown. Very good, very sharp. The present, well, he endures it like all of us.' His mild gaze returned to Emmet who, with a glare, let him pass.

'What was that about? You know him?' Agnes asked.

'I heard about him. People like him take up too much space. It'd be better if it was freed up.'

'I don't think he's important. You're not going to get hung up on him are you?'

Emmet shook his head. 'Only a few words for my satisfaction.' He lowered himself beside her on the far end of the sofa. A clumping sound from the corridor, accompanied by Sinclair's voice, averted any further discussion of the matter.

The gleaming top of a completely bald head appeared in the doorway, followed by an upraised fleshy face presiding over a corpulent body which inched forward laboriously on two crutches. Alakhin's upper half was clothed in a voluminous striped red and black dashiki, his lower half in incongruous white duck trousers. His right eyelid drooped more than normal and, as the further consequence of a minor stroke, the corner of his mouth had taken a downward turn. Agnes rose to go over and help him to his chair.

'Please stay, Miss Brown.' He paused. 'I'll be with you in a twinkle, as Sinclair here would say. Though no doubt the picture of youth, and if I may say so such charming youth, helping crabbed old age would have greatly appealed to him. He takes a sentimental view. Perhaps you'd be so good as to bring us some refreshments, Cameron. A diversion or two. I can manage by myself from here.'

Half turns of his feet swivelling between his supports brought him across the floor to his chair into which, with Agnes looking on solicitously, he gradually lowered himself, resting his crutches beside him. 'I see you have a daughter's concern, Miss Brown,' he continued. 'I find that entirely fitting. Good day, Mr Briggs. My apologies for not greeting you immediately. I trust you are well and in good spirits. I know of you, of course. Your name was often mentioned to me in the past, but fate decreed we wouldn't meet until today. Now, I see you still go about in the world while I, well, you can see for yourself.' He broke off as Sinclair re-entered, carrying a wooden tray, which he laid on the low glass coffee table. It contained, to Agnes's surprise, a plate with three indisputable joints and a box of outsize matches. 'Now may God look kindly on our heedless pleasures and forgive me for the impropriety of mentioning his name,' Alakhin murmured. 'Leave us, Cameron. We can fend for ourselves from now on. Miss Brown, if you'd be so kind as to light one and pass it to me. Mr Briggs?'

'Not for me.'

Agnes put one of the spliffs gently in her mouth, lit it and passed it over. She then lit one for herself.

'What a treasure that man is,' Alakhin said when Sinclair had gone. 'How indefatigable. Once, under my command, he fled to pursue his own life, then four years ago he suddenly returned, determined to observe and note the last paltry scintilla of my impending demise.' He took as deep a drag as his lungs would allow. 'As you see, I'm truly blessed. A few grams of hashish. A shared silence with strangers. In the time I have left, time has lost its meaning for me, but my chronicler is at hand. He resides in the house.'

'I need to ask you some questions,' Agnes said. 'It's why I am here.'

'Go ahead. You have my attention,' Alakhin replied, 'but please also ask yourself why you have come and why someone like Mr Briggs is with you.'

'I'm not sure I follow you.'

'Mysteries and crimes, Miss Brown. The public prefers the former; Mr Briggs, no doubt, the latter. Did you arrive in Greenlea and decide to pay me a visit, a man you had never heard of? No. Someone directed you to me. Someone whose motives may not be the same as yours.'

'Chance Company directed me.'

'A large organisation. A convenient umbrella, which might well shelter an individual or individuals pursuing their own agenda. But please forgive me. I don't mean to interrogate you. Tell me why you have come and I'll help you if I can.'

'I'm looking for my father. Chance Company indicate he could be in Greenlea. I believe you may have information regarding his whereabouts.' She stopped. Alakhin took another drag and waited. Carefully controlling her voice, Agnes went on, 'His name is René Darshel. You may know him as Joe May or even Fernando Cheto Simon.'

'The sins of the fathers, how troubling they are! I knew the man you speak of. Indeed, we were partners in an enterprise briefly many years ago. Sunrise Tea & Coffee. You may have seen their stalls. They provided me with a convenient cover of listening posts through which to glean and sift the gossip of the city, its comings and goings. Information is all, Miss Brown. Detection counts for very little. Your father had money to invest, but our alliance was temporary. He departed. I never saw him again.'

'But you still receive information.'

Alakhin smiled. 'Look around you. You've formed an impression of how I exist. I see practically no one. Sinclair attends to all my needs. Apart from you, nobody calls. My police days are in the past.'

'But you heard what happened to him,' Agnes persisted.

Alakhin smiled 'We die, Miss Brown. It happens to all of us. Your father, like some others, used to try and resurrect himself in a new persona, but none of us can cheat time.'

'Are you saying he's dead?'

'I honestly don't know, but I will tell you what is dangerous.

It is the printed word. It's a mistake to write your memoirs. Oh, I know I am as guilty as anyone. I was tempted by the money, insignificant as it was. Your father, on the other hand, I believe has a sneaking love for notoriety. He resembles the arsonist who can't resist pretending he's an innocent spectator, while all the time he's inwardly proclaiming, "Can't you see. It's all my own work."'

Agnes thought of the manuscript of the life of Fernando Cheto Simon. Did it go on to detail the crimes Alakhin hinted about? She took two quick puffs then laid her joint back on the plate. Beside her, Emmet seemed closed within himself, showing no interest in their conversation. 'What was he like? Was he your friend?'

'No. I won't lie to you. He was not my friend.' Alakhin breathed out smoke. He reflected for a moment and then said, 'Once, when I was sixteen or seventeen, I did have a friend. His name was Taji Mohammed. We went to night school together where we studied Mechanics.

'It was our custom to while away many a late afternoon and early evening down by the port. We'd leave our bicycles at the foot of the outer mole, climb up and walk along its slender curve to the beacon at the end. There, outward bound ships passed close enough for us to see clearly the men on board, and we felt that one day we, ourselves, would be on that deck, looking back, as they did, at two figures standing by the light.

'At that time, my family expected me to become an engineer, a designer of press tools. You smile, but really it was my own idea, which my father encouraged. You see, in those days, sailors used to leave their magazines in the barber shop where he worked. The ones he thought suitable he brought home. So, whilst he learned to distinguish the latest Pontiac from the latest Chevrolet or Plymouth, I returned again and again to devour the contents of two—they were battered with several pages missing—copies of *Mechanics Illustrated*. My interest delighted him, for he wanted me to better myself and avoid following in his own haphazard footprints.

'Taji, though, came from quite a different background. His father had died when he was only three. His mother, in the circumstances, had gone back to her family home. When I met him, his uncles were well-to-do. They ran a furniture-making business, which had become increasingly profitable in the recent past, and they lived in two large houses in town, as well as sharing a villa at Majoul.

'Since Taji had always obstinately refused to learn cabinet-making or to have anything to do with the business, they had given him an ultimatum—study for a profession or get a diploma in something practical. As their previous loving indulgence now seemed at an end, Taji had listed the disciplines which required the shortest times to complete and, closing his eyes, had let the point of the pencil he was holding come to rest against Mechanics and Dynamics. Thus our meeting was decreed.

'His real love, however, was music, and as we chatted, looking over the confines of the harbour, about the girls we met or the women we had seen and desired, he would sing the faltering, broken lines of a ghazal or tap out on the stone parapet the pulse of a lament for long lost Al Andalus.

'One night, when we were filing out of class, he took me to one side and said, "Let's not come tomorrow. Put on your European suit, you've got one haven't you, and meet me outside the Ciné Raspail at eight."

'His invitation, as luck would have it, ensnared me in a string of subterfuges before I was able to leave our apartment the following evening without my mother seeing my unaccustomed mode of dress. All my precautions at concealment, however, proved in vain because no sooner had I reached the alley below than a swarm of neighbourhood kids surrounded me, plucking at my sleeves and jeering, *"Ouan beau!"* Their taunts and cries drew every curious eye to door and window, no doubt including hers, making any further explanation I had to offer doubly ridiculous.

'The evening was fine, I remember. As I walked, the walls of the town turned to ochre in the last rays of the sun. Pink surrendered to violet in the onrush of dusk to night. On the boulevards, the raw smells of gasoline and horse manure mingled with the scent of lemon trees. Starlings chattered incessantly above the revving engines and braking squeals of the traffic, and to my surprise and delight, on rounding the corner of Rue de la Grande Armée, an oriole flew off from a pile of abandoned packing cases. A light breeze fluttered the line of tickets in a lottery seller's outstretched hand as he paraded up and down in front of the Café Picpul, where French women held onto their hats when a sudden gust of wind ruffled and stretched the green and gold awning above the *terrasse*. Glancing down, I could see that my finely polished shoes of a quarter of an hour ago and my trouser bottoms were covered in fine dust. I stopped at the nearest bench and flicked off what I could with the edge of my handkerchief, feeling every eye was following my slightest move.

'Taji was already waiting when I got to the Ciné Raspail. He was dressed in a Prince Edward check suit with a fawn gabardine, which I found incongruous, draped over his arm. We embraced and, not for the first time, he kissed me full on the lips. He outlined his plan as we sat and ate an ice cream in Zaforiano's. Tomorrow was his eighteenth birthday. His uncles had already given him money, and, by the shape he made between his fingers and thumb, it was a sizeable amount. He proposed, therefore, that we celebrate the occasion by going to a brothel patronised by the French—not the very grandest, that would have been foolish and provocative—but a chic one which catered for lesser functionaries and, as he put it laughingly, "*Le doux papa de la table soigné.*" Needless to say, he would pay for everything.

'His idea intrigued me. I confess I felt a stirring in my genitals as he spoke, but the risks were high and the dangers of a beating or police arrest strong possibilities. Not even money can open certain doors.

'"Let's go where the sailors go," I counselled, but Taji was adamant.

"Aren't we at home?" he said. "Isn't this our city?"'

Emmet raised himself from the sofa. 'I'm going to have a word with Sinclair. Don't worry,' he said, noting Agnes's concerned look. 'I'll behave. Be back in a mo.'

'I could see how determined he was not to do anything for his own good,' Alakhin continued when the door closed. 'A light shone in his eyes and I realised he must have smoked some kif before our assignation. "Where will we find this brothel of yours?" I asked him, for although, like everyone else, I knew where the houses of *grand luxe et volupté*, frequented by court and government circles, I was ignorant of those discreet places visited only by foreigners.

'"Don't concern yourself," Taji said. "I already know of one."

'He then explained how he had followed certain men, whom he had singled out as likely clients over the last few weeks. One of them had turned out to possess a regular four o'clock habit between his sojourn at the café and his return to his agency. The brothel was on the second-floor right of an apartment building three streets away.

'"Didn't he spot you tailing him or hanging about?" I asked.

'Taji smiled and shook his head. "They look at us briefly," he said, "but they don't see us. One Arab face or another is of no importance."

'We left Zaforiano's. On the way, I tried to tell him about the oriole, but he wasn't interested. Out of curiosity, I asked him why he had brought a raincoat when the weather was set fair. "It's best to leave something" was his cryptic remark. I learned his reasoning was it would give them something to do when they opened the door. "Like a kind of cloakroom, you mean," I said. He nodded.

'By now, we were facing a six-storey building in a quiet side street. Wrought-iron balustrades protected its crescent-shaped balconies. A *Défense d'Afficher* inscription was painted in white at the height of a man's head to the right of the entrance. The front door itself was decorated with more wrought iron twisted into thin interlacing tendrils. The glass behind looked heavy and opaque.

'My heart began to thump erratically as Taji pulled the door open. I followed him into the darkened hallway. He groped along the surface of the wall until his hand found and depressed a button, which yielded us momentary light. My palms were clammy. My lips felt as though they were sealed together with gum. Treading as lightly as I could, my shoes still clumped against the floor then hammered on the polished wood of the stairs, sending their clatter to the uppermost part of the building. The light went out. I stood motionless, while Taji went back to the first-floor landing and pressed again.

'Our footsteps recommenced. Surely by now the whole place was at the ready. *"Défense d'Entrer Arabes!"* Taji began to sing loudly. If I remember rightly it was a little French love song then in vogue. *"Tu me plaîs et je te plaîs, pourquoi pas balader ensemble?"*

'I understood then that he thought his music would open up the brothel door and that the proffering of his coat would keep it open, and I realised exactly why he was my friend and that his courage and gaiety would sustain and nurture me as long as we were together.

'At that very moment, he turned to me and grinned. His finger hit the bell beside the supposed brothel door with one easy, confident jab. That's how I keep seeing him, at the beginning of that youthful spree, savouring the joy of expectation before the door opened to him, just as he hoped a woman's thighs would open for him and she would take his money like anyone else's and listen, perhaps with some pleasure, to his song as she washed.'

Alakhin paused. He stretched out his left hand as if he expected it to come into contact with something.

'What happened?' Agnes enquired, not sure whether to be relieved or not that there were no raised voices to be heard elsewhere in the bungalow.

At the sound of her words, Alakhin returned from wherever he had been and fixed her with his rheumy eyes. He gestured that the joint, which had almost slipped from his right hand, needed relighting. Agnes struck a match and leant over.

'You can imagine. It didn't end well. A man might shrug and turn away, saying there are other days and other people, things change, but in youth humiliations cut deep and for Taji it was worse because he had brought me there.

'The place was indeed a brothel. His detective work had borne fruit. A woman dressed in black, her blonde hair fixed in a chignon, her face—surprisingly without make-up—alabaster pale, as though her cheeks and forehead had never felt the sun, opened the door. From within, we could hear the strains of a foxtrot, played in strict tempo, coming from a radio or a gramophone, its syncopation accompanied by the murmur of voices above which a woman's rich laugh evoked the pleasures yet to come.

'The mouth before us, however, did not laugh. Its lips parted to show two even rows of white teeth between which its tongue started out in astonishment. Taji stammered something about money and could we come in. In an idiotic gesture he handed her his coat. There was a tiny instant of stasis before rage and hysterics distorted her features and convulsed her body. It was a second of fleeting calm during which, somewhat perversely, I found her one of the most desirable Europeans I had ever seen. She wasn't conventionally beautiful. Her body was stocky and wide-hipped and yet it made me want to preserve her image—an image to which I returned in my later masturbatory fantasies when I held her close to me, feeling her breath on my face, the texture of her nipples against my lips, the tip of my tongue on her pubic hair. Then the image was shattered and she was transformed into the vituperative bearer of hate and loathing, outraged that the other, the uninvited was here, daring to enter her territory.

'Others came out quickly at the sound of her screams. Two men hurled themselves on Taji and began beating him with their fists. He raised his arm. His coat, which was poised between himself and the woman, fell to the floor. I started pulling him away. A girl's voice yelled, "Get the police! Do the fuckers!" Despite my efforts, Taji was down. One of the men kicked him in the ribs. I didn't feel the other one's punches, though I saw them coming. The fear that more people in the building would rush out and overwhelm us gave me renewed strength. I managed to drag Taji back. By then, both men were breathing heavily. Slowly, they reverted to what they were—two French businessmen of a certain age and lack of fitness.

'A dark-haired woman came to the threshold. "He's got nice skin," she said, looking at Taji. "Let them go. We're wasting time."

'One of the men swore, but I could see for the moment it was over. A justified thrashing had been administered. Trouble among *les domestiques* had been put down *et voilà* the world was righted. Now, they could resume their interrupted dalliances and afterwards, at their club or in the corridors of the Stock Exchange, the shocking incident would make a salty interjection to leaven the boredom of exile.

'The pale woman with the blonde hair regained her composure. They all went back inside. The door closed. I helped Taji to his feet and supported him down the stairs. The light went out. He mumbled something to me, but his swollen lips made it unintelligible. We reached the hallway. Nothing in the building stirred. With my handkerchief, I wiped the blood away from his mouth and dabbed at a cut on his cheekbone. The light came on. Someone higher up began to descend. Taji gestured that he wanted his coat. Propping him against the wall, I hurriedly retraced my steps. His coat lay where it had been jettisoned. The brothel door was tightly shut. Footsteps sounded louder. I snatched up his coat and ran. Once at the bottom, I draped it round his shoulders. Swiftly, I guided him out to the safety of the street.

'Within minutes, a taxi dropped us off at the foot of the Medina. I extricated some of the notes from Taji's wad and paid the driver. Ibrahim, our night school friend from Rabat, let us into his rented room in Water Seller's Alley. He comforted Taji while I stripped more notes from the bundle.

'When I got back, I put the kif I'd bought in a bowl. Ibrahim attended to the first pipe. As neither he nor I were musical, he asked a girl downstairs if she would sing in the courtyard, and, after a second pipe, she did, not well but adequately.'

Alakhin shut his eyes. The heat of the room was beginning to make Agnes feel drowsy. The imagined cool of the courtyard beneath Ibrahim's room was an attractive alternative. She was about to get up and go to the loo for some water when Emmet opened the door and Sinclair entered, bearing a jug of mint tea and three glasses. Without speaking, Emmet resumed his seat on the sofa. Sinclair poured the tea and left.

'I was reading about a man called Taji Mohammed,' Agnes said. 'He was a musician in the court orchestra of Rabat. Maybe he was your friend?'

'What happened to him?' Alakhin watched them drink, ignoring his own glass.

'He committed suicide in Muret, a town in southern France.'

Alakhin laughed. 'Where did you read this?'

'In a manuscript about my father's early life. A woman who calls herself Elizabeth Kerry, but whose real name is Evangeline Simpson, gave it to me.'

'An impetuous young woman. She hasn't learned to live with her money.'

'She's rich?'

'Oh yes, but wealth derived from her mother's involvement with Chance Company, to her, is tainted. She's prey to all kinds of fads and obsessions.'

'If you'll forgive me for saying so, you don't seem very upset if it truly was your friend who committed suicide.'

'You're a bearer of bad tidings, Miss Brown. One should always laugh in their face. Now, as I have nothing further of use to say, I'd prefer if you both finished your tea and took your leave. Mr Briggs is a professional. He continues in the world, unlike me. You must take the consequences if you go on making him your companion. For my part, I hope your search does not succeed. Goodbye, Miss Brown. Mr Briggs.'

When they were outside in the welcome cold air on their way to the car, Agnes said, 'What was that all about with Sinclair?'

'I wanted to clear up something that happened in Veldar when he and Alakhin were there. It was nothing to do with your father.'

'And?'

'People lie, Agnes. People lie.'

The chair should have been empty. The screen on the fixture in front of it unutilised. Instead, while Harvard watched with growing distaste, Sonny Ayza sat hunched over the keyboard, busy with God knows what. The man was virtually irredeemable. Everyone else looked forward to their vacations, whereas here he was ignoring leave and now returning unbidden to work.

'A word in my office, please,' Harvard said. Other heads swivelled round and looked up as Sonny got to his feet. Could this be my second possible mistake? Harvard thought. First randomly picking Emmet Briggs to accompany Emily, then choosing a supposedly absent operator in charge of her file.

'What do you think you're doing? Didn't I make myself clear enough,' he said wearily, when they were both seated in his room, 'when we spoke last night? The boundaries are straightforward. Leave is leave. Work is work. This building and its resources are not an extension of your living room. I don't want to get heavy but as your boss you give me no choice. I'm ordering you home.'

'There's no problem, Harvard. I'll soon be off. I only dropped in for a little while. Something's been puzzling me and I wanted to sort it out for the company's sake.'

Before Harvard could reply, the telephone rang. He picked it up. 'Yes. I haven't forgotten. I'll be with you as scheduled. Goodbye.' He replaced the receiver. 'Sorry about that. I've got a meeting in a quarter of an hour. You were saying something about the company.'

'It concerns a recent client. I can't find out who authorised and set up the file, and nobody here seems to have a record. I was almost on the point of concluding she was the victim of a hoax but

315

for the fact that she told me she was installed in one of our flats in Tara Village.'

'She? What's this woman's name?'

'Emily Brown is the file allocation.'

'Means nothing to me. Aren't there the usual backup papers?'

'The original approach was made by the company in the States. A guy called Harry Fulton wrote to her. That's as far as I got. He, by the way, is not listed in our accreditations for the Eastern States.'

'So, you wanted to safeguard the company. Very commendable. I'll get Mary to dig around and cover the bases if necessary but as I said, Sonny, leave is leave. Staff relations and all that shit. But a hoax? You think somebody's trying to misuse our name?'

Sonny looked embarrassed. 'The truth is, Harvard. The other night, in here, there was a telephone call. You weren't on duty and as I was the only one around, I answered it. A woman called Elizabeth Kerry dictated a strange message. That's why I asked you about Amadeo Cresci. She said she was ringing on behalf of the Amadeo Cresci Foundation. She didn't mention your name so I thought if it was important and it was really you she wished to speak to, well, she would phone again.'

Harvard got up from his chair and stood for a moment gazing out of the window. 'How long have you been in Greenlea, Sonny?'

'Six years. You know that.'

'I liked it when my wife and I came here. Greenlea wasn't the most brilliant posting I could have hoped for, but the place held an individual allure. I used to enjoy getting lost in some of its old areas. Now it's much of a muchness like everywhere else. The company's right—we need an added inner frisson before we're stimulated by our surroundings.' He returned to his seat. 'I'm glad you told me about this. It's a private thing, but there's no harm in me telling you that this woman is a menace. She's been hounding my wife, who you know is not always in the best of health, and myself with crazy stuff about Cresci and others she claims were deliberately ruined by the company.' He sighed. 'Well, god knows we all run into sad cases and weirdos, and I guess you've had your share.' He glanced at his watch. 'Now I mustn't miss my meeting, and you really shouldn't be here. By the way, can you remember what it was she said?'

Sonny nodded. 'The strange thing is I found it's connected with the Emily Brown file I was telling you about. I ran into her last night, Emily Brown that is, and she asked me if I knew of a man called Fernando Cheto Simon. I said no, but his name was also mentioned by Elizabeth Kerry, and, you'll find this laughable, I actually met him this morning. His name these days is Andrew Guthrie and he claims he owns an interest in the Sunrise Tea & Coffee stalls.'

'Never heard of him. He's not one of our clients is he? No. Well, thanks again for telling me. If this woman keeps on pestering I may have to inform the police. Let me see you down part of the way. I've got a marketing pitch I need to sit in on.'

After they had said their ciaos and Sonny had promised not to come back to the building until his leave ended, Harvard looked in briefly on the publicity team then returned by lift to his own floor. In his office, he swallowed two indigestion tablets and waited for the acid burn to abate in his stomach before consulting the Greenlea and District telephone directory. Four Andrew Guthries were listed. None of them were likely to be the man he sought. He jotted down Sunrise's head office number and leant back in his chair. 'You'll find this laughable,' Sonny had said, but he was not laughing. Instead he was beginning to feel physically sick. Another story we tell ourselves, he thought wryly, but this one hopefully would never find its way onto a cassette tape. He still had time not to act. He could continue to let Evangeline make the running and watch *que sera sera* unfold.

His finger punched out the number. After all, it was not the final step. There were still plenty of details needed before his choice was irrevocable.

'Sunrise Tea & Coffee. How may I help you?'

'Jack Sherman here from Weintraub and Ellis. I've just arrived from New York on a flying visit. Would you put me through to Andrew Guthrie?'

'Mr Guthrie is not available, Mr Sherman. Could you tell me the nature of your business? I'm afraid we don't know Weintraub and Ellis.'

'We import and roast coffee beans. Andrew and I met in the States a couple of times. We have a new line of Costa Rican single estates I'm certain Andrew would be very interested in at the price I'd be able to offer. I'd call him at home, but it appears I've mislaid his number and I know he's ex-directory.'

'Sorry, I can't help you. May I suggest you contact Lisa Martin, our head buyer.'

'No, it's Andrew I need to talk to. Will he be in later today? Perhaps his secretary can help.'

'Putting you through.'

Harvard stared at the words he had quickly scrawled while Guthrie's secretary had politely corrected his stab at a previous address. She had shown no surprise at his tale of past encounters in the States. Guthrie, it seemed, was a constant traveller. The level of security at his house in Massard was someone else's problem. A recent photograph was, however, a direct necessity, either that or a verified sighting.

Choices within choices, he reflected. An emitted belch gave him some hope that his burning pain might relent. Crunch time was approaching. His feet were dangling in the Rubicon, its waters as icy as he had imagined. Leaking parts of Evangeline's grotesque manuscript, highlighting the passages she claimed to have heard from the oracle's mouth as an autobiography, then upping the ante by saying the Joe May revelations were due to appear, had progressed his strategy. His timing had been great. Important and influential people had long memories. These solutions were not entirely uncommon. After all, money could not solve everything. A long-standing nuisance finally removed and advancement switched to the fast track were mutual benefits.

He left the building. On the corner, he rang the Salonika Street number from a public phone. 'Get your operative to stand ready,' he told Walter, after he had supplied the name and address. 'Identification will follow. I'll see to it myself.'

'Tell me about Llomera.'

Sonny and Agnes walked together across the grassy bank that descended from the balustrade of the Belvedere to the road winding through the small wood below. The ground was lumpy and uneven. The earth beneath it hard. Street lamps came on in the now enveloping dusk, creating a bracelet of light around the park. Agnes stumbled slightly and leant against him for support.

'Are you cold?'

'Yes,' she replied, 'but there are worse things. Let's keep on walking.' She looked down at the trees ahead. 'As there's a Belvedere, presumably there's a famous view.'

'Over the estuary and the ships. You can see Panalquin, Massard, the upland beyond. As far as the hills round Veldar on a good day.'

She fell silent, as though she had forgotten her earlier injunction about Llomera, while they shifted leftwards in order to bypass a clump of whins. Knee-high mushroom-style lights at broken intervals on either side lit their progress when they gained the pathway. Up ahead, a small clearing was visible among the bushes and trees. Ivo and his companions would have been about here, Sonny reckoned, when they caught sight of the family group, which consisted of Monica Randell, her son and her husband. Of course, the whole thing might have been pure fiction. After all, Sylvia had described it as a story she had been told. In which case, the clearing existed alone.

'I was born in Llomera.'

'I know. At least, I figured out you might have been.'

'Why are you interested in it? It's a very small place. Not many people have heard of it, even inside Miranda.'

'Humour me, Roberto. Tell me about it and the people there.'

'It's in the east. Inland from the coastal plain among the mountains they call the Master's Domain. Llomera lies on one of the foothills. It's somewhere between a large village and a small town. I guess the population would be around three and a half thousand. We moved away during the war when I was still very young. I expect it's changed greatly.'

'You knew people though. Tell me about some of them.'

'Most would be dead. People of my generation would mostly have left to seek work. Some, no doubt, will still be there.' He refrained from telling her that most days he wandered its streets and talked to its inhabitants through the revivified image of his father. 'There was Paca Ceret. She used to keep one of the little wine shops where the men of the place congregated and played cards. They had a weekly market in the main square. The stallholders went to Paca's as well. In the old days, there was a nightwatchman who patrolled the streets ostensibly to keep the place quiet and do communal repairs. He was known as My Son by everyone because he called every man he knew My Son, and there was Tony Pigeon. Again that wasn't his real name. He worked on the roads when there was work. Sebastian Marva, my stepfather, you could say was Llomera's most famous son. He was a composer, one of the foremost in Miranda at one time. There wasn't much history about, but there were a few Romanesque chapels in the area and a meadow they called the heretics' field because Cathar shepherds from France had once grazed their flocks there. The war affected it, of course. Less than a lot of Miranda, but people were dragged into it, or in some cases threw themselves into it. No one escaped unscathed.'

'Batiste Cheto. Did you meet Batiste Cheto?'

Sonny looked at her. She walked at his side calmly taking in, like himself, the swirls of moths above the mushroom-stalk lights. They passed a couple of young lovers wrapped in a passionate embrace. 'From what my mother told me, I used to be his inseparable companion when I was little. I dogged his footsteps, by her account.

She said he took me places I shouldn't have gone to. He was a famous skirt-chaser and had a local reputation as a philanderer. He took me all over in his father's tractor or in a broken-down pick-up truck he used to drive. My mother claimed the reason he put up with my attention so much was because he hoped to use me as bait to get himself in the good books of his intended victims. We went on all sorts of jaunts to see the miller's wife at St Mateo and he let the girls at The Crystals in Ligac make a fuss of me. I met him again when I was older and we were living in Orias. Sebastian Marva was a professor there. Batiste's hair, which I had thought of as very blond, was darker then. He brought us some things from my father who had died in France near the end of the war.'

'Antonetta Simon. What about her?'

'Not a name I can recall from my childhood. I've no picture of her at all. Llomera, as I said, was a very brief episode for me. Most of my growing-up was done in Orias.'

Agnes stopped. Sonny stopped with her. 'Do you have family there, Roberto?'

'My sister and her husband and their three kids live there. My mother's in a home. She has Alzheimer's. My father, as I told you, died a long time ago. Sebastian Marva, too, is dead. He had a stroke and then a few years later a fatal heart attack. I haven't been back. Once I left Miranda, I left for good.'

'She was my grandmother. Batiste Cheto was, or is, my grandfather. Since my mother died this year I thought I was alone in the world. My father ran away from the two of us when I was a child. Now, I find I have relatives who I didn't know existed, and they come from a country I was barely aware of and places I'd never heard of. I've got to tell you they seem very foreign to me and I don't know how to feel or what to do about it. Do you have children?'

'No. I don't.'

She leant forward and touched his arm. He found and held her hand for a moment and then let it go. 'So, you, too, are part

Mirandan. Strange strangers. Foreign foreigners. Something we all are to others no matter where we are. Is this why you asked me about Fernando Cheto Simon? You had discovered he was your father before your mother died.'

'No, she didn't know. I only found out for sure today, and that's not all. My father has masqueraded in a series of different identities. You work for Chance Company. You knew him under the name of Joe May.'

The news Sonny had been on the point of tentatively divulging after some discreet questions stayed frozen in his gullet. He needed time to think. 'Why did you come to Greenlea, Agnes?'

'I promised my mother I'd find my father if he was alive. She seemed certain he was. In truth, I wanted to punish him if it was at all within my power. I've got more than I bargained for though.'

Sonny glanced at his watch. 'They lock the gates at five in winter. We need to leave. I'd like to talk to you again tomorrow if it's okay with you.'

Agnes nodded. 'Phone the flat in the morning. I'm going out tonight. You know, these drawings of yours, I keep sensing I saw them once before when my father was living in the house.'

'It's a habit of mine. I've done it ever since I first went to school. I used to practise them a lot. Whenever I got a spare moment and there was a piece of paper and a sharp pencil, that's what I'd do. They started without me really being aware of why I was doing it. Then I began to polish them up. I suppose they're a form of release.'

'Do you keep them?'

'No, that's not their purpose.'

They reached the gates. Agnes shook his hand then awkwardly kissed his cheek. 'I must learn to be more Mirandan,' she said. 'Thank you, you've helped.'

Sonny kissed her on both cheeks in return. They went their separate ways.

Sylvia's imagined face, trapped in the shuddering rectangle of the adjacent tram window, reflected back at him.

Begin with her face, Lucas told himself. Only hold on to her face then everything will come right and develop naturally. Sylvia was the embodiment of substance: a substance that could overcome his previous emptiness and fill and sustain his newly regained existence.

He found it easy to visualise her face. It floated unhindered wherever he looked. It seemed as though Greenlea itself was becoming impregnated with her features. Her eyes stared down towards him from each billboard they passed. Her mouth opened wide and inviting at each entrance, beneath the sequential concrete bridges, while her presence haunted the flyovers above and infiltrated their one-way systems. At the street intersections and beyond the traffic lights, her lips parted to connect the city's flow with the intake and exhalation of her breath. She was visible everywhere. Buildings were defined by the stamp of her lineaments. Vacant lots were transformed by her beauty. Under her benevolent gaze, Antoine Viall disappeared and Lucas Jones emerged reborn.

'Come to the Rag Market,' she had said, and now here he was on his way, earlier than she had expected. Her words, her affirmative, 'Yes I will see you,' formed a descant to the ubiquity of her features and his retrieval and acceptance of his true past. They were a welcome refrain, an easy burden, a thread, which was leading him note by note into an unforeseen future while simultaneously changing and remedying all his previous deeds of bad faith. Walter and Emmet Briggs were no longer of any importance. Sylvia's existence had cancelled them out. He felt so intoxicated with the prospect of meeting her, allied to his own newly found sense of being, that he decided to get off the tram and walk the rest of the way.

His knowledge of the city centre, apart from the immediate surroundings of Salonika Street and the Rag Market, was rudimentary. Walter and he had travelled everywhere else by car. The tram, he reckoned, had deposited him somewhere still to the north of his intended destination. As he walked, he searched the building walls for a street name but found none. Guessing which way was to the south, he continued following the tramlines to the nearest corner.

Through the door of a lit grocery store, he watched fascinated as Sylvia, her back towards him, reached over and picked an item from the topmost shelf. Farther along, beyond the narrow tiled entrance to a Turkish Baths, he imagined her rise resplendent from the water of its cold pool. Draping herself in a yellow towel, she greeted him, as she had already done that morning, with an eager embrace. He passed a cheap hotel, and looking upwards there she was, framed in the third-floor front bedroom window: the same kind of hotel where, after a single night, she had sat in her room, knowing that even its modest tariff was too great for her diminishing funds. Next door, above the Excelsior Cinema box office, the title of the now playing attraction *The Loves Of Martha Hanrahan* melted letter by letter into *The Loves Of Sylvia Manjon*.

The loves of Sylvia Manjon. Lucas had an uneasy feeling. The grocery store. The Turkish Baths. The cheap hotel room. Sunrise Tea & Coffee. A benefactor. Her words about him: 'His only reward.' He struggled to get the niggling possibility out of his mind. WENDE WILL BE FREE! The white painted slogan sprayed on the wall of H. Mavor & Sons Glove Manufacturers halted his speculation, but he failed to see Sylvia's hand anymore around the aerosol, nor did her image immediately materialise in the adjoining stationer's window. He turned the corner, looking for someone to ask for directions, and suddenly there she was, up ahead in front of two groups of pedestrians, her hair swinging in time to the rhythm of her shoulders, not as a figment of his wish fulfilment, but in the flesh with a green knapsack hanging down against her back. Exultantly, he quickened his pace and threaded his path between the men and women coming towards him. She was not alone when he managed to get a clear view. Andrew Guthrie, the man at the coffee stall, her benefactor, was walking and talking beside her.

The lobby of the Old Russia Hotel had seen better days. Sometime in the last decade someone had tried to bring it up to date, but with skewed results. Swirling patterns of declamatory oranges and equally strident blues made messy bedfellows on the walls and carpeting. High-backed tapestry-covered easy chairs appeared marooned in the large, unresolved space between the doors, the concierge desk and the stairs.

At the untended counter, Andrew Guthrie pressed the bell and waited impatiently until a pregnant brunette in a loose-fitting black and grey smock came out of her inner sanctuary. As soon as he asked for a room things moved quickly. She made out a bill for a one night stay and, with a cursory glance at Sylvia's knapsack, shuffled the key to room 234 across to him, putting his cash payment in the till drawer.

He let Sylvia stride on ahead up the stairs. The sight of her loping vigour and youth intimated the promise of a sustained erection. In the corridor, her buttocks jiggled in front of him under the thin covering of her black Chinese peasant-style slacks. When he joined her in front of their door and turned the key, her small, bra-less breasts stood out in relief against her gauzy top.

The room was like thousands of others he had been in, designed precisely to utilise the same restricted space and provide the same standard, uniform fittings. He switched on the light of the bathroom crammed in the corner and inspected the washbasin mirror, WC and half-sized bath with a showerhead above the taps. When he returned, Sylvia had emptied the contents of her knapsack on the table by the bed: a packet of condoms, a tube of KY jelly, a circle of black masking tape and a pair of nail scissors. She had divested her top and dropped it on the floor. Her breasts were bare with her nipples as yet not erect. She slipped off her slacks and her minimal panties, while he removed his jacket, shoes, socks and shirt. Waiting until he, too, was naked, she cut off a strip of tape and, stretching up on tiptoe to reach his mouth, affixed it firmly to his lips. 'Please keep it on,' she said.

The tape tasted strange. How long did she want him like this, unable to speak? He breathed through his nose. He tried to caress her, but she avoided his grasp. Moving back towards him, she suddenly reached down and cradled his balls in both her hands. His eyes glanced over to the condoms on the table, but she shook her head. She knelt before him, her lips parted as her fingers continued to massage and rub the base of his extended member. He stroked her scalp and kneaded the nape of her neck and shoulders when finally her mouth closed in its O of acceptance. A perfect O, but an O which did not move, did not exert any pressure. It simply enclosed that which it had within its circumference. By now her hands had abandoned their cargo. He propped himself gently within the space which he sensed by common consent he would only partially fill. Her eyes were open but abstracted, as though in a void, her lips had simply formed an O to let the stuff of the world, whatever it was, enter unhindered for a second. He came. She received then withdrew her mouth without swallowing. His semen flowed, moistening his still erect penis. Drops fell on the carpet. Sylvia rose and went into the bathroom. He heard her run the tap and spit into the sink. The sound of the water continued for a moment or two then she returned and lay down on the bed, her arms behind her head.

In turn, he washed and dried himself, fitting on one of the condoms. He wanted to speak but knew while they were together they would not do so.

Even though his tongue was a prisoner, he put his head down to her bush. She pushed it away and gently did the same when his fingers tried to find her clitoris. Raising her legs, she grasped the small of his back with her thighs and moved against him as he thrust inwards. No sound came from her mouth. There was no change in her all-seeing eyes. He understood then that she was not going to let him have any of her youth or beauty. She was going to deny him any opportunity of worshipping at her altar. This was only a transaction between them, but a fuck was a fuck and in the way of the world he was as willing a fucker as any.

'You must be hot in those stockings.' His father's hand had stayed on her slim, young leg a fraction longer than the conventions of hospitality allowed. Madame Morsom had audibly grumbled. Juliette had blushed then turned away. Batiste winked, a compliant wink, a wink of man to boy saying you desire her, but you see I can do this. Forgive you father for you have sinned.

He started to come. He raised his head away from hers. Still she made no sound. There was no possibility of recognition in her eyes. There was only her pelvis continuing to throb, only her receptive vagina wanting his cock, any cock perhaps that met with her choice. He withdrew and watched as she finished masturbating beside him, careless of his presence. Not even a tiny sigh escaped her lips at climax. Their eyes met again. She looked across the room to the chair where he had draped his trousers and for a moment her eyes held his fixedly until she inclined her head. In compliance, he got off the bed and unthreaded his belt, holding it coiled in front of him. Her eyes neither signalled yes nor no. Skirting the bed, he went into the bathroom, slipped off the used condom and dropped it in the bin. His reflection in the mirror held him trapped and pensive after the act. The stupid tape. He felt like ripping it off there and then, but whatever happened between them he knew he was committed to carry out her wishes to the end. Forgive her for she knows not what she does.

When he returned, Sylvia had rolled over on to her front. He climbed on the bed beside her. Tightening his grip and making sure the buckle of the belt was held in his palm, he rested it dangling gently against her cheek. Contrary to his expectations, she did not turn her head to kiss or caress it nor moisten it with her lips. He struck her lightly twice between her shoulder blades then moved it down to stroke her ribs. He had always adored the backs of women, the curve and hollow of their spines down to their waist and the jut of their buttocks. A hand always fitted there. His hand had rested there time after time before and after copulation. Suddenly in anger because of her relentless passivity, he slid his legs over the side of the bed and dragged her listless body across his. Her buttocks were apple-shaped. He hit their summit with the flat of his hand and struck again harder on their fullness. Her head was pressed against the sheet. She made no attempt to wriggle free. He realised whatever he did she was going to accept it. He felt for the belt and brought it down hard on her. She gave no sign of feeling any pain. Numbly, he knew he could thrash her until she cried for mercy or at least betrayed some sensation, but at the same time he knew he could not do it. The nearness of her sex had given him another erection.

He slid her off him and got out another condom. When he turned, she had not changed her position. He fitted on the condom, picked up the jelly, rubbed it over the sheath and gently massaging and moving the cheeks of her behind, pulled her into position and inserted his penis. Forgive me mother for I have sinned.

How he had wanted to overcome his timidity when Juliette opened the cupboard door and bent down in the enclosed space to search for the right bottle. How he had wanted to place, only to place, his hand on her thigh, to go no further because that was out of the question and beyond his boyish powers. Even without touching her, he had felt her heat, the overpowering warmth of her body. Then she had found the bottle, straightened up, turned to him and laughed, seeing his embarrassment as she looked pointedly and good-naturedly at his stiffening crotch. For we do these things. Thrust in. Thrust again. Had Taji Mohammed died in a room like this? No, not like this. His would have been an even simpler room with linoleum on the floor, a cheap cast-off wardrobe against the wall and a bed with a sagging mattress. He did not have a girl with him to fuck before he killed himself, not even one of the whores hanging about the Passage Ducasse. Not even his trombone was with him. It had stayed locked in its case where he had left it at the station. He, though, now had this beautiful young woman to fuck, to traduce, to defile, just as he had expectantly opened the case and wonderingly pressed his lips to the mouthpiece, letting his fingers play over the stops. The sound, the sound, the beautiful sound that you could make but never really hear for yourself, not even with the aid of heroin as others had told him. The sound that only your listeners could hear, and most of them did not truly listen. They were preoccupied with other things so the sound faded away and, though it might be reprised or re-made, it was never the same. The last time he had lain with Sula. The last time, without saying anything, he had left, and now this young woman's arse, whose every contour, every facet, he could say he saw and absorbed as it twitched and turned to the drive of his cock, yet was still unknown to him, beyond his powers of comprehension, just as Sula, himself and Sylvia here under him totally were.

Again he was done. He had signed the contract, as they used to say in Miranda. It was over. He withdrew and released her. At the same time, he tugged the tape away from his mouth, but he did not speak. His mouth held the taste of overripe figs. His lips exuded gunge.

Sylvia lay on her back, her eyes staring at the ceiling, showing no discomfort as if he had never beaten her. 'Wee wee,' she said in a forced childish tone then added, 'pee on me,' in Mirandan. He shook his head and went into the bathroom. She said it again when he came back.

He spoke for the first time. 'No. It's not possible.'

'You pee here.' She laid the tip of her index finger against each of her eyelids then closed her eyes. Wearily, he discarded the condom and raised his penis onto her forehead and trailed it down her nose. 'I can't.'

'Think of water. Think of a watering can sprinkling a rose bush. Its finest spray reaches the bloom.'

Forgive me mother for at heart I am a no good bum, a nomad, who until now has never unpacked his things, his gathered detritus of the world.

A dribble of urine lay on her left eyelid. A splatter fell on her cheek. He raised himself, his cock in his right hand. He aimed it over her face, against her neck, across her breasts, down to her navel and into her bush then over her legs, each foot and back, after anointing the sheet, to those eyes, which, although shut, would see more than his, long after his had ceased to see. Bless you daughter for yours is the kingdom of heaven. Now there's only the coda left, he thought.

Sylvia rose and went into the bathroom. Guthrie listened while he heard the shower beat against the enamel of the bath. The water would soon sluice away the traces of his urine. Its flow would restore her body, sluice by sluice, into whatever it was she planned for it this evening and night, whether to be with her lover or to be by herself, or to be once more with someone like him.

She re-emerged still naked with a towel in her hand. 'Dry me,' she said.

He was grateful for her words. He draped the towel over her shoulders and rubbed it gently against her skin. Her buttocks still bore the red marks he had given her. He knelt down and dried the fronts and backs of her legs. When he finished with her feet, he lifted his head to kiss her ankles and calves, but she forbade him. 'Don't kiss.' She leant down and took the towel from him, drying her breasts and her sex. When she finished, she moved across to her knapsack, took out her wallet, counted out some notes and left them on the table. 'For the room,' she said. 'I don't have enough for the service.'

He did not say anything, but he knew he would pick up the money. It had to be.

'Now I no longer owe you.'

'No. You don't owe me anything. What will become of you in the world?'

'I'm not your daughter. You don't have the right to be concerned about me. I expect I'll do well enough, to answer your question.'

'I think so too.'

'You did what you wanted. Nothing more.'

'More or less,' he agreed. 'Don't think badly of me.'

'I won't think of you, at all.'

She began to dress. He lay back on the bed and closed his eyes. For the first time, he would be the one to stay here and hear her close the door. He would wait in this room. Then, when she had left the hotel, he would get up, dress and turn off the light. Downstairs he would hand in the key and return the inquiring stare of the pregnant concierge. Strangely, for the first time in a long time, ever since his off and on sojourns in Greenlea, he felt almost positively happy. Wilson Loumans was in town. Tonight he could go and talk with Wilson. The obscure ties that bind, he thought. The chance encounters that in spite of ourselves determine our lives.

Across the street, from his vantage point in the window of the Hunan Long March restaurant, Lucas Jones watched Sylvia come out of the hotel. Stifling his desire to rush out and accost her, he gloomily stayed where he was and waited for her companion to catch her up. Nobody else appeared. Sylvia, without a backward glance, was already out of sight.

It was 3.57 p.m. At least three hours remained before their proposed evening meeting. Lucas finished his last acrid dumpling, as the menu translation described it, and called for the bill.

The Old Russia, from his observation, catered neither for tourists nor for business people. It had no doorman, and items of luggage did not feature with those who entered and exited. In spite of the two courses he had consumed, there was an empty feeling in the pit of his stomach. Reluctantly, he accepted Antoine Viall would have weathered the situation better than he could. Antoine would simply have shrugged his shoulders and set off in pursuit of another woman or would have ignored her dalliance, a favourite Viall word, in order to bed her again. After all, Sylvia had given him no promises. She was completely free to do as she wished, and it was not a case of her being coerced. Indeed, during the brief time of his following them, she had seemed to take the lead in choosing the venue for their . . . He left the word unresolved, trying to blot out any pictures of the room or their actions. What to do? Say nothing and meet her as planned or challenge her and risk their hopefully future relationship? The image of the couple on the bed when the trembling hands of the deliverer laid out the guns for Walter's and Emmet's inspection floated above his uncleared bowl and chopsticks. He relived Emmet's scornful look when he had spoken up and selected one for himself. But that was Antoine Viall who had intervened—Antoine Viall who had owned a gun in New York and who had visited places like the Bronx. The fact was, however, the gun was still in his flat. Walter was flying out tomorrow. He need never see Emmet again, and before he finally got rid of it, which he definitely intended to do, it might be put to some use. He smiled at the thought of what Emmet's reaction would be if he found out that it was he, Lucas Jones, who could use a gun as a persuader, who could effectively warn someone off, make sure they disappeared. It would only be a little warning. Nothing more than a bargaining chip that would tilt the balance back in his favour and at the same time maybe dent Emmet's complacent aura of superiority. Take care of what matters now, he thought. It still need not go further. When he comes out the important thing is I'll be waiting.

He pushed back his chair, rose from the table and left a tip. In his new-found certainty, he knew exactly what he was going to do. He was going to keep a close eye on Mr Guthrie, follow him home if possible and then, well, time would tell.

Emmet downed his whisky. The small brown jug of water Margie had placed on the table remained untouched beyond his glass.

'You're back to your usual I see,' she said as she brought over a double and watched him swallow a gulp undiluted.

'Water's fine in its place, but it wastes good spirit.' He set the tumbler down. He needed to take it steady. The days were long gone since booze was automatically free. The enervating heat in

Cheb Alakhin's hideaway hole and his fruitless conversation with Sinclair, who had denied all knowledge of Corinne's mother and had stuck to his tale of being mostly based in Greenlea when his boss was in Veldar, plus chasing Jacky Millom all over town, had tired him.

He had hit Jacky several times before he had handed him the automatic. The price he accepted was lower than what he would normally have demanded, but circumstances were different. The key thing was he had got rid of the gun and word to that effect would spread around. A safer, untraceable weapon was essential if he was going to carry out the final part of Walter's commission.

The phone on the corner of the bar counter rang. Margie let it ring while she finished serving a group of four customers, then she answered it. 'Emmet, are you here?' she called over with her hand clamped across the mouthpiece. He nodded.

Walter spoke fast when he picked it up.

'Slow down, brother! They haven't called the final boarding for your flight just yet.'

The irony of his use of brother seemed lost, however, because Walter continued to gabble in his ear.

'My memory's good. Don't worry about that. There won't be any trace now you've told me his name and where he lives.' This is the get out stakes for both of us, Emmet thought. He cannot wait to scurry back. Only now he's scared he won't be able to finesse the shit if things go wrong, and this is probably my last chance to win the fat city prize.

'I must have the key, Walter. No, I want you to listen, citizen. I need the key to the deposit locker otherwise it's no show, and you and your Old Man and his nameless friends can fuck yourselves.'

'You're asking the impossible, Emmet. It's not mine to give. It's beyond my control. Of course, I want you to have it, you know that. I want you to have the money, but his death must be verified first. Trust me, it will be settled. There's too much at stake to cut you out.'

The line went dead.

Emmet returned to his booth. There was no point in calling back. His call would not be answered. A visit he was certain, would only confirm hurriedly vacated premises. While Walter remained in Greenlea he had a chance of tracking him down, but it would take time and effort, and besides he believed Walter had told him the truth. The key was not in his possession. Someone else had it and knew the all-important location of the second half of his fee. Wait for further information, Walter had instructed, and wait was what he was going to do. It was something he was used to, even if now it was in the service of tourists.

Three whiskies later, a motorcycle courier dressed in a helmet and black leathers came into the now crowded room. After speaking to Margie, he approached Emmet's table. 'Mr Briggs?'

Emmet nodded.

The courier handed over an envelope. Emmet scrawled his signature and prised it open. The photograph inside showed two men standing side by side looking at what appeared to be chalked figures on a pavement. An inked arrow pointed to the man on the left. Emmet grunted to himself. Make the face leaner, take away a few pounds round the waist, and there was the likeness of Agnes's father, the man he had met off the train at Veldar.

'Why, it's Rose.'

The woman's voice surmounted the already animated conversation of her two companions. They and the new arrival formed a protracted knot of greeting which obliged Agnes to say excuse me and thread her way past their embraces.

She was lost: not disastrously so but enough to be uncertain about which direction to take. A plaque informed her that part of the Medical Faculty inhabited the building on her left. The Veterinarian Hall had to be somewhere close by in these grids of streets, which seemed mainly occupied by university departments. She looked round for someone to ask, but there was nobody. The women she had passed were nowhere to be seen. If she had thought, she could have asked them.

'Why, it's Agnes.' Who would say these words to her? Certainly not him, if she ever found him, no matter how much she might long for that spontaneous, casual, everyday recognition. No, instead, she would have to say them for him. 'It's Agnes.' This time she said it out loud. Like a cartoon character, she imagined the phrase solidifying within the bubble of her visible outflow of breath. Not yet thirty, she thought, and here I am speaking to myself in the street like some ranting, demented bag woman. This is what he is doing to me. The sooner I meet and challenge him, the sooner I can get out of this depressing place. 'Your daughter.' She might even have to add that explanation, for what had he retained through his transformations from Fernando to René to Joe to whoever he might dissimulate under today? Had he ever, apart from his biological connection, truly been her father? Would the outcome be any different if she simply arraigned the next male stranger she saw and vented her spleen on him? The man coming towards her now, for instance. In the street light, he looked too young to possibly be her father, but what did it really matter?

'Yes, it's just a block away. Turn right and right again. You can't miss it.'

She thanked him. Up until her mother's death, she had suited herself and it had suited her well enough. She had lived in the present and had looked forward to the future. The past had been none of her business. Then one day she had laid her hand on her mother's hand and had felt the burning of her skin and said, 'It's alright. It's Agnes.' But all too soon that skin was cold. Her mother stopped being with her on earth, and, as a consequence, the possible continuing existence of her father inexorably wormed its way back into her future.

She followed the directions she had been given, but on rounding the corner there was still no sight of the Veterinarian Hall. The street culminated in a T-shaped cul-de-sac. Before its containing wall, two alleyways led off it: one to the left, the other to the right. Both looked dismal and uninviting. Light shining from a coffee stall at the end of the one on the left drew Agnes towards it. As she approached, she recognised its striped awning as belonging to the Sunrise Tea & Coffee Company whose outlets she had seen in other parts of the city, though why people wanted to drink out in the open in winter was beyond her.

A man and a woman stood with their backs to the counter facing her. They were conversing in what sounded like Mirandan. She ordered a coffee and asked if the Hall was nearby. The attendant apologised and explained that this was her first stint at this particular location and she did not know the area well. 'It's just I feel I'm going round in circles and never getting there,' Agnes said. 'I'm beginning to wonder if the place really exists.'

'It exists all right,' the woman customer said. 'You've come the wrong way. Go back and at the top of the street turn left. It's on the right side. You won't miss it. Are you going to a film or a concert there?'

'A concert. Wilson Loumans, an American pianist, is playing there tonight.'

'Ah. I teach at the Music Conservatory just behind us here. I'm Monserrat Selle. Everyone calls me Monse. This is my husband, Albert.'

'Emily Brown.' Agnes put down her cup. They shook hands.

Albert smiled. 'A cock with two hens,' he said. 'Perhaps before dawn I'll have managed to round up some more.'

Monse dug him playfully in the ribs. 'Behave, my sweet. This macho preening never leaves them. Really, they're mummy's boys afraid to show how feminine they can be. Take no notice, Emily. Do you work in Greenlea or have you come specifically to hear Mr, what was his name?'

'Loumans. I'm on a visit, but my father once played with him and it's a coincidence not to be missed.'

'Your father's a musician, a famous one?' Albert asked.

Agnes shook her head. 'Famous no, but he used to play a lot

when I was young.'

'Ah, youth,' Albert murmured and added something in Mirandan.

'You're both Mirandan?'

'We are,' Monse said. 'Do you speak the language?'

'No.' Agnes paused. 'This may seem a strange question, but have you ever heard of a man called Fernando Cheto Simon? I'm sorry. It's a stupid idea.'

'Not at all,' replied Albert. 'Things collide. People bump into each other. Two days ago I would have said no to your question, but only the other night a friend of ours mentioned the same name. However, as we told him, we don't know the person.'

'And your friend who asked?'

'A fellow countryman—Sonny Ayza. Monse's known him since he was a youngster.'

'It's time we went,' Monse said. 'Nice meeting you, Emily.'

'Time we weren't here,' Albert added. 'Enjoy your concert.'

When they had gone, Agnes finished her coffee and retraced her steps. Something Alakhin had said, something about the possible danger of others finding her father as well as herself, slipped into her mind. Roberto Ayza had been busy making inquiries on his own account. Only today, she had begun to treat him as a friend. Was she right to do so or had he motives she had yet to understand? The answer still eluded her as, obeying Monse's instructions, she spotted a stream of people entering a glass doorway across the street.

She was late. She had arrived ten minutes after the concert was due to start. Directed by an usher, she shuffled past the knees of the already seated people to her place at F8. The auditorium was noisy. There was a chill in the air, making her wish she had not left her coat in the foyer cloakroom. On the raised platform in front of her, a Bosendorfer grand piano awaited Loumans. The green velvet curtains behind it betrayed no movement. Above her head, the ceiling receded into a stained glass cupola.

'O mortals listen here!' A deep male bass voice seemed to

337

emanate from the rear of the narrow hall. While heads turned towards it, the curtains parted and a slight stooped figure of a man in a long white tunic began to blow energetically into the open strings of the piano, alternating his breathing with downward jabs of the heel of his right hand. 'O mortals attend within. It is in the making numinous!' The voice spoke for a second time and then was silent. Loumans moved away from the piano strings and seated himself at the keyboard. For a moment, he appeared lost in contemplation, oblivious of his audience, then he tapped his foot and began to play an ever rising tumult of notes. Hunched over the keyboard, his absorption was total. Sweat glistened on his forehead as traces of melody emerged and disappeared amid the clusters of chords and extended runs of his right hand. Dissonances refused to be resolved as he introduced them over and over until they, too, subsided into short lyrical bursts which gave way to more sustained crescendos.

Agnes had literally heard nothing like it. Although her mind switched off from time to time, the fury of Loumans' attack and the coaxing tenderness he evoked, which occasionally seemed to plead for more space, drew her into the music to a degree that surprised her.

After about twenty minutes, he stopped briefly before continuing. A hesitant scatter of applause gathered momentum into a few shouts and whistles while some other members of the audience got up and left ostentatiously. The sound of their retreating feet and the slight creak of the door springs punctuated the opening calmer mood of his second piece. Agnes thought about her father playing with him. No doubt, the music was different then. 'I felt he was getting ready to leave the life. To tell the truth, his heart wasn't in it.' The words of the young drummer on the tape came back to her. Loumans, in contrast, was thoroughly committed. He was what he was doing. His concentration was total. His whole being was focused on the execution and realisation of his task. Variations of notes were pursued and pursued until, momentarily satisfied, he let them fade and the theme re-emerged. He lives for this expression, Agnes realised. In his case, the music was his name and identity.

After the concert was over and Loumans had not reappeared to play an encore, Agnes waited in her seat until her row was clear before venturing backstage. She was not sure whether her presence would be welcomed or her questions answered, but in the end she had no choice but to press forward. She, therefore, made her way to the foyer and, showing her pass, asked for the artists' room. The front of house attendant checked it then pointed to the flight of stairs which led to the basement. Agnes descended them and paused in front of the third door in the dimly lit passageway. She knocked twice. There was no answer. She knocked again. This time a youth opened the door. His body blocked her view of the interior, apart from the dark-blue patch of paint visible beyond his head.

'Emily Brown. I've an appointment to see Mr Loumans.'

'That's okay,' a voice said.

The youth stepped aside. Agnes went in. Loumans was seated on a disintegrating imitation leather sofa. He was naked from the waist up except for a white towel draped about his shoulders. A bottle of cognac and four plastic glasses were on a low table in front of him. 'Come in, Ms Brown,' he said. 'Fetch her a chair, Jimmy. This,' he pointed to the sofa, 'like me, has seen better days. Do you take alcohol?' Agnes nodded. 'Good.' He poured out a measure. 'I always did say I'd have a drink with Emily Brown one day. Lovable, huggable Emily Brown. Miss Brown to you,' he sang the last phrase. 'That's right, Jimmy, put it here. You can leave us now. We'll both be fine. No offence, Emily.' He waited until Agnes sat down and took a sip of her drink before asking, 'Are you a critic or a music lover stroke thesis researcher? I'm too old and last decade's thing to have groupies come and visit me.' He took a long pull at his glass and mopped his sweating brow with the towel. 'Seriously, nobody's called Emily Brown these days.'

'No, you're right. Emily Brown's not my real name. It's a dress, a suit I've been given. Bespoke or ready to wear, I'm not sure which. I'm Agnes Darshel. I was hoping,' she paused, 'hoping my father might be here. It's ridiculous,' she gave a nervous laugh, 'because to tell you the truth I don't know what I'd do if he were.'

'Upset yourself if it helps. I've got time enough, though you might not think it. But tell me where you acquired this name.'

His eyes were red-rimmed round their dark-brown irises. Agnes guessed he had probably been drinking before his performance as well. 'Chance Company. I've paid up for a fortnight.'

Loumans laughed. 'It goes round and nothing's private anymore. The hucksters get to know and, sure as shit follows sunrise, they sell it back to you. Well, Agnes, I once met a guy who called himself René Darshel. It's an unusual name, and you just could be connected. I also met him before when he was known as Ferdy Simon. Now, he used to talk about Emily Brown. It was a way of his. Instead of saying like everyone else he was slipping off to take care of business, he'd say he'd gotta git go. Emily Brown's train's due or Emily Brown's waiting on the corner so I can't be late, and you know what a stickler for punctuality she is. Then you wouldn't see him for a day or two or longer, but that wasn't unique. There's a lot of disappearers in life. The things of the world discourage them and sometimes obliterate them.'

'Did you like him?'

'Are we talking about your father?'

'Yes, I believe so. In fact I'm sure.'

'Then I'm glad you've come.' He replenished his glass and moved the bottle towards Agnes's. She placed her hand over it. He put the bottle down. 'There's people you don't hear about anymore. They don't get together like they used to. Nobody expects us to be home buddies and stick around the old neighbourhood, but once we were like family, all the musicians, and that's when I met your daddy. Yeah, I liked him alright. He was open to the new thing as some called it. He studied trombone with Mahlik Ali, a cat I'd known since high school in Pittsburgh. It would be in the winter of '59 or

'60 in New York City when we hung around. I used to needle him by saying he should stick to Mirandan music alone. You got those deep soul singers and mean guitarists I'd say; go mess with them. Well, he'd pretend to get fired up. "You've heard me sing," he'd say. "Am I playing the guitar like the kid from Whahawha?" Then he'd fit his mouthpiece and give me an imitation of the bullpen stare. We were both young.'

'I hear you recorded together.'

'Yes. As far as I recall, he was on a nonet date. Usual shit for the time. We'd rehearsed for about a month in an empty floor of a press tool plant on the Lower East Side. Frank Hayes, our altoist, got us a recording date with a new independent label. Then when we arrive the guy wants us to play standards, and he gives the thumbs down when he hears us take off. Frank got mad. He was a sweet guy normally, a family man, but he'd played gigs down home and been on the territory road so he knew how the mustard had to be cut. Anyway, he pulls a big, scary revolver out of his satchel and tells the producer guy, "We're gonna roll with or without you man. You dig?" Silence. It was silence like the mortician's waiting room. Willie Peabody, the bassist, I think it was Willie, says, "Sweet Jesus, baby, music sure does soothe the savage breast," and he starts up arco. Well, the upshot was we laid down seven cuts. We never were paid, but a record came out. Poor tonal quality, no publicity, the standard practice shit.'

'Do you have a copy?'

Loumans shook his head. 'No. I rarely listen to my own work. What's done is done. How much do you know of your father?'

Agnes told him what she had found out. He nodded here and there. 'When you're little, grown-ups are like giants,' she said. 'They loom over you. Their smell lingers in your room and pervades the whole house then they stride away from you as if they were wearing seven league boots. As you get older they shrink to manageable size. This happened with my mother, and finally when she was terminally ill I felt, as we probably all feel, that she had become the child and I had become the adult she looked up to, but with my father that couldn't happen. He had absented himself. He had chosen not to be with us. So you see, he's still a vague shape to me. In many ways, he's a figure of my imagination, an unknown kind of non-reality on which I can pin anything I wish. I promised my mother I would seek him out, and now, for my own sake, I need to see him in the flesh. I need to reduce him to human stature—back to someone I can choose to reject or embrace.'

Loumans smiled. 'It's tough to be human in this life. Some people don't even try. You say he might be here in Greenlea. Well, I don't know anything about that, but let me tell you about some of the things I do remember from the old days. Picture it. I guess it wasn't long after the record date I was speaking about, he's scrabbling around trying to pay the rent, like the rest of us, when he runs into this society lady who takes a shine to him. She'd seen him around the Village and up in Harlem. Funnily enough, God knew her as well. Let me explain. God was a young guy who roamed the streets and avenues of the district. You'd say hello God, and he'd say hello Wilson and you'd tell each other the news, but I digress. Anyhow, as well as the thing they locked on together, she introduced him to some of her business associates. Her name was some gospel number or other: Evangelina or Evangeline. Of course, at the time none of this amounted to a barrel of shit, but later I knew from your father it was really the minors debut of Chance Company. All sorts happened then in the early sixties, especially in New York City. Their particular angle was they thought business could be the new narrator of the times, the provider of manufactured illusions, and they figured if they invented a mythical founder he would lead them to the majors. You mentioned the name they dreamed up, Joe May, and with it they gave him tailored suits and money. Believe me, he lived in some high-style apartments when the owners, friends of theirs, were away. I've been in them. It's a view you don't get easily from the street. He was file zero, a kind of prototype. Their idea was for people to pay for an assumed identity for a fortnight or a month, and they would hire others to collude in the fantasy and charge them a percentage from the fee they paid them. As he outlined it to me, he was in on the deal, and they were going to market a franchise after they got it up and running. Then I split for the West Coast and didn't see him for a few years. I did okay in the studios, still playing the music around LA and in the Bay area. When I came back to New York, I asked God if he knew anything. He still talked to the gospel lady. In fact, she'd offered him a job, but he said, "You can't give God money. God's not for hire." Then one night after hours in a little town upstate, your father turned up again. "They're going to kill me off, Wilson," he said. "I got a tip-off. The easy life is on the slide." Well, it so happened a guy I knew from California, Liam Fitzhugh, had also come to catch my set. He and your father got yakking. I laid out for a while, but when I came back they were still at it. Later, when I was up in Seattle, Fitzhugh told me they had brokered a deal together through a Japanese gangster he knew and some European operator, who had been put forward by a local cop. According to him, your father met them, but something went wrong. I don't know what. That kind of shit is bad news, and the energy needed is misplaced.'

He stopped talking as the door opened. Agnes half turned, expecting to see that Jimmy, who had brought her chair, had returned. Instead, a middle-aged man stood in the doorway. 'Wilson,' he said.

Loumans got to his feet. After a moment's silence, he said, 'Oh, what spirit is conjured up!'

'Aren't you going to embrace me?' the man said.

Agnes felt her hand begin to tremble. She lowered her glass to the table, shifting her chair the better to see the newcomer straight on.

The two men enveloped each other in a bear hug. 'Baby,' Loumans said.

There was no doubt. Agnes felt none of the hesitation, the uncertainty, she thought she might have experienced during her protracted search. Loumans had taken a minute to recognise him. She had sensed his presence immediately as soon as she had turned her head to look.

'Sit down here beside me,' Loumans said. 'Have a drink.' He passed over the cognac bottle.

Agnes saw he was about to introduce her, but did not quite know how to go about it. 'Emily Brown,' she said. 'Mr Loumans was giving me a history lesson.'

The man stared at her without replying or touching his drink. She was aware how closely he was inspecting her from her hair down to her shoes.

Loumans polished off the brandy left in his glass and poured himself another. 'What should I call you, spirit from the depths, for I think you have journeyed here from the underworld?'

'What you've always called me, Fernando Simon.'

'Well then, Fernando Simon, tell me whether love is the answer as in the sublime music of Wolfgang Amadeus?'

'Yes, Wilson, love is the answer, but am I confronted with yourself and a Pamina or is this a joke you've cooked up between you?'

'No joke, Orfeo. No joke at all.'

'I've been reading your life, Mr Simon,' Agnes said, deciding she could no longer listen to their male banter, 'or, should I say, Fernando Cheto Simon, because one mustn't forget the Cheto part.'

'Who are you?' Fernando looked to Loumans for guidance. Wilson's eyes led him back to the fixed stare of the calm face opposite.

'It's Agnes. Agnes Darshel.'

'Did you know this?'

'She told me before you came in.' Loumans got up and put on an olive-green T-shirt he found on the floor behind the sofa. 'I'm tiring,' he said. 'Did you catch me tonight?'

'The last twenty minutes. It's you who should be Orfeo. You've kept the flame while I . . . ' His voice trailed off. 'What is it you want me to say, Agnes, for I believe it is truly you?'

'Nothing. There is nothing you can say to me. Did he ever talk about me, talk about his wife, during those wonderful times you were telling me about, Mr Loumans, when you discussed music and art and the birth of Chance Company and the squalid seizure of a life up for grabs? Did he never mention the cruel trick he had played when he came back to a house others thought was a home and from which he walked away without any explanation, without any warning, as if it and the people in it were not worthy of a backward glance? Oh, you see, Fernando Cheto Simon, I've become a great listener and an assiduous reader because of you. I know all about your life in Llomera and when you went to France with your father. I know how you fell in love with music and could have become a human being. I know about the man whose valve trombone you inherited and how you went to the States. I've seen huge photo portraits of you when yet again you weaselled yourself into a new persona. I've heard enough about your exploits from Mr Loumans here and a crazy woman called Evangeline, as well as from a criminal and a cop, to last me a lifetime, but no, I don't want to hear anything from you.'

'You hate me.'

Agnes shook her head. 'No, I don't hate you. I might if you were my father and I was your daughter, but that's no longer the case.'

'I never denied you or your mother, Agnes. I want you to know that.' He took a vigorous pull at his brandy and, seeing she did not interrupt him, went on, 'There must be some mistake. Today must really be All Souls' Day, for the ghosts have gathered round me with a vengeance. First of all I bump into Sonny Ayza, who I had never met before, but whose drawings used to plague my childhood, then in this hall that madwoman you mention, who keeps turning up and claiming she's my daughter, and now you, Wilson, and you, Agnes, who are really my daughter. Neither of us can change that. I see a lot of Sula in you, in your eyes and round your chin. You're more of her than me, but once you were ready to entrust your hand

345

to mine, to let me pick you up and carry you in my arms. These are memories I've always kept.'

'Emily Brown,' Loumans said. 'I was thinking of all the times you pretended to go and meet Emily Brown, and there she was waiting for you somewhere else. Who is this madwoman? Is she still around?'

Fernando shrugged. 'That's a long story. She claims to be my daughter. You knew her mother, Evangeline Simpson. The weird thing is this woman has got the same name. Sure, we used to have a thing, her mother and I, but her date of birth is all wrong for me. Besides, I knew the guy who was her father.'

'You'd do better with her than me,' Agnes said. 'She worships you. She's written, or had commissioned, a testament of your life. She lives for you. She wants to inhabit your innermost being. If you think you have a daughter, choose her.'

'Help me, Wilson. Tell her we do stuff we regret, that sometimes people are better off without us.'

'There's no point, Orfeo. You can't look back at your Eurydice. You'll have to handle the present and see what future it makes possible.'

'Sula's dead. Did you know that?'

Fernando bowed his head. 'No I didn't, Agnes.'

'It's why I'm here. To tell you this and go.'

Loumans got up and crossed the room to the door. He opened it and called out for Jimmy twice. A distant voice answered. Loumans asked him to get a cab. 'I'll leave you to it,' he said to them both. 'I'm tired. I'm going back to the hotel. I've an early flight tomorrow morning. You know what it's like, Fernando. It costs to maintain that feeling. I'm pleased to have met you, Agnes. I just wish it had been sooner.'

'Come back with me,' Fernando said when they were alone. 'You can't simply leave it like this. I own a house in Massard. We still have time to catch the last ferry. I need to know more.'

'That's rich coming from you. Where's your sense of irony? No.

I'm going back to my flat.'

'Tomorrow then. Surely you can spare an hour to tell me about Sula and let me know something about yourself. I understand why you want to punish me, but the truth is I still love you both. Wilson's a good man. You would have been better off with someone like him.'

'She loved you. You were all she spoke of at the end. Perhaps she always loved you. I don't know why, but it would be wrong of me not to acknowledge it. She wanted us to be together. She saw you all over the hospital, in her room, up on the ceiling, in the corridor, out of the window.'

'Did she suffer?'

'Yes. She suffered.'

Fernando buried his face in his hands. When he raised it he said, 'Thanks for telling me. You needn't have said it. What do you want to do, Agnes? I recognise I've long since abandoned any right to make demands on you.'

Agnes got up. He looked so dejected and defeated for the moment that she softened towards him. 'I will come tomorrow morning. Give me your address. What did you think when you walked in here and saw me with your friend?'

'I thought I might be interrupting something, but then I got a lot more than I bargained for.'

'And when I turned round and looked at you?'

He did not reply. She took the address he had scribbled on a piece of paper. 'It would have been nice if you had been able to say, why, it's Agnes,' she said softly.

Wait a moment.

Now, you can see again. Your eyes are accustomed to the light.

Slit the last bean pod open with your thumbnail and detach and add its contents to the pile already in front of you on the table. Sprinkle the grains of salt on to them through your fingertips. Cut a hunk of bread and eat. It is never too late to try and gain sustenance.

347

'You still have appetite,' Vincenz says. 'It gladdens my heart, Manolo.'

At the counter, Tony Pigeon puts down the tattered pages of an old *Jim, The Fastest Draw in the West* adventure. Vincenz slices an onion with his knife. His head bent over his stick, Uncle Jaume, seated on the bench, grumbles over the past only he now remembers. Paca stoops, opens the tap of the barrel, and fills a glass jug with wine. Nowadays, there are more chemicals in it than before, but none of that stops it from being raised aloft and poured in a stream down accepting throats.

Tian sits opposite you. Here, he feels somewhat out of place, like yourself. He yarns about the old singers from the golden age, the days and nights of wild sprees that rich men organised, the music he alone was gifted to write. Vincenz talks of the pig he slaughtered the other week up in the foothills beyond Ligac.

'Nolo,' Tony Pigeon says, 'I swear I thought it was you. We were down on the road, breaking it up then resurfacing it, but Orange Miguel told me no, it was someone he knew from the forge at St Mateo. These days my sight plays tricks on me, for I truly seemed to see your gait and the way you carry your head.'

The jug is in your hands. Tilt it and clear the dust and the ruins of time that coat your gullet.

Swallow your fill then pass it to Vincenz as he scrapes off a sliver of dried cod. He remembers when the three of you were boys together, standing on the sloping shelf of the cave mouth, watching torrential rain sealing off its entrance.

Speak to Tian. Tell him direct. This is as good a time as any other. You have spoken before in here. You managed to speak to Iusebio in the night streets outside and to My Son, clanging at a water pipe with his spanner. Your throat is clear. You have the necessary saliva. Perhaps the spurt of unaccustomed wine has loosened your tongue. Say now what you must have said privately to Rosario. Say openly to Tian what you must have discussed with him before you departed.

No words come. No words it seems will ever come. The confines of Paca's cannot accommodate them. The survivors here can neither see nor hear you. The past may loiter on in this obscure corner, but, outside the door, times have changed, and the world wears a new sensibility in which you are no longer a man with a voice to be heard.

> May the Divine Shepherdess
> keep me company
> for I am without the warmth of anyone
> in a strange country.

Fine snow was blowing out over the estuary. Sonny Ayza stayed at the rail, listening to the tape of Forest Mushroom he had bought yesterday on his rarely used Walkman. The song was a siguiriya: the couplet once made famous by El Nitri, a fabled singer of the previous century. Flakes landed and melted on the iron between his hands. Ahead, the same line of tankers he had seen on his previous journey weighed at anchor. Astern, Greenlea's slopes vanished into the murky lowering of the sky.

'You won't be able to leave. No matter where you go.' Forest Mushroom's words spooled back like an unrecorded guitar accompaniment to the austere bleakness of the lament. Out here on deck, open to the elements, he thought of Albert's confession of fear. 'Man overboard!' Would the cry, heard or unheard, be so terrible in his own case?

> To the graveyard I am destined.
> For God's sake, companion,
> don't let me die alone:
> I wish to die by your side.

Thanks to Tian's tuition years ago, he recognised Forest Mushroom's final couplet as belonging to Curro Pablas, a contemporary of El Nitri. Fernando Cheto Simon awaited him in his house in Massard on the Panalquin side, but he was neither a divine shepherd nor a companion, although their parents had seemingly intertwined their respective childhoods through the sending and keeping of his beloved sketches. In addition, they both shared Llomera as a birthplace, while otherwise they remained strangers who had never bumped into each other until their chance encounter with Jacob Kemmer. All the time their relationship had been known yet unknown: known through the spate of Joe May stories and iconography in which Chance Company recruits once were inducted; yet unknown, until Agnes had divulged it, in respect of who Joe May really was, and known as well, in a sense, by his daily attendances at the Sunrise Tea & Coffee stalls where, without being in the slightest way aware of the identity of their owner, he had contributed to the other's livelihood.

The compilation tape rolled on. The repertoire changed first to faster paced bulerias then to some saccharine renditions of commercial hybrids, which had characterised Forest Mushroom's later career. On his brief shopping trip, he had been unable to unearth any Antonio Escobar recordings. No doubt, if any had been extant, Monse would have mentioned them in her notes.

He switched off the tape and removed the headphones, slipping them and the Walkman back into his coat pocket. Panalquin docks came into sight round the rust covered stern of one of the tankers. He thought of the cave in the hinterland above Cirit and the three boys temporarily confined there. Had the bond between them, especially the bond between Manolo and Tian, been forged there or had it already always existed? Rosario told one story; Tian another. Now Tian, too, was dead, and, in Veri's occasional accounts from Miranda, Rosario, day by day, recaptured less and less of what had been and who exactly she was. Only he shuffled them around in his mind and made them speak in half-remembered Llomeran streets and in Paca Ceret's wine shop whose topography, to tell the truth, he had partially invented. How often had he actually been permitted to go inside when Tony Pigeon read his comic book or when My Son tipped his cap brim back and ordered another drink and one for My Son over there? True, he did clearly recall squinting into its mysterious interior from the safety of the doorway, but what had he really glimpsed apart from the total lack of light and the rise and fall of indistinguishable voices? If he was honest, Iusebio was nothing more than a name to him: a name which Rosario sometimes invoked as a stalwart and loyal companion to her dead husband, and Paca, herself, was really only a hazy amalgam drawn from a gallery of old women, all of whom dressed in omnipresent black. Amongst them, Batiste alone had re-emerged after the war and given himself a concrete existence. Fernando, his son, in practice, knew the place and its inhabitants far better than he did. Manolo had wanted their safety. He had entrusted his family to the man he knew secretly loved his wife. There was no going back on it. The dead were dead, but for some reason he would not let them rest. 'We'll disinter the bones and give our upbringings a proper funeral,' Guthrie/Fernando had said. This morning he would find out if such a thing was truly possible.

The dock drew ever closer. He looked down from the deck at the knot of people standing on the quay, waiting for the ferry to berth, then joined the line of passengers gathered at the exit from which the gangway would soon be lowered.

Stepping ashore, still trying to banish any thought of Manolo and Tian and what they might have said to each other, he made his way beyond the quay to the taxi rank. At this hour, fares appeared to be scarce, because a long line of cabs stretched back towards him from the head of the queue. As he passed, several of the cabbies, in spite of the continuing flurries of snow, were leaning against the doors and boots of their vehicles, engaged in conversation. Determined not to repeat yesterday's circuitous and idiosyncratic journey, he was glad to see his erstwhile driver was amongst them. When he reached the first available taxi, he got in, and, as well as giving his destination, he instructed the driver to take the east town intersection. The man nodded. They pulled away.

While they moved in stops and starts along the boundary of the newly pedestrianised shopping centre of north Panalquin, the driver broke the prevailing silence with a sequence of what he obviously considered were topics of common, current interest. What did he think of the Kraus fraternity phenomenon? Were they political or was it a new advertising strategy as some said? Had he heard the latest news bulletin about Albert Wende threatening to go on hunger strike? Did he know what it was costing to keep him and his brother banged up month after month? Sonny replied tersely and mostly in the negative. He would have preferred not to have been asked, but at least it was better than listening to hackneyed myths about Minty Wallace and the Bird Woman of Massard.

Outside the window, the snow was abating. The surface of the road was slushy and wet. The driver switched off the windscreen wipers. Buildings, people, cars, street furniture, overhead sign gantries, surrounded them. Sonny leant back in his seat and contemplated the things in the world. Like the driver, he also had to pass the time. Lights changed. Traffic moved on. The driver broached the topic of the forthcoming railmen's strike. Everything proceeded. Everything went somewhere. The things in the world were in unstoppable motion. 'Happy to be there. Happy to be here.' He thought of Sylvia's face as she had said the words, her calm certainty as she related the story of Monica Randell. 'It may not happen,' he said in response to the driver's last question.

The turn off for Massard appeared ahead. The cab jockeyed into the filter lane. Soon, they were beyond the highway and descending the tree-lined avenues to the privileged enclave.

'You wanted Bayford?'

Sonny nodded. 'Number 11.'

'Most of them have names. They don't think numbers fit the bill round here. Bayford's on the right. Want me to take you to the door?'

'No. I'll walk the rest. Exercise will do me good.'

He paid the cab at the foot of the driveway and watched as it turned and drove off. After the initial bend, an extensive lawn spread to his left, leading up to a substantial two-storey villa built in the hunting-lodge style. A monkey-puzzle tree, its symmetric branches sticking out in the now wan sunlight, rose from the middle of its turf. On the other side, banks of rhododendron bushes concealed what lay beyond. He gained the front door and rang the bell. There was no answer. The only sound was the chirping of some unseen bird. He rang again. Looking through the nearest window, he saw what looked like a study. There was no one in it. He rang once more, sensing a replay of his experience at Old Station Yard. Again there was no response. He walked round the gravel path at the side of the house to its back. More lawn sloped down past an ornamental pond to the boundary fence and a wooded dell. Three people stood in a glass conservatory attached to the rear of the building. Fernando and Agnes faced him. The other man had his back towards him, but his figure was familiar. He turned the door handle and walked in. As he had surmised, Antoine Viall, Chance Company's serial client, was the third person.

Something was very wrong. He read it at once in the expressions on Agnes's and Fernando's faces.

'Roberto,' Agnes said in a husky, unnatural tone. Fernando raised his eyebrows in way of a silent greeting. Viall turned slowly. He was holding a small gun, which he quickly swivelled back to train on Fernando.

Sonny was so surprised he muttered something about stopping play-acting before being at a loss for words.

Fernando said, 'Whatever your grievance is I can sort it out. Now, with Mr Ayza here as well, you can see how ridiculous the situation has become. I sense you already know this man, Sonny. Perhaps you can shed some light on our present predicament.'

'I think I can. He's possibly carried away with the melodrama of his assumed identity. Lucas, I . . . ' He did not finish because there at his side, having burst in with extreme rapidity, as if out of nowhere, was Agnes's companion of last night, Emmet Briggs.

Time seemed to go crazy, slowing down implausibly while Emmet looked at Agnes, stared at Fernando, a smile crossing his face, then hurtled himself into a blurred vortex of action as Viall's finger tightened round the trigger. Agnes moved in front of her father and Emmet seized Viall's wrist. A shot rang out. It was a sound Sonny had never heard properly before. The gun dropped to the floor, and as it did so Emmet hurled Antoine into the corner, where he crumpled against a stone-circled water feature, his nose covered in blood.

Pain. Unbearable, excruciating, unimaginable pain roared through and clawed at Sonny's entrails. He realised it might be a good idea to lie down but found his back was already pressed hard to the floor. A blur flashed past him, and he heard a distant voice say, 'Let him go.' Pain, tearing zigzagging pain. When he had sufficiently rested, he would get up and go. They could call a cab. He would be on board the next ferry in, what was the phrase? Two shakes of some animal's tail. Dogs, that was it. The world was full of dogs with different names. Pain. Someone was screaming. The ludicrous thought surfaced that it might even be him. He saw the waves cream past the rail. Over the spume, a tilting, tossing buoy was clanging out its sonorous bell. Pain. An intense furnace was burning his gut into molten lead. Back in his own room, a bottle of brandy and a mound of tablets were waiting for him on the table. He swallowed hard. He must get up and walk. Organise himself, that was the watchword. There was a strange taste in his mouth. A taste he could not recognise properly due to the pain. In its horrendous grip, the screaming stilled. Christ, he thought, I hope I haven't shat myself. Safety. Manolo had wanted safety for him, Veri and Rosario. The letter they stole need never have been read. Pain. The pain was something awry to time. It was making the words he heard people say into gibberish. A cat. A cat was there to help him. A cat with its paw raised and its Japanese miaows. What a joke it had been. What a joke it would be if it was not for the pain. A telephone rang;

only it was not a telephone. Batiste took off his jacket and draped it over his bare shoulders. A woman's face bent over him. It filled the whole world alongside the now shrieking pain. Whose face was it? He struggled to make it out; then it became clear. His eyes were still okay in spite of the agony. It was Mado's face, her every feature so discernible, now so vividly etched in his memory. He tried to get his lips to form what he wanted to know. 'Who is Vera Sowenwell?'

Agnes raised herself from Sonny's prone body. Viall, in the meantime, had staggered to his feet and fled. 'Emmet,' she said. 'I can't feel his pulse.' She turned and looked round when there was no reply.

Fernando came back into the conservatory. 'The ambulance is on its way. I've also called the police.' Emmet stared at him. He had picked up Viall's gun and wrapped his handkerchief around its butt.

'Don't bother with that now. It's not important. I need your help,' Agnes told him. 'Stupid as it is I think Roberto may be dying. Please come.'

'Shouldn't you leave his gun where it was for the police to find?' Fernando said.

Emmet emitted a deep sigh. The steady trickle of water splashing on the stones in the corner reminded him suddenly of the kid and his uplifted hands. 'Manny said we'd be picking up your bones when we last met at Veldar, but in the end you just upped and walked away. Today he's dead and you're still alive.'

'For God's sake, Emmet,' Agnes cried, 'this is serious.'

With a lingering stare at Fernando, Emmet let the gun drop. He knelt down beside Agnes. 'He's far gone,' he said, after he had felt in vain for a pulse. 'I don't know if he can be revived.'

'You wish someone ill for years and then it happens. He only came because I invited him, an invitation I very nearly didn't give,' Fernando said, almost as if he were speaking to himself.

Emmet stood up. 'I'm going to go. I've no place here.' He touched Agnes's shoulder. 'Tell them I wasn't here if you feel able to, or else I was, but you had never seen me before. Say that Ayza struggled with Viall. Either way just give me some hours and I won't be in Greenlea. After that it all depends whether they believe Viall when they catch up with him.'

'Why on earth should we do that?' Fernando said quietly.

'I'm asking your daughter not you. You must do whatever you want. My silence, however, is in your interest if you wish to go on living this existence.'

Agnes nodded. 'I won't say you were here.'

Taking a long, last look at Fernando, Emmet left. Agnes started to cry softly. She laid her forehead against Sonny's.

'Would you have felt like this if he had managed to shoot me instead?' Fernando asked. 'After all, for some obscure reason known only to him, I was his intended target. No, I know it's a tactless question, a selfish one, one I've no right to ask.' The ring of the doorbell interrupted whatever else it was he was going to say. He left to answer it and returned immediately with two paramedics carrying a stretcher.

'I'm afraid we're too late. He's already dead,' one of them pronounced as he got up from the body. 'As he has been shot, and as I understand the police are on their way, we can't move him. I suggest we don't touch anything in here and wait for them in another room.'

'I don't want to leave,' Agnes said.

'I understand how you must feel. Is he a relative? Your father perhaps? But it's best we go. You can see that, sir.'

A police siren sounded in the distance. Agnes reluctantly joined Fernando as they retired to the dining room next door, leaving the paramedics in the hallway.

'Stay with me, Agnes,' Fernando said. 'I've got this house and a good business. We could share them both until you found something better to do. Please let me try to make amends.'

She shook her head. 'I never asked Emmet exactly why he was here. No. Your suggestion isn't possible. We'd both be living a lie. It would be the same as playing at a Chance Company scenario, a faked case of father and daughter. I won't do it.'

'What will you do?'

'I decided on it last night. Once all this is over, and I've told the police about the four of us being here, I've decided to go back to the beginning.'

'I don't understand.'

'I'm going to go to Miranda, to Llomera, and I'll take it from there. I'll find my relatives. Some of them must still be there, and I'll visit Roberto's. I need to tell them what happened to him, describe to them what they didn't see, but what will you do?'

The doorbell rang again. They listened while the paramedics opened it and admitted the police. 'What I'm accustomed to doing,' Fernando said. 'I don't think I can change now.'

<hr>

The phone rang. He walked back into his office and picked it up.

'Harvard Smith.'

Silence gathered at the other end. He repeated his name, then, after a pause, Evangeline replied.

'We've found him, Harvard. I saw him again last night. He's not greatly changed. I knew if we put Loumans and Emily Brown together it would work out fine. We talked about the book, and I told him how I'd managed to get into his thoughts. I just want to thank you for your help. Believe me I won't forget it. It's a wonderful thing you've done. I'll be thinking of you, and, of course, when the book of his life is published I'll reserve a very special copy just for you. Be in touch soon.'

He put the phone down. Standing at the window, he looked across the precinct to the Issa Tower. Someone there, framed in a window at the same level as his own, was gazing downwards to the concrete below. A faint ray of sunlight sparkled against the glass eliding his image. Harvard returned to the paperwork piled on his desk. All he had to do now was to sit tight and wait for confirmation.

APPENDIX

MAIN CHARACTERS

Roberto 'Sonny' Ayza: a self-exiled Mirandan, working for Chance Company.
Fernando Cheto Simon: a Mirandan man of many parts.
Agnes Darshel: a daughter seeking an errant father.
Emmet Briggs: an ex-gangster.

IDENTITIES

Emily Brown
Elizabeth Kerry
Joe May
Renè Darshel
Andrew Guthrie
Antoine Viall

TELL-TALES

Sylvia Manjon: a coffee stall attendant.
Corinne: a native of Veldar.
Forest Mushroom: a Mirandan singer.
Jacob Kemmer: a pavement artist.
'Cheb' Alakhin: a retired detective.

Manolo Ayza: Sonny's dead father.
Rosario: Sonny's mother.
Veronica 'Veri': Sonny's sister.
Sebastian 'Tian' Marva: Sonny's stepfather.
Madeleine 'Mado' César: Sonny's ex-lover.
Antonetta Simon: Fernando's mother.
Gloria: Antonetta's sister.
Iusebio: Gloria's dead husband.
Batiste Cheto: Fernando's father.
Rafael: Batiste's father.
Guillermina: Batiste's mother.
Jacinta: Batiste's sister.
Paca Ceret: a tavern owner.
Thérèse: a French traveller to Miranda.
Sula Darshel: Agnes's mother.
Hallie Briggs: Emmet's wife.
Harvard Smith: a Chance Company manager.
Evangeline Simpson (the second): Harvard's ex-lover and opponent of Chance Company.
Evangeline Simpson: her mother and co-founder of Chance Company.
Selly Rycart: Chance Company co-founder and father of Evangeline (the second).
Walter Sembele: a political fixer.
Lucas Jones: a serial client of Chance Company.
Jacky Millom: a procurer of illegal firearms.
Monserrat 'Monse' Selle: a music professor.
Albert Roig: an owner of a printing firm. Monse's husband.
Wilson Loumans: a pianist.
Leo Manners: a Chance Company part-timer.
Taji Mohammed: a former court musician.

ORISHAS

Ogun: the spirit of the forge.

Olokun: the spirit of rivers and sea.

Elegba: the messenger of God to humans. The embodiment of Creativity and Chaos.

Ifa: the bringer of the 'logos' to humans.

THE AUTHOR TAKES HIS LEAVE

On this page, his traces may linger in Glasgow, Kilmarnock, Auchmithie, Barcelona, Peñiscola, Granada, Paris, Hammersmith, Battersea, Bromley and Twickenham.

By happy chance, Eric Dolphy, Thad Jones, Johnny Griffin, Teddy Wilson, Leslie Caron, Barbara Bray and Patrick Magee spoke to him. He was fortunate to speak back with them.

Workmates aver he was a relatively civil—unlike Brian O'Nolan—civil servant in Unemployment Benefit Offices, union meetings and training rooms. Others claim to have witnessed him in antiquated telephone exchanges and film-cutting cubbyholes.

Years, wasted or burnished in pubs, bars, picture houses and at racetracks, slid away imperceptibly, while Stendhal and Dickens remained his two stalwart guardian angels, and John Huston's movie, *The Asphalt Jungle*, provided the blueprint for all he wrote or would write.

Food intake largely consisting of fish and chips, relishing the memory—with older readers in mind—of Alf Tupper, *The Tough of the Track*, who will surely win Olympic gold provided Wilson doesn't turn up. Also, following the preference of Leopold Bloom, offal was appreciated, especially tripe—*callos picante*—and Scots black pudding.

So, all in all, a serious scribbler, worthy or unworthy of your attention, who, if he didn't exist, might entice someone, Quentin S Crisp perhaps, to invent him.